SHELL GUIDES

edited by JOHN BETJEMAN AND JOHN PIPER

CORNWALL *John Betjeman*
DORSET *Michael Pitt-Rivers*
THE ISLE OF WIGHT *Pennethorne Hughes*
LINCOLNSHIRE *Jack Yates and Henry Thorold*
NORFOLK *Wilhelmine Harrod and C. L. S. Linnell*
SUFFOLK *Norman Scarfe*
WORCESTERSHIRE *J. Lees-Milne*

edited by JOHN PIPER

DERBYSHIRE *Henry Thorold*
ESSEX *Norman Scarfe*
GLOUCESTERSHIRE *David Verey*
KENT *Pennethorne Hughes*
LEICESTERSHIRE *W. G. Hoskins*
NORTHUMBERLAND *Thomas Sharp*
SHROPSHIRE *Michael Moulder*
MID WESTERN WALES *Vyvyan Rees*
NORTH WALES *Elisabeth Beazley and John Brett*
SOUTH-WEST WALES *Vyvyan Rees*
WILTSHIRE (third edition) *J. H. Cheetham and John Piper*

NORTHAMPTONSHIRE *Juliet Smith*
THE SHELL PILOT TO THE
SOUTH COAST HARBOURS *K. Adlard Coles*

A Shell Guide
North Wales
Caernarvonshire, Anglesey, Denbighshire and Flintshire

The splendour falls on castle walls
And snowy summits old in story:
The long Light shakes across the lakes,
And the wild cataract leaps in glory:

Blow, bugle, blow, set the wild echoes flying,
Bugle, blow; answer, echoes, answer, dying.

O hark, O hear, how thin and clear,
And thinner, clearer, farther going!
O sweet and far from cliff and scar
The horns of Elfland faintly blowing!

TENNYSON, from *The Princess*

A Shell Guide
North Wales
Caernarvonshire, Anglesey, Denbighshire and Flintshire

Elisabeth Beazley and Lionel Brett

Faber & Faber 3 Queen Square London

First published in 1971
by Faber and Faber Limited
3 Queen Square London WC1
Reprinted 1975
Printed in Great Britain by
Billing & Sons Limited, Guildford and London
All rights reserved

ISBN 0 571 09756 1

Although sponsoring this book, Shell-Mex and B.P. Ltd would point out that the authors are expressing their own views

"To have no errors is a Privilege above the Condition of Humanity; under it, Happiest is he who has fewest of them."

Henry Rowlands' preface to
Mona Antiqua Restaurata, 1723.

© 1971 by Shell-Mex and B.P. Ltd

Contents

List of illustrations   6

Introduction   9

Caernarvonshire: Gazetteer   17

   The five ranges of Eryri   48

   The Lakes   58

Anglesey: Gazetteer   65

Denbighshire: Gazetteer   99

Flintshire: Gazetteer   126

   The English Maelor or Flintshire Detached   141

Bibliography   144

Maps *following* 144

Index   145

Few of the houses in North Wales are open to the public and mention in this guide does not imply that they are. Some may be seen on written application to their owners; this also applies to monuments on private land.
The gazetteer is based on civil parishes except where this may cause confusion. Only if a place may be otherwise impossible to find is the National Grid Reference given.
Prehistoric dating is that of the new carbon 14 chronology.

Illustrations

Front endpaper
  Rock face in Cwm Tryfan
  John Piper

Frontispiece
  Cwm Pennant
  Lionel Brett

Title page
  Llanrhwdrys, churchyard gate
  Elisabeth Beazley

Page
15 Ynyspandy slate mill
   Lionel Brett

CAERNARVONSHIRE

16 Aber Falls
   Vernon D Shaw
17 Abererch
   E. Emrys Jones
18 Abersoch
   Lionel Brett
18 Aberdaron
   Lionel Brett
19 Bangor, University College
   Lionel Brett
20 Bethesda churchyard
   Lionel Brett
20 Beddgelert
   Lionel Brett
21 Betws Garmon
   Lionel Brett
22 Betwys y Coed, three views
   Lionel Brett
23 Betwys y Coed, Swallow Falls
   Lionel Brett
24 Borth y Gest
   Lionel Brett
25 Caernarvon Castle
   Lionel Brett
26 Caernarvon Castle
   Lionel Brett
27 Clynnog Fawr church
   Lionel Brett
28 Conway
   E. Emrys Jones
29 Conway, Telford's and Stephenson's bridges
   Peter Burton

Page
30 Criccieth
   Lionel Brett
31 Conway Mountain
   E. Emrys Jones
31 The Conway estuary
   E. Emrys Jones
32 Gwydir Uchaf chapel
   Peter Burton
34 View from Yr Eifl (The Rivals)
   Lionel Brett
34 Yr Eifl
   E. Emrys Jones
35 Llandegwning
   Lionel Brett
36 Llandudno, three views
   (above) *Lionel Brett*
   (centre and below) *G. Douglas Bolton*
37 Llangelynin
   Lionel Brett
38 Nantlle, Talysarn
   Lionel Brett
39 Nantlle, Dorothea slate quarry
   Lionel Brett
41 Penrhyn Castle
   Lionel Brett
42 Port Penrhyn
   Lionel Brett
43 Portmadoc Quay
   Bruce Watkin
44 Sarn-Mellteyrn church
   Lionel Brett
45 Llanrhychwyn church
   Peter Burton
46 Tremadoc
   Lionel Brett
47 Tremadoc, Peniel chapel
   Lionel Brett
48 Eryri from Traeth Mawr
   Lionel Brett
49 Moel Hebog
   Roger Mayne
49 Y Garn and Drwys-y-Coed
   Roger Mayne
50 Cnicht, two views
   Lionel Brett

Page
52 Glyder Fach
   John Piper
53 Glyder Fawr
   John Piper
54 Tryfan summit
   John Piper
55 Tryfan from the east
   Lionel Brett
56 Snowdon, two views
   Roger Mayne
57 Snowdon, two views
   G. Douglas Bolton
59 Llyn Edno
   Lionel Brett
59 Llyn Idwal
   Lionel Brett
60 Llyn Gwynant
   Lionel Brett
61 Llyn Nantlle Uchaf
   Roger Mayne
61 Llyn Llydaw
   Roger Mayne
62 Llyn Mymbyr
   E. Emrys Jones
63 Llyn Peris
   Lionel Brett

ANGLESEY

64 Llanallgo, limestone wall
   John Piper
65 Field wall near Llanddona
   John Piper
66 Aberffraw, three views
   (above) *Elisabeth Beazley*
   (centre) *E. Emrys Jones*
   (below) *G. Douglas Bolton*
67 Aberffraw, benches in St Mary, Tal-y-llyn
   Elisabeth Beazley
68 Beaumaris, Victoria Terrace
   Elisabeth Beazley
69 Beaumaris Castle
   Peter Burton
70 Bodwrog
   Elisabeth Beazley
71 Brynsiencyn, Llanidan old church
   Elisabeth Beazley

Page
73 Holyhead, the Irish boat
   E. Emrys Jones
74 Holyhead, South Stack
   G. Douglas Bolton
75 Holy Island, Holyhead Mountain
   Elisabeth Beazley
76 Holy Island, Trearddur Bay
   G. Douglas Bolton
77 Llanbadrig
   G. Douglas Bolton
78 Llanbadrig, three views
   Elisabeth Beazley
79 Llanddaniel Fab, sandstone quarry
   Elisabeth Beazley
81 Llandegfan, Maen Hir
   Elisabeth Beazley
81 Llanddaniel Fab, Bryn Celli Ddu
   G. Douglas Bolton
82 Llanerchymedd, chapel
   Elisabeth Beazley
83 Llanfair-Mathafarn-Eithaf; chimney piece at Glyn
   Elisabeth Beazley
84 Llanfairpwll, Britannia Bridge
   Edward Piper
87 Llanfairpwll, Plas Newydd
   Elisabeth Beazley
88 Penmon Priory, dovecote
   Peter Burton
89 Llangoed, inside of dovecote at Penmon Priory
   Roger Mayne
90 Llaniestyn, St Iestyn
   Elisabeth Beazley
90, 91 Llangoed, the cross and font at Penmon Priory
   John Piper
92 Menai Bridge
   Elisabeth Beazley
95 Newborough, Llanddwyn Bay
   Elisabeth Beazley
95 Newborough, Llanddwyn Island
   Elisabeth Beazley

Page
97 Plas Penmynydd
   E. Emrys Jones

DENBIGHSHIRE
98 Abergele, Gwrych Castle
   Peter Burton
99 Abergele, Kinmel Park
   Peter Burton
100 Betwys-yn-Rhos church
   Lionel Brett
101 Bodnant
   Peter Burton
102 Capel Garmon, burial chamber
   Peter Burton
103 Cefn Mawr, Pont Cysyllte
   Edward Piper
105 Chirk, viaduct and aqueduct
   Edward Piper
106, 107 Chirk Castle
   Edward Piper
108 Denbigh
   E. Emrys Jones
109 Denbigh, tomb in Whitchurch
   Lionel Brett
111 Gresford
   Edward Piper
113 Hafodunos
   Lionel Brett
114 Eglwyseg Mountain, Craig Arthur
   Edward Piper
115 Eglwyseg Mountain, Trefor Rocks and quarry building
   Edward Piper, Elisabeth Beazley
116 Llanrwst bridge
   Lionel Brett
116 Llangwyfan
   Elisabeth Beazley
117 Pistyll Rhaiadr
   Lionel Brett
118 Llantysilio, Valle Crucis Abbey
   Elisabeth Beazley
119 Rosset, corn mill
   E. Emrys Jones

Page
120 Ruthin, Congregational chapel
   Lionel Brett
121 Ruthin and the Clwydians
   Edward Piper
121 Ruthin, St Peter's Square
   Lionel Brett
122 Wrexham church
   Edward Piper
124 Brymbo Steel Works near Wrexham
   Edward Piper
125 Towyn church and school
   John Piper

FLINTSHIRE
127 Bodelwyddan church
   John Piper
128 Near Cwm, the Vale of Clwyd
   Edward Piper
129 Near Dyserth
   Edward Piper
130 Flint castle
   Edward Piper
131 Halkyn church
   John Piper
132 The Dee estuary from Brynford Hall
   Edward Piper
135 Drybridge Lodge, near Mostyn
   Elisabeth Beazley
136 Fferm, near Pontblyddyn
   Elisabeth Beazley
137 Plas Teg, near Pontblyddyn
   Edward Piper
139 Rhuddlan castle
   E. Emrys Jones
140 Brynbella, near Tremeirchion
   Elisabeth Beazley
142 Bettisfield church
   John Piper

143 Anglesey farm
   Elisabeth Beazley

Back endpaper
   Waterfall on Snowdon
   Roger Mayne

Acknowledgements

A great many people have given most generously of their time and knowledge in the compilation of this guide. Any scholarship it may claim is theirs or comes from the books listed in the bibliography. We are particularly grateful to Lord Anglesey, Professor M. L. Clarke and Lt.-Col. H. M. C. Jones-Mortimer not only for patiently checking the sections of typescript but for the many useful suggestions that they have made.

No guide to North Wales could be authoritative without the advice of Mr Clough Williams-Ellis, which was most generously given; nor would it have so much beauty to record without his tireless activities. Canon B. F. L. Clarke lent us essential books and Prof. M. L. Clarke gave freely of his specialist knowledge of Welsh Church architecture. Mr Peter Howell and Mr Vernon Hughes disinterestedly put at our disposal their invaluable card-indexes of 19th-century building in Wales; Dr M. J. T. Lewis gave much useful information on industrial archaeology as did Dr Mostyn Lewis on medieval glass; much of the material on the Menai bridges and the Holyhead road came from Mr L. T. C. Rolt; Mr E. Beavan-Evan's knowledge of both industrial and Iron Age Flintshire was also much appreciated. Mr J. P. Gaudin made many useful suggestions on the proofs.

Others, who have been particularly helpful in giving historical information and in telling us where to look for the detail which brings a guide book to life, include:

The Marchioness of Anglesey
James and Roland Beazley
Mr and Mrs Gwyn Brown
Mr Michael Burn
Mr James Greenwood
Mr Colin Gresham

Mr N. Squire Johnson
Mr Jonah Jones
Mrs H. M. C. Jones-Mortimer
Mr Roger Lloyd
Mr P. M. Padmore
Mr R. F. Powell

Mrs Ramage
Mr Vyvyan Rees
Miss Cynthia Swan
Mr Arnold Taylor
The Rev. E. Whitford Roberts

The Keeper of Prints of the National Library of Wales, The Anglesey and Denbighshire County Librarians, The Flintshire County Archivist, The Librarians of the University College of North Wales and the Royal Institute of British Architects have been ever helpful as experience has led us to expect. We are very grateful to them all.

There are many others, unfortunately too numerous to mention, nor do we always know their names. They include the invaluable people who look after churches and chapels and who keep the keys, and others who told us where these people live. For security reasons, many of these buildings are now locked and the keys are no longer kept under the mat. (It would be very helpful if incumbents could put a notice in the porch telling would-be visitors, like ourselves, to whom to apply for the key.) We should like to thank them not only for their help on the guide but for cherishing the buildings which we enjoy. This, of course, applies equally to the owners of houses who so hospitably showed us round. We beg readers to take note of the paragraph on page 5 regarding access.

Elisabeth Beazley
Lionel Brett

Introduction

THE LAND

Geology and rock-climbing originated in North Wales—two ways of getting to grips with its outstanding physical fact. This is the natural fortress to which the British historically retreated for their last stands, and to which they still retreat from their softly contoured lowlands and smoggy cities for harder living and Atlantic air. The material of these mountains was built up on the floors of unseen seas 500 million years ago, then overlaid with the marine sediment which was to become the limestone of Anglesey and the Clwyd escarpment, then twisted and compressed by ferocious volcanic action into the famous slate strata, penetrated by veins of gold and crystal and the ores of copper, lead, zinc and iron, and lifted above the hot seas to form the smooth hills of Wales, and finally carved by wind and rain and scooped by glaciation into the sharp edges and deep cwms of Snowdonia. Wales has always attracted the prospector as well as the tourist, and both have left their scars.

The rivers, except for the eccentric and convenient Dee, run mostly northwards from the east-west watershed of central Wales, so that you could most easily penetrate the region, like the Romans from their base at Chester, along the north coast or up the Dee towards Bala. The northerly route along the broad Dee estuary gives a first impression of continuous industry. But by turning up any steep lane off the main road one is instantly in a different world. Here is a remote limestone interior only a hundred yards above the grimy coastal plain; blackberries and stone farms in surrealistic juxtaposition to the steel and chemical works, cooling towers and industrial housing immediately below. Not so long ago lead mines riddled these limestone uplands; from Elizabethan times they, and later coal, had made Flintshire the richest part of North Wales.

If you enter the Principality a little further south, the Wrexham area provides landscapes equally stimulating, or awful, according to one's mood: slag heaps and pit-head machinery, dairy cattle and deep woodland, ironworks and shiny Ruabon brick housing and plain cottages and farms, all within a stone's throw. Either way, as you move west, the landscape grows wilder and more "Celtic". In Flint and Denbigh, the Clwydian range could be Somerset, the Berwyn moors could be Yorkshire, and the innumerable valleys have a Devon-like snugness and domestication. But west of the Clwyd the moors take over, the land becomes poorer, dark conifer forests spread their shadows across the high ground, and Snowdonia itself mixes with the clouds in what seems an unattainable distance. The wooded cleft of the Conway is the natural frontier between moorland and mountain. But a last wall, the Carnedds, mountains in scale but not in shape, interposes before we reach the unmistakeable peaks, each of which turns its blackest and most savage face in our direction.

The landscape of Snowdonia is a minor miracle of illusionism. It lacks the bosky Arcadian beauty of the English Lake District, but because its peaks are more pointed they seem twice as tall. The small scale of their lakes and cascades, their delicate clothing of stunted indigenous oak and birch, the narrow walled lanes just wide enough for an English car, all conspire to magnify these mountains, and it is only when the photographer has his film developed that he finds he has been deceived. With this deception goes the boon of accessibility. Distances are always less than you expect, ferocious mountain walls less impregnable than they look, and only the presence of a huge cow in a tiny field exposes the miniature scale of the foothills, with all their intimate complexities of black heathery knolls and bright green mounds and rocky outcrops and hanging woods and steep ravines loud with falling water.

This climax is by no means the end of the

story. Beyond Snowdonia is the Lleyn, a region as remote in feeling as the west of Ireland, where isolated peaks, each capped with a prehistoric fortress, rise up in series against the sunset, sandy estuaries and coves provide a dodgy anchorage, and twisting lanes walled in by wild flowers drop down into hollows where semi-tropical gardens flourish. Finally the landscape ends on a quieter note as it began, with Anglesey, long known as Mona the Mother of Wales, the granary that fed the garrisons of Snowdonia.

The first impression of the island, the wooded banks of the Menai Straits which separate it from the mainland like a great tidal river, could now hardly be more misleading although it probably reflects its prehistoric face. Today most of the island is windswept and bare, outcropping rock and brown marshes breaking its undulating greenness, with Snowdonia, a splendid backdrop, in the ever-changing distance. Here and there wedge-shaped clumps of salt-bitten sycamore shelter an isolated farmstead or church, or one of those unexpected mansion houses which nearly always look plain Georgian whatever their date. Between are deep lanes (like the Lleyn) or patches of moor, or tiny lakes; a slow world to explore. The coast, and there are well over 100 miles of it, is infinitely varied: tremendous stretches of beach, estuaries alive with shifting light as the tide ebbs on their sand and mud, sandy pebbly bays with secret hoards of cowries and tiny coral-coloured fan shells, or immense cliffs, wild with sea birds and suddenly terrifying when you are alone. Telford's Holyhead Road lies ruler-like across the island. One cannot help hoping that the majority of tourists will continue along it, bound for Ireland, as they have for centuries. Anglesey is an island for the happily unsophisticated and for the connoisseur of surprises.

One's preferences among these landscapes will be a matter of taste and mood and above all weather. On some days outdoor North Wales is a washout, and the grey terraces, the drowned campers and the invisible mountains can be dispiriting. This can happen as suddenly in August as in December. But hold on, because as suddenly the Atlantic wind will roll the clouds away and unwrap a vision which for brilliance, for contrast of delicacy with savagery, for sculptural form, and above all for colour, is unexcelled by any landscape in the world.

THE INVADERS

Like the rest of the British Isles, North Wales has been repeatedly colonised from beyond its borders. The first to make a positive architectural mark in this remote region were the neolithic pioneers who began to filter up the western seaboard from the Iberian peninsula around 3500 B.C., and their successors who worked in bronze. They brought with them the worship of a mother goddess and the astounding discovery that they might hope to reap in the summer if they sowed grain in the spring. With them, the neolithic revolution arrived in Wales: settled life was at last possible and it was no longer necessary for man to devote his whole energy to hunting and food gathering. There was even time to construct those strange megalithic monuments which survive in such abundance. Indeed, it seemed imperative to do so: man's very existence was too often at stake. Having discovered the secret of farming he evidently possessed the wisdom to realise that this was not the secret of life.

Anglesey then, and until the years just before the Norman Conquest, held a key position on one of the great trade routes of the western world. As in recent history her geographical relationship to Ireland, then a most vigorous cultural centre, was all important. It is hardly surprising that some of the greatest chamber tombs or temples of these people should have been built on the island (Bryn Celli Ddu, Barcloddiad y Gawres) but it is astonishing that, in 1910, as many as 54 tombs were known to have existed in Anglesey alone (20 are now recorded).

Not only do the cromlechs of these mysterious, practical Iberians survive. Their physical characteristics are still much in evidence: dark-haired people, short and strong.

Waves of settlers succeeded each other like

the waves of the sea which brought them, but they came in relatively small numbers: there was plenty of space. Finally, in the 7th and 6th centuries B.C. the extraordinary shunting movement of Indo-Europeans which had started from central Asia in the late second millennium brought a new race to Wales, the long-headed, fair-haired Celts. They brought with them iron and war: much of Europe was now in turmoil; no longer did there seem to be enough room. As soon as the new people settled it was necessary to throw up fortifications. The Welsh coast and particularly Anglesey and the Lleyn were very vulnerable, and as the centuries went by inland strong-points also had to be fortified. Most of the surviving coastal and hinterland hill forts date from this Iron Age, which includes that tenuous Roman occupation that produced the forts of Caerhun and Segontium.

The Druids were the priesthood of the Celts. They worshipped chiefly in groves, leaving no architectural remains, but the Welsh feeling for poetry and music is closely linked with this tradition. Tacitus described Anglesey as the place where young men aspiring to the priesthood were sent for training in philosophy, poetry and religion (from far-away Gaul among other places). They were as distant in time from the builders of Stonehenge and the cromlechs as we are from them. They handed down their culture by verbal tradition; nothing seems to have been written down. How "civilised" they were is hard to tell, but there is no reason to suppose that their poetry and music were not of a high standard simply because their religious rites included human sacrifice and prophesy from human entrails. But if the unsqueamish Romans, usually tolerant of native religion, decided Druidism should be stamped out and felled the sacred groves, it must have had little obvious attraction. The visual art of the Celts developed later to become that of the early Christian church.

The missionaries of this Celtic church were the next arrivals. Again they made use of the sea routes, as the siting of remote parish churches often inconveniently close to the sea is a reminder. Such churches may mark the spot where, traditionally, a saint embarked or landed. Later it may have become a monastery (like Bardsey or Penmon), or remained simply a seafarers' shrine. The Celtic church seems to have been generously disposed towards the creation of saints and many chieftains adopted this title on their conversion. The church allowed its priests to marry and it took many years and synods to bring them into line with Rome.

Between the 9th and late 13th centuries Welsh sovereign princes held sway over the north. Much has been written of this period—its high hopes and bitter disappointments. Welsh independence was tolerated by the Plantagenets for just as long as the Welsh princes behaved prudently, and it was finally the rashness of Llewelyn and the deviousness of David which gave Edward I his chance to subdue and colonise their principality of Gwynedd in 1283. From that time, except for Owen Glendower's brief but brilliant defiance of Henry IV, the Welsh lived in sullen subjection, eventually somewhat mitigated when their own Henry Tudor captured the throne of England in 1485. Now for the first time they could identify themselves with the crown, a loyalty which was to persist throughout the Civil War. Churches were enlarged or rebuilt even in the more remote-seeming parishes. On the border, peace plus a market for its mineral wealth produced prosperity and with it a social pattern more or less English, with the professional classes and factors becoming country gentry. But the interior of North Wales was very different. The middle classes, which had been growing steadily in England, scarcely existed here. It was a country of shepherds and crofters living precariously from harvest to harvest, and of big landlords, often absentee. Their loyalty to the royalist cause did them little good.

And so remote Gwynedd was largely forgotten and it might have remained so had it not been for the dauntless English tourist. Thomas Pennant of Whitford, whose pioneering *Tour in Wales* was published in 1778, was a naturalist and antiquary. His successors, many of them ladies, were less dutifully scientific. For in the second half of the 18th century, with the stirrings of the romantic movement, Wales, and particularly the mountainous north, suddenly lost its uncouth reputation and was found instead to be very picturesque indeed. Sublimely so, some found. Others, both painters and poets, were happy to record its awful melancholy. This reversal of taste occurred just before the Napoleonic wars were to make European travel awkward, so it was not long before the enthusiasm was widely established.

With this enthusiasm came the industrial revolution and the happy coincidence that what was awful or sublime was also rich in slate, copper and lead. Snowdonia and Parys mountain, the cotton mills of Flintshire and the foundries and mines of Denbighshire were included in the tour for their industrial fascination. A Welsh and English middle-class to work and manage this new industry settled, built themselves appropriate gentleman's residences and became as devoted to the Principality as to their Iberian and Celtic neighbours, who were themselves rapidly adjusting to the facts of industrial Wales.

The dearth of Anglican clergy in the previous century and the growth of the Sunday School movement (in which reading and writing were taught as well as scripture) led to a great reverence for education which was based on the Nonconformist Chapel, the focal point of 19th-century village life, whether it was an agricultural, quarry, iron or coal community.

The coming of the railway made the Principality yet more accessible as the wealth of 19th-century building proves. Tens of thousands came for holidays, and others to retire. The seaside was undoubtedly the first attraction, but soon a more serious-minded tourist was to explore the peaks of Snowdonia. The Victorian mountaineer is a period piece in his own right. The first recorded ascent of Snowdon was in 1639, and Pennant explored the central ranges in 1781. But it was not until the 1850s that climbing became a ruling passion of the male Victorian intelligentsia, and those holiday parties of deeply shy but hearty dons and schoolmasters and their favourite pupils began to gather round the big fire at Pen-y-Gwryd—the forerunners of today's classless technicians with their nylon and stainless-steel equipment.

Last of the settlers was that other explorer, immortalised by appearing on the front of the pre-war 1 inch O.S. series in tweed knickerbockers and cap, with his sandwiches in a knapsack on the ground beside him. For many he will epitomise North Wales at week-ends for ever. Not well-off, at heart a countryman, but bound for economic reasons to pass his working life in the grimy city, he scans the promised land of Wales planning exploration on foot or bike or by elderly motor-car. He returned year after year as regularly as the migrant wheatear to give his suburb-based brood a glimpse of reality. Now he has retired to a small village, marked in his mind long before he set off to war in 1939, where he and his wife, with their English voices and English beliefs, are courteously received by the indigenous community. By intermarriage and the process of time their children's children, who too will migrate, may return to be accepted as part of that place, as have other foreigners who, as servicemen and women, or prisoners of war, married and settled where war had brought them. North Wales has thus been absorbing its explorers since Neolithic man first appeared in his precarious skin-covered coracle.

THE BUILDINGS

As with the climate, lovers of architecture must make a mental adjustment before they come to North Wales. English standards do not apply. West of Denbigh, there are no important examples from the classical 17th or 18th century which most people regard as the great age of English architecture. And pre-classical domestic architecture is mostly represented, as one would expect from the medieval poverty of the country, by vernacular buildings which by sophisticated standards are primitive or even pathetic—and none the less moving for that. Right from the start it was the invaders—Neolithic and Iron

Age chieftains, Roman commanders, English kings and their staffs—to whom the most durable monuments were due. Comparative prosperity flowing from industrialism and tourism only reached Wales with the railway. So the architecture of North Wales is predominantly the architecture of the Railway Age: the man-made scene is Victorian. To some, this may be an acquired taste: as a holiday pastime it is certainly a taste worth acquiring.

Within these limits one can divide the buildings of North Wales into seven fairly distinct groups. First the *fortified towns and castles*, reaching back through Roman Segontium into prehistory and forward through the Celtic keeps of Criccieth and Dolwyddelan to the great Edwardian castles of Conway, Caernarvon, Beaumaris, Rhuddlan and Flint, built swiftly by a master mind, the legacy of nearly half a century's experience of military architecture in Europe. At the same time came the building or rebuilding of many of the border castles of the Lords Marcher, of which Chirk must be the most remarkable.

Next the *medieval churches*. The Celtic church had its own pattern long before the Roman missionaries made their mark. Nearly every Welsh medieval church is sited on some tiny cell dedicated to a Celtic saint, who in his turn had planted his cross in the ground on this spot because he wished to preach there. Churches, particularly in the west, may therefore be remote from human settlement. This applies specially in Anglesey and where there are few villages in the English sense, the Celtic pattern of settlement, scattered farms and hamlets having persisted.

Everywhere great building activity followed the Tudor accession. The splendid Perpendicular churches of Gresford and Wrexham are good border examples; these are thorough-going rebuildings. Often it was a case of adding a new aisle to a church which consisted only of a nave, often without a chancel. This gave rise to the unusual plan of a double-aisled church (since one cannot talk of twin-naved). The inevitable duality is disconcerting till you get used to it. This plan is typical of much of North Wales away from the border where the more conventional English plan persisted (with exceptions like Chirk, double-aisled and almost in England). The great church builder of the Tudor period was Lady Margaret Beaufort (of the Boat Club at Cambridge), widow of Edmund Tudor and mother of Henry VII; she built the shrine to St Winifred at Holywell and several outstanding churches, including Gresford. In the Vale of Clwyd the best of the 15th and 16th century two-aisled churches are the Whitchurch at Denbigh, Llanrhaiadr yn Cinmerch, Llanefydd, Llanynys and Llangynhafel, and in Caernarvonshire Dolwyddelan, Llanengan and Llangwnadl. Also of that age, and on no account to be missed, are the Gwydir Chapel at Llanrwst and the monumental parish church of Clynnog Fawr on the north coast of Lleyn. At the other end of the scale of size are the tiny late medieval churches of Llanrhychwyn, Llangelynin and Llanfaglan.

In Anglesey the humility and siting of some of the medieval churches is most moving. Some indeed may not be medieval; one of the charming things about the remoter parts of Wales is its usual oblivion of architectural fashion. Fifty to a hundred years can often be added to normal dating. The wayside chapel of St Mary's, Tal-y-llyn, or the island church of Llangwyfnan, or Llanrhyddlad (not even named on the 1 inch O.S.) are among many worth seeking out, not primarily for architectural reasons. If they bore you, do not look further. But to plunge deep into the Middle Ages in one short step, leave the bright light reflecting from the waters of Menai for the dim nave of Penmon Priory: eight hundred years dissolve without trace.

Pre-Victorian *domestic architecture* is thinly represented, with Plas Mawr in Conway the outstanding example of an Elizabethan town house, rare enough anywhere in Britain. The end of the 16th and the early 17th centuries produced some outstanding country houses in Flintshire: the combined result of peaceful times and mineral wealth: Plas Teg and Nerquis Hall are the most spectacular but others combine quality with domestic charm. In Caernarvonshire there are a number of minor manor houses such as Maenan, Bodwrda and Vaynol Old Hall. Plas Berw, in Anglesey, a rebuilding of this period, is certainly astonishing to come upon. Unfortunately most of the Georgian great houses in the border country have been burnt, like James Wyatt's Wynnstay, or have just crumbled or been demolished, or improved beyond recognition. But the influence of the 18th century estate here is still apparent. The interior is quite different: it was not considered the place to build, being far too wild and uncivilised. Plas Newydd, by James Wyatt and Joseph Potter, on the Menai Straits is a notable exception.

In the early 18th century, outstanding wrought iron, as good as any in Britain, was produced by the Davies brothers of Bersham. Their work includes the famous Golden Gates of Eaton Hall as well as the splendid but less known screens at Chirk Castle and Leeswood Hall. These have the great advantage of being entirely visible to the public.

The romantics discovered Wales at the end of the century. Madocks' villa at Tremadoc (1800) set off a fashion for similar Regency retreats within an easy ride of the "British Alps", several of them designed by members of the prolific Wyatt family. The fantastic castle followed, Gwrych, Bryn Bras and the formidable Penrhyn. Later, with increasing wealth, Welsh and English industrialists stepped up the scale of their Celtic seats. Nantclwyd and Glynllyfon were rebuilt, Bodelwyddan, Hafodunos and Rhianva created, and Kinmel, grandest of all, brought to completion.

The next group is what we now call *industrial archaeology*, for which the region is outstanding. This is largely because of the juxtaposition of three outstanding facts. First, the political need to improve the route from London to Dublin brought into focus by the Act of Union, 1801, and the troubles which preceded it. Second, Thomas Telford's appointment, a few years earlier, as Surveyor to Shropshire. He was one of the most inventive engineers of all time and ceaselessly pioneered the use of the new material, iron. Third, the development of the border coalfields and iron foundries literally on his doorstep and close to the site of some of his most astonishing works.

Before the Holyhead Road became an issue, Telford was involved in the English canal system. The beautiful Llangollen Canal, with his famous iron aqueduct, Pont Cysyllte, and the earlier Chirk aqueduct, was virtually a navigable feeder to this system. Then came the road, itself an engineering feat (the fact that its gradients are hardly noticeable is proof of this). The Menai suspension bridge which carries the road over to Anglesey was, like Pont Cysyllte, an engineering work of international importance. Telford's bridge, at Conway, though less dramatic was a dress-rehearsal for Menai; it still has the original wrought-iron chains.

Less than a quarter of a century was to pass before the railway thundered in. Stephenson's huge Britannia Bridge was indeed a prodigious feat: he too had a dress-rehearsal at Conway.

Numerous 19th-century iron windows, of surprising variety and great charm, still survive in cottages and factories and sometimes in grander houses, particularly in north-east Wales and the border country. In Anglesey, simple and very attractive iron field gates are still used on many farms; some have been skilfully adapted to the widths necessary for modern machinery.

The other major industrial influence on the landscape of North Wales is the slate industry, "the most Welsh of Welsh industries," says Prof. Dodd, because of its inaccessibility to English capital and labour. The two great slate seams run S.W.–N.E., the Cambrian to the north of Snowdon (Nantlle to Bethesda), the Ordovician to the south (Ffestiniog to Penmachno). Originally, like other building materials, a local hand-craft, slate grew to a national and then a booming export industry, with the opening-up of North Wales in the early 19th century. The two colossal quarries, Penrhyn and Dinorwic, were wholly exploited by local improving landlords, the Douglas-Pennants and the

Assheton-Smiths—both, incidentally, heirs by marriage into Welsh families. Each built his own roads, towns, railways and ports. By 1850 200,000 tons a year were being shipped out of Caernarvon, Port Dinorwic and Port Penrhyn. Artificial substitutes have since contracted the industry almost to insignificance: the Dinorwic quarry closed in 1969. But its haunted ruins are imperishable.

Alongside the monuments of industry are the *industrial towns and villages*, the scattered lead-miners' settlements in Flintshire, and the colliery and iron-founders' villages both here and clustered around Wrexham, and the slate quarrymen's townships like Bethesda and Pen-y-Groes. Here chapels predominate over churches, some simple and charming, others elaborate and hideous—all locked and cherished, but with the key hard by in the caretaker's house sensibly built to match the chapel.

The other characteristic urban community is the *seaside resort*, once despised by architectural snobs, but now coming into its own. From Llandudno right through the scale of size to Criccieth and Llanfairfechan, North Wales can show outstanding and unspoilt examples. To these we can now add the pop scenes of Pwllheli and the medieval orange and blue of the tented camps, bravely sitting it out against the black precipices of Nant Ffrancon.

Finally, in all these towns and in the tiniest rural communities the *Victorian churches*, from the naïve 1840 "Commissioner's Gothic" of Welch or Alexander through Kennedy's conforming if seldom inspired High Gothic to Douglas's beautifully finished and occasionally hilariously non-conforming work near the border. Then there are the marble confections of Trefnant and Bodelwyddan, the solidly competent work of G. E. Street at Towyn and Bettisfield and, everywhere, restorations by Kennedy or Scott: a remarkable testimony in their quantity and quality to the local pride of those new Anglican communities.

Ynyspandy slate mill, CWM PENNANT

Caernarvonshire: Gazetteer

The number after each entry refers to the square on the map following page 144 *where the place is situated.*

Aber (10). Most spectacular and remote of Caernarvonshire waterfalls, the 170 ft. mare's tail is reached by a pleasant two-mile walk from the roadhead through a romantic wooded glen.

Pen-y-Bryn, glimpsed from the main road just east of the village, has an attractive 17 c. round tower.

The coastal escarpment on both sides of the village is beautifully wooded and much prettier than the shored-up precipices further east.

◁ Aber Falls
▽ Abererch

Aberdaron (4). The last hamlet of Wales' land's end, with a magnificent windy beach. In the spacious barn-like church on the cliff edge, with a weather-worn Norman doorway, Bardsey pilgrims dossed down while they waited for a boatman to take on the dangerous currents of Bardsey Sound. The Old Kitchen opposite kept them fed. The Post Office is by Clough Williams-Ellis.

Two miles on one can drive to the crest of the National Trust's *Braich-y-Pwll* headland, "a vast precipice, black and tremendous", 524 ft. sheer above the restless sea, with magnificent views inward to Lleyn and Snowdon and outward to Ireland. Bardsey Island (q.v.), a fraction higher, is a mile and a half off-shore. Pennant tells of a freshwater spring below Braich-y-Pwll uncovered at low tide.

Just visible from the main road one mile out is *Bodwrdda*, a beautiful Elizabethan manor house with stone centre and brick wings, the home of the Edwards family since 1749.

Abererch (8). The neat grey and white village, mercifully by-passed by the A.497, climbs from the bridge over

the Erch to where the restored medieval church, with some 15 c. joinery, and the attractive red and white Ebenezer Chapel face each other at the top of the hill.

Abersoch (5). A gay and growing sailing and bathing resort, with scores of yachts moored off-shore in spite of the lack of shelter from the east. From the sands are superb views of the mountains from Snowdon to Cader Idris, and off-shore are the grassy *St Tudwal's Islands*, with the remains of an oratory and a disused lighthouse. A mile up the main road to the north is *Castellmarch*, a Jacobean stone manor house with an unusual portico (not open).

Bangor (10). Best visited at high tide, the small cathedral city on its furrowed site has a distinctive Victorian personality, best preserved in the airy and richly wooded suburb that looks across the Menai. The long, delicate pier is worth the walk for the view from the Menai Bridge right round to the keep of Penrhyn Castle silhouetted against the high Carnedds.

The centre is a muddle but is redeemed and dominated, despite recent competition from academic skyscrapers in the valley below, by the powerful tower of *University College*, designed by Henry T. Hare in 1906 and undoubtedly his best work. It is in his favourite free version of the English Renaissance, here handled more romantically and less fussily than elsewhere; the inner quadrangle is particularly successful aesthetically if not functionally. Of the many new buildings added to the College since 1950 none have been architecturally distinguished, but it is at least encouraging that to our eyes the latest (by Sir Percy Thomas and Sons), which completes Hare's outer quadrangle, seems the best. Of modern outlying buildings, Plas Gwyn by David Roberts (end of Menai Avenue), is outstanding.

The *Cathedral* of this the oldest diocese in the U.K. (81 years senior

◁ *above* ABERSOCH
below ABERDARON

BANGOR, University College

to Canterbury) is low-lying and tree-wrapped. It was almost wholly destroyed in the 11 c. and 15 c., then transformed from a largely Perp. building to a Dec. one by Sir Gilbert Scott and his son between 1868 and 1880. They rebuilt the transepts, re-roofed and restored the whole and began a central tower intended for a spire. The result is a conscientious but lifeless interior, with some good Victorian glass, particularly the west (originally east) window by David Evans (1838) and

◁ *above* BETHESDA
below BEDDGELERT

BETWS-Y-COED ▷
p22 above left Telford's Waterloo Bridge
above right Bridges on the Machno
below Picturesque cottage on the road to Capel Curig
p23 The Swallow Falls

the east window by Clayton & Bell (1873). Near the north door is the 15 c. or early 16 c. "Mostyn Christ", a movingly austere woodcarving. Bishop Skevington's 16 c. west tower, a less robust version of Clynnog, is the most effective external feature. The Bishop Rowland's almshouses, south of the Cathedral, were built in 1805. The Town Hall, north of it, formerly the Bishop's Palace, has been much altered: it has a good 18 c. staircase and ceiling.

Of minor churches, *St James'* (1866), opposite the Hospital, is by Kennedy; *St Mary's* (1864), to the N.E. of the Cathedral, is by Horner of Liverpool; and *St David's*, on the Caernarvon road, is a dullish work (1888) of Sir Arthur Blomfield.

A few pleasant 19 c. houses survive in the High Street, as well as two splendid 1860 banks, one Tudor (Lloyds), the other Venetian (National Westminster). The modest 18 c. Tanrallt has a staircase in a local version of Chinese Chippendale.

Bardsey Island (4). 2 miles off the tip of the Lleyn Peninsula, now a bird sanctuary, has all that an island should: sheltered anchorages, a mountain, a ruined monastery and a lighthouse. It was an important place of pilgrimage from the 6 c. and it is believed that the monks from Bangor Is-coed settled here. The lighthouse, on the low-lying tail of the island, attracts countless migrant birds on passage down the west of Britain. It was designed by John Nelson (1821). The turf here is sheep-grazing, short and springy; oyster-catchers nest among the thrift. North of the island's waspwaist, where the anchorage nearly cuts it in two, a farm road has been built below the mountain. Rock, gorse and heather above, farmland and small withy-beds by the stream below. The 3rd Baron Newborough rebuilt the farms on the island, 1870–5, to a model plan. Four are in semi-detached pairs sharing yards in giant walled enclosures which were built to give shelter from the relentless south-westerlies. There was then a small but thriving community of farming-fisher families. Now the Bardsey Bird and Field Observatory uses the old school house for its work. The island has breeding colonies of sea birds and is an important ringing station.

Beddgelert (13). The only true mountain village in Snowdonia, with an atmosphere of hob-nailed boots, wood-smoke gathering on autumn evenings and the close presence of peaks felt rather than seen. The chunky stone vernacular of the region is nowhere better seen than in

▽ BETWS GARMON

the inns and cottages surrounding the diminutive bridge, which all must hope will be by-passed and preserved.

In the flat fields to the south nothing remains of the oldest monastery in Wales after Bardsey but the restored church of its successor, an Augustinian priory of the 12 c., and this is largely late 19 c. in character, with the important exception of the 13 c. east window, with three slender lancets, and the north transcept arcade; both rather sophisticated features for this part of the world.

A mile south of the village is the pretty and popular little defile of *Aberglaslyn*, in which turn left at the bridge for a landscape, dominated by the sharp peak of Cnicht, as beautiful and as characteristic as any in Snowdonia. A mile east of the village, on the left of the road (best climbed from the east) is *Dinas Emrys*, Iron-Age and Roman hillfort and site of a 12 c. Welsh keep; a prominent and mysterious crag closely connected in legend with Vortigern and Ambrosius. Excavation shows the layout to be closely similar to that described in the earliest legends. The pool is the spring where the dragons prevented Vortigern building his palace.*

Beyond Llyn Dinas the peak of Snowdon is briefly seen towering at the head of Cwm y Llan, and beyond Llyn Gwynant is the entrance, right, to the National Trust's *Hafod Llwyfog*, a characteristic 17 c. Caernarvonshire farmhouse of the larger sort.

Bethesda (10). Radiating in long white and grey terraces from the great stucco chapel (1840) from which it takes its name, the famous slate town is a model of how to build in the landscape of North Wales. At its heart is the rather dull mid-Victorian *Christ Church*, Glanogwen, the sober black headstones in long rows in the tall grass of its beautiful sloping churchyard. Of several grandiose chapels, the 1872 *Siloam*, with Corinthian frontispiece and polychrome slate back and sides, is perhaps the best. Facing the town across the valley is the well-placed steeple of *St Ann's* (Goronwy Owen, 1865), with a beautifully cared-for Victorian interior. *Capel Bethel* at Tyn-y-Maes has some of its Regency fittings intact.

The great terraces of the *Penrhyn Quarry* dominate the landscape. The industry was built up from a manorial craft by Richard Pennant of Liverpool, who married the heiress of Penrhyn and was created Baron Penrhyn in 1783. Each terrace is 60 ft. high and from floor to topmost gallery the immense excavation is 1,140 ft. deep—the deepest slate quarry in the world.

South of the town "the most dreadful horse path in Wales",* now Telford's Holyhead road (opened to coaches in 1819), passes on the right Benjamin Wyatt's Regency Gothic Dairy Farm of Penisarnant (hidden in jungle), before starting the long straight climb into the heart of the savage rock scenery of Nant Ffrancon. The fine cwms to the right were all scooped out by glacial action.

Betws Garmon (6). Scattered alpine village romantically situated below

* M. Lewis, K. Watson.

* Pennant.

BORTH-Y-GEST

CAERNARVON

the precipice of Mynydd Mawr. Good granite church of 1841 by George Alexander.

Betws-y-coed (14). The Victorian honeymoon resort, with a feeling of the Trossachs and many well-built 19 c. hotels and villas. Its most notable features are its three bridges: the rugged, basically medieval Pont y Pair, Telford's beautiful cast-iron Waterloo Bridge, unfortunately no longer painted white, and downstream beside the old church a later and delightful white-painted iron suspension footbridge. The church itself is humble and unspoilt, with a naïve 13 c. font, and a Welsh knight who fought for Richard III recumbent in full armour. The mid-Victorian New Church (Paley and Austin, 1873) has a richly handsome interior, with polished marble font, pulpit and reredos, spoilt by weakly corbelled chancel piers.

The wooded hills around are now all stuffed with Christmas trees, but the famous beauty spots—the white Swallow Falls, the brown Conway Falls and the Fairy Glen ravine— are unaffected. All are best seen in May or October, when there are fewer people. Less popular and equally picturesque are the falls of the Machno beside Pandy, reached by a lane (right) half a mile up the Penmachno road. The pretty 'Roman' bridge over the Machno is evidently not Roman. Good walks to wooded lakes to the north and south of the Llugwy Valley.

Bodfuan (8). Behind a rather forbidding façade, Kennedy's neo-Norman church of 1894 has an impressive red sandstone cross-shaped interior, containing some cool classical monuments of the Wynns of Bodvean, who built the church. Beside the west door are four marble slabs, the grey about Death, the red about Judgment, the white about Heaven, the black about Hell. Beyond, in richly wooded grounds, with huge beeches and rhododendrons, is the early 18 c. Victorianised Hall.

Borth-y-gest (9). A pretty village built in a semi-circle round its sandy harbour, which dries out at low tide, with good bathing coves to the west. Three miles across the now subtopian Morfa Bychan (where a Mephites* emerged to burn the crops and astound the population in the 18 c.) are the vast Black Rock sands, smooth as silk and hard as

* Presumably **marsh-gas**.

25

marble, where hundreds of cars can lose themselves.

Caerhun (11). Site of the Roman fortress of Canovium, marked by grass banks in elmy pastures on the left bank of the Conway. The medieval church at the far corner of the square vallum is of little interest.

Caernarvon (6). The "Castle in Arfon", very congested on Saturdays. It is worth crossing the Seiont to Coed Helen to see the full stretch of Edward I's grandest castle (1283) "the most magnificent badge of our subjection",* with its polygonal towers and finely coursed masonry perfectly reflected if the tide is in and the day calm. Then park if possible on the Slate Quay and climb the dangerous slope, past the little gesticulating figure of Lloyd George,

* Pennant.

◁ CAERNARVON
▽ CLYNNOG FAWR

into the handsome but traffic-infested Castle Square (Y Maes), its basically calm Georgian scale foolishly disrupted by 19 c. rebuilding.

The Castle is entered in the centre of its north side, whence the granite Roman Doric County Hall of 1863, with a figure of Justice on the pediment, is worth a glance. The Castle's empty interior, with tidy official lawns, is far less beautiful than its exterior. It is fully labelled.

Beneath it the little walled town is exactly as Edward laid it out, except that its protection by two rivers has been diminished by infill and embankment. Straight from the east gate the narrow High Street leads to the west gate where one emerges spectacularly upon a generally smooth sea. It and the more cheerful Palace Street contain a few mutilated 17 c. and 18 c. houses. In Palace Street is the stone-faced Covered Market built by Lord Anglesey in 1836 (John Lloyd, architect), with an airy cast-iron and timber interior; in Market Street the huge 19 c. Conser-

vative Club. The street names are carved in slate. The 14 c. church of *St Mary*, partly rebuilt by Benjamin Wyatt in 1814, is neatly and originally fitted into the north-east angle of the walls, using the corner tower as vestry.

Outside the walls the best things in the town centre are the view from Twt Hill, stony Chapel Street with its primitive Gothic chapel of 1826, and the *Moriah Chapel* in South Penrallt, also 1826, whose severe Tuscan portico conceals a beautiful classical interior with a fine built-in organ encased in Corinthian pilasters. The bleakly English *Christ Church*, in North Road, is by Anthony Salvin.

Roman *Segontium* (A.D. 79), furthest north-west outpost of the Empire, is a rectangular fort on high ground astride the road to Beddgelert (A.487). Excavated by Mortimer Wheeler in the 1920s, it is of considerable historical but no visual interest. There is a small museum of local finds at the entrance. The smaller

fort of *Hen Weliau* close by has a section of Roman wall 12 ft. high.

Two hundred yards beyond, opposite some decent modern flats, is the rather dull parish church of *St Peblig*,* mainly 14 c., with a pair of Regency lodges in front of it, and a stepped battlemented tower. The interior is Victorianised and very dark, but the Vaynol Chapel contains the finest altar tomb in the county.

Capel Curig (14). The best centre for Snowdonia climbers, but not in itself a particularly attractive place. The view of Snowdon from the old Royal Hotel (built by the first Lord Penrhyn and now a physical education centre) is famous but often invisible. Neither the picturesque old church with its two fine yews nor the 1883 one by Goronwy Owen are of architectural interest.

Within easy reach are the two historic climbers' inns, *Pen y Gwryd* at the head of Nant Gwynant and *Ogwen Cottage* (now a climbing school) at the head of Nant Ffrancon (see mountain section). The drive as far as the latter, in which the beautiful mountain Tryfan makes its sudden appearance on the left, should on no account be missed. If making the road circuit of Snowdon itself, always go *down* the lovely Nant Gwynant, which unlike most mountain valleys is best seen looking downstream, and come *up* the darkly sinister Llanberis Pass, its converse in every way. At the crest (Pen y Pass) is Gorphwysfa, the rough inn (no longer so used) which served as training headquarters for the Everest expeditions.

Clynnog Fawr (8). Easy to miss this hamlet astride the dead-straight A.499. It contains the best Gothic church west of the Conway.

St Beuno (7 c.) "no doubt ranks among Welsh saints second only to St David".* His well is still visible on the roadside a short way west of the church and his cult, sensibly established at a convenient stopping-place on the pilgrim's road to

---

* Perhaps Publicius, son of the Emperor Maximus and Empress Helen—the St Helen (of Coed Helen), whose well is in the grounds of Llwyn Helen, South Street.

CONWAY. Telford's and Stephenson's "medieval" bridges from the castle ▷

* Rev. R. D. Roberts, Vicar 1950–5.

CONWAY

CRICCIETH

Bardsey, must have largely financed the building of this noble late Gothic church. The strength of its square tower is emphasised by the diminishing storeys, and the exterior with some fine Decorated tracery composes well from all angles. Through a huge studded 18 c. door one enters the plain, light, whitewashed interior, which is entirely free of Victoriana. There is a good hammer-beam roof. The oak choir screen is well restored, and behind it are rough-hewn stalls, with linenfold and double-headed eagle panels. To the left of the altar is a primitive 17 c. altar tomb. St Beuno's Chapel, less interesting, is reached via a crude stone-roofed passage from under the tower.

Half a mile along the lane south of the church and close to the cliff edge there is an impressive neolithic burial chamber.

Conway (11). Essential to approach from the east across the rather heavy new road bridge which masks Telford's elegant suspension bridge of 1822, boldly anchored into the Castle walls. Beyond is Stephenson's castellated tubular rail bridge of 1846, leading to Francis Thompson's attractive Station. Both bridges were dress rehearsals for the much more spectacular exercise of bridging the Menai (see under Anglesey).

The *Castle*, contemporary with Caernarvon and by the same architect, Murray's Guide rightly considers "the most elegant of all the Welsh fortresses, though less grand than Caernarvon". It is remarkable that Conway's perfectly picturesque form, now dark but in the Middle Ages whitewashed, still holds up against the onslaughts of generations of engineers. This castle, unlike many, should be entered and explored. Each tower is isolated by a timber bridge so that it could fight alone. The Chapel Tower at the north-east corner is the most worth climbing. It contains at first floor level Queen Eleanor's little groin-vaulted Oratory, and from the top one has an exciting introduction to the geography of the Castle itself, of the walled town, of the three bridges, and of the river and mountain backcloth. The Castle's own features are fully signposted.

Edward's walled town, the most perfect to survive in Britain, climbs to a high point at its west corner, and the perimeter is still virtually complete and not over-restored. Within is a rather shabby and, at present (pending a controversial bypass), desperately congested little town. ("A more ragged town is scarcely to be seen, within; or a more beautiful, without".—Pennant.) High Street and Castle Street contain the best old houses, notably Plás Mawr,

the lately restored and important Elizabethan town mansion now occupied by the Royal Cambrian Academy of Art, with pretty courtyards and much naïve and powerfully modelled plasterwork of the 1580s; Aberconway, a modest wattle-and-daub oversailing house of similar date, now well cared for by the National Trust; and the Black Lion pub, also 16 c.

The mainly 14 c. but much restored *Church* on its rather forlorn green surrounded by backs of houses was converted for parochial use when Edward I removed the Cistercian abbey, a century after its foundation in 1185, to Maenan. It contains a 15 c. (restored) screen and carved choir stalls, a 16 c. recumbent lady (now known to be Archbishop Williams' daughter) worn to a moving simplicity, and a good head of himself by the early Victorian sculptor, John Gibson, a native of Conway.

In the suburb of *Gyffin* to the west the little church has some faded 15 c. ceiling paintings of saints.

Criccieth (9). The compact Victorian town spreads round a large central

above Conway Mountain ▷
from DEGANWY
below the estuary at CONWAY

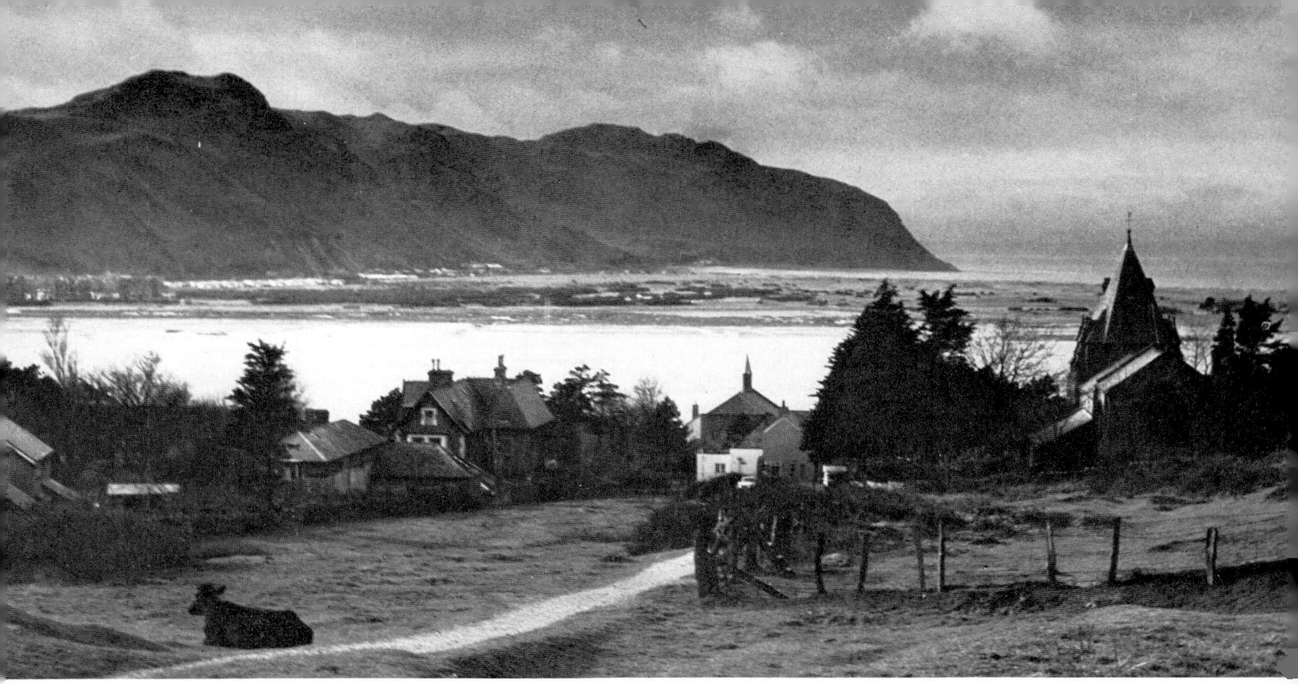

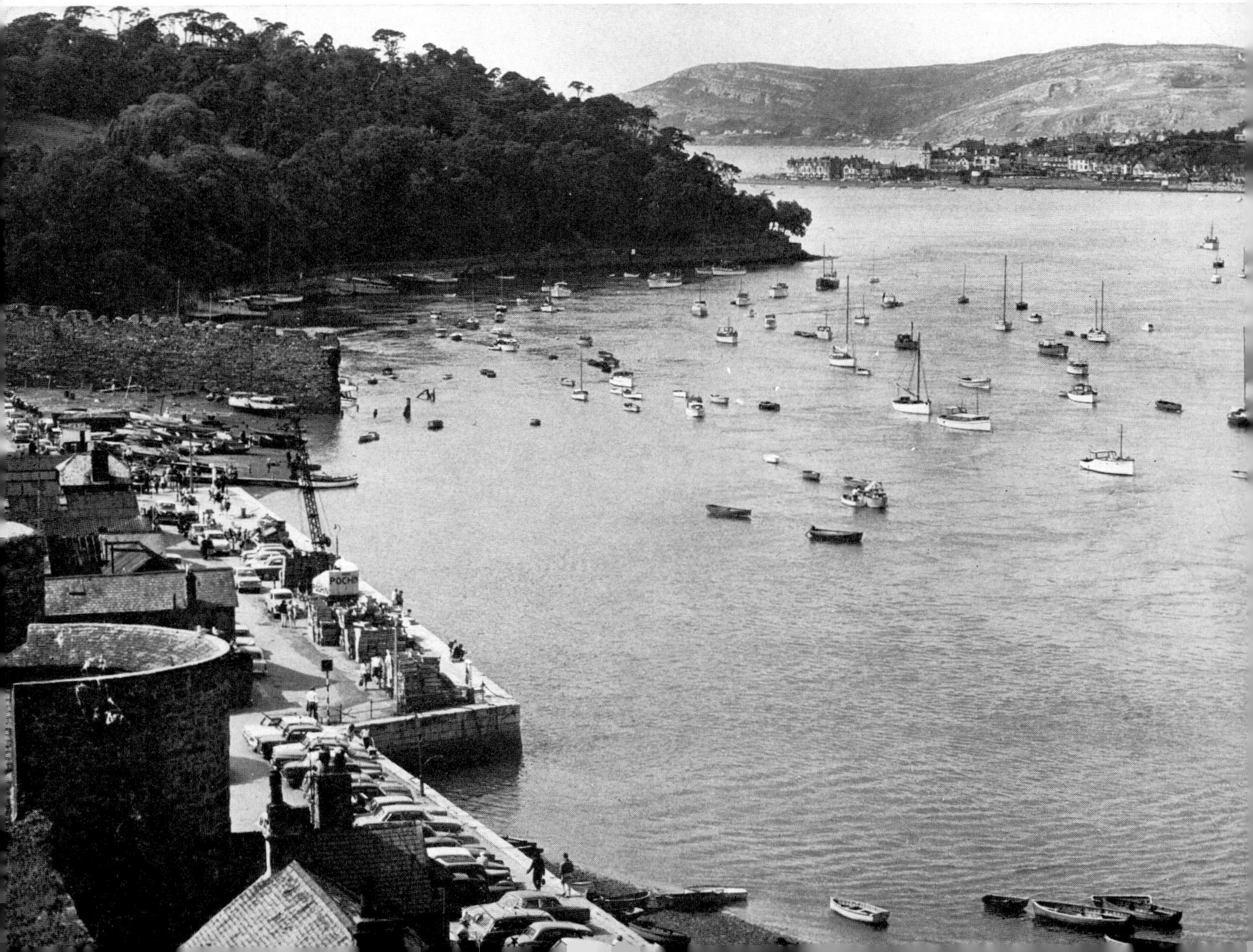

green, wisely withheld from car parking, which slopes steeply down to the sea, the Merioneth mountains across the bay and the Castle on its great round rock. Built in the 13 c. by the last of the free princes of Wales, i.e. not by Edward but against him, it has a Celtic freedom of form, and a vertiginous view from its walls, with the convex slope plunging into the waves far below. To east and west are sand and pebble beaches, the latter overlooked by a modest esplanade. A few older cottages nestle amid the spiky Victoriana. The church (Douglas of Chester, 1884), forbidding outside, has a rather good interior.

Deganwy (11). Now a suburban outpost of Llandudno with a hilltop castle site (demolished by Llewelyn the Great) commanding panoramic views. All Saints' Church, designed by Douglas of Chester in the free Gothic of the nineties, is well-placed behind ilexes, and has a romantic tower showing Lethaby influence.

Deiniolen (Llandinorwic) (13). Largest of a group of quarrymen's villages looking across Llyn Padarn to Snowdon. The finely sited copybook church was built for the community by the Assheton-Smith family in 1857. At a respectful distance is the contemporary rose-windowed chapel. The steep lane down to Llanberis has many snug cottages commanding sensational views.

Dinas Dinlle (5). Seaside earthwork of 100 B.C., much eroded. Best seen silhouetted against the horizon from the gates of Glynlliffon. Closer approach reveals extensive bungalopia alongside.

Dolbenmaen (9). A modest but attractive group of cottages at the entrance to Cwm Pennant, with a tiny church approached through a gabled 18 c. lych-gate. There is a sundial on the belfry and some fragments of old glass. The early 19 c. vicarage is entirely appropriate.

Garndolbenmaen, the 19 c. village on the hillside above, is of no architectural interest, but the many white-painted cottages, deriving from 18 c. and 19 c. small-holdings, give the landscape between here and Pen-y-groes a distinctive character.

Dolgarrog (11). Hydro-electric power station and council housing.

Dolwyddelan (14). A compact community half-way up the beautifully wooded valley of the Lledr. It used to be said that a squirrel could travel through the oak forests from Conway to Dolwyddelan without touching the ground. Two miles after leaving the A.5 the road passes under a highly picturesque Piranesian viaduct, whence a track ascends two miles to the National Trust's Ty Mawr, the birthplace of the Bishop Morgan, who translated the Bible into Welsh. Turn left in the town centre for the Old Church, perhaps the most perfect of the little churches of North Wales, consistently 16 c., with slate floor and limewashed walls, carved Gothic screen, some exquisite fragments of 16 c. glass and a fine Wynne memorial tablet. The pulpit and benches are 18 c. On a bluff one mile beyond are the twin keeps of the *Castle*, where Liewelyn the Great is said to have been born. Further up the valley opens to disclose a fine view of Snowdon with the "great bending mountain Siabod"* in the foreground.

Glynllifon (5). The huge and gloomy grey stucco mansion of Lord Newborough, rebuilt in the Palladian style after a fire in 1836, is now the County Agricultural Institute and College of Further Education. Dying conifers and young plantations. On a hilltop in the park, amid shackery, is the sadly derelict Fort Williamsburg, one of the two† erected by Newborough in the late 18 c., from which he planned to defend North Wales against Napoleon.

Gwydir Castle (14). Built by Wynnes through several centuries from the materials of Maenan Abbey, this picturesque pile was gutted by fire in 1912 and 1922. Only the low 17 c.

* Pennant.
† The other, and much finer, is Belan Fort, commanding the entrance to the Menai and now Lord Newborough's residence. It is not open.

central block with 19 c. stair turret contains two plain original rooms.

A short climb through the Forestry Commission's spruces, *Gwydir Uchaf* chapel lies beside a Regency cottage used as a Commission office. It is wholly as left by Sir Richard Wynne in 1673, with wood-mullioned clear glass windows, a rugged painted gallery balustrade and a remarkable painted ceiling with primitive cherubs and scrolls as in Carinthia.

Llanaelhaearn (8). A dull village at the foot of Yr Eifl (*angl:* The Rivals) with a 12 c. (restored) cruciform church. Its endearing low interior has a 16 c. rood screen and attractive 18c. spindle-backed box pews. Inscribed 6c. stones inside and outside the church suggest that it was a station on the Saints' Road to Bardsey. High above it at 1,590 ft. is the remarkable British walled hill-town of *Trér Ceiri*,* occupied as late as 400 A.D. It is best reached by a delectable grass path (marked) leaving the Nefyn road a mile beyond the village. On a clear day (essential) the view from the central Fujiyama-shaped Rival is the most beautiful mountain-top panorama in Wales, with the whole of the Lleyn, its hills rising one behind another, miles of sea north and south, Holyhead mountain, and the majestic silhouette of Snowdonia.

Llanarmon (8). Just a 15 c. church and school in the quiet country behind Pwllheli. The church, pointed externally in a Pop-Art style, has a graceful arcade between its two aisles and a primitive 15 c. rood-screen.

Llanbedrog (8). Sheltered from the prevailing winds by a sheer cliff, clothed with rich woodland where it overhangs the village, this snug and sandy cove has recently become popular and built-up, but immense trees muffle it all. The restored church, entered through a tiny lych-gate, is close to the beach, but so embosomed in trees that in summer it is hard to find. It contains a graceful 16 c. carved screen and some fragmentary 15 c. glass in the west window lighting the little minstrels' gallery. The old village inland of the main road is less attractive.

* Town of the Giants.

◁ Gwydir Uchaf chapel,
  GWYDIR CASTLE

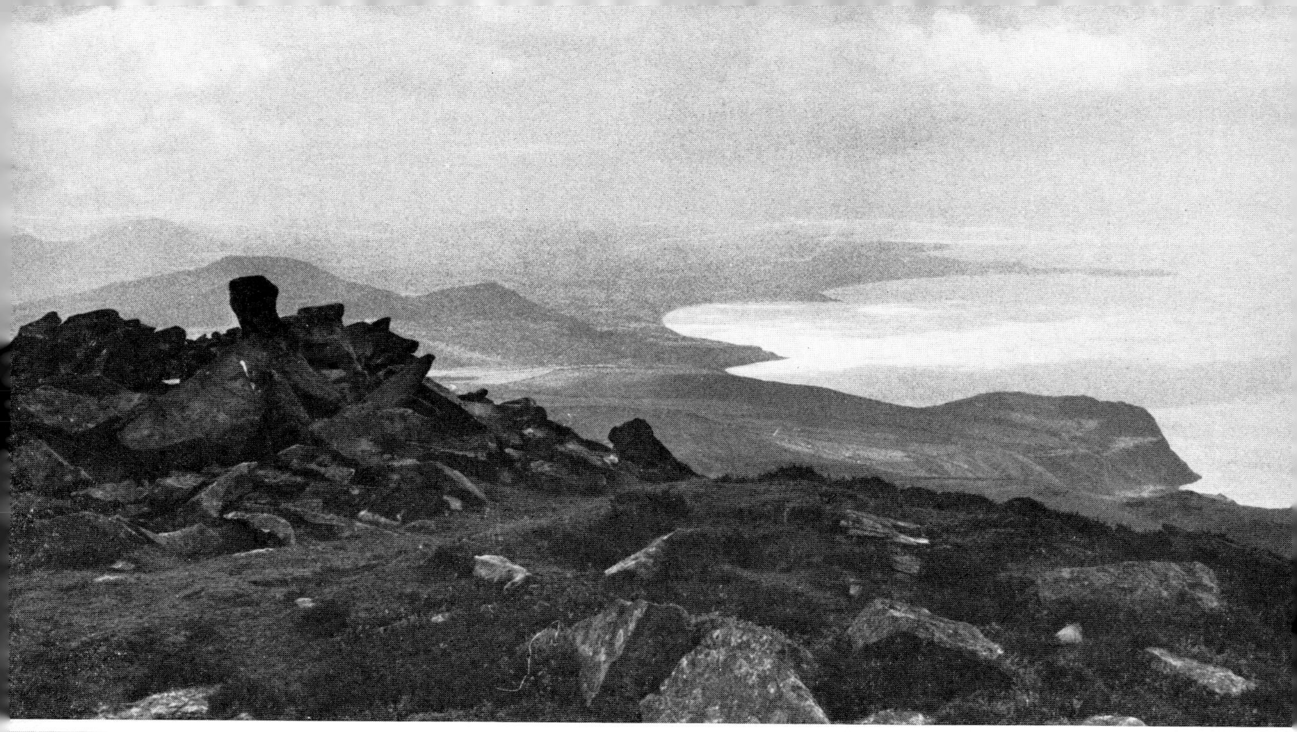

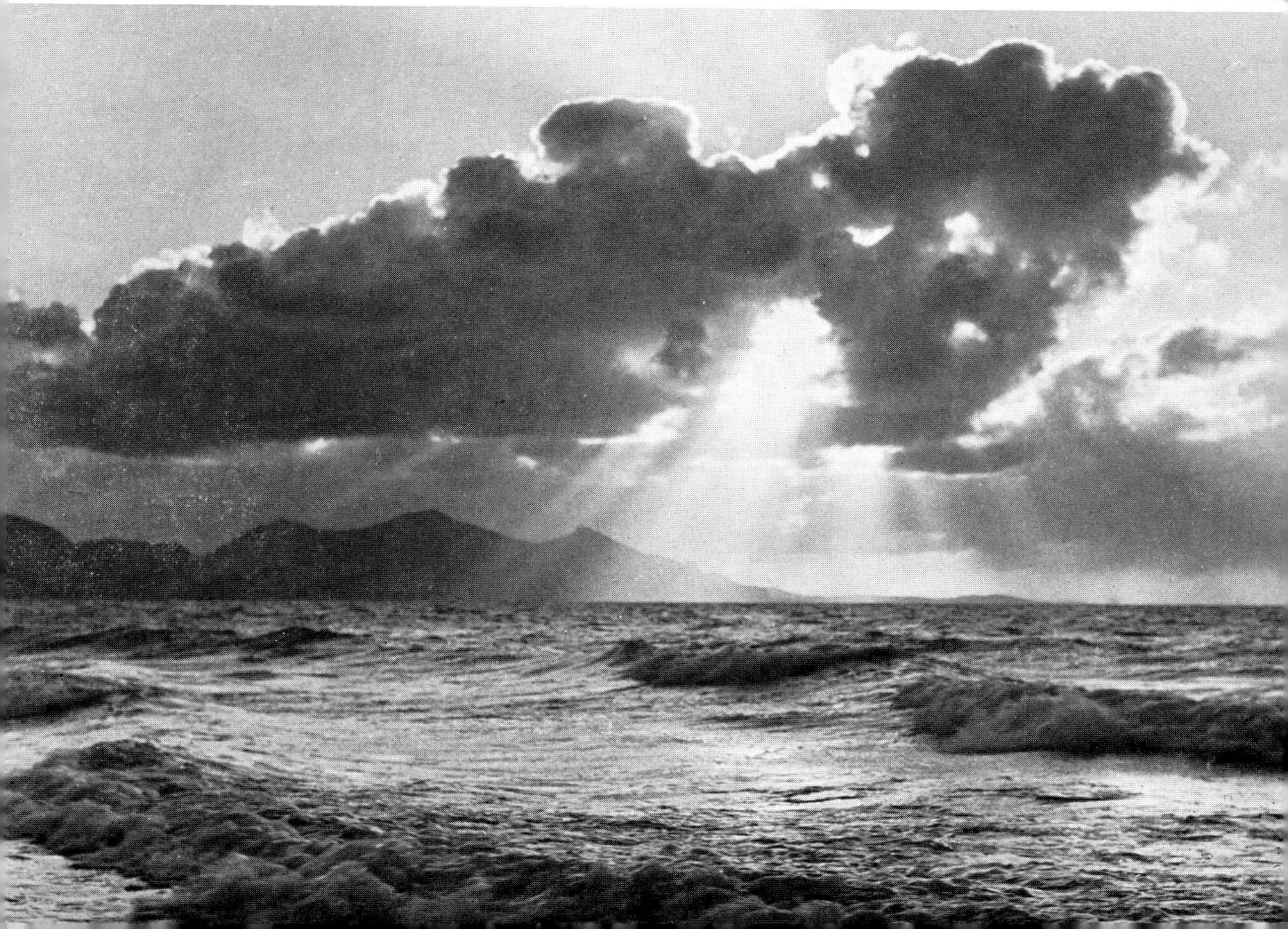

The landmark of *Foel Fawr*, 1½ miles inland, is an old mill given to the National Trust by the Misses Keating. The view on a clear day is magnificent.

Llanbedr-y-Cennin (11). A whitewashed hamlet above the Conway with a well-placed church among yews, restored by H. Kennedy in 1842.

Llanberis (6). Touchingly described by an 1881 guide as "the Chamouny of Wales", Llanberis retains a good deal of Victorian charm, now overlaid in the summer season by ice-cream vans and queues for the Snowdon Railway. Dolbadarn Castle (13 c.), godsend to generations of water-colourists, is best seen at a distance, and there is no need or chance to avert the eye from the immense Dinorwic quarries which cover 700 acres and spill straight into Llyn Peris from a summit level that is often in the clouds.

The original quarry buildings can be reached on foot by the private road between the two lakes, and are very handsome, particularly the main front facing north-east. The lane should be followed northwards at least as far as the beautiful flooded "twll", or pit, of the earliest quarry. There is a very fine 50 ft. waterwheel (1870).

St Padarn's Church of 1885, designed by a pupil of Gilbert Scott, ugly outside, has an unusual interior with a large central space.

Llanberis was the home of Margaret Evans, who, according to Pennant, was "at the age of 70 the best wrestler in the country, and few young men dared to try a fall with her. At length she gave her hand to the most effeminate of her admirers."

Nant Peris, at the foot of the Pass, has the tiny medieval parish church, with a modern chancel, overhung by the immense dark cwms of the north ridge of Snowdon.

Picture this whole gorge filled to the brim with a slowly grinding mass of ice a thousand feet deep. "While

◁ *above* The view westwards from the summit of Yr Eifl, LLANAELHAEARN
below Yr Eifl
LLANDEGWNING ▷

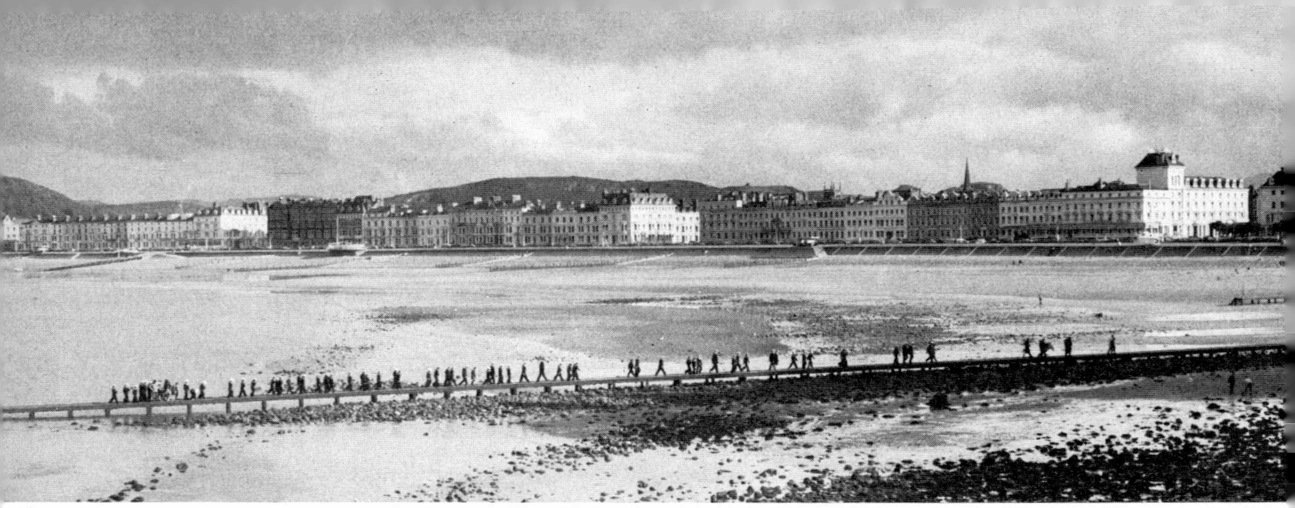
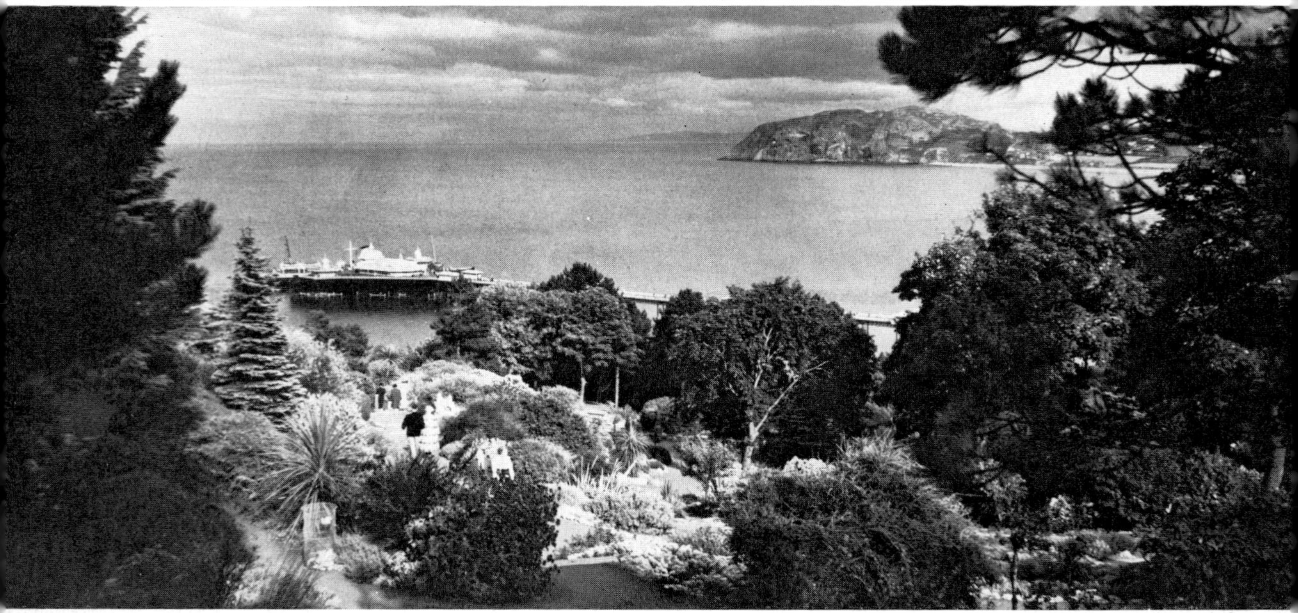
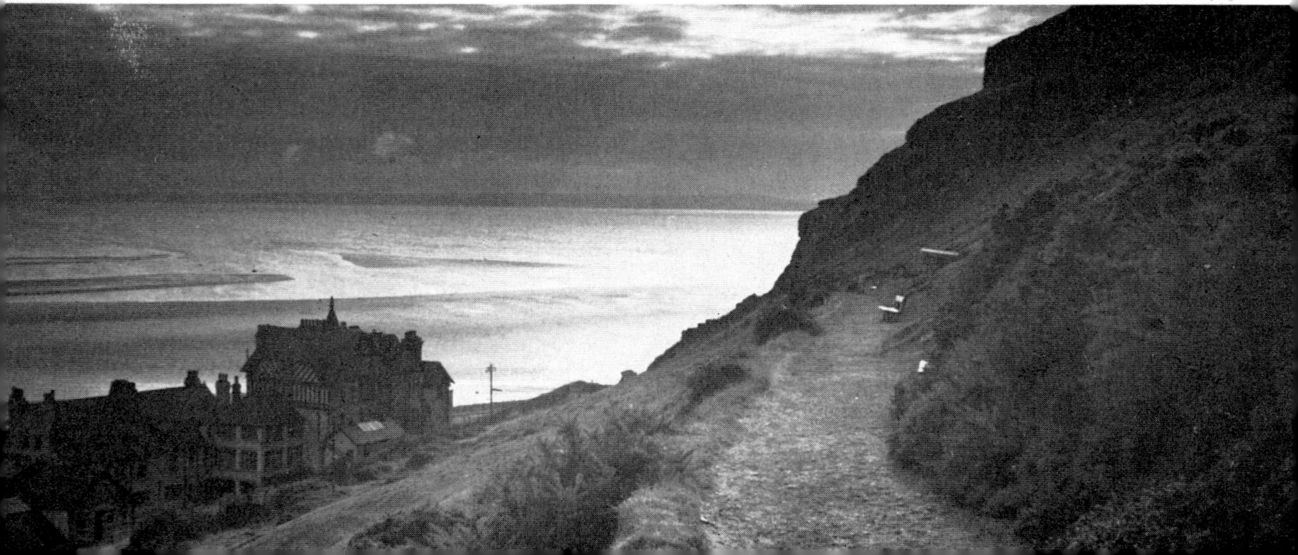

LLANGELYNIN

the tourist, who sees something in scenery beyond mere external form, is often puzzled to account for the numerous blocks that, perched on precarious points, seem as if they ought to have taken a final bound into the lower valley, the well-pleased eye of the geologist versed in ice at once detects that they were let gently down where they lie by the melting of the diminishing glacier." (A. C. Ramsay 1860.)

Llandegai (10). Lord Penrhyn's model village at the Castle gate. The layout is Picturesque and the cottage designs deliberately varied. The restored church at the end of a fine yew avenue has a 15 c. alabaster tomb with effigies of a knight and lady, Archbishop Williams kneeling in his niche with his helmet and spurs beside him, and a respectful quarryman, paired with a figure of Hope, grieving at the tomb of the first Lord and Lady (by Westmacott).

◁ LLANDUDNO
The navy goes ashore
The Happy Valley
Great Orme

Llandegwning (4). Charming toy church of 1840, with a round tower and conical spire. At *Nanhoron* to the east is a good Regency house and lodge, and the tiny *Capel Newydd*, 1769, the earliest surviving Nonconformist chapel in North Wales, hard to find at the end of a grassy lane at 286309 (turn off the main road at pt. 233). The simple barn-like structure has an earth floor and box pews.

Llandudno (11). One of the most perfect and unspoilt of Victorian watering places, the town was admirably laid out by Lord Mostyn in 1849 along the crescent-shaped beach between the two remarkable limestone headlands of the Great Orme* and Little Orme, with wide streets and a great boulevard (Gloddaeth Avenue) linking its south-facing and north-facing beaches, now terminating in the War Memorial obelisk at the north end. Cleanly painted from end to end, the great cresent of hotels and houses has no discordant element, and ends in a fine pier of 1876 from which steamers ply to Liverpool and Holyhead. Perched boldly beside it is the Grand Hotel by J. F. Doyle. Parallel and one block inland Mostyn Street, with sensible iron-and-glass arcades, contains the main shops "much frequented in summer by the Liverpool people" (Murray, 1885) but never congested. Of the numerous undistinguished 19 c. churches and chapels, John Welch's *new Parish Church* of 1840 on the lower slopes of the Great Orme has an attractive east window, and *St Paul's* of 1895, by J. O. Scott, the son of Sir Gilbert, bleakly situated on the half-developed flat land east of the centre, has a rather grand interior with marble columns.

The Great Orme has at its near end the prettily landscaped Happy Valley and at its far end *St Tudno's* much-restored medieval church. The one-way motor circuit of the headland (starting at the pier end) is best done at sunset.

On the main road to Colwyn Bay, a precarious oasis in suburbia, is Penrhyn Old Hall, a small Tudor manor house now a restaurant, and on the Conway road (1 mile out) is *Llanrhos* Church, wholly Victorian-

* Norse: *Orma*—a serpent.

37

ised but containing a 6 c. inscribed tombstone, 17 c.–19 c. Wynne and Mostyn memorials and a good early 19 c. window. There is a well-designed early 19 c. schoolhouse opposite. *Bodysgallen*, the Tudor stone Mostyn mansion, is hidden in the richly wooded limestone landscape nearby, and across the valley is *Gloddaeth*, with a Tudor great hall, restored by Nesfield. It is now a school.

Llandwrog (5). Worth the brief detour off the A.499, Lord Newborough's charming Gothic village of the 1830s has some pleasant almshouses and an elegant spired church of 1860, perhaps his best work, by Henry Kennedy of Bangor. Entered through the tower, the excellent Gothic Revival interior, complete with appropriate fittings, has some beautiful 18 c. Wynne monuments in the chapel right of the altar.

Llanengan (5). The square-towered church (the tower dated by inscription 1534), the most important in Lleyn, is at present in a state of precarious beauty, emptied of all furniture. The twin-aisled interior, untouched by the Victorians, is remarkable for its two carved late Gothic rood-screens, with delicate galleries above and primitive stalls below. The Communion rail in the south aisle is 16 c.

Llanfaglan (5). Isolated and hard to find at 455606, protected by a walled enclosure and wind-bent trees in a field on the edge of the vast Menai sands, this little medieval church, untouched since the 18 c., gives a vivid idea of the sort of building the Victorian restorers longed to get their hands on, and generally did. The lintel on the inside of the door is the tombstone of the late Roman Antemorius.

Llanfairfechan (11). A pleasant grey and white village in a steep wooded combe, with an untouched mid-Victorian seafront. Christ Church (1855) has a bright and gay interior of no architectural distinction but considerable polychromatic charm. St Mary's, up the hill, is of less interest.
The "Druid's Circle" (see under Penmaenmawr) can be approached part-way by car via Mount Road.

Llangelynin (11). A remote little crouching church high on the sheep runs above Conway at 752737. To reach it, a tiny rough lane climbs

Dorothea slate quarry, NANTLLE ▷

800 feet out of the hamlet of Henryd; the last stretch best done on foot. Key at Garneddwen Farm. The interior is beautifully plain, with earth floor surviving in the transept. The women stood (the earliest bench was dated 1629) in the 12 ft. wide nave, the men in the parallel aisle alongside. The chancel has a timber barrel-vault as at Gyffin. In the corner of the sheep-cropped churchyard is the saint's well. A mile south-east at 740718, on the Roman Road across the moors from Canovium to Segontium, is a fine cromlech.

Llangian (8). Pretty white village beside a stream, popular with Abersoch holiday-makers. The long, narrow church, Victorianised internally, has a good 1760 memorial to Timothy Edwards of Nanhoron. In the churchyard, north of the church, is the tombstone of the late Roman Melius Medicus.

Llangwnnadl (7). An airy and beautifully cared-for three-aisled Perp. church, with rough stone interior. The carved Gothic lettering on the

Talysarn, NANTLLE

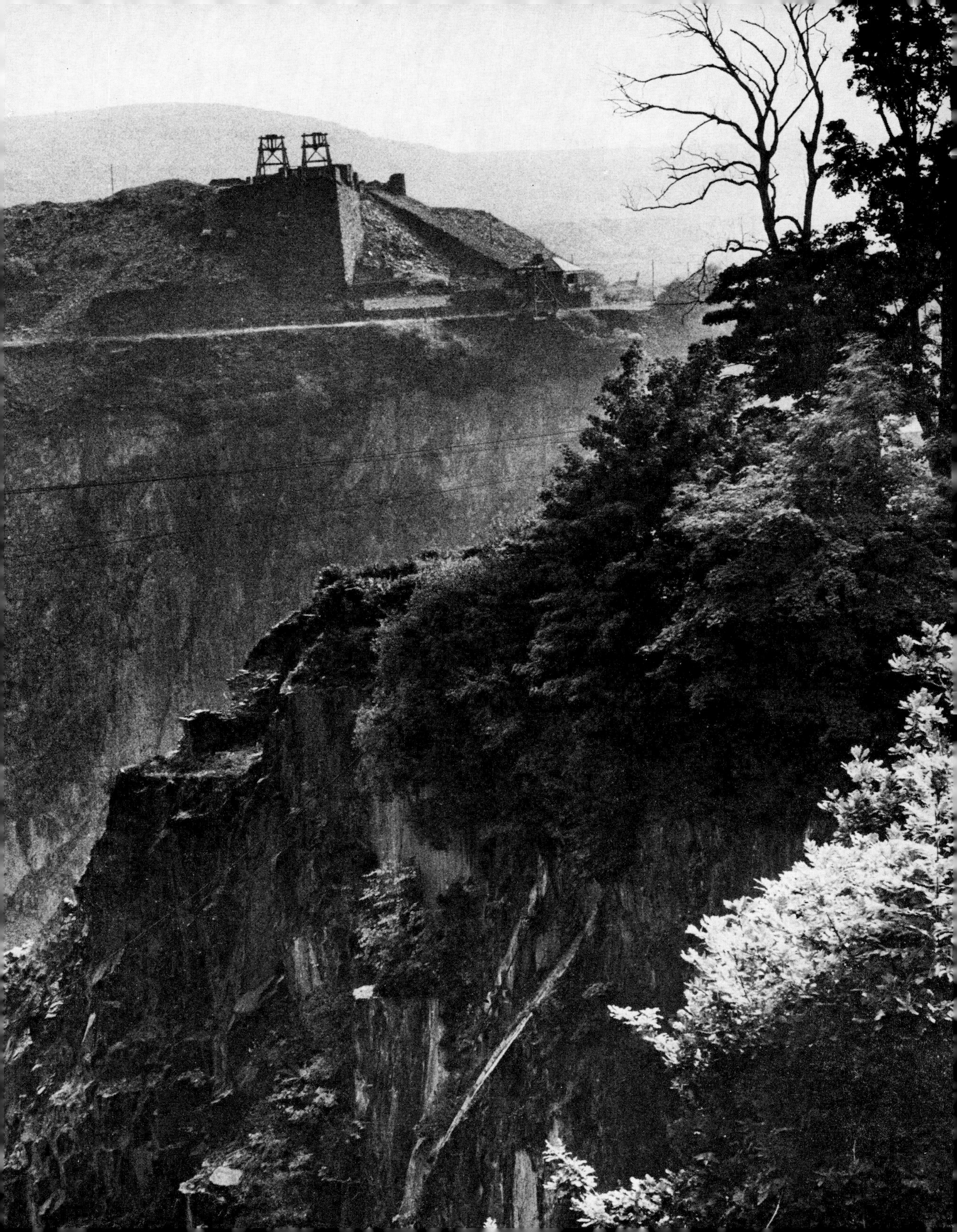

piers record the date of building as 1520. Every hassock has a different design in *gros-point*. The church is all alone in a sheltered cranny, and a mile beyond it there is a quiet bathing cove at Porth Colmon.

Llangybi (8). St Cybi, 6 c. Cornish saint, founded churches in Wales and Ireland. Behind the simple church in this quiet place a path leads down to his well (Ffynnon Cybi) enclosed in a roofless megalithic structure with rough niches, overhung by a beech grove. East of the church an equally simple group of 1760 almshouses.

Llaniestyn (7). Peaceful, sheltered spot at the foot of the conspicuous 1,200 ft. Carn Fadron with its important Iron Age hill-fort. The church, like so many in Lleyn, is beautifully looked after. It has an unusual musician's gallery and a delightful rococco memorial to an 18 c. fellow of Jesus College, Oxford.

Llanllechid (10). A quiet quarrymen's village near Bethesda, with magnificent mountain views. The monumental granite church, an early work (1846) of Henry Kennedy in an eccentric and effective Norman style, is approached through a solemn yew avenue lined with slate headstones. The east window is by Clutterbuck. "Little", wrote the Ecclesiologist, "can be said for its correctness. This comes of the same architects essaying Church architecture who deal in the revived Pagan." Kennedy was later to put this right. A mile away, *Cochwillan* was a 15 c. manor house, is now a barn.

Llanllyfni (6). Quarrymen's 1860–90 tight-knit village on the A.4085 between mountains and sea, with a long main street. Of several chapels, Capel Ebenezer (just beyond the north end of the main street) has an original 1826 interior with box pews and gilded Corinthian centrepiece, Capel Moriah (1871) a charming Gothic front with monkey-puzzle. In the churchyard wall of St Gredfyn is a slate tablet inscribed (in Welsh) "The stone which cries out from the wall".

Llannor (8). A farm hamlet inland from Pwllheli. The church has a bold plain tower with stepped gables. There is a late Roman tombstone in the porch and various 19 c. monuments in the Victorianised interior. Nearby are several good old houses, including the tall austere Bodvel, where Dr Johnson's Mrs Thrale was born in 1741, and the more cheerful 18 c. Bodegroes, with a Regency verandah.

Llanrug (6). Typical linear quarrymen's village near Llanberis spoilt by 20 c. building. At the far west end is the beautiful churchyard on a small hill, with a restored and stuccoed church which retains its 15 c. roof. The bridge over the Rhythallt is recorded as by "the modern Inigo, Harry Parry".

To the north, romantically placed against the mountainside, is the early 19 c. *Bryn Bras Castle*.

Llanwnda (6). Main road subtopia with an 1848 "Norman" church by G. Alexander, containing a primitive 17 c. monument and an elegant 18 c. one.

Llanystumdwy (9). Spoiled main-road village near Criccieth where Lloyd George lived, with a good old bridge over the rocky Dwyfor. His memorial by Clough Williams-Ellis overlooks the rushing river from its east bank and is linked by a curving drive with piers and a wrought-iron gate to the Lloyd George Museum by the same architect. The wholly appropriate 1862 church, dull internally, is by Kennedy.

Llithfaen (8). Exposed village with wide views on south slope of Yr Eifl (see Llanaelhaearn). A steep lane, part motorable, runs north to Vortigern's Valley, scene of his legendary death, a sinister hanging valley cut off between sea and mountain, now scarred by quarry workings. In its bottom, reachable on foot only, is an abandoned hamlet.

Maenan (11). Site of the abbey evacuated from Conway by Edward I when he decided to rebuild and fortify the town, and since then an enclave of Caernarvonshire. Maenan Hall, on the slopes above, is rare in N. Wales in retaining its late medieval hall.

Originally the property of a worldly monk, it was embellished in 1582 by his son Maurice Kyffin with plasterwork no doubt by the same bold hand as Plas Mawr in Conway. The 1790 W. Front, until lately a farmhouse, was restored by the Aberconway family in the 1950s. On the crest behind is a gazebo no doubt of similar date, also recently restored

Nantlle (Talysarn) (6). The long white terraces hug a sunny slope right up to the slate tips, with Snowdon walling in the head of the valley. The Talysarn village street runs under a bold arch straight into the quarry, with a fine flooded twll to the left and the immensely deep working Dorothea pit to the right. The latter can be visited from the main road entrance at 594527 and is well worth it. Unlike the terraces of of Penrhyn and Dinorwic, Dorothea has vertical sides, and perched on their edges great dry slate bastions to hold aerial ropeways, looking like Assyrian fortresses.

Nefyn (8). A snug little town with a comic church rebuilt in the 1820s, villa accretions and magnificent sand beaches sheltered from most winds. Beyond and across the impeccable golf course at Morfa Nefyn one can reach on foot the cluster of white cottages at the yacht anchorage of Porth Dinllaen, the natural harbour from which Madocks hoped to run the Irish mail, and to which the dead straight Pwllheli–Nefyn road was directed for this purpose.

Penmachno (14). Quarrymen's village in central-Wales-type pastoral landscape, easily reached from A.5. The church has some 5 c. and 6 c. inscribed stones and a triptych by an unknown 16 c. Flemish painter. There are good 17 c. farmhouses (e.g. Hafod Dwryd) on the surrounding slopes.

Penmaenmawr (11). Mr Gladstone's holiday spot, now throttled by main road and railway. St Seiriol's Church (1868), on the road leading to the Sychnant Pass, is entered beneath its saddleback tower; it has a two-tone brick interior of considerable character by Waterhouse, perhaps

PENRHYN CASTLE ▷

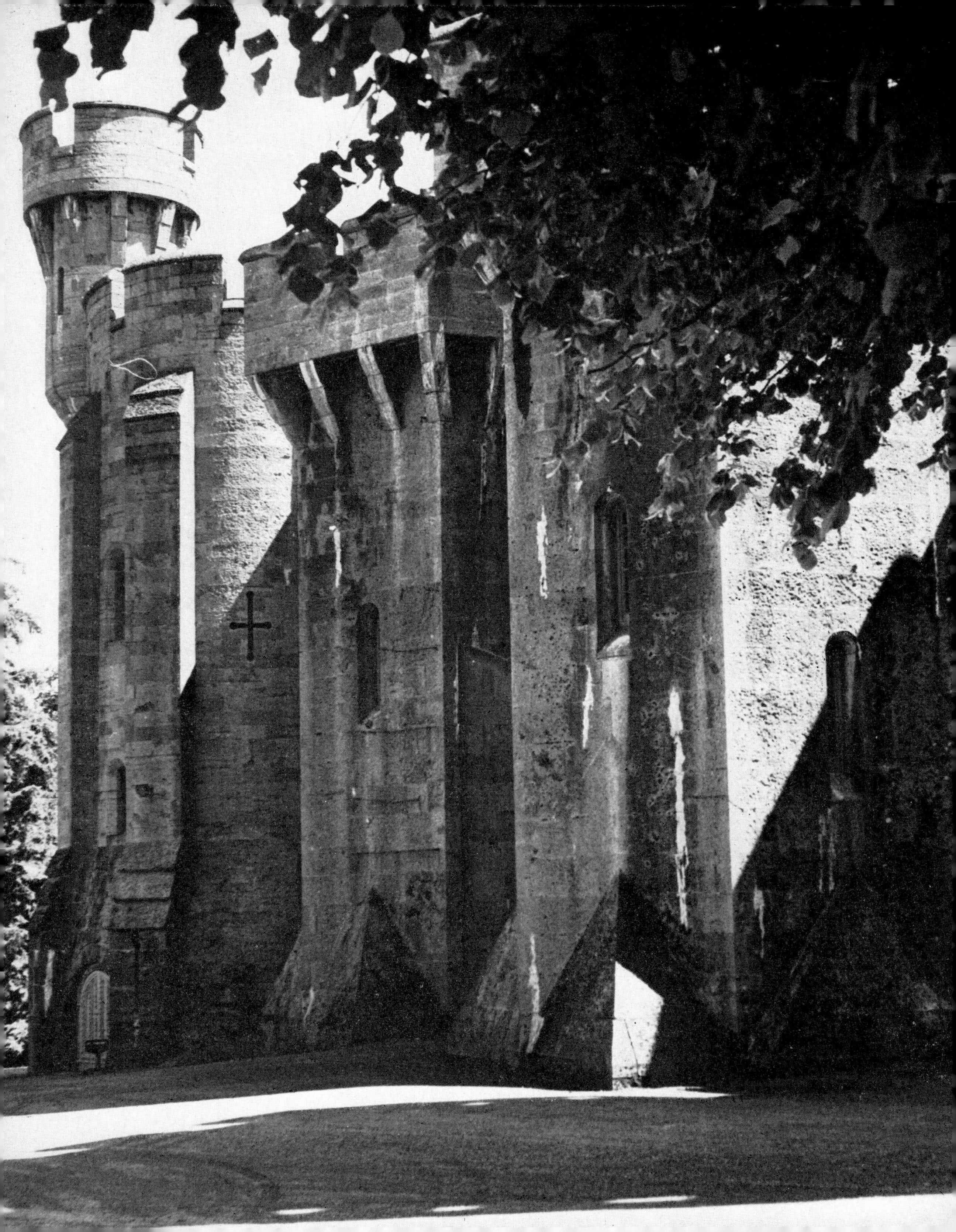

under the influence of Butterfield. The suburbanised village of Dwygyfylchi has at the head of its valley a "Fairy Glen", with a cascade descending a richly wooded ravine. The sands along this whole coastline are vast and safe.

On the crest of the escarpment at 723746, 1,200ft. above the town, and an equally stiff climb from Penmaenmawr or Llanfairfechan, is the "*Druid's Circle*", one of the great many Bronze and Iron Age remains on these northern slopes of the Carnedds. Stone axes from the factory here have been found all over Britain. The great camp on Penmaenmawr itself was destroyed by quarry workings.

Pennant, Cwm (9). The most peaceful of Snowdonia valleys, because its head is closed by a semicircle of peaks, and to many the most beautiful. "Oh God", wrote the bard Eifion Wyn, "why didst thou make Cwm Pennant so beautiful and the life of an old shepherd so short?" It is well seen from the main road south-east of Dolbenmaen, with the Victorian folly tower of Brynkir (from which a cow was recently seen looking over the battlements) peeping out of its clump of trees.

To the east, below the dull side of Moel Hebog, is the lonely reservoir of Cwm Ystradllyn, and on the way to it at 549433 the conspicuous and dramatic ruined slate mill of Ynyspandy (see page 15), built by an English syndicate in 1864 to exploit the Gorseddau quarries and the water power of the lake below them. The slate was brought in at high level on the bold curving embankment and sawn and dressed on the floor below. By 1870 the enterprise had failed to repay excessive investment and the mill was stripped and ruined: it is now one of the most impressive of the ruins of Wales.

The valley is full of remote and extraordinary relics of the slate industry, all of which enhance rather than damage the beauties of nature. Note for example the cyclopean masonry at 570454, the waterfall, tunnel and "dragon's pool" at 522452 and the melancholy remains of the Prince of Wales' quarry on the pass that leads from the head of the valley over to Rhyd-Ddu, with the bleak barracks where the men spent their weekday nights.

The whole valley is worth a long day's exploration on foot: only the telegraph poles and one new house spoil the impeccable scene. There is a good Regency cottage at the bottom bridge over the Dwyfor. The Victorian church of Llanfihangel-y-Pennant is of no architectural but some scenic value.

Penrhyn Castle (10). Staggering insight into the mind of the Romantic age, this megalomanic granite pile by Hopper (on the site of a late 18 c. Gothic mansion by Samuel Wyatt) is said to have cost the second Lord Penrhyn £$\frac{1}{2}$ million of his quarry profits and 14 years of his life (1827–40). "It is to be regretted," sighs Murray (1885), "that . . . recourse should not have been had to a later style than Norm." To our eyes its solemn platitudes and heraldic glass admirably set off the mainly late Victorian furnishings, some of which are appropriately horrendous. There is a slate bedstead and in the stables an entertaining locomotive museum. The estate now belongs to the National Trust, and the picturesque park, with winding gravel drive, commands views along the coast to the Carnedds.

The great empty dock of *Port Penrhyn* now shelters a few fishing vessels. The pretty late Georgian Port Office is by Benjamin Wyatt, brother of James and agent to Lord Penrhyn.

Port Penrhyn, The Port Office

Holiday housing on PORTMADOC Quay

Pentrefelin (9). Roadside hamlet near Criccieth with a modest church and vicarage (1912) by Clough Williams-Ellis.

Pen-y-Groes (6). Compact and now colourful quarrymen's townlet on the western approaches to Snowdon. Pen-y-Gaer (750693) is an Iron Age hill-fort. The 19 c. settlements in this area are named biblically after their chapels, e.g. Nebo, Nazareth, Carmel, Caesarea.

Pistyll (8). On the north Lleyn coast with sea views and caravans. The very plain church, part 12 c., has a powerfully buttressed west front, bold roof timbers and a fine 12 c. font.

Port Dinorwic (6). Stucco townlet with one long street on the Menai and a yacht marina. The locks and quays where the slate was loaded are now richly wooded but deserted. Note the polychrome slate harbourmaster's office. Pastoral Anglesey with its white ferry terminal looks enticing across the water.

Portmadoc (16). While building Tremadoc (q.v.), William Madocks embarked on the even more ambitious enterprise (occasionally discussed ever since the 17 c.) of building a causeway across the mouth of the beautiful Glaslyn estuary and so at one blow reclaiming 3,000 acres of the Traeth Mawr, providing a rail link from the Ffestiniog slate quarries to the sea, and offering a huge short-cut on his abortive route to Ireland. After many adventures it was done, and in the process it was found that the Glaslyn had scooped out a natural harbour which was named Portmadoc in happy double commemoration of its founder and the legendary Madog who is said to have sailed to the New World from this spot. By the mid-century the port was crowded with shipping and handling 50,000 tons of slate a year. It is now a growing yacht centre.

The view of Snowdon from the Cob, as Madocks' causeway is locally called, was saved at a cost of £2 million by burying the 275 k.v. power line that crosses the estuary. It is the most beautiful of all the prospects of Snowdon. All the same, few will dispute Peacock's judgment on the scenic damage done by the draining of the Traeth:

"Vast rocks and precipices, intersected with little torrents, formed the barrier on the left: on the right the triple summit of Moelwyn reared its majestic boundary: in the depth was that sea of mountains, the wild and stormy outline of the Snowdonian chain, with the giant Wyddfa towering in the midst. The mountain-frame remains unchanged, unchangeable: but the liquid mirror it enclosed is gone."

Fortunately it need not be gone for ever. The role of the Cob could be reversed.

The town is of wholly mid-Victorian character. It has eclipsed in size and prosperity its little Regency neighbour, and there are several grandiose chapels and a fine granite Midland Bank in the busy stucco High Street. A decent 1933 R.C. church stands on the hill up to Borth-y-Gest, with one of the few Regency houses (where Madocks once lived) behind it, and there (1968) are new holiday cottages by John Phillips on the quay.

Pwllheli (8). Created a borough by the Black Prince, railhead and market town of the Lleyn peninsula, this small Victorian watering-place has never got big enough for its boots—the vast sea-front, and the bleak areas around its equally vast and muddy harbour. The old High Street is one of the few in Wales that is not a through traffic route, and hereabouts are what pleasant buildings the town possesses. The best of several large chapels is Penlan, 1863, standing back from Gaol Street behind a large ash tree, with a spick-and-span interior and impeccable woodwork. Seawards are the usual windy stucco terraces and council housing, with a (modern) stone circle in the recreation ground. Pressing on you will reach what remains of the Gimblet Rock, the town's one landmark, nibbled away to provide roadstone for Lloyd George's harbour works. Close to it a well-designed modern yacht club.

Pwllheli does a brisk trade with the 12,000 patrons of the large Butlin Holiday Camp, 3 miles east, where flagpoles and pop art enliven a featureless stretch of main road. Nearby, buried in semi-tropical Victorian gardens, is Broom Hall, a large plain early 19 c. stucco block with American style verandah round three sides.

Rhiw (4). A hilltop hamlet near the tip of Lleyn, with wide views. Tucked away in the shelter of the 1,000 ft. Mynydd Rhiw is Plas-yn-Rhiw, a 16 c. manor house with Regency roof, windows and verandah, given to the National Trust, with other properties nearby, by the Misses Keating, who show the house on certain days in April, May and June. The square stone house, now stripped of its stucco, looks calmly across the bleak and forbidding Hell's Mouth to the Merioneth hills and distant Cader Idris. Below, sheltered by great trees, an outstandingly romantic little garden, with cobbled court, falling water, box and yew hedges and rioting roses, fuchsia, azalea, magnolia and camellia—a movingly human response to the dour and hostile environment.

Sarn-Mellteyrn (7). A depopulated

◁ Sarn-Mellteyrn
    Llanrhychwyn church, Trefriw ▷

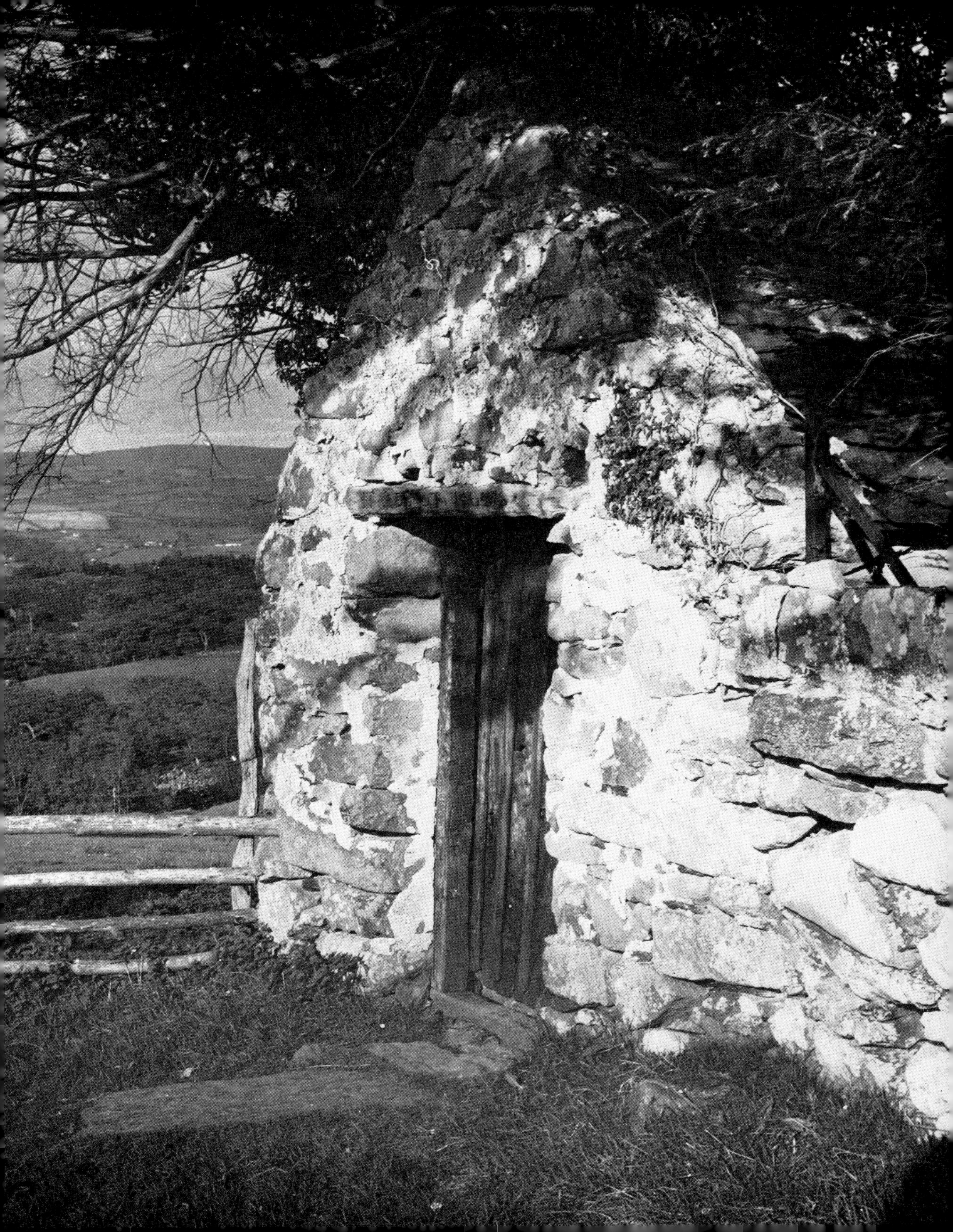

TREMADOC

village in a sheltered dell on Lleyn, with some shackery. Beautifully situated above it is H. Kennedy's little sharply pointed 1848 church, which earned this compliment from *The Ecclesiologist*: "It is consoling to see anything like a revival of ecclesiastical propriety in this forlorn district where the old churches are generally mean in their architecture."

Talysarn (See Nantlle)

Trefriw (14). A nearby chalybeate spring led to the growth of this jumbled village clinging to the wooded west slope of the Conway valley, with a Victorianised church and a number of ugly villas. It is the point of entry to the Crafnant valley with its pretty boating lake and also, up a steep lane climbing 1½ miles through the forest, to 'Llewelyn's old church' of *Llanrhychwyn*. You reach this across the meadow from a kink in the lane (marked) and pass under a little 1762 lych-gate among yews. The interior is touchingly simple, with white-washed walls and square columns, slate-slabbed floor and a pale timbered roof. There is a decent 17 c. pulpit and reading desk and some fragments of old glass, including a Trinity of about 1460 in the York style.

Tremadoc (16). The classically planned townlet was created and almost wholly erected in the first decade of the 19 c. under the direction of William Madocks, M.P. for Boston, on reclaimed land forming part of his Tan-yr-allt estate. Madocks, bon viveur, romantic, and practical improver of restless energy, conceived the idea of opening up a new mail route to Ireland (united with England in 1801), by driving a road across the Lleyn to the natural harbour of Porth Dinllaen and so by-passing the obstacles of the Conway, the Menai, and the crossing to Holyhead Island. Tremadoc was to become the last inland staging-post before the Irish Sea (hence "London Street" and "Dublin Street") so benefiting the locality and attracting the gentry. At the head of the symmetrical Square and hard up against a rocky backcloth stands the Madoc Hotel and the accidentally off-centre Town Hall (now a Crafts Centre) in a provincial Inigo Jones manner. On a hillock to the south is the miniature Gothic church of 1806 with an elaborate Coade stone lych-gate and forlornly empty graveyard. Beyond and west of the road is the bold Tuscan portico of the Peniel chapel of 1811 (which has an unusual raked interior). Madocks assured the

Peniel Chapel, 1811, TREMADOC

Bishop of Bangor, who expressed some surprise at this comparatively lavish provision for Dissenters, that while the church was built on rock, the chapel was built on sand.

In the woods above the main road 1 mile east of Tremadoc is *Tan-yr-allt*, the first "Regency" house in North Wales, largely built by Madocks in 1800. It has the low-pitched roof and deep eaves characteristic of his work and made possible by the better slates then coming out of the quarries. It also characteristically has a window over the drawing-room fireplace. The house was rented by the Shelleys in 1812–13 during the poet's brief period of enthusiasm for Madocks' enterprises. *Queen Mab* was written in it.

The old parish church, prettily situated down the lane south of the village of *Penmorfa*, has some 15 c. glass in its west window and a memorial to the Welsh Royalist Colonel John Owen.

"In former times," sighed Pennant, "this neighbourhood abounded with gentry."

Tudweiliog (7). Hilltop village on the exposed north coast of Lleyn, with a dull church rebuilt by Sir Gilbert Scott in 1850. Close by *Cefnamlwch*, buried deep in ancient woods, was originally a substantial house of the Griffith family, and has an early 17 c. gateway. On the green slope of the Mynydd to the south is a fine cromlech; on its north flank the little church of *Penllech* is untouched since the 18 c. East of the village at 274368, in a beautifully kept enclosure in open farmland, is the tiny medieval church of *Llandudwen*, with early 19 c. glass lighting its pretty interior. The octagonal font of local granite is probably of the 10 c.

Vaynol (6). Superb park and gardens. The old stone manor house, with fine rough 17 c. staircase, now incorporated in the stable block. (Not open.)

Ysbyty Ifan (14). Central village of the National Trust's great Penrhyn Estate sheep-walk on the borders of Merioneth. Its name derives from "Hospice of St John" of Jerusalem: "so styled (says Pennant) from having formed, in the then inhospitable county, an asylum and guard for travellers under the protection of the knight who held the manor and made its precincts a sanctuary. After the abolition of the Order, this privilege became the bane of the neighbourhood; for the place, thus exempted from all jurisdiction, was converted into a den of thieves and murderers." It is now a very quiet place, of no architectural interest.

The Five Ranges of Eryri

The section that follows is no substitute for the *Climbers' Guides* or for such comprehensive walkers' handbooks as Rowland's *Hill Walking in Snowdonia*.* All it tries to do is to indicate some attractive ways up the most attractive mountains, for those whose taste lies midway between the rock-climb and the long, dull slog. Snowdonia is admirably laid out for such persons. Up all the major peaks there are rocky ascents, easily reached by car, that give a sense of achievement without terror, and all to be had in the space of even a winter's day. Unless otherwise stated, it is best to go down the way you came up (and nowadays anyhow you have probably left a car there).

All such accounts have to start with a warning. It is quite easy to kill oneself on these mountains, most often by straying on to territory beyond one's capability. Exposed rock faces and old quarries are the obvious traps, but even innocent-looking grass can in Snowdonia be steep enough to be dangerous, particularly if it is very dry or very wet. Low clouds or high winds double the hazards. You may be striding in mist along the smooth green back of Trum-y-Ddysgl, feeling as if you were on the South Downs, and go straight over the edge of a near-vertical 500 ft. precipice like a figure in a comic strip. Or a gale may blow you off balance on the airy crest of Crib Goch. So stick to the well-worn paths on doubtful days, and if mist does descend, take a compass bearing on your line of retreat. As well as this compass and the 1 in. map, take an extra sweater and some chocolate, wear thick socks and strong boots or shoes with studded or rubber-ribbed soles, and remember it will be ten degrees colder at the top. Only the experienced should climb alone, and he should take a whistle in case he sprains an ankle and leave word of his route. But one should not be too apprehensive: the main mood of these mountains is pure pleasure.

For some reason not given by the geologists, the five ranges of Eryri nearly all present rather tame slopes to the west and darker faces of varying degrees of savagery to the east. So one tends to lose the sun shadow and to come up into the prevailing wind as one hits the crest, but also to be greeted, on good days, by a shining expanse of seas and peninsulas. Each range is surrounded and almost too accessible by main roads. We take them in turn moving round them anti-clockwise from Caernarvon.

above Moel Hebog ▷
below Y Garn and Drwys-y-Coed from Mynydd Mawr

* The Cidron Press, Tremadoc, 3s. 6d.

Eryri from Traeth Mawr

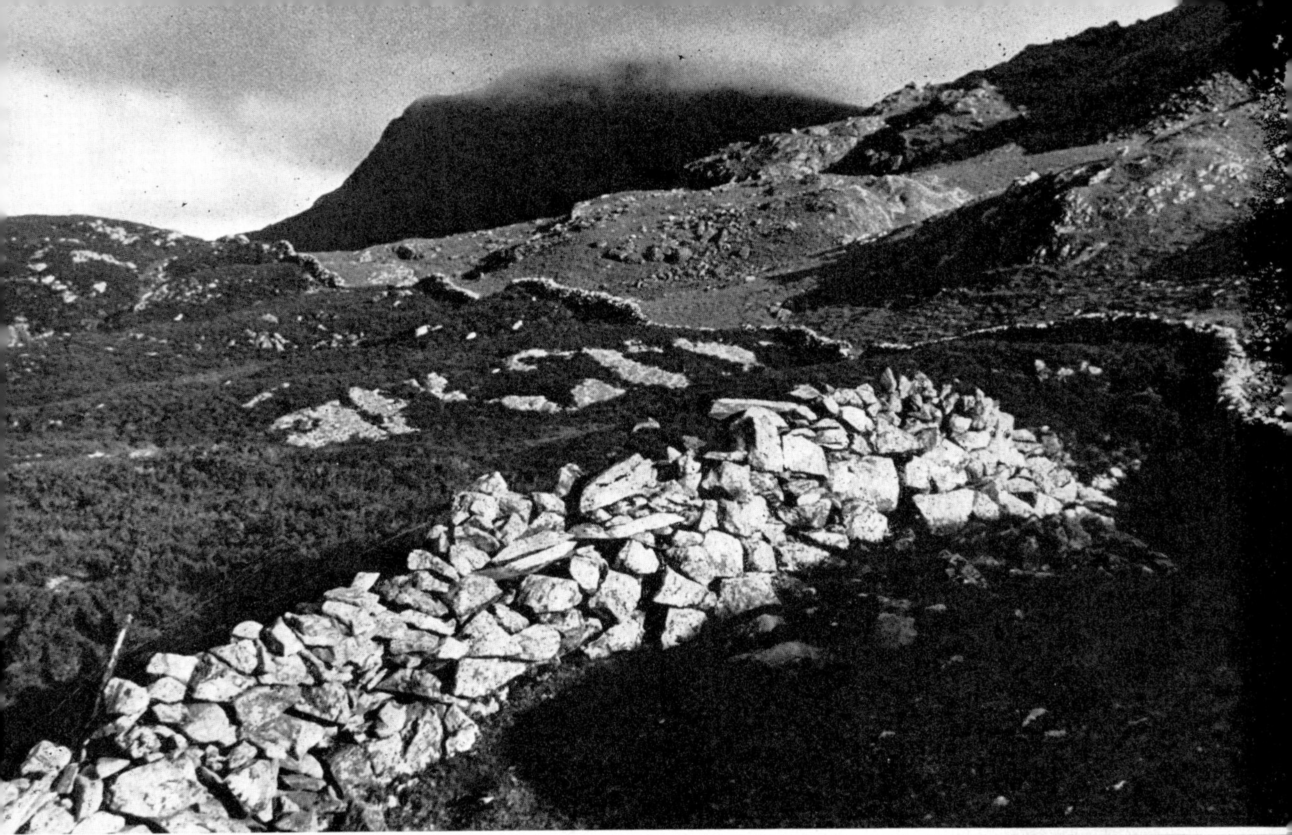
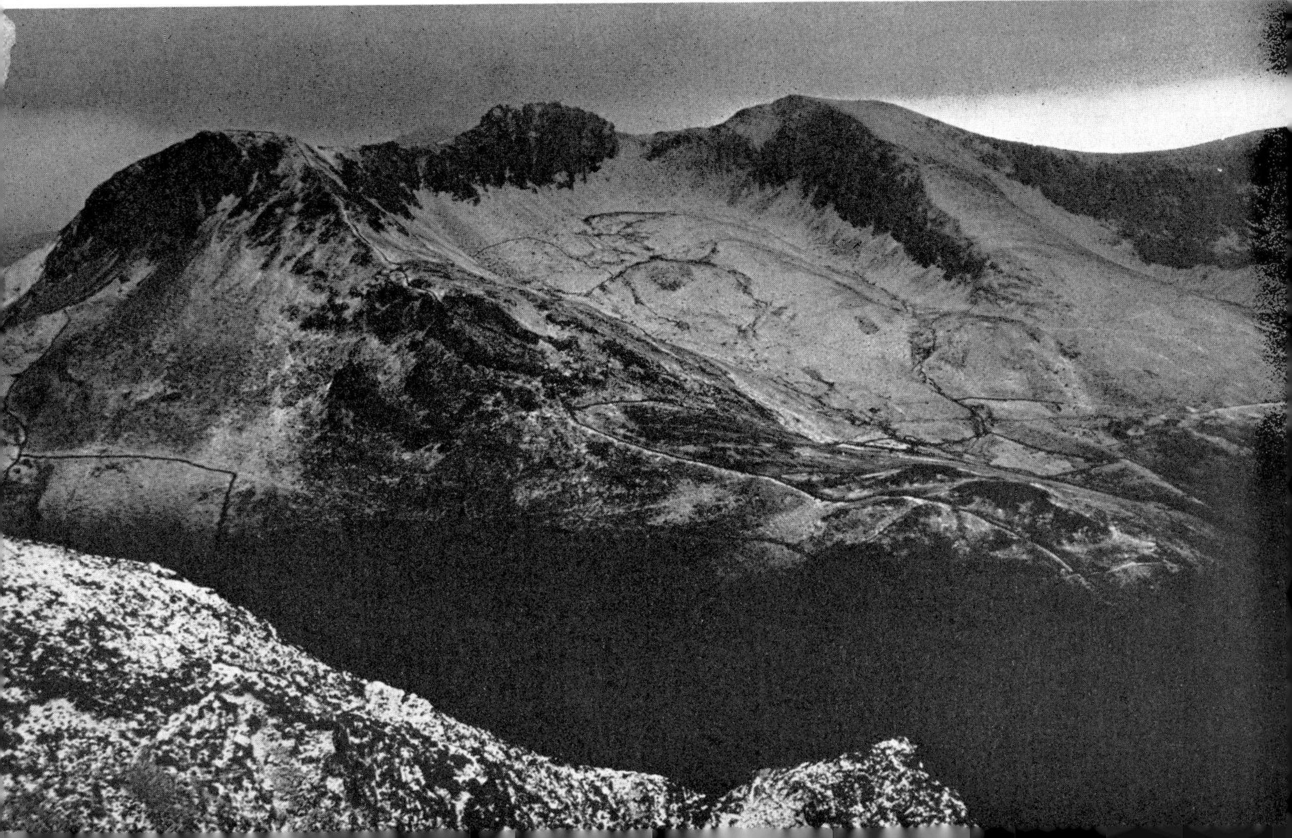

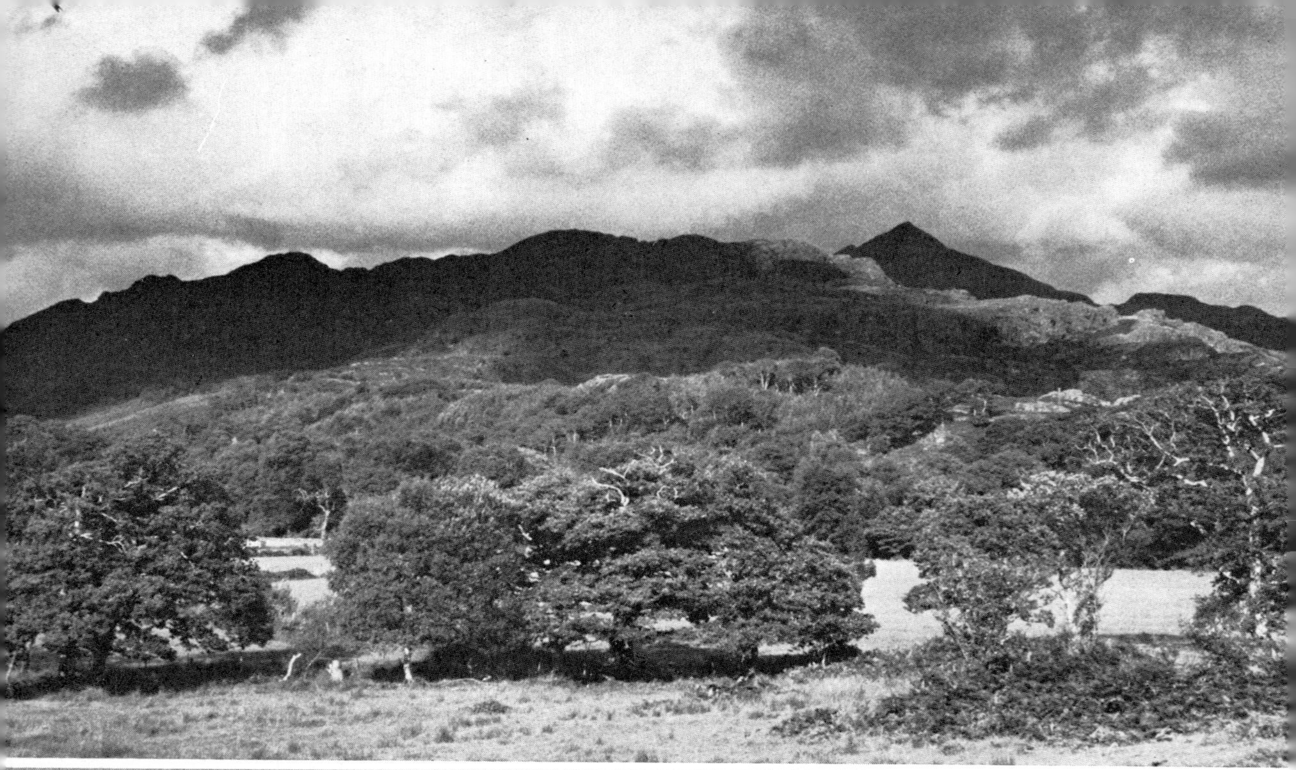

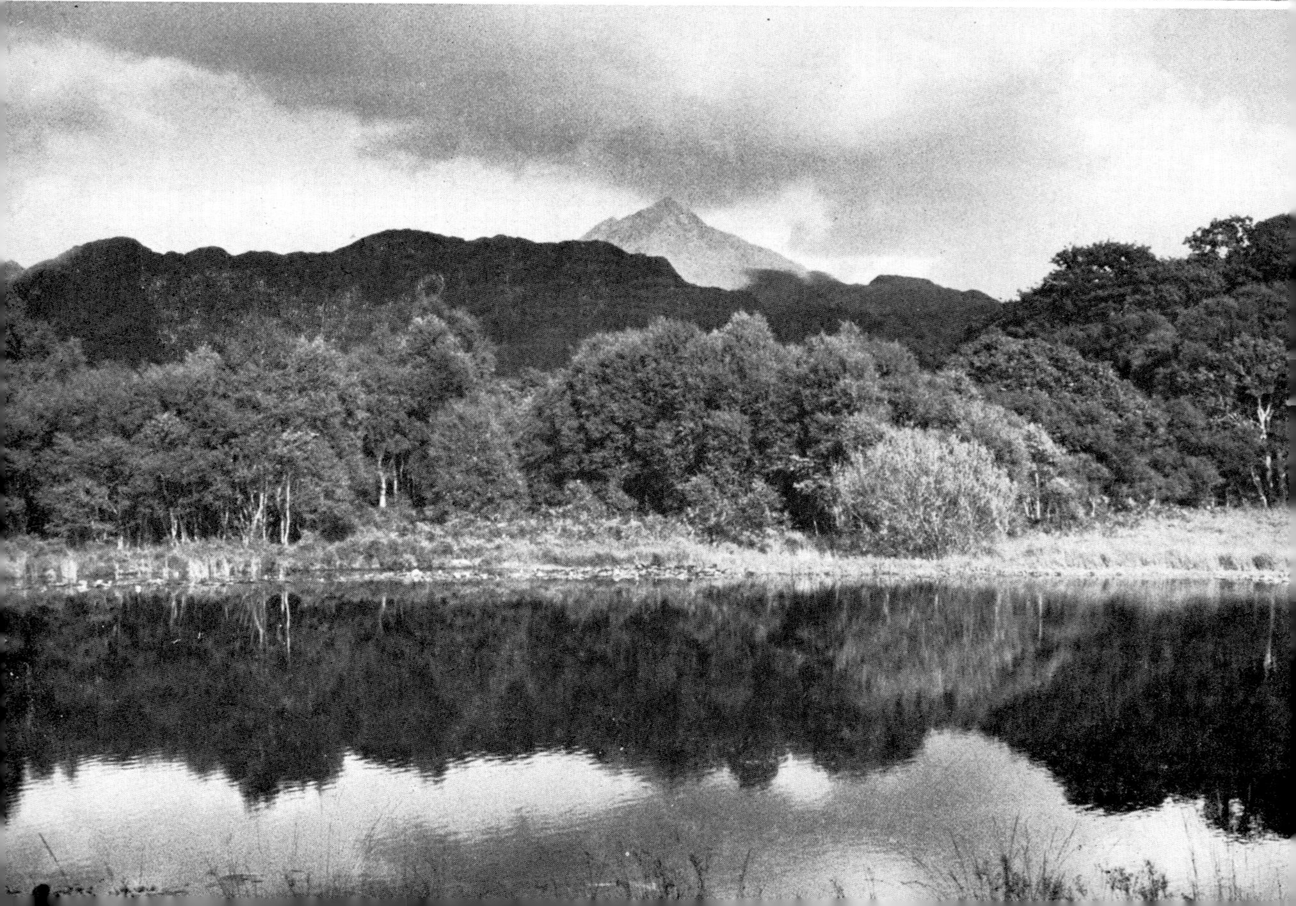

1. THE HEBOG GROUP

This is a horseshoe of peaks around the head of the romantic Cwm Pennant, with one outlier, Mynydd Mawr, away to the north beyond the Drws-y-Coed pass. They are deceptive hills, to be avoided in mist, with smooth green slopes suddenly cut by black cliffs, and the complete ridge-walk is no walk at all. The views westwards over the Lleyn and the sea are superb and several peaks worth climbing.

Mynydd Mawr (2,291 ft.)
The normal and best route starts 800 ft. up on the crest of the Drws-y-Coed pass at the attractive Llyn-y-Dywarchen with its legendary floating island, but this is at present obstructed and walkers must gain the east ridge via the forestry plantations above Llyn Cwellyn. The grassy ridge steepens where the trees end and needs care. From the first cairned peak it is an exhilarating 10 minutes to the summit with the shattered cliffs of Craigybera falling away to the pass and the precipices of Y Garn across the way. Caernarvon Castle is conspicuous in the wide sea view.

Mynydd Drws-y-Coed (2,329 ft.)
A deceptively smooth-looking mountain seen from Beddgelert, its face brutally disfigured by high-level plantations, with precipices at its back. Can be climbed either from Rhyd-Dhu by taking the marked path south-west across the moor then up the steep shoulder of Y Garn (itself a magnificent airy viewpoint) with a sharp drop on one's right all the way; or more easily from the head of Cwm Pennant, taking the same path from its opposite end and bearing left up the inviting grassy ridge.

Moel Hebog: "Hill of the Hawk" (2,566 ft.)
Dull seen from the south-west, beautiful from the north-east and best climbed from that direction. From the Goat Hotel at Beddgelert or from A 487 gain the north-east ridge opposite Cwm Cloch farm,

◁ Cnicht from Nantmor

then head for the rocky (false) summit, with precipices to the right at first, to the left later. One of the best viewpoints in Snowdonia.

2. THE SIABOD GROUP

So-called from its outlying and highest peak, this is a wide expanse of moor, tarn and bogland, relieved by a few picturesque peaks facing the finest escarpments of Snowdon. Two of them are in Caernarvonshire.

Cnicht "The Knight" (2,265 ft.)
Park the car by the chapel in Croesor village and take the track up on to the ridge, then climb *ad lib* with the sharp peak dead ahead. At the foot of the final pyramid, best to bear right up easy rocks. The views to Snowdon and sea-wards are equally lovely, and the descent into the sunset exhilarating.

Moel Siabod (2,860 ft.)
An isolated peak best seen from the east, with a vast view. Cross the cascades of the Afon Llugwy at Pont Cyfyng and take the marked path, often boggy, to the north-east ridge, which you follow to the summit. It needs care in places, and if in doubt it is safer to bear right than left.

3. THE CARNEDDS

As the Pennines to the Lake District and the Grampians to the western Highlands, this massive and rather featureless range walls in the whole of Snowdonia on its eastern side. No elegant peaks here, but a sense of limitless space on a clear day. Avoid in mist.

Creigiau Gleision (2,213 ft.)
The most attractive expedition from the Conway valley side. From the last farmhouse beyond the head of Llyn Crafnant climb steeply through bracken and scrub woodland to the skyline between rock outcrops and a breath-taking view of Tryfan and the Glyders, then bear right across trackless moorland to the furthest rocky peak, with its fine view of the screes of Pen Llithrig plunging into the depths of Llyn Cowlyd. Resist temptation to descend an easy valley into impenetrable Gwydir Forest.

p52 Rock piles on Glyder Fach ▷
p53 The Castle of the Winds (*above*) and another rock 'sculpture' on Glyder Fawr

"I would therefore rather consider this mountain to have been a sort of wreck of nature, formed and flung up by some mighty conjunction, which has given these vast groups of stones fortuitously such a strange disposition. . . . The elements seem to have warred against this mountain: rains have washed, lightnings torn, the very earth deserted it, and the winds made it the constant object of their fury." (Pennant).

Carnedd Llewelyn (3,485 ft.)
A hard day, for peak-baggers only, but unquestionably the best circuit on the Carnedds. Cross the Ogwen outlet and strike up the rocky face of Pen-yr-oleu-wen, the savage corner bastion dominating the pass. When finally, after several false crests, you collapse exhausted on the summit, you have broken the back of the day. An easy ridge walk to Carnedd Dafydd, and bear right to the rounded summit of Llewelyn, noting on your way, to the left, the precipices of the Black Ladders. The view, says Pennant, is "very disagreeable, of dreary bottoms or moory hills, and of no waters of any consequence", and on dull days it can seem so. Descend due east and then south-east across a fine narrow crest, with the great Craig-yr-Ysfa rockface to the left and a steep drop to Ffynnon Llugwy to the right. From the last summit, Pen-yr-helgi-du, one swings easily down the long slope to Tal-y-braich farm.

4. THE GLYDERS

Granite and heather characterise this bare, weather-beaten range, lying in the heart of Snowdonia and hemmed in by mountains on every side: no prelude of leafy dells or pastures full of lambs, but the compensating advantage of a start from 1,000 ft. or so, so that the tops are less hard-won. And nothing could look more worth winning than the beautiful peak of Tryfan as it reveals itself to the traveller from Capel Curig, or the great *cirque* of mountains that enfolds Llyn Ogwen. Ogwen cottage is the best base for all ascents, and of a wide choice we recommend this, perhaps the finest expedition of those we describe. A clear day is essential,

51

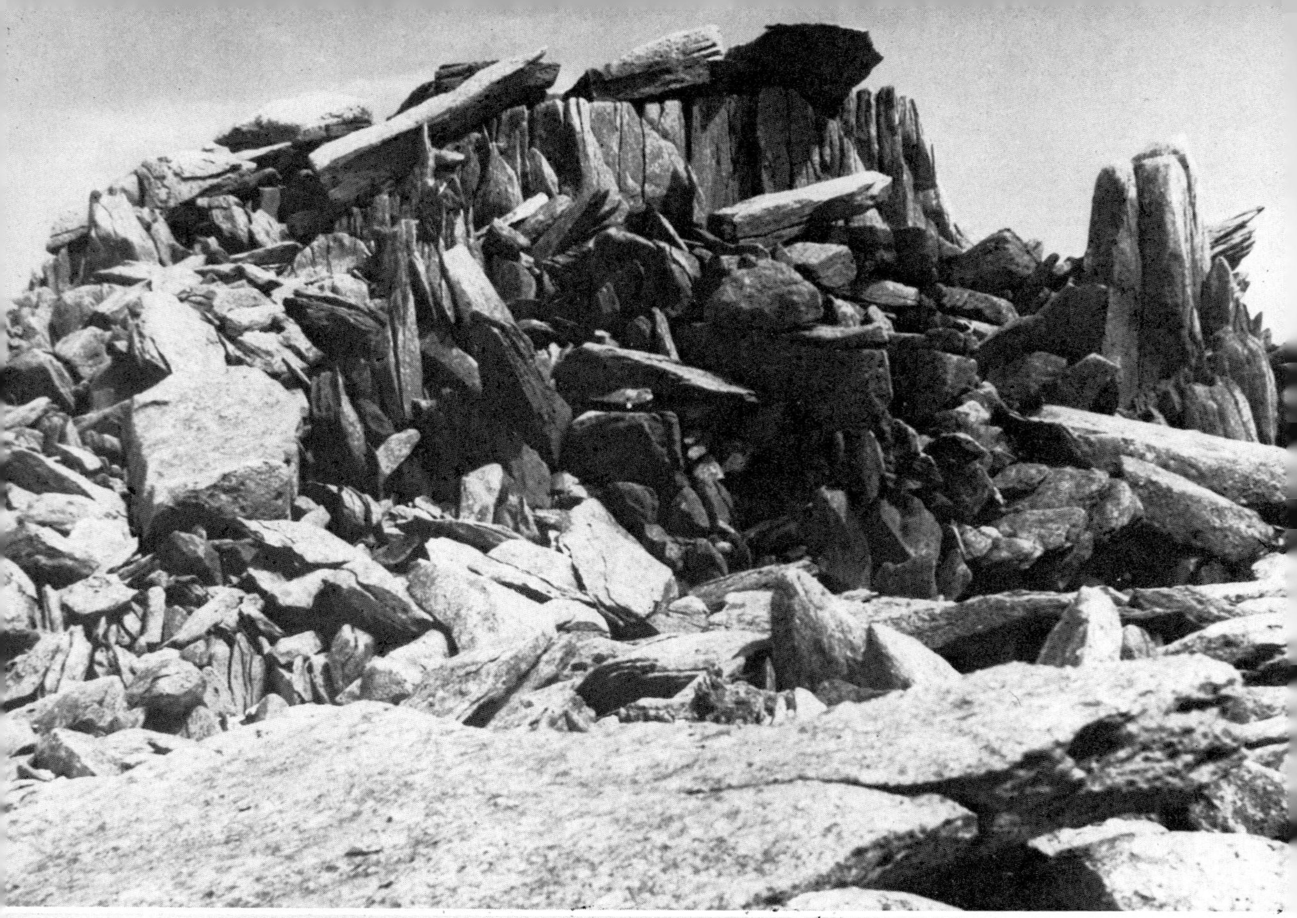

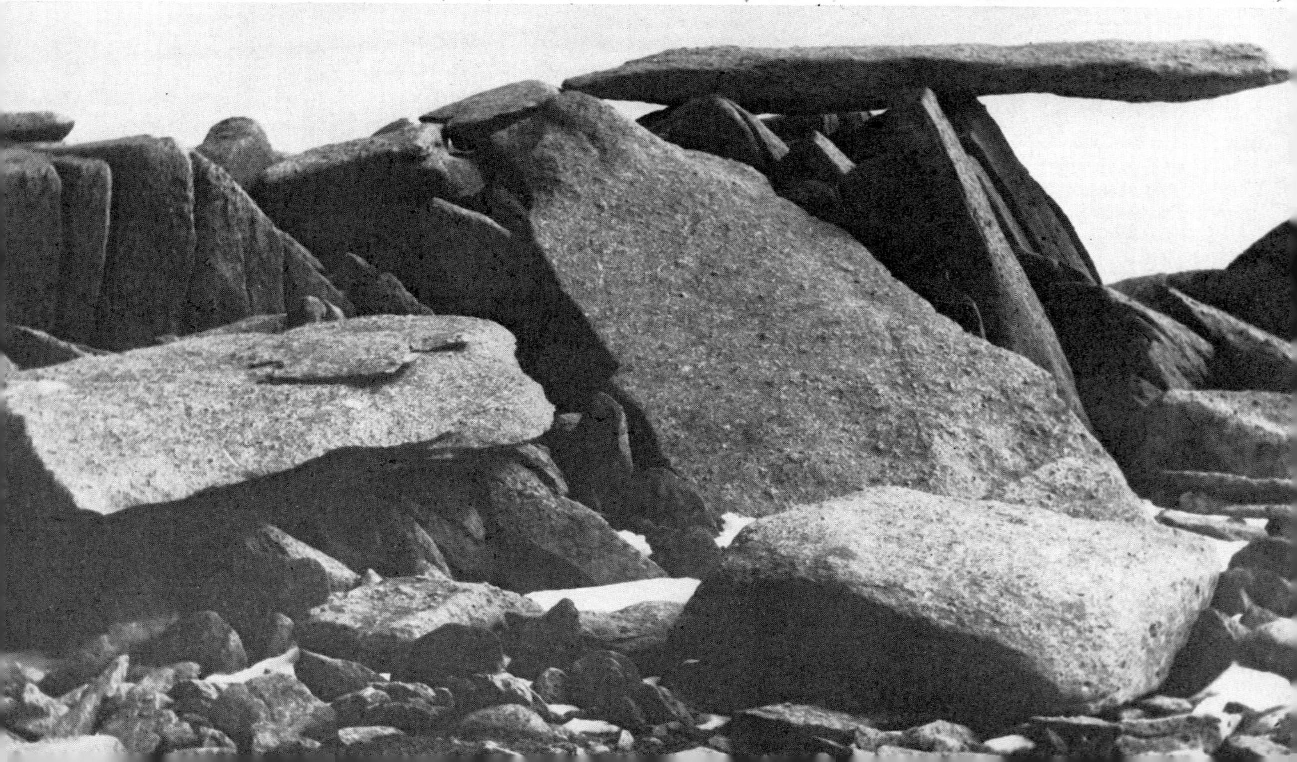

53

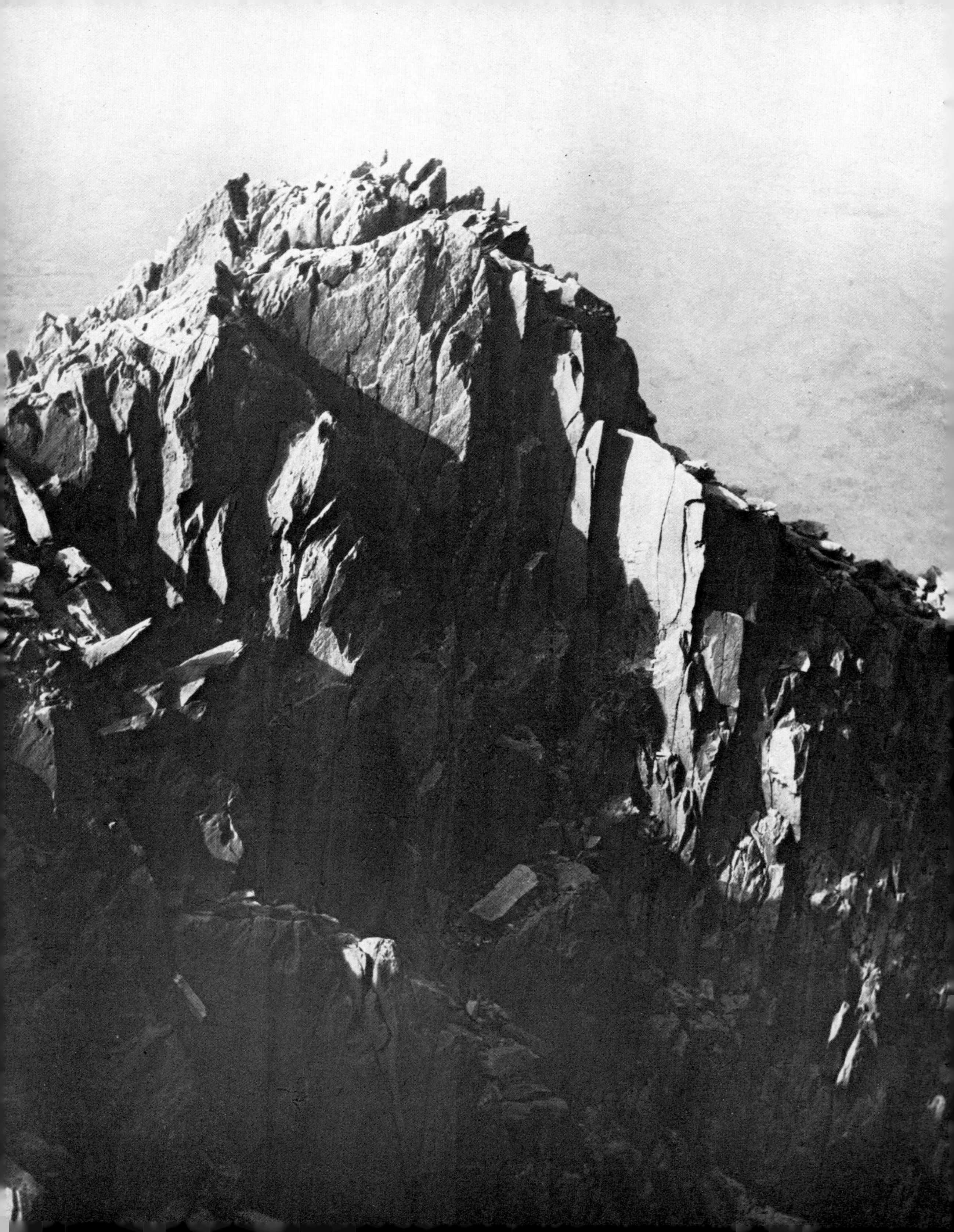

since in this range a round trip is far more rewarding than a return by the same route.

Take the track which hugs the east margin of dark Llyn Idwal, past the foot of the famous Idwal Slabs, then conspicuously traverses the cwm-head, passing close to the bottom of the Devil's Kitchen chasm which you leave on your right. After gaining the crest leave Llyn-y-Cwn on your right and climb *ad lib* to emerge on the eerie tundra that stretches a mile ahead. From the triple crest of Glyder Fawr (3,279 ft.) make straight for the fine summit of Glyder Fach along the line of cairns, with Snowdon rising grandly beyond the Llanberis Pass. Then about turn, and pass the superb rock sculpture known as the Castle of the Winds, to the narrow grass col. There leave the track and bear right across a green crest to a conspicuous single cairn, from which the Gribin ridge descends. The first couple of hundred feet need care, and as you approach the foot of the

◁ Tryfan Summit
▽ Tryfam from the east

ridge bear right to avoid climber's territory.

Strong walkers can extend this round to take in Y Garn (3,104 ft.) at the beginning (climbed by striking due west from the Idwal outlet, keeping the deep cwm seen from below on one's left) and Tryfan (3,010 ft.) at the end (climbed by carrying on east from Glyder Fach, then taking the marked track back to Bwlch Tryfan). The direct descent from Glyder Fach to the Bwlch by the Bristly Ridge should be avoided, as should the north ridge of Tryfan itself. But really both Y Garn and Tryfan are better to look at than from.

5. SNOWDON

The Welsh and English being what they are, one can say without exaggeration that no mountain in Europe is so legendary or so loved in intimate detail as Snowdon. Luckily the glaciers shaped it well for such a role—better than many Alps three or four times its size. A starfish of sharp ridges and steep cwms, it is accessible from half a dozen directions and can be traversed in innumerable ways. But, of course all routes meet at the top, *Y Wyddfa* (3,560 ft.) Armies of teenagers take the foot-slog as part of their education, and so (to the unspeakable horror of Victorian romantics do the more sedate patrons of the rack-and-pinion railway. So hill-walking misanthropes stay away, preferring to stare at the graceful peak than sit on it, or they climb out of season: the mountain is never more beautiful than in November.

Your route and timing is consequently a matter of taste, and you will find the main alternatives listed in all the guide books. On the principle that, logistics permitting, it is a pity in the case of Snowdon to go up and down the same way, we offer the following selection:

To appreciate the full scale of the

On SNOWDON ▷
p56 above Y Wyddfa from the slopes of Crib Goch
below Clogwyn d'ur Arddu
p57 above Llyn Cwellyn and the westward view from the summit
below Glaslyn, Llyn Llydaw and the eastward view

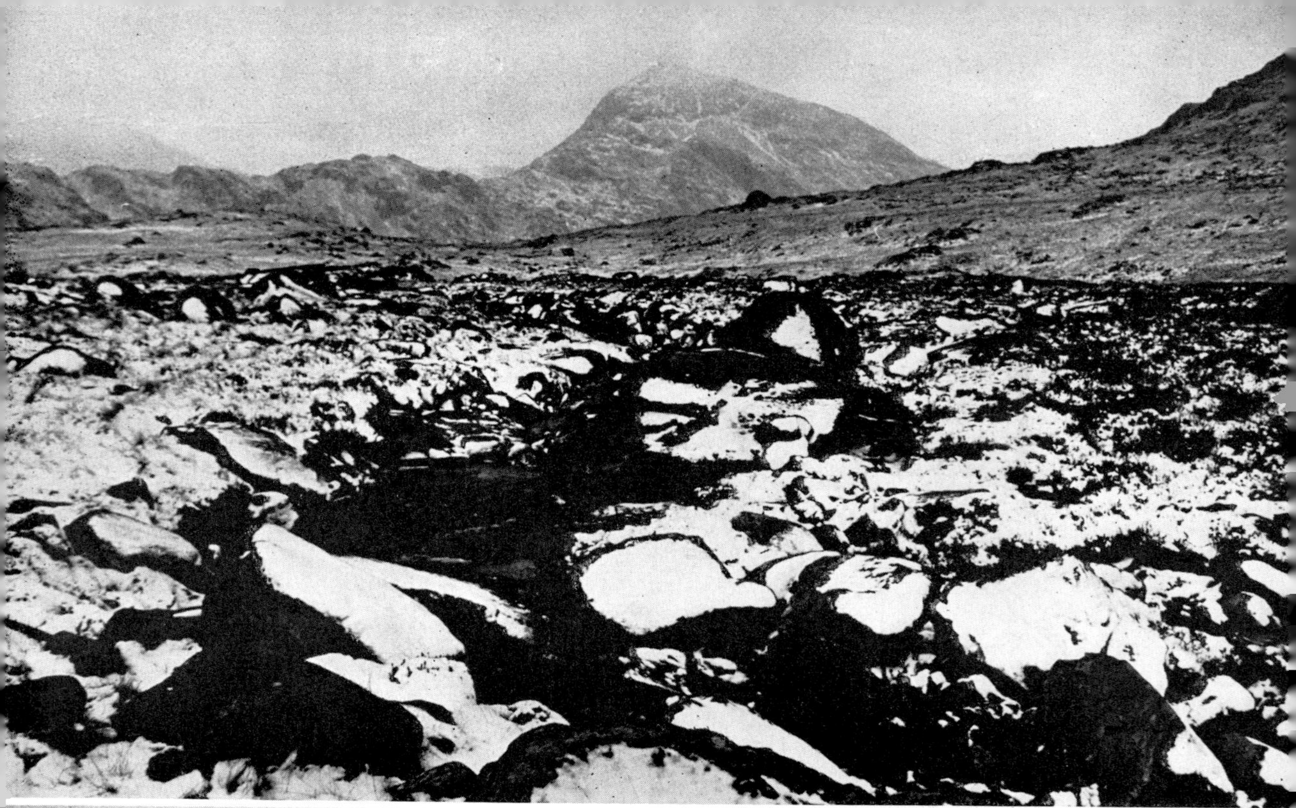

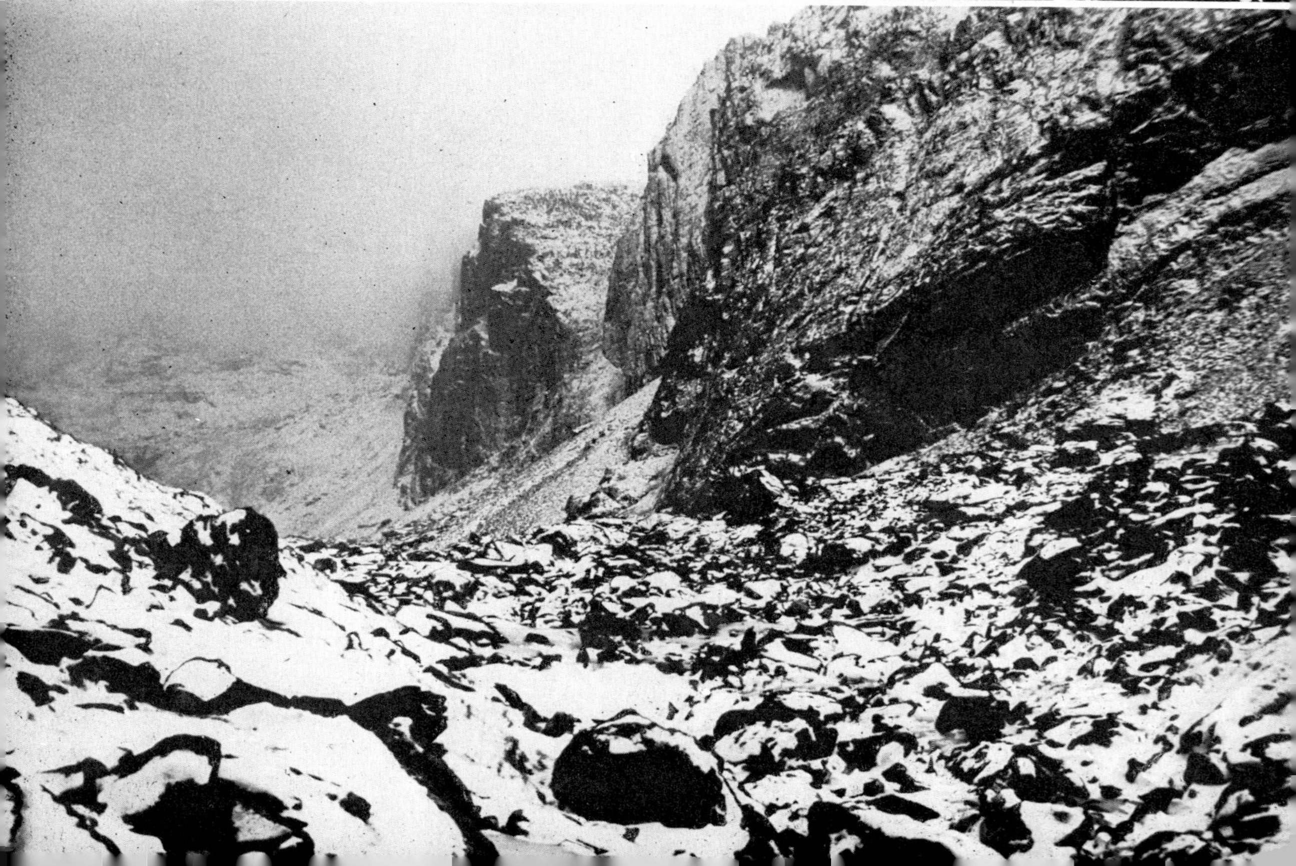

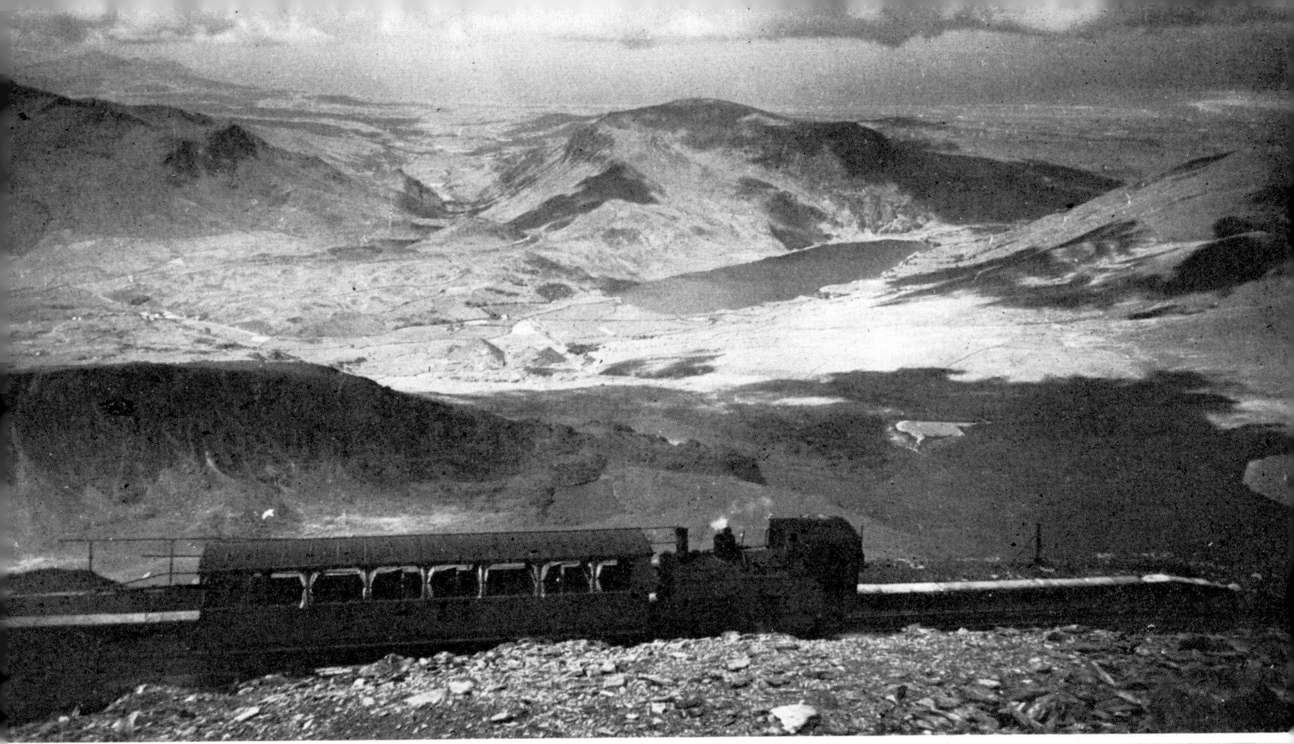

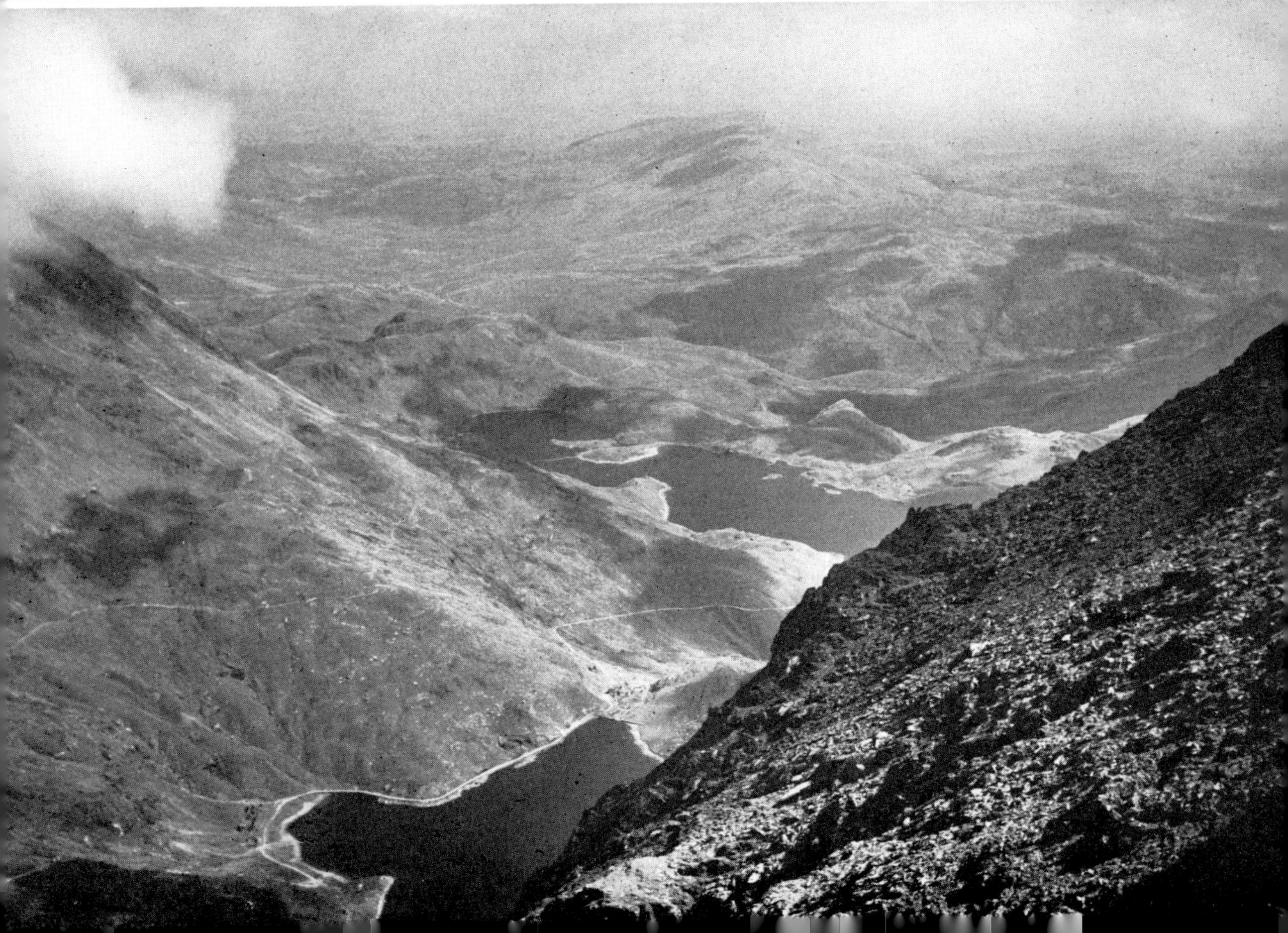

mountain, start at the bottom, not a third of the way up. Take the easy Watkin path from 627506 as far as the quarry buildings in Cwm y Llan, passing on your way the moving memorial to Mr Gladstone's great gesture at the age of 83. Where the quarry buildings come into sight, bear left on a turf path across bogland, then take a bee-line for Bwlch Cwm Llan (605522). On the bwlch turn right and follow the ridge line to the summit. Descend into the sunset via Llechog and the Beddgelert track.

To penetrate the mountain's innermost (but by no means lonely) recesses, take the stony highway from Pen-y-Pass across the causeway of Llyn Llydaw to the shores of Glaslyn and the zigzags to the summit. Descend either into Cwm-y-Llan as above or (more dramatic) start down Bwlch Main, turn left at a cairn down the screes to Bwlch y Saethau, traverse Lliwedd and descend either north-east or south-west from Gallt-y-Wenallt.

Finally, a route for the connoisseur: the only one on which you have to find your own way from the start till you hit the Llanberis track near the top. Park at Ynys Ettws and climb straight up between the streams into the glaciated Cwm Glas. You soon reach an easing of the slope, a great shelf of turf and boulders. Ahead is a cliff with a rock like a toad on top. Climb steeply left of this, to emerge at Llyn Glas (q.v.) upon a second shelf, with the Parson's Nose dead ahead. Here you either bear left and head for the nick in the ridge right of the Crib Goch pinnacles and thence via the Horseshoe to the summit, or bear well over to the right and climb the slope *ad lib* till you hit the Llanberis track over the skyline. This second alternative is incidentally the shortest of all routes from the base to the summit.

The only Snowdon ridge that is not accessible to the ordinary walker is the famous Crib Goch though, of course, it can be done by a sensible pair with good heads on a still day.

Do not believe the accounts of fabulous views from Snowdon embracing the Wicklow Hills in Ireland, Isle of Man, Scotland, etc. The chances of such a day are so remote as to be negligible.

The Lakes

We list in this section by no means all the lakes of Caernarvonshire (there are over 250 in the National Park alone) but those which we think have a special individuality and are therefore most worth seeing. On days when the peaks are inaccessible through cold or heat or mist, there is a lot to be said for making a mountain lake one's objective. All are at their best on windless days. An (F) after the name means that it can only be reached on foot. These seem to possess an air of mystery verging on the sinister, and it seems natural that so many of them in North Wales should be wrapped in legend.

The first two figures in the grid references give the N–S line, the second two the E–W one.

L. Bochlwyd: 6559 (F from Ogwen) 1,800 feet up between Tryfan and the Gribin ridge, the deep tarn is often a dazzle of sun against the black Glyder precipices. Sheltered despite its altitude, it is popular with botanists (rare alpines) and campers accessibility to climbs).

L. Conwy: 7846 (F easily from main road)
High on the moorland plateau of Migneint, this windy sheet of water, the source of the Conway, has a wide panorama of the Snowdonian skyline. No better stopping-place on a spring day.

L. Cowlyd: 7363 (F from rough track) Relentlessly steep slopes on both sides plunge into the dark water to make this by far the deepest in N. Wales. Good fishing, gloomy scenery. According to Frank Ward (1931) "there is reported to be a Water Bull residing in the depths". The witch of Pen Llithrig was another former resident of this sinister landscape.

L. Crafnant: 7561
Reputed to have the largest trout in Snowdonia until its accessibility made it popular with small boat sailors and picnickers. It is certainly the prettiest of the group of lakes on the E. side of the Carnedds, its pastoral setting enlivened by a backcloth of little peaks.

L. Cwellyn: 5655
A grand, deep, clear lake, with a largeness of scale enhanced by the plain and powerful forms of Mynydd Mawr and not diminished by the dark conifer plantations that plunge down to the waterside. Swimming not allowed! Char lurk in the depths.

L. Cwm Silin: 5150 (F)
Up a wooded ravine and across a stony moor you reach this remote pair of hidden lakes, the far one hard up against the craggy face of Craig Cwm Silin. Much more rewarding than the more accessible Llyn Cwm Dulyn.

L. Cwm y Stradllyn: 5644
A fine gloomy sheet of water below the easy S. slopes of Hebog, with interesting but dangerous quarry workings at its head.

L. Dinas: 6149
The smaller and less dramatic of the two lovely lakes of Nantgwynant. Perfect for boating on summer evenings. Best to go ashore on its S. side and wander up into the easy hills behind, with their great views into the heart of Snowdon. Moel Hebog stands up finely to the southwest.

L. Diwaunedd: 6853 (F)
A secluded figure-of-eight among the soft and generally boggy slopes W. of Siabod, best approached from Roman Bridge.

above Llyn Edno ▷
below Llyn Idwal

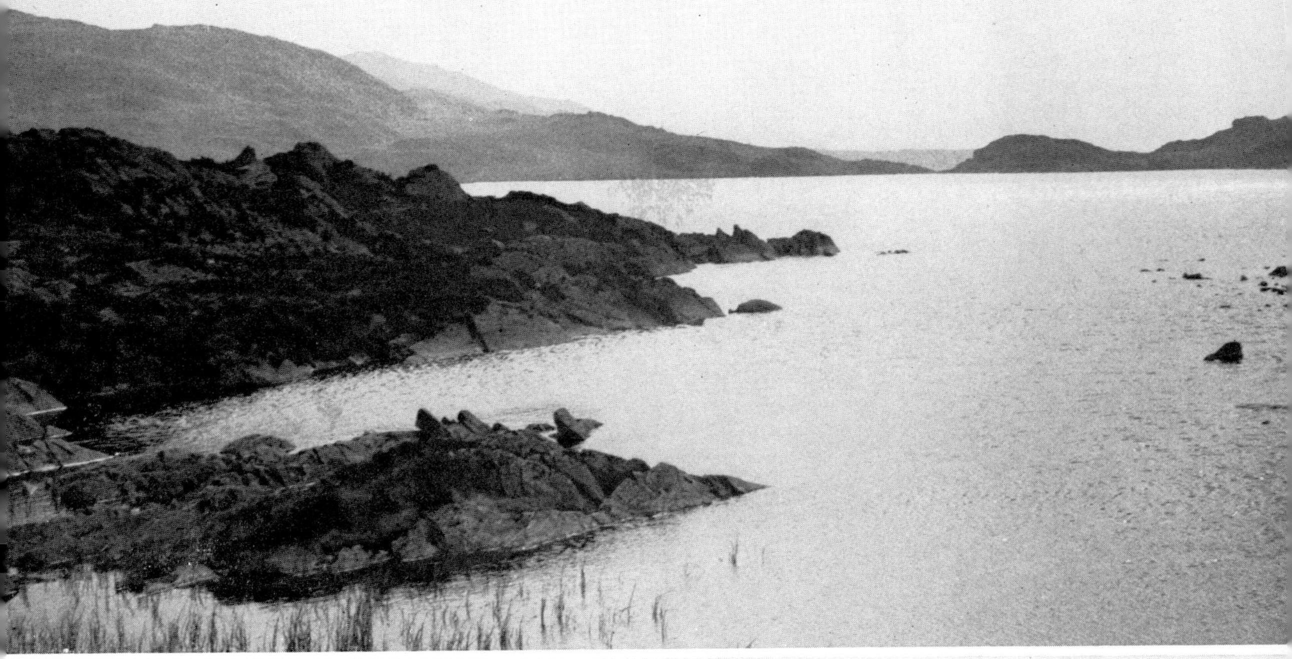

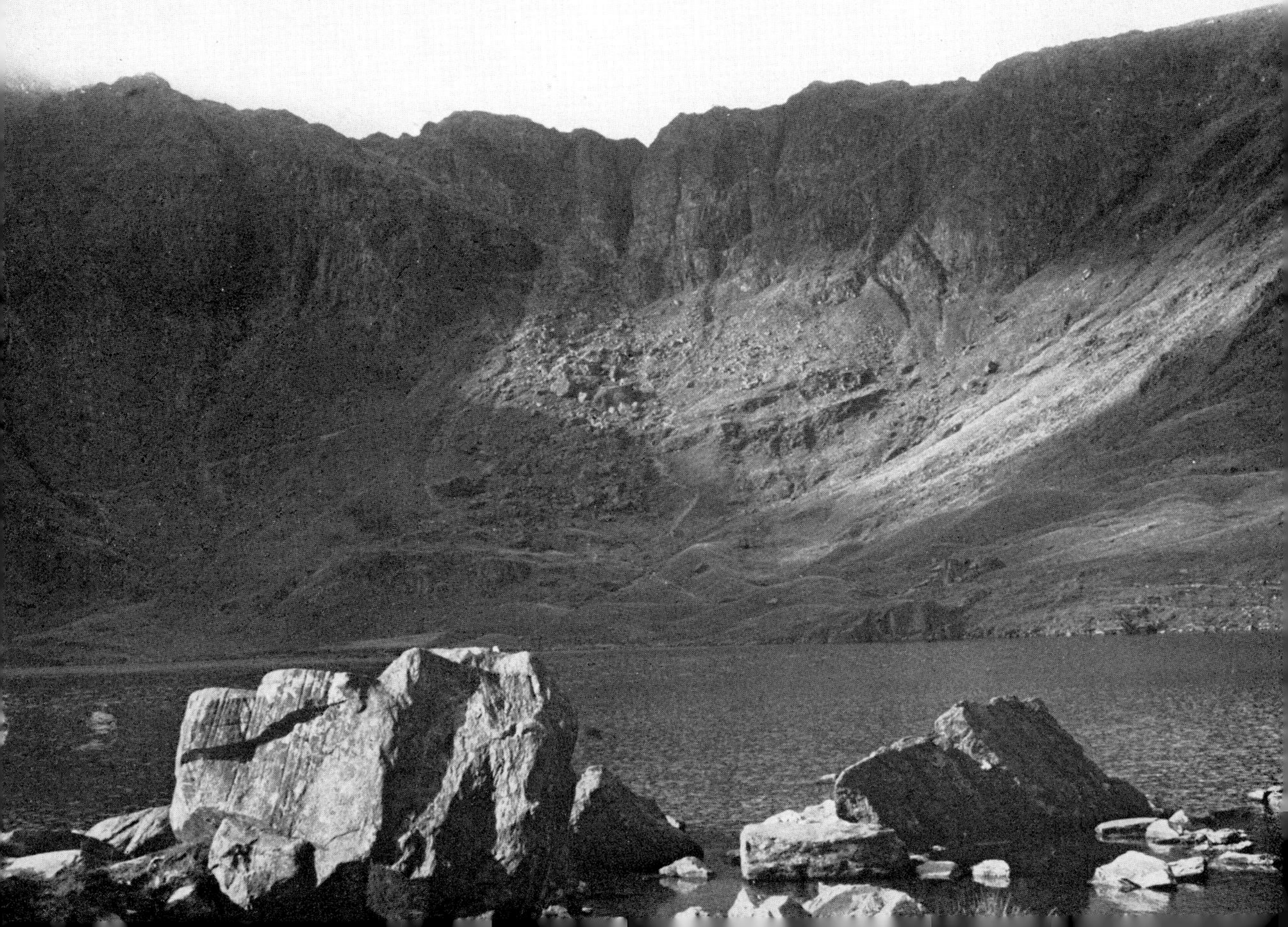

L. Dulyn: 7066 (F)
Very remote but reachable by a rough track from Dolgarrog, the black, crater-like lake, overhung by the precipices of Craig Dulyn, is 55 ft. deep a yard from its western margin.

L. dur Arddu: 6055 (F from the Snowdon Railway)
Like its twin Glaslyn the other side of Snowdon, this turquoise blue pool is commonly seen from above, seldom approached. For background it has the vertical black precipice of Clogwyn dur Arddu, with some of the severest rock pitches in Europe.

L. Dywarchen: 5653
Now strongly defended against fish poachers, this little lake above Rhyd Ddu was visited by generations of naturalists and tourists on account of its floating (peat) island, first noted by Giraldus in 1188, now vanished. The present rocky islet is no relation.

L. Edno: 6649 (F)
A thousand feet of gentle climbing from the head of Nantmor, through a knobbly brown fawn and grey rock and heather landscape, will bring you to this spacious windy lake, with fine prospects of Snowdon and Siabod from the surrounding hillocks. Moel Meirch, a couple of hundred feet above the lake, is a splendid belvedere.

L. Elsi: 7855 (F from St Mary's Church)
The more alluring of the two larger lakes on the plateau above Betws, with islets white with nesting gulls in May, and a monument to Lord Ancaster. Magnificent views all round, particularly of Moel Siabod, but the foreground cut about by the Forestry Commission, which is rapidly transforming this whole landscape, probably for the worse.

L. Ffynnon Lloer: 6662 (F)
The smaller but more beautiful of

above Llyn Nantlle Uchaf. ▷
(Richard Wilson's view of Snowdon)
below Llyn Llydaw

the two moraine lakes in the southern cwms of the Carnedds, and not spoilt, as is Ffynnon Llugwy, by water works. It is named "the Well of the Moon", because it reflects the full moon to the summit of Carnedd Dafydd high above. At 2,225 ft. it is the most elevated of the "crater" lakes of Snowdonia.

L. Geirionydd: 7661
Craftnant's shy twin, now attractively afforested. It is easily reached from the old church at Llanrhychwyn, and from its head the lane leads on into the pinewoods above Betws y Coed.

L. Glas: 6155 (F)
Not to be confused with Glaslyn, this lovely tarn, overhung by the great black beak of the Parson's Nose, is no trip to attempt in bad

Llyn Gwynant

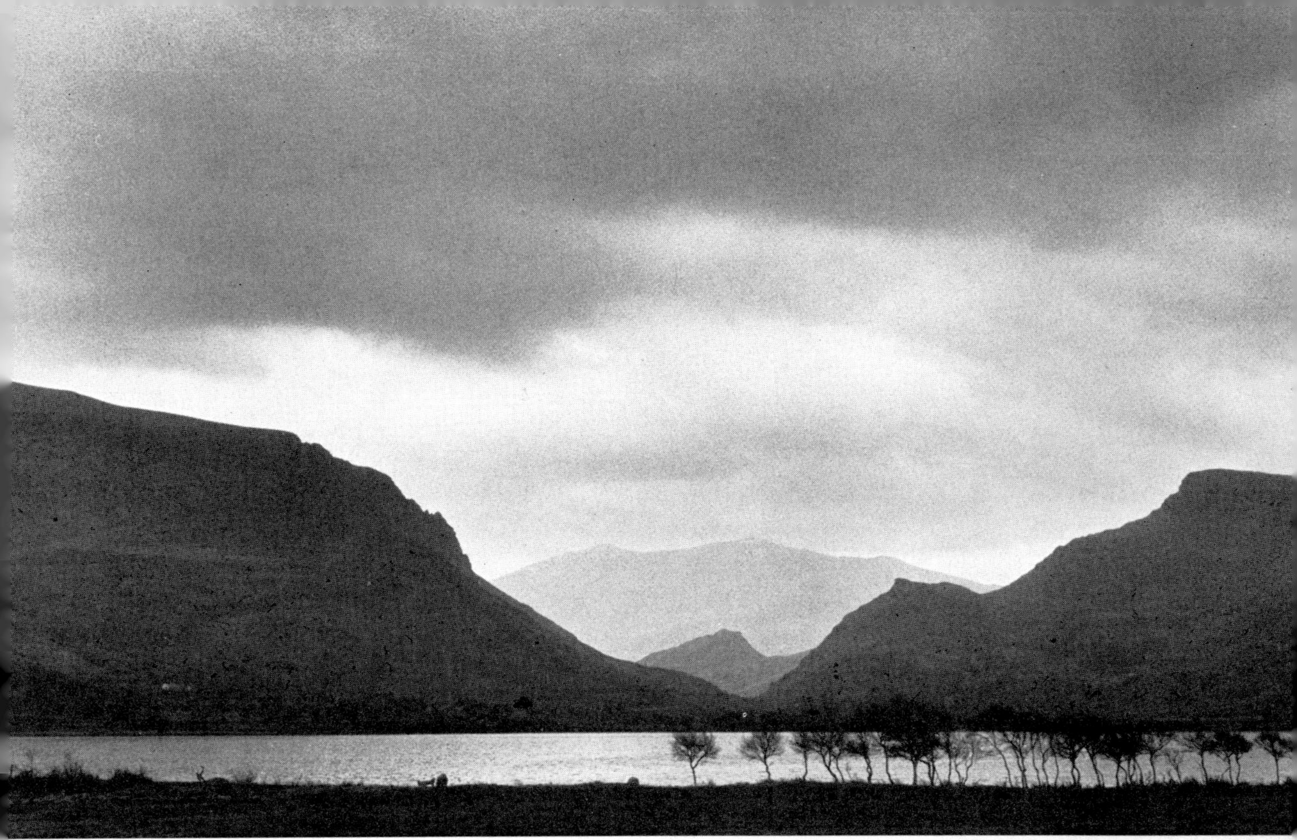

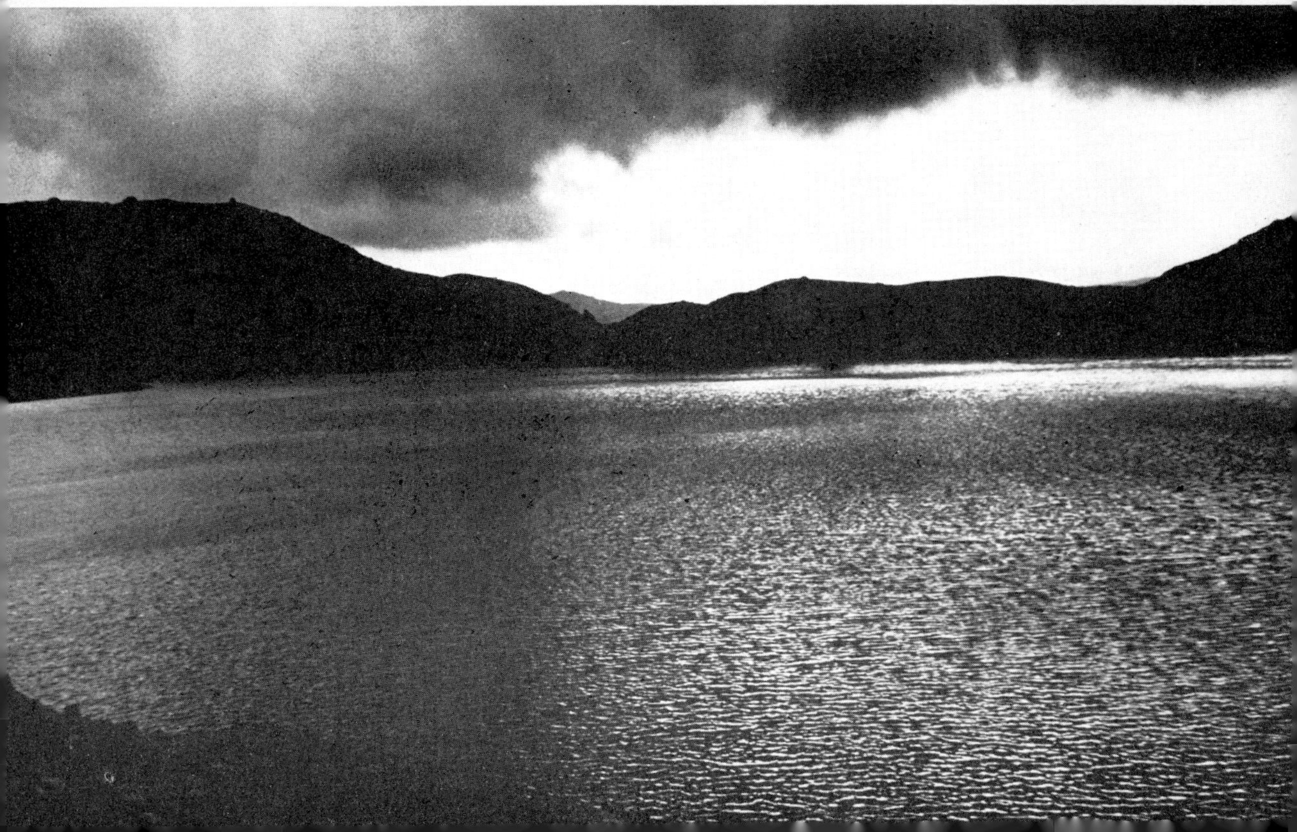

Llyn Mymbyr

weather, but when the sun shines one can lean against an ice-worn boulder and watch through binoculars the climbers on the Crib Goch pinnacles. The trees on the little island surely cannot, at 2,100 ft., be self-sown. It is worth the ten-minute extra climb to tiny, crystal clear Llyn Bach to the W. of the Nose.

L. Glaslyn: 6154 (F)
Claustrophobically situated beneath the ferocious E. wall of Y Wyddfa, an almost vertical drop of 1,600 ft. A rainfall of 246 inches (ten times London's average) was recorded in 1912.

L. Gwynant: 6451
Best seen from a steep grass mound a few yards off the main road at 650523, whence lake and woodland and mountains have a Chinese felicity of composition.

L. Idwal: 6459 (F)
The legendary birdless lake in a setting of savage grandeur below the north wall of Glyder Fawr. The easy circuit of this shallow but sinister mere is well worth making. Anyone who has done this in full moonlight will know why the mountain opposite, seen from this black cwm, is named Pen yr Oleu Wen: "the hill of the white light".

L. Llagi: 6448 (F from head of Nantmor)
The most accessible of the group of tarns on the delectable N.W. slopes of Cnicht. Walled in by cliffs on one side, it is wide open on the other to a fine view up Cwm y Llan to Snowdon. Atop the cliffs is Llyn yr Adar, with an even vaster panorama. Llyn Edno, a mile N.E. is worth the extra effort.

L. Llydaw: 6354 (F)
Somewhat spoilt when its level was lowered to facilitate the building of the causeway in the 19 c., but still the finest of the high lakes, and a necessary foil to the grim north face of Lliwedd, where the classic climbs are. The moraines and debris of the glacier that filled Cwm Dyli are evident on the slopes beside it and below. From above, the copper in the water makes it a brilliant turquoise on a sunny day.

L. Marchlyn Mawr: 6162 (F)
A rough drive up to the deserted quarry at 602627 followed by a boggy bee-line to the cwm-head brings you via Marchlyn Bach to this gloomy "crater" lake in the shadow of the crags of Elidir Fawr: best on a summer's evening.

L. Mymbyr: 7157
The twin Capel Curig lakes, once bleak but now effectively afforested and popular with canoeists. For two centuries they have served romantic painters as foreground to

Llyn Peris

a wild view of "Snowdon and all his sons" 5 miles to the W. The featureless moorland ahead, now strung with power lines, was in Pennant's time "enlivened with the busy work of hay harvest".

L. Nantlle Uchaf: 5153
The beautiful pastoral lake, with its classic prospect of Snowdon, is often missed by the hurrying motorist merely because it is behind a wall. He should stop where the main road crosses the outlet. 'It is from this spot Mr Wilson has favoured us with a view as magnificent as it is faithful" (Pennant). The picture is now in the Walker Art Gallery at Liverpool.

L. Ogwen: 6560
This shallow and slowly silting mere appears just when the eye needs it at the head of the bleak Nant Ffrancon pass. It is best enjoyed from the fisherman's path on its N. bank, whence the peak of Tryfan seems to plunge straight into the water. Here the pale arm "clothed in white samite, mystic, wonderful" rose out of the water to grasp King Arthur's sword Excalibur, cast away by Sir Bedivere on Merlin's instructions.

L. Padarn: 5661
The largest of the Snowdon lakes, and to many the most beautiful. From its peaceful outlet the view towards the Llanberis Pass has been much sketched and photographed. The glaciated rock-and-heather hillside on its northern flank has a special charm. This is one of the four lakes that contain char.

L. Peris: 5959
Originally continuous with Padarn, then cut off by silt from Afon Arddu, then stuffed with debris from the Dinorwic quarries. It is still very fine, and best seen from the foot track that crosses its outlet on the far side of Dolbadarn Castle.

L. y Cwn: 6358 (F)
A tarn at 2,300 ft. above the Devil's Kitchen. Giraldus relates that all its fish "wanted the left eye", but when Pennant climbed up to investigate, there was "not a fish in it to disprove the relation".

L. y Foel: 7154 (F)
A rocky lake with rocky islets below the summit cone of Moel Siabod.

L. y Gadair: 5652
A marshy, inaccessible mere on the main road near Rhyd-Dhu.

L. y Parc: 7958 (F from Pont y Pair)
Up through dark pinewoods and cascades one reaches this wild but sadly diminished sheet of water in a forest setting, like a Canadian lake after somebody has breached the beaver dam.

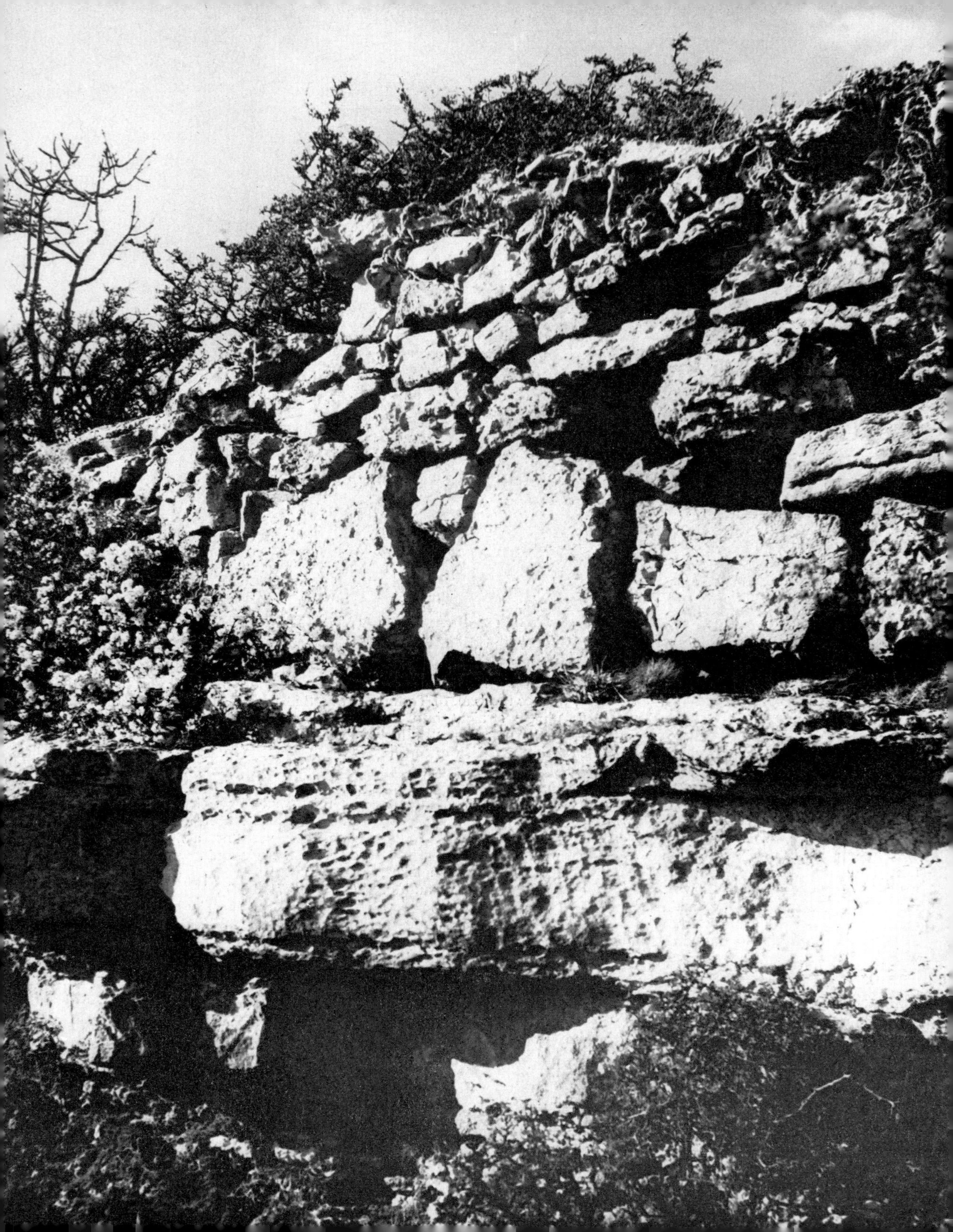

Anglesey: Gazetteer

The number after each entry refers to the square on the map following page 144 *where the place is situated.*

Aberffraw (5). A quiet grey village on one side of the shallow tidal Ffraw, which is spanned by a single arched bridge (1731); geese wander below, farmland behind, enormous warren with dunes in front. Has much more sense of place than most Anglesey villages, and its new council housing (Alex Gordon and Partners) has been carefully integrated. But Aberffraw's medieval glory, when it was the seat of the Princes of North Wales, has vanished. Their palace was presumably timber, and timber was taken from Aberffraw for the repair of Caernarvon in 1317. Village bakery survives so you may smell fresh bread.

St Beuno's church: outside unprepossessingly rendered in smooth cement; twin-aisled, divided by a light 16 c. arcade. A late 12 c. round arch carved with chevrons and animal heads survives, rough but attractively bold; perhaps then typical of the island, or maybe more sophisticated than most since this was the royal capital. The church was repaired and re-roofed in 1840 (Thomas Jones of Chester) and again restored *c.* 1868 (Kennedy and O'Donoghue).

Three miles north of the village near Llyn Padrig is the wayside chapel of *St Mary*, Tal-y-llyn. Small, sturdy and simple. The tiny door momentarily changes its scale, but the whopping timbers of the roof truss instantly cut it down to size again. Diminutive nave (12th–14th), chancel (late 16th) and south chapel (17th century) have been very sympathetically restored (1968) by the Friends of Friendless Churches and the County Council. Bench pews (one dated 1786) are planks halved over the wall footings. Communion rails 1764.

Llangwyfan church: on an island in a bay (curlews and cowries) one mile west of the village. Cut off by high spring tides. Sense of remoteness not quite shattered by the presence of Ministry of Defence Establishment on the opposite headland. Best seen in evening, mid-summer, when low sun streams through the north windows; warm sense of refuge and murmur of the sea. Now a single cell dating from the 12 c.; the arcading in the north wall was blocked up when the 16 c. north aisle was demolished. Restored 1893 under H. Hughes. Annual service early June.

Porth Trecastell, more commonly

◁ Limestone wall at Llanallgo
▽ Field wall near Llanddona

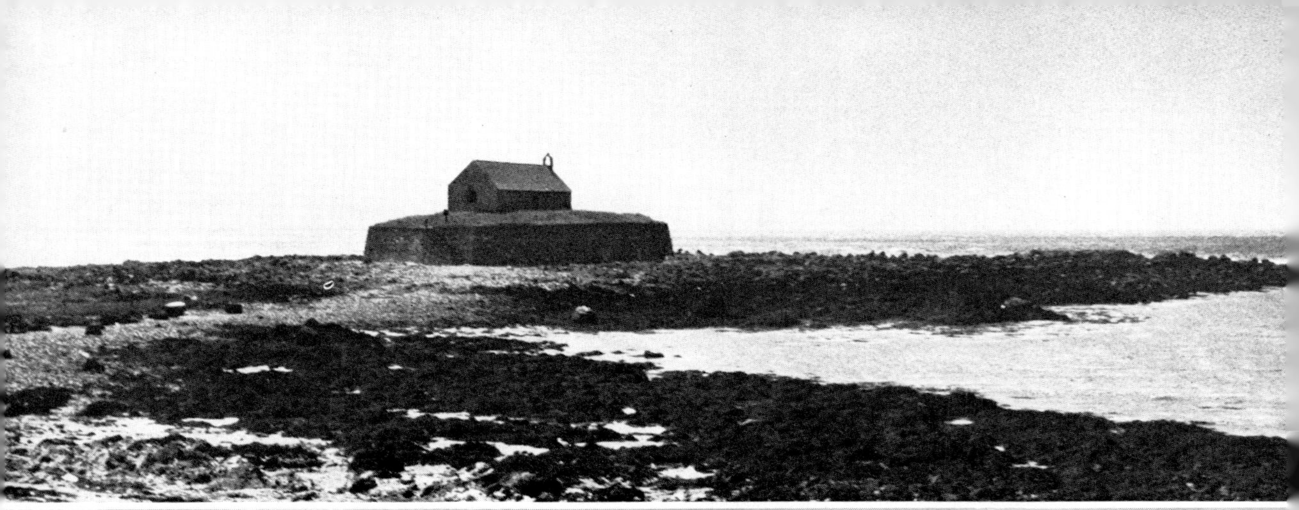

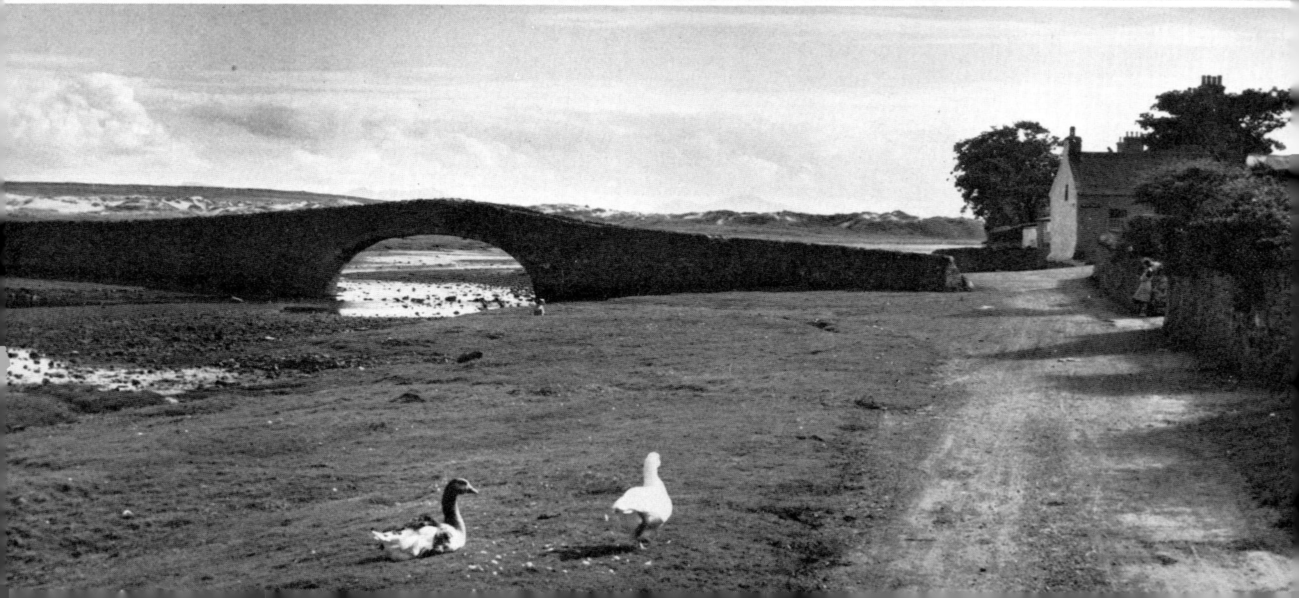

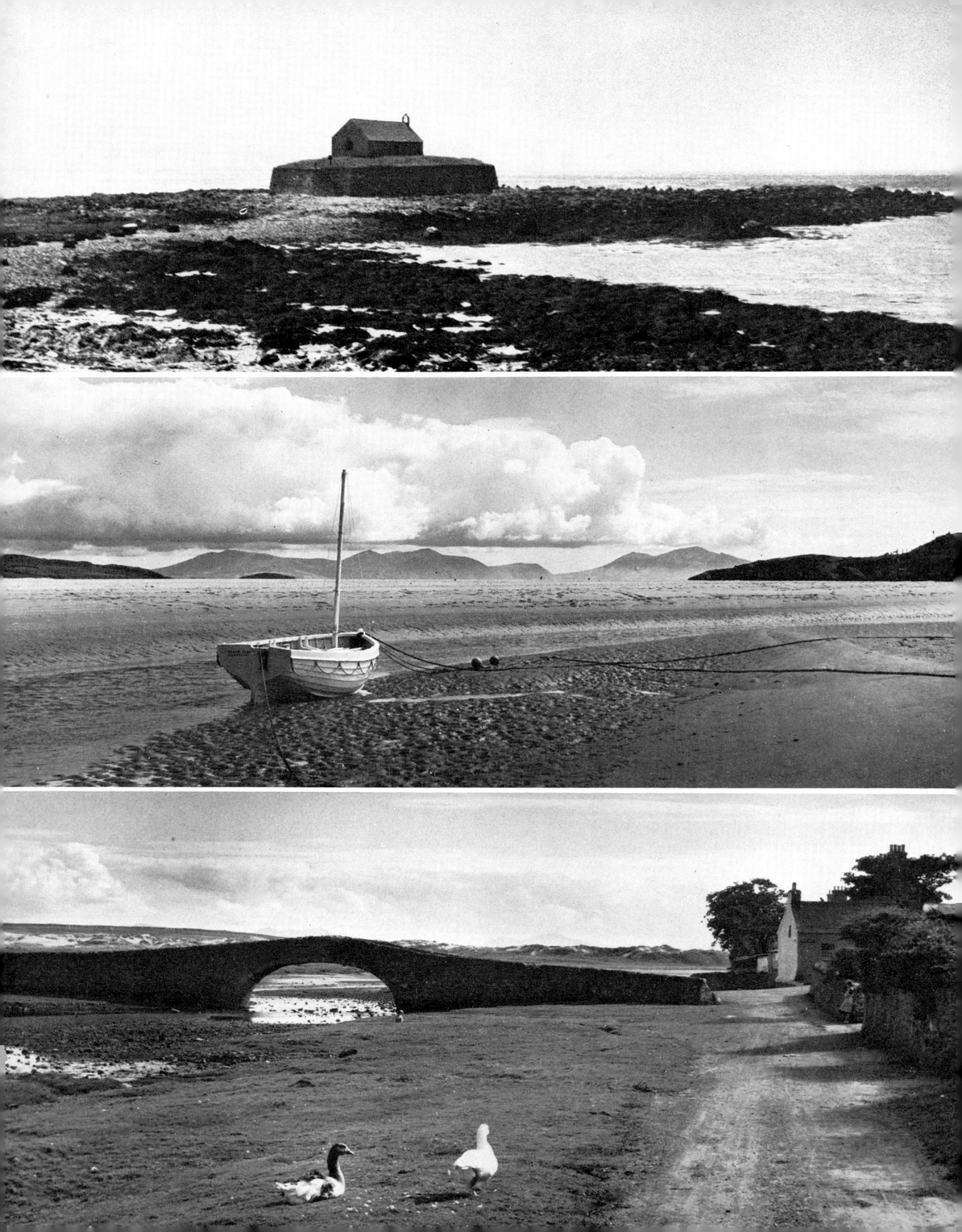

◁ Three views at ABERFFRAW: the church on the beach is Llangwyfan

Cable Bay (the telegraph line to Ireland was laid here), is sheltered and sandy but rather cold-seeming, walled in by abrupt headlands; a road runs close to the beach with obvious results.

Barcloddiad-y-gawres: Neolithic or early Bronze Age, in another world on the north headland. This burial chamber was excavated and buried in 1953, so instead of the standing stones of the cromlech you now see a big green hump. A 20 ft. passage leads to the central chamber. Stylistically the carved patterns are said to be closer to New Grange, County Meath, than Bryn Celli Ddu the only other surviving burial chamber in the United Kingdom with megalithic mural art. A remote-seeming site, specially on a windy day when waves crash on the rocks below. Holyhead Mountain to the north; the Lleyn Peninsula across the sea to the south-west. A good place to be buried.

Din Dryfol burial chamber (395725). Late Neolithic or early Bronze Age. Lies 1½ miles northeast of the village through the farm of that name, in hummocky limestone country of little fields under a high natural outcrop. The stones, though partly collapsed, are unfenced, giving a timeless impression impossible behind railings. Probably a passage grave at least 50 ft. long. A lone stone stands to the east.

Amlwch (2). A tiny creek on the north coast. The Harbour Act was passed in 1793 and Amlwch then claimed, with justification, to be the world's most important copper port. It is said to have had a population of 4,977, and 1,025 ale houses. Now village-size, but according to the signboard Amlwch still "invites industry", and the famous copper mountain is again prospected.

The parish church was erected by the Parys Mine Company: grey, classic and civic; 1800, by a "Mr Wyatt of London". Unfortunately Gothicised in 1867 (Kennedy and O'Donoghue). Headstones in the graveyard reflect the business of the town: captains, smelters, surgeons, and coal merchants lie here; also a bookbinder, and the Marquis of Anglesey's Assay Master. The epitaph of Jonathan Roose refers to the famous strike believed to have been made in March 1768 when, after seemingly hopeless prospecting, a wonderfully rich seam was discovered in *Parys Mountain*. This day became an annual festival for miners. Today the mountain is a lunar landscape riddled with mine workings. It is fascinating, private, accessible and extremely dangerous. Desolate; not a bird. Brown, ochre, mauve and pink rock; sinister shafts; a curious absence of scale. Romans dug copper on the north side and it was mined in Elizabethan times, but the late 18 c. saw its hey-day. Nearly nine million Amlwch penny tokens were cast. It was then found that the richest copper could be won by precipitation; hence the numerous ponds formed in the mountain. The ruined windmill near the summit was for pumping the water. Parys Mountain soon became an important feature of the Welsh tour; Sandby, Ibbetson and many others drew the miners swinging from their whimsies at the cliff faces, and recorded the desolation of the land (the vicar of Amlwch was paid £15 per annum for "smoke trespass"). To alleviate the poor rate, women wearing yellow spotted handkerchiefs were given the job of breaking up the lumps of ore while children picked them over.

Beaumaris (3) basks on the shore of the Menai Straits. It has a distinctly English feel: 19 c. Georgian, seaside and regatta. Painted plaster and stone terrace houses and hotels. It has entirely English origins, having been founded to settle English immigrants by Edward I when he sited his castle here in 1295. Whenever possible he chose castle sites for comfort as well as strategic potential, with some outpost of civilisation nearby, in this case Llanfaes Friary.

Facing the Straits are several pleasant, plastered and painted terraces of unknown origin, before you reach The Bulkeley Arms (Hansom and Welch, completed 1835; extended by R. G. Thomas 1873). On New Year's morning the Lady Patroness of the Anglesey Hunt showers hot pennies on the populace from the hotel balcony. This tradition has been undermined by devaluation; only the aristocracy

Benches in St Mary, Tal-y-llyn, ABERFFRAW

and gentry now trouble to pick them up. Victoria Terrace (Hansom and Welch, 1830–5), grand in scale and manner, look across the straits to Snowdonia; hydrangeas. Edge of Green Terrace (John Hall of Bangor, 1824–5) next door is a complete change of scale and character; much humbler. Pretty trellissed verandah; geraniums. Unfortunately now drably plastered.

Long before Beaumaris took on the role of a Tenby or Brighton of the North, it was the gathering place of Anglesey gentry, being the assize town of the island. Local travellers and those going between England and Ireland crossed the Straits at Beaumaris. From medieval times until the 19 c. it was the chief harbour of Anglesey.

Beaumaris Castle, on its low-lying site, seems at first more domestic than military. This is partly due to its unaggressive levelness at battlement level; the tops of the towers were never finished. But it is indeed excellent military architecture: being the eighth (and last) of Edward I's Welsh castles, a lifetime of experience lies in this most perfect concentrically planned castle in Great Britain. Every inch of wall is covered by the cross-shots from its turrets. There is also an impressive ruined hall with big windows looking over the green lawn of the inner bailey; and a tiny chapel as delicate as all else is robust.

When building started in 1295 labour was diverted from all parts of the realm. Soon, 400 masons and 2,000 labourers, as well as smiths and carpenters, were at work. But it was not a straightforward job. The Masters of the King's Works in Wales held no sinecure. When, on 27th February 1296, he wrote to report to the Barons of the Exchequer on the state of building at Beaumaris, he finished:

"As to how things are in the land of Wales, we still cannot be any too sure. But, as you well know, Welshmen are Welshmen, and you need to understand them properly; if, which God forbid, there is a war with France and Scotland, we shall need to watch them all the more closely...

"P.S. And, Sirs, for God's sake be quick with the money for the work, as much as ever our lord the king wills: otherwise everything done till now will have been of no avail."

The Parish Church, civically sited in the middle of the town, was built in the early 14 c. for English immigrants. Chancel added, and aisle walls raised and battlemented *c*. 1500. The misericords brought from Llanfaes Friary are the same date. Inside it is high, wide and handsome, but has been fiercely restored (harsh pointing in the nave) by G. F. Bodeley, 1902. Fine alabaster Bulkeley tomb (late 15 c.) in north aisle. In the porch an inscription (1808) explaining the history of the sarcophagus of Princess Joan (daughter of King John, and wife of Llewelyn the Great) which "having been conveyed from the Friary of Llanfaes, and, alas! used for many years as a horse watering trough, was rescued from such indignity, and placed here for preservation, as well as to excite serious meditations on the transitory nature of all sublunary distinctions". 19 c. glass includes some by Kemp.

The Court House (from 1614) opposite the castle, is the oldest

Victoria Terrace, BEAUMARIS

BEAUMARIS CASTLE ▷

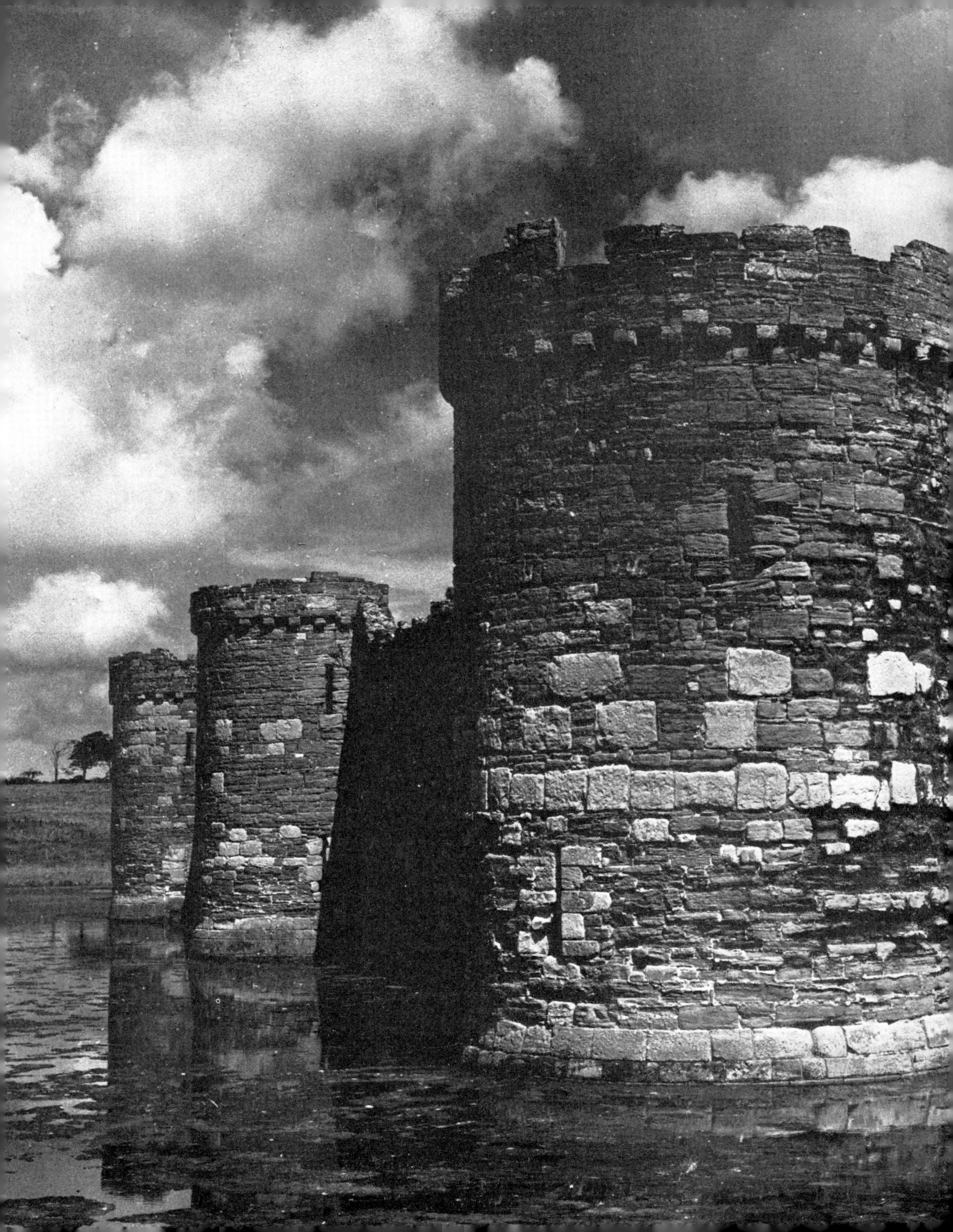

BODWROG

court still in use (Petty Sessions and Assizes). In the Great Court Room an iron railing divides the public from the business of the Court. It is handsomely fitted with original and 18 c. furniture, boxes, etc., restored and added to in early 19 c. when the windows were Gothicised. Then, when horrible penalties were inflicted for the most reasonable crimes, leniency could be expected in cases concerning smuggling, an activity in which the island gentry were as interested as everyone else.

Beaumaris Gaol, 1828–9 (to see, ask at the Council Office), is by Hansom (who designed the carriage and was the first Editor of *The Builder*) and Edmund Welch. Architecturally effective, but in human terms claustrophobic and despondent. It has a treadmill for raising water. For public hangings prisoners walked a plank from the main block to a high-level door in the outer wall. Last time this happened all the children (i.e. the grandparents of some of today's citizens) were taken out of the town. The prisoner, who proclaimed his innocence, cursed the church clock with continuing effect. The prison walls contain fascinating fossils.

Baron Hill (not open), seat of the Bulkeley family, stands above the town: Samuel Wyatt (1776) with mid 19 c. additions by David Moore, was partially gutted by fire during World War II. The nearby almshouses (much altered) date from 1613. See also *Llanfaes*.

Bodedern (2), a no-nonsense towny stone village on the last stage of the old Holyhead road. Then a small woollen manufacturing town with a branch post office. The church is at the T-junction in the middle of the village; its stone looks green in the rain. Although in a "neat and creditable state" in 1851 it was extensively restored twenty years later by Kennedy and O'Donoghue. Lately it seems to have suffered from paint manufacturers' enthusiasm.

The grand pump under its classical pediment was presented by Lord Stanley of Alderley, 1897. Until recently it pumped "the best water on the island: far better than the piped". About one mile along the Llangefni road one of Telford's gates (presumably from the suspension bridge) is hung on a drive entrance.

Presaddfed burial chamber, Neolithic, just south of Llyn Llywenan (birds, reeds and trout) stands alone in a field: the two sets of stones are probably part of a long chamber.

See also *Caergeiliog*.

Bodewryd (see Carreglefn).

Bodwrog (2), a central parish straddling the old main road. No village. The lonely church stands high on a grey outcrop. Campion, yarrow, ragwort, cow-parsley, feathery grasses and green bracken thrust from every crack in the rock. A great field, new yellow and smooth as a lawn when the hay has been carted, sweeps up from the north. A benign bull's face looks down from the hooded lintel over the south door; inside bluebottles buzz and miles away sheep bleat. It seems a very long way to the sea. A single cell church, late 15 c., more quietly restored than most. Victorian box pews. Gas-lit. Slab floor.

At *Bryntwrog* (2 miles north on Llanerchymedd road) is an attractive small chapel: stone, with pointed windows but straight glazing bars; the lower panes have been painted in pinkish pearly wash. The caretaker's garden has Sweet William and neat rows of potatoes. Also on this road is one of the few surviving whitewashed cottages with a grouted roof, typical of Anglesey until 1939. Cherished and trim.

Brynsiencyn (6) is a definite village in the Straits parish of Llanidan (described here). A.4080 twists determinedly through its grey stone and rough-cast main street, which is dominated by the immense Calvinistic Methodist church, 1883. Another building of personality is a humble 19 c. cottage, which curiously has survived in an otherwise entirely renewed council terrace.

This wooded, peaceful parish is steeped in bloody history. The site where, in A.D. 61, Suetonius' infantry crossed the Straits in their flat-bottomed boats to defeat the Druids, is believed to be at Griffith's Crossing below Porthamel Hall. It is indeed a blessing that Tacitus' account survives to give them substance: the romantic 18 c. image of the Druids, combined with that given on television by the Bards at the 1969 Investiture, is too clearly imprinted on one's hopelessly confused mind. He describes how, having crossed the Straits, the Romans found the British Army "in close array, and well armed; with women running wildly about in black attire with dishevelled hair, and like the furies brandishing their hands to heaven, and pouring forth the most dreadful imprecations". The Romans seem to have been numbed by this horrid sight, and took time to overcome their initial shock, but eventually "overthrew all who opposed them, and flung them into their own fires . . .". (Pennant's translation.)

Llanidan (*old*) *church* lies between the Straits and the village. Closely sheltered by trees; romantic and ruined; a sense of green seclusion. Was founded by St Nidan, A.D. 616. The never-failing well close by in the walled garden of Llanidan House probably gave the site religious significance long before the Christian era. Llanidan became an off-shoot of the Augustinian Priory at Beddgelert (q.v.); after the Dissolution it became the parish church. In 1696 Henry Rowlands, the antiquarian later famous for *Mona Antiqua Restaurata*, became vicar ("This prodigy of learning"—Pennant). Most of the church was demolished in 1844 when the new one was built by the main road. This left standing only the two western bays and the ruined arcade which separated the aisles. The east wall of the present 14 c. church was then constructed to seal it off. The north aisle (and perhaps the south porch) were late 15 c. additions to a 14 c. single cell church. Water in the stoup in the south porch always maintains its level, unless actually baled out to be taken away by over-enthusiastic visitors who believe it to be particularly holy.

Llanidan (*new*) *church* lies to the east of the village. Architect John Welch (see St George's, Llandudno), 1843, but the inside unexpectedly feels a century later. No aisles, but shallow transepts with high pointed arches at crossing. A spacious, bright, cherished building; the varnished pews gleam like kippers. Clear glass in south windows gives glimpses of Snowdonia. Some fittings moved from old church, include bells and an early 13 c. font.

Caer Leb (473674) an enclosed settlement occupied during the 3rd century, on marshy ground near a stream. Buttercups and orchids; and remains of earthworks, presumably defensive. These formed an irregular pentagon 200 by 160 ft.; a

Llanidan old church, BRYNSIENCYN

round hut 18 ft. diameter was found towards the middle.

The *Bodowyr burial chamber* (464683), Neolithic–Early Bronze, is a fine cromlech absurdly encased in fencing.

Castell Bryn-gwyn (464671) is a fortified earthwork, rather confused by big hedges and farm buildings, dating from Neolithic times. The last evidence of occupation is about the time of the arrival of the Romans.

Caergeiliog (Bodedern) (2). A small village on A.5. An original tollhouse survives. The Calvinistic Methodist chapel and adjoining house make a satisfactory L-shaped group opposite the post office.

Carreglefn (2). An inland agricultural parish north of the new Alaw reservoir.

Bodewyrd Church has a primly trim churchyard (macadam paths with concrete kerbs). Inside are three fine 18 c. brasses; simple and shiny. By the road ⅓ mile north is an attractive, 4-gabled dovecot still inhabited by squatters, but crumbling; probably 18 c.; has a pretty site by a miniature cleft. Plas Bodewyrd, the farm to which it belongs, has been modernised inside. *Rhosbeiro Church* (19 c.) seems to be out of use; reached by overgrown path, a miniature avenue of sycamore and cow-parsley.

Cerrigceinwen (2). A long, thin agricultural parish, 2½ miles southwest of Llangefni. No village; but Mona, once an important halt on A.5, was the scene of the famous foot race depicted by Cruikshank. This was run along Telford's Holyhead road, after a meeting of the Anglesey Hunt Club at the Mona Inn in 1873; post boys held candles in bottles to light the course. In 1934 the Club Committee, inspecting their stock of wine, found it to be undrinkable. It was minuted after their next meeting that it had been sold to a famous London store.

The church is attractively sited in a sheltered hollow; rebuilt in the 19 c., having already been refitted in 1839. The south door lintel is a 12 c. grave slab: a crude cross with a circular head and four-petal pattern. Boldly carved 12 c. font; two simple and elegant six-branched brass chandeliers.

Gaerwen (6), in the parish of Llanfihangel Esceifiog (q.v.), is a linear village dating from the opening of A.5. An iron milestone survives near church. Once thatched cottages now boast modern roofs and metal windows. The church was built by the main road in 1847 under H. Kennedy, who "in the kindest manner consented to carry into effect the plans of an amateur architect and to improve them by his own taste and experience". Restored 1897 by P. S. Gregory. Total result pointed and towny; more like Birkenhead.

Gwalchmai (2) (parish of Trewalchmai) was described in 1833 as "being on the newly opened line of road, neatly built but small". It has grown and produced a wide variety of places of worship. The parish church, like that of Heneglwys, was rebuilt by the rector, J. Wynne Jones (1845), who took the east window from Heneglwys for Gwalchmai. The Methodist church (1780, 1849, 1925), rather hideous outside, is well grouped with flanking houses. Very grand inside; semi-circular seating focused on elaborately carved pulpit; gallery supported on Corinthian iron columns; pews dark violin varnish. Roman Catholic church recently built; mid 20 c., new town style.

Heneglwys (2) a hamlet between the two Holyhead roads, east of Gwalchmai. Civil airfield. The church was rebuilt in 1845 by the Rector (J. Wynne Jones). He re-used windows and doorways, but took the old east window for Gwalchmai.

Holyhead (1). This small port, long an important link between Dublin and London, is now mostly driven through by tourists using car ferry. Has a slaty Edwardian–Victorian feel; more seaside and yacht club to the west. A regular packet service was licensed in 17 c. Passengers, e.g. Jonathan Swift, frustrated by gales, found little to see. Nor did the Rev. Bingley who in 1814 wrote, "Though Holyhead is much resorted to by company to and from Ireland, it possesses very few attractions for the traveller on pleasure". At first glance this might still seem true; an impression that may be reinforced by Rio Tinto's giant zinc smelter which will shortly dominate the scene. But 19 c. development and restoration provide great variety. A new harbour was recommended by John Rennie (1801), and the *Admiralty Pier* (Salt Island Pier) was constructed (1821) with a lighthouse on its tip. Here the drive-on ferry now operates. The Doric Memorial Arch (Thomas Harrison, 1824) commemorates the visit of George IV (1821), who was detained for five days by contrary winds. Eventually he abandoned the royal yacht for a steam paddler, recently introduced. The pleasant small Customs House and Port Offices (1830) are also by Harrison. In 1831, a 300 ft. chain was laid across the harbour entrance as a grapple, since the sea bed had been so much raked that anchors would not hold. The present Lifeboat Station (visitors welcome) is beyond the car-ferry entrance on Salt Island. Salt was extracted from sea water here in 18 c. To the west *Skinner's Memorial* (1832) commemorates that admirable mail-packet captain who did more than anyone to bring about harbour improvements.

In 1845 work started on the railway station (Hotel 1880) and the great *breakwater*, which formed what was to be described in *Parry's Railway Guide* as "one of the most splendid refuge harbours and packet stations in the universe". Stone was quarried from under Holyhead Mountain and brought along a railway to the workshops near Soldier's Point. Here the chief contractor built himself the castellated, turreted mansion. In 1853 Queen Victoria came to witness blasting; 20,000 tons of rock were brought down in one gigantic operation for her entertainment.

It is a 1½ mile walk to the lighthouse, last manned 1962, at the end of the breakwater (brass clockwork machinery, 1873, survives). It is a massive structure built at two levels, a railway for servicing running below.

Trinity House Depot (near the 1845 breakwater) services Cumber-

HOLYHEAD: the Irish Boat

land coast—Cardigan Bay. All buoys have a replacement here; superb shapes, spick and span in rich oil paint; black, white, scarlet. Far-sounding, lonely names: Chester Flat, Coal Rock, Point of Ayr . . . (ask Shore Bos'un for permission to view).

Holyhead's importance goes back at least to Roman occupation. *Caer Gybi:* a small coastguard fort, now occupied by St Cybi's churchyard, is just off the High Street. Almost certainly Roman, but never excavated. Stands on a low cliff once washed by the sea; remains below have suggested a quay. It may have been part of a system of coastal forts which operated in conjunction with the Fleet against Irish marauders (see Hen Weliau, Caernarvon). High walls and corner bastions, restored at various times, clearly mark its boundaries; constructed in rubble with diagonally pitched bonding courses. Below: steamers, trains, and Rennie's harbour.

The *parish church*: St Cybi, a much-travelled, aristocratic, and perhaps quarrelsome monk, founded his monastery here *c.* 550, sensibly choosing the protection of the Roman fortifications. But this did not prevent its sack by the Danes (961). Present building much restored by Sir Gilbert Scott (1877–9); south aisle by C. L. Baker (1896). Great sense of height and light when compared with the humbler churches of the island. Airy four-centred arches and high ceilings (late 15 and early 16 c.) to nave and aisles contribute to this. Elaborate carvings of the south porch and parapet of south transept: early 16 c. Fine 19 c. glass includes a pomegranate window and pre-Raphaelite figures by William Morris and Burne-Jones. The organ came from the library at Eaton Hall (Alfred Waterhouse). Immense Stanley tomb is by Hamo Thorneycroft. *Capel Llan-y-gwyddel* (Capel-y-bedd) by the south gate is what remains of the nave of a medieval chapel, which was converted to a school in the 18 c.

The *Library and Exhibition Room* (1968), pleasantly grouped with a primary school just off the High Street to the north of St Cybi's, house a permanent exhibition of local finds and frequent exhibitions of topical or regional interest. The huge buildings at the top of the town is *Le Bon Sauveur Convent* (mother house at Caen), a girls' school. The aloof spire nearby belongs to *St Seiriol*'s; grey, spiky, withdrawn and locked. (Charles Verelst, *c.* 1853).

Holy Island (1). For the last ten miles or so along A.5 the traveller is lured westward by Holyhead Mountain; although only 720 ft. above the sea it has the isolated majesty of something far greater. This bare, rocky land, though hardly hospitable, was easier to settle than much of the densely wooded, swampy main island, and through pre-historic to early Christian times Holy Island held a key position on one of the great traffic routes of the western world. Remains of much of this activity abound.

The *Stanley Embankment* (1822), Telford's last major work on the A.5 was constructed for the crossing to Holy Island. The tide is concentrated into one narrow tunnel, which crazy canoeists occasionally try to shoot. The Embankment, which now also carries Stephenson's railway, forms the northern end of the shallow Inland Sea (invisible from the road because of massive wall to railway). This great tidal lake, bounded to the south by Four Mile Bridge, is a haunt of herons and human fishermen. Low tide: marvellous, melancholy mud. Three tracks are marked across the sands to Holy Island on Evans' map (1795): all where the water was wide but shallow. One lies to the north of the Stanley Embankment; a second about half a mile above Four Mile Bridge; the third a mile up from Cymyran.

Holyhead Mountain. Several paths up are marked on the Ordnance Survey map. No climbing necessary. One of the most satisfactory starts at the enormous limestone quarries west of Holyhead; beware the abyss if you miss the path on the return journey. To the north and west

73

the mountain drops by tremendous cliffs into the sea. *Caer-y-twr*, a 17-acre hill fort crowns the mountain. Not excavated, but presumed to be about the same age as the Ty Mawr hut group below. Defences make use of natural precipices, elsewhere a massive dry-stone wall protects the enclosure, still standing 10 ft. in places. On the summit, Pennant found what he thought to be a pharos.

Hut group near Ty Mawr (to north of road to the South Stack Lighthouse). A remarkable group of 2–4 c. hut circles and small rectangular buildings bask in the afternoon sun on the south-west slope of the mountain looking towards Snowdonia; a 20 c. speculator's dream site. About twenty huts survive from a much larger settlement. Cultivation terraces can also be traced. Huts vary in plan from near-perfect circles to elliptical and roughly rectangular enclosures. Some still have raised shelves and fireplaces. In most cases the walls stand to about 2 ft. and are capped with heather, stonecrop and foxglove, and the floors make a clean contrast of short nibbled turf. A short distance above this site another track leads to an easy path to the summit of Holyhead Mountain.

The *North Stack* cliffs have long been renowned for sea birds and these, and the great cave in Gogarth Bay, were very popular with intrepid 19 c. boating parties. The 19 c. Telegraph Station (see Llanryddlad) was about midway between the North Stack and the summit of the mountain. There is now a new unmanned signal station on the point.

The South Stack Lighthouse. Off the west tip of Holy Island. The construction of this lighthouse was no sinecure, since the bridge connecting its rock to the mainland did not then exist. A contemporary painting, inscribed to the architect, Daniel Alexander, shows the ingenious pulleys and hoses slung across the gap to carry workmen, materials and water. Work began in August 1808, and the first light shone six months later.

Alexander was a versatile architect whose works include the early buildings of Princetown Prison, the flanking blocks and colonnades to Inigo Jones' Queen's House, Greenwich, and some ecclesiastical work in Gothic. *The Visitor's Handbook for*

The South Stack Lighthouse, HOLYHEAD

Fortifications on Holyhead Mountain and Holyhead breakwater, HOLY ISLAND

Holyhead, 1853, describes how the keeper had to cross over in the cradle "the bellowing ocean raging below to swallow him"; but later a rope bridge was thrown across which "although considered perfectly safe and convenient, was by no means agreeable to the affrighted Tourist". The suspension bridge constructed in 1827 has now been replaced. The lighthouse is usually open from 1300 hours to 1 hour before sunset; not on Sundays. From the path down to the bridge there is an excellent view through a narrow gap of the intense folding of the rock in the opposite cliff face; also often of razorbill, guillemot and kittiwake.

Between the South Stack and Rhoscolyn there is very good cliff scenery, though the land itself is much lower—around the 50 to 100 ft. contour, with hummocky outcrops and a few sandy bays.

Dinas Promontory Fort, due south of Holyhead Mountain on a headland to the east of Porthdafarch. Almost an island; perilous cliff defences; still connected by a narrow neck of rock just above high-water line. A low grass bank ran across the headland on the land side.

Porth Dafarch. The nearest sandy bathing bay to Holyhead on the south coast. In an attempt to improve the Irish mail service, a small quay was built here in 1820 for the use of sailing vessels when contrary winds made Holyhead impracticable. Remains of this and a road-cutting above can clearly be seen on the west side of the bay. The introduction of steam packets and the build- of Rennie's harbour put paid to this scheme. Immediately inland from the bay are traces of another hut group.

Trearddur Bay: an inter-war period piece; middle-class detached holiday ideal. English, white houses, grey slate roofs. A few vast pre-1914, suggesting annual Edwardian exoduses from Liverpool complete with staff and linen. Hummocky topography of out-cropping rock and rockbound sandy bays help to tie it together, but it is now overbuilt.

Trefignath Burial Chambers, 2000–1500 B.C. One mile south-east of Holyhead on road to Trearddur farm. Probably consisted of three or more chambers strung together, the whole making a structure about 45 ft. long.

Penrhos House, to the east of Holyhead, has been mostly demolished. It was the home of the Stanleys of Alderley. Gothicky 19 c. ruins of a late 18 c. house (James Defferd, who also designed Bodorgan House) and a battery on the coast survive.

Llanallgo (3). A tiny parish in the north-east of the island. Is best known for the wreck of the *Royal Charter* (October 1859) which is commemorated by a dingy obelisk in the churchyard, and also by Charles Dickens in the *Uncommercial Traveller* (he stayed at the Rectory to cover the event). The ship was

Trearddur Bay, HOLY ISLAND

wrecked on the Moelfre Rocks with the loss of 140 lives, with "an enormous quantity of gold; a considerable part of which was the property of fortunate diggers who were returning home to enjoy their fortunes". The church has been ruthlessly and often restored.

Moelfre: a village for seaside and retirement to one's dream bungalow. Shingly cove among shelving rocks bright with beach-balls, windmills and ices.

Llanbabo (2). An agricultural parish towards the north-east, partly submerged by the new Alaw Reservoir (stocked with trout). St Pabo is thought to have been a chief of the North Britons who, around 500, led an army against the Picts; later he sought asylum in Anglesey. The fine 14 c. low relief, re-set in the north wall of the church, represents Pabo: a crowned king with his sceptre, he stands under a cusped arch wearing a long cloak with stylised pleating. Rosettes decorate the background; a perfect use of space and surface pattern (see Llaniestyn). This small church lies by a stream and a stone bridge.

Outside it glows with virginia creeper; inside colour-washed like a green dairy. Single cell with 12 c. origins, a 14 c. window, and tough medieval roof trusses. It jangles with electric fittings. A grave, traditionally that of the unfortunate Princess Bronwen, is now being excavated on the banks of the Alaw.

Llanbadrig (2) on the north coast is one of several places from which St Patrick may have set sail for Ireland. It includes some of the most splendid of Anglesey's coastline, the enormous Wylfa Atomic Power Station, and the small resort of Cemaes Bay. Llanbadrig church, with some snug cottages and a farm, is at the end of the farm road near the sea. Llwyd described it as being "most inconveniently on a cliff . . .". "In certain winds," he claimed, "the waves break over it with such violence as to interrupt, and frequently prevent the performance of divine service." Even funerals were held up for some days. This 14 and 16 c. building has been astonishingly restored. Outside, dreary rendering; inside, it is reminiscent of a church converted to a mosque. A mixture of blue light from the east window and tiling below it; white walls; a small cusped canopy (14 c.) encrusted in whitewash so that it looks like sugar. Hardly surprising to be told that the restoration (1884) was by the Lord Stanley of Alderley who became a Moslem. He was that eccentric uncle of Bertrand Russell who married the same Spanish lady four times, twice by Mohammedan rites, once in a Roman Catholic church and once in a registry office, only to find that all ceremonies were equally invalid as she had another husband living. There are handsome benches in the porch (probably 18 c.). A boldly carved stone with a very original cross pattern (9–11 c.) stands at the west end.

Most of the coastline from the church to Cemaes belongs to the National Trust, so is accessible.

Cemaes Bay, a cheerful seaside holiday village to which the power station builders have given winter life. The story of Wylfa Atomic Power Station is told in a centrally-heated viewing tower (a useful place for wet walkers to dry out?) by a bi-lingual golden voice. It is the biggest nuclear power station in the world (1969) and uses one million gallons of sea-water per hour for cooling. (Architects: Farmer and Dark. Landscape architect Sylvia Crowe.)

Dinas Cwynfor: an Iron Age promontory fort on superb stretch of coast (to east of the church). The fort itself belongs to the National Trust (a footpath is marked to it). Far below yachts race; on top bees buzz in the bell-heather among the limestone outcrops; looking inland the foreground is closely grazed, making curving patterns in the dark bracken. To the west, the great bulk of **Wylfa**. The fort, an area of 700 by 300 yds., has formidable natural defences: cliffs of up to 200 ft. drop sheer to the sea; to landward the marsh. In summer the man-made defences which reinforce this side are lost in deep bracken: two lines of limestone block walling and a defended entrance to the south-east. Clay was dug here. The ruined remains of the tiny port from which it was exported lie at the head of *Porth Llanlleiana*, immediately west of the head. Curious walls, curved on plan, run just above high-tide line.

On the other side, *Hell's Mouth* lies under very steep cliffs which run round the lovely wide bay of *Porth Wen* with its pink/mauve shingle (accessible by paths from the main road). The deserted brickworks, with their angular quay, rounded ovens and tall chimneys, are most satisfying in form, like some middle-eastern mosque with embryonic domes and minarets. The bricks are a harsh texture.

Llanddaniel Fab (6) includes the most idyllic and secluded stretches of the Menai Straits, whose wooded reaches make the Druid's groves easy to visualise. The inland village and church (rebuilt mid-19 c.) are not the most interesting architectural features of this agricultural parish.

Bryn Celli Ddu, one mile east of the village, is a very well-preserved tomb or temple (Neolithic or Early Bronze). Complex religious ceremonies evidently took place within the four concentric stone circles which now lie in pleasant farmland among outcropping rock with fine views to Snowdonia. The original mound covered most of the present fenced area. In the burial chamber, reached through a 20 ft. passage, stands a pillar stone (8 ft. 3 in. overall height) whose whole surface has been carefully smoothed: this phallic symbol is really much more impressive than the famous central stone with its incised pattern (now in the National Museum, but replaced by a realistic cast).

LLANBADRIG

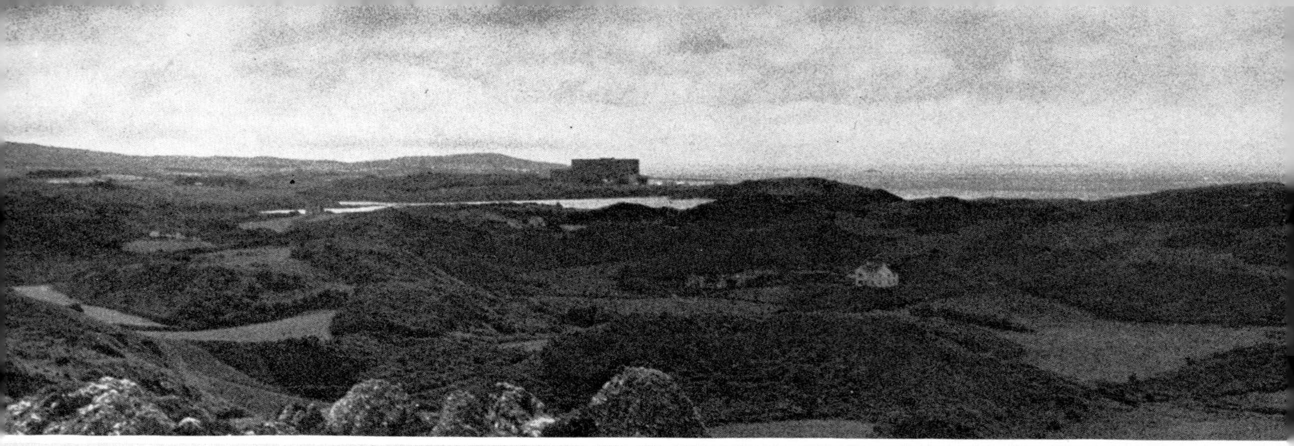
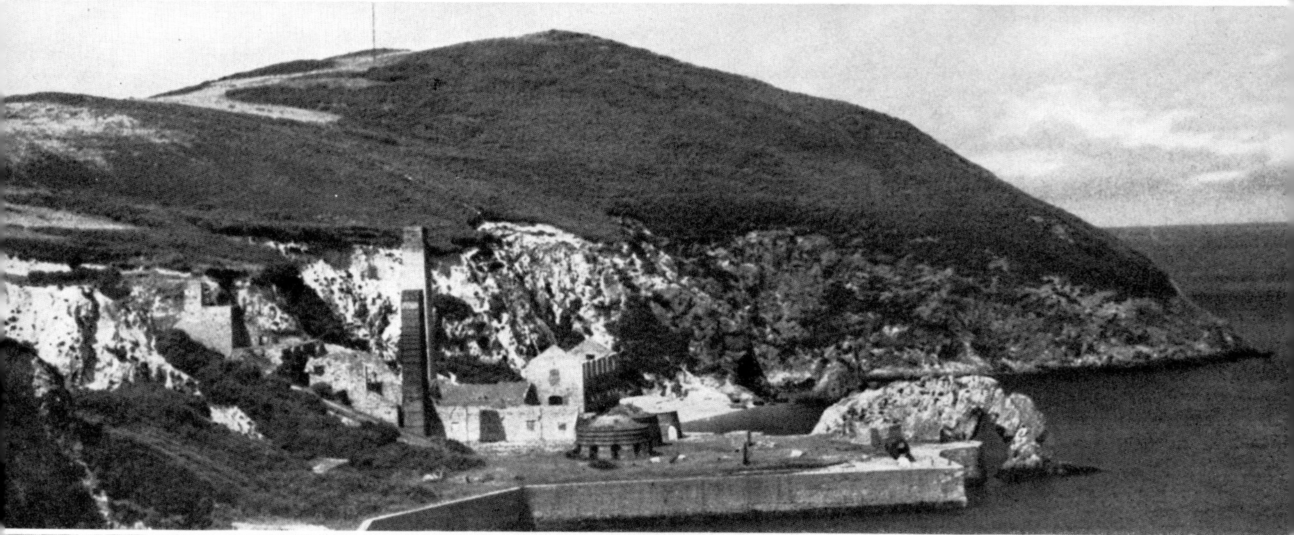
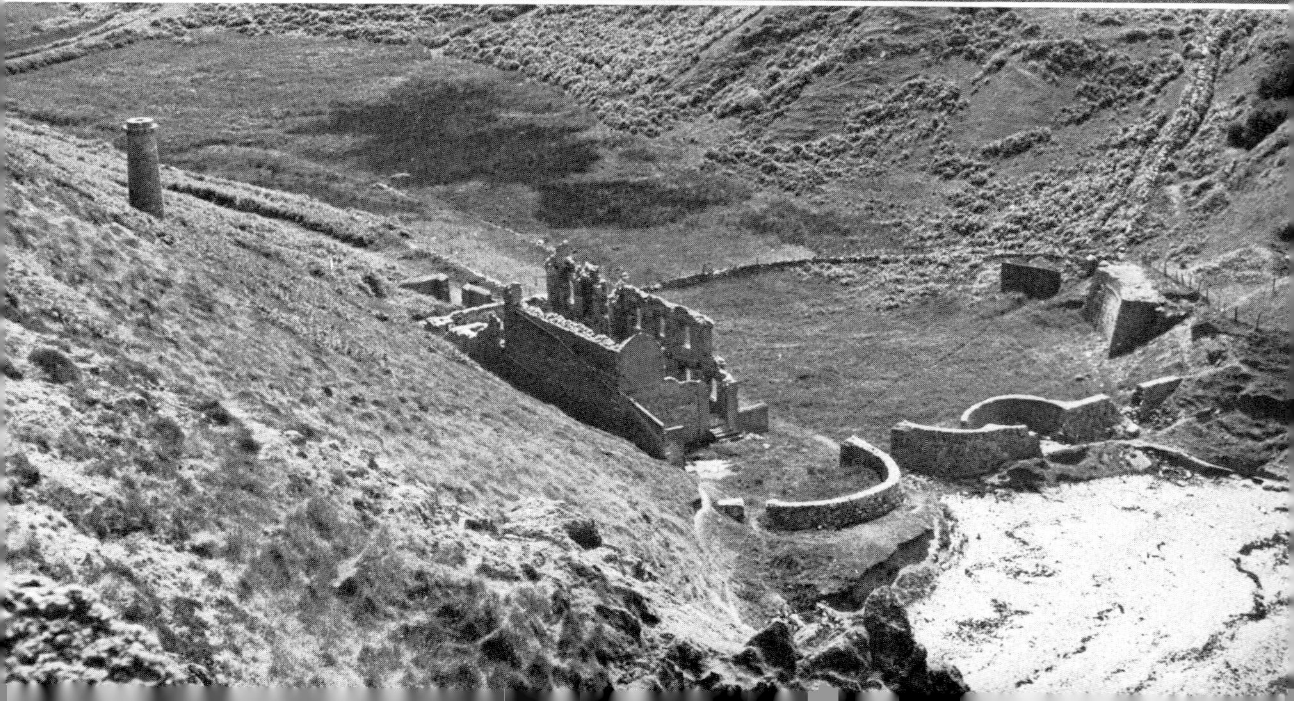

◁ At LLANBADRIG
above Wylfa atomic power station
centre Porth Wen
below Porth Llanlleiana

Llanidan Methodist church (about ½ mile south): a very simple group of buildings: church, caretaker's house, coach house and stable, round an unadorned yard. The cottage garden (rows of peas, beans and potatoes) is cherished in the same dateless way as the plain Georgian 19 c. chapel.

Plas Coch, 16 c. house with extensive 19 c. additions made with confusing skill, is now a holiday caravan centre. The road leads on to the old *Moel-y-don ferry*, once an important crossing to the slate port of Port Dinorwic (q.v.). It was here that three hundred of Edward I's followers were slaughtered in the winter 1281–2. The king was away in Conway, and the wily Welsh had sensibly retired into Snowdonia. The restive English, camped in Anglesey, built a bridge of boats ready to attack. This they did prematurely with disastrous results.

Plas Newydd (see Llanfairpwll).

Llanddeusant (2). An inland parish in the north-west. Church was rebuilt in 1861 by "a native amateur architect who shrinks from the public gaze"; rather forbidding, large and pointed. *Cellar Mill* humble and attractive, the only working water-mill left in Anglesey: overshot wheel, grinds maize mostly, has been run by the same family for four generations. Ask at house for permission to see. *Llynon Mill*: was the last working windmill of the many once active on the island, structurally very unsound but machinery still in position.

Llanddona (3) on the east of Red Wharf Bay. Cliffs climb steeply above the bay to the 500 ft. contour near the village. Wooded to the west. Biggish village above the bay, stone cottages survive. *Llanddona church* lies in hamlet below, down steep lane. 1873, by the Rev. Peter Jones who "acted as secretary and treasurer . . . furnished the plans, and acted as Clerk of Works". It cost "barely £600".

Do not miss *Llaniestyn church* ½ mile east of the village (page 91).

Wern, a music-holiday colony built in inter-war years by the Verney family, lies above the bay.

Llanddyfnan (3). An agricultural parish north-east of Llangefni, with pretty stretches of marsh. The church has an attractive site down a farm road, but it is only used for funerals so is locked. Its chief interest is the carving of the south doorway, c. 1500. A niche on each side and one above the door, integral with the carving of the frame, shelter figures of the Virgin, St John and the Trinity (without the dove). The spandrels of the arch are carved with a hart and two dogs. But none of this is visible without the key. Inside are plain 19 c. fittings. The tumulii on the Pentraeth road are camouflaged by hay.

Plas Llanddyfnan (not open) is one of those most likeable and typical Anglesey mansion houses from 16 c. with 18 and 19 c. improvements. Unpretentious Georgian white-washed roughcast, with gritstone quoins, slate roof and dormers. Dreaming and withdrawn in parkland, now fields. Sturdy barns in home farm.

Llandegfan (3). Between Beaumaris and Menai Bridge, includes the stretch known as Millionaire's Mile. The Beaumaris road was constructed by Lord Bulkeley in the early 19 c. Virtually a narrow shelf in the wooded banks of the Straits; inevitably widening alters its carriage-drive character. Several imposing mansions were built between it and the water, making this stretch excellent hunting ground for Victorian domestic architecture: Craig-y-don, Rhianfa (Charles Verelst, *c.* 1859), Glan Menai, Glan-y-garth. . . . Recent flats (Percy Thomas and Partners) aim to preserve the idea of a wooded reach unbroken by small plots, but their giant scale and size dominate the Victorian development, disrupting the 19 c. composition.

The inland church is much mellower outside than in: brown stone and lichen. Sturdy tower given by Lord Bulkeley, 1811 (see Llanfaes). Restored during the 19 c., and generally gone over again 1901–3. A pretty chandelier, and a nice 1649 effigy of Thomas Davies, King's Messenger to Charles I, with the

Sandstone quarry, LLANDDANIEL FAB

Royal Stuart arms across his chest, survive.

A maen hir (554739) ⅔ mile southwest of the church, in a field near the road. A great stone stands alone in a wide empty field, marvellously silhouetted against the mountains. Low down, where sheep have rubbed, smooth like oiled wood. Higher up, dry and greenish-grey with yellow lichen.

Llandrygarn (2) (383796) church lies down a long straight track to the south of the old main road, grass down the middle, sheltered by a bent hawthorn on the west, curving like a tunnel. It stands above a brown marsh, sheltered by ash trees among hummocky outcrops. The re-sited 13 c. doorway just fits under the gutter. Likely to be locked. Heavily restored within, so architecturally not worth finding the key. Better to enjoy the curlew.

Llandyfrydog (3) church lies in a wooded hollow, pleasantly grouped with the old school house and farm (horse-drawn hay rake still in use, 1968). Very inland feel, so it is surprising suddenly to see sandhills when you emerge to take the road to the village (i.e. shop and council houses and fine view to Mynydd Bodfan). The church feels broad and open; nave and chancel about equal, linked by generous 14 c. chancel arch. Nave windows step up in oddly attractive arrangement. Pleasant 19 c. box pews and pulpit. Restoration 1862, Kennedy and Rogers.

Llandysilio (see Menai Bridge).

Llaneilian (2), the north-east tip of Anglesey: fine rocky coast, a few sandy bays. The parish includes Point Lynas. The lighthouse (first shone 1781) may be seen on written application to the Mersey Dock and Harbour Board. Vessels bound for Liverpool pick up their pilots off Point Lynas, so the pilot-boat can be seen cruising off-shore. When the Mersey is fogbound, ships from all parts of the world may be waiting their turn here. One of the Liverpool telegraph stations (see Llanrhyddlad) was on Mynydd Eilian.

The *church* is interesting by any standards. Late 15 c. chancel and nave with battlemented parapets, linked by passageway to St Eilian's chapel. 12 c. tower (with spire) has been defaced by cement rendering. Inside: bold 15 c. rood-screen and loft; sturdy 16–17 c. choir-stalls; musicians playing flutes and bagpipes spring from the corbels of the chancel roof.

Traeth Dulas bounds the south of the parish. A lovely landlocked estuary, almost sealed from the sea by sandbanks (sea-lavender and other dune plants). Now remote, once busy. Clay was cut from the low cliffs on the north shore, and colliers called at the now-derelict quays with fuel for the brickworks; shipbuilding and lime-burning (note kilns). A very dangerous coast to sailing vessels. The tower with a conical top (1824) on *Ynys Dulas* was both a landmark and a refuge, food and drink being left for shipwrecked mariners who might be stranded there.

Llanwenllwyfo (*old*) *church* (medieval: restored 18 c.) now ruined, is buried in the woods of Llysdulas House (B. Woodward, 1856, Ruskinian with amazing carving; private). Tips of slate tombs surface in the sea of undergrowth.

Llanwenllwyfo church, 1856, can be spotted by its very sharp spire. Unrelenting exterior. Dingy interior, but splendid collection of Flemish glass (mostly 15 and 16 c.) given by the owner of Llysdulas in 1887, probably brought from France. Landscapes, townscapes and tiled interiors; figures exactly express tranquillity, exhaustion, awe.

Llanerchymedd (2) was once the market town of the north of the island which Mr Bulkeley referred to as "that great greedy-gut place" on account of his opinion of the butcher's bills. Nice sequence of townscape as you approach downhill via the Bull Hotel from Llangefni, but the pleasant square has been opened up on one side by a garage.

The *parish church*, reached through a dilapidated lych-gate from the square, stands well but seems dark and impersonal inside. Rebuilt, except the tower, by H. Kennedy, 1856. The *Welsh Presbyterian Church of Jerusalem* is cheerful, grand, white and square, with a hipped roof. Some of its windows still have iron Gothic tracery. Galleries round three sides; pulpit high, varnished and lightly Gothicised. The *Baptist Church* is a simple sash-windowed building, with a lovely brass thumb-latch on the main door.

Llaneugrad (3) on the east of the island has barely ¼ mile of coast.

Traeth Bychan is a jolly seaside bay with the club-house of the Red Wharf Bay Sailing Club, and a caravan site (carefully cherished plots complete with individual planting and paving). A very different scene from that in 1939 when H.M.S. *Thetis* (later H.M.S. *Thunderbolt*) was beached here after salvage. She had failed to surface when on her sea-trials in Liverpool Bay and only four men had escaped.

The little *parish church* is in the well-wooded Parciau estate. 12 c. chancel and nave, and 16 c. transept heavily restored. In a niche in the north wall of the nave is a 13 c. crucifix; roughly carved and grotesquely agonising. *Parciau dovecot* can be seen from the drive on the way up to the church. Early 17 c., almost unaltered. Two storeys rising from cow-parsley covered mound. Honey-brown gritstone, with four gables crowned by a cupola which repeats the pattern with four tiny gables.

Llanfaelog (5) includes a short stretch of the south-west coast; attractive and accessible. Llanfaelog church (in the village) stands on rising ground, partly sheltered by windswept sycamores; valerian grows from the garden walls. The old church was replaced by a plain Victorian nave and chancel in 1848 (H. Kennedy). On the north wall there is a nice marble which refers to "the fifty-six unfortunate persons who lost their lives in crossing the River Menai on the Fatal fifth day of December 1785".

Ty Newydd burial chamber (probably Neolithic–Early Bronze): in the corner of a field ½ mile north-east of the church (344738). A giant capstone on three uprights. When excavated, 110 pieces of broken white quartz and a tanged flint arrowhead were found on the floor.

Rhosneigr: a cheerful Edwardian-

Maen Hir, LLANDEGFAN

onwards holiday village on the coast, uninhibited by good taste. Few old cottages survive. Sheltered bays; attractive stretch of rocky coast without high cliffs. English families have migrated here annually from late Victorian times for happy, unpretentious seaside holidays. Sandy picnics, optimistic fishing, boating, secretive birds round reed-fringed Llyn Maelog. Bounded by dunes to Valley airfield (jets roar over) and the great sweep of Cymyran Bay to the north. A shore road from Cymyran is marked on the 1795 map, running south to the Barcloddiad-y-gawres headland thence across land eventually to Aber Menai.

Llanfaes (3) nearer the mouth of the Straits than Beaumaris (q.v.) was the village nearest to the crossing until Edward I built his new town. In 1237, Llewelyn the Great granted the Franciscans a site for a Friary here (no architectural remains, but see tombs in Penmynydd and Beaumaris churches). The parish church was rebuilt by Weightman and Hadfield (1845) and a spire added to the 1811 tower. The expensive, rather precious character of the design of this Sheffield firm comes as a surprise in Anglesey. North Chapel 1885, R. G. Thomas, and south aisle 1890 by H. Kennedy.

Bryn Celli Ddu, LLANDDANIEL FAB

The Welsh Presbyterian Church of Jerusalem, LLANERCHYMEDD

Llanfaethu (2) in the north-west of the island has views of both the Skerries and Snowdonia. The church of *St Maethlu* has been frequently restored, and is much more interesting inside than out. The rather grand pew in the nave has been re-made from a 17 c. box pew, and the octagonal font is 1640. The only sizeable clump of trees in this part of the island shelters Careglwyd, a pleasant 17 to 18 c. mansion house (not open). The coastline is rocky, with big sandy bays. At *Porth Trefadog* there is a very attractive farmhouse with gabled dormers, right by the sea, and a small squarish promontory fort; wild flowers before archaeology.

Llanfwrog church is Victorian, light and unmysterious.

Llanfair-Mathafarn-Eithaf (3). A coastal parish to the north of Red Wharf Bay. Outcropping limestone and plenty of trees help to absorb the extensive caravan and bungalow development. *Benllech* is a popular holiday resort.

The old parish church stands by a stream in a quiet leafy valley, sheltered by miniature limestone cliffs. Very restored. The poet Goronwy Owen (1723–69) was curate here; and the new pulpit, result of world-wide appeal, commemorates his bi-centenary. His cottage, visited by George Borrow and countless other admirers, is near *Brynteg*.

Glyn, an early to mid 17 c. farmhouse (open on written application) sheltered in a silvery beechwood, has unique plaster decoration. Very vigorous and bold: a frieze of firearms and two over-mantel panels, one depicting a potentate sitting under two palm trees receiving an ambassador (?), perhaps an incident in the owner's life. There is also a charming slate chimney-piece, engraved with naïve plants; date unknown.

The *Pant-y-saer burial chamber* (510824), late Neolithic, is on a limestone ridge made even more inaccessible by gorse and brambles (find stile in north-east corner). A lovely site, with sweeping views from the Great Orme through Snowdonia. Outcropping pavings of limestone: cinquefoil, thyme and orange lichen grow on the capstone (slightly collapsed). It covers a pit cut in solid rock. Remains of thirty-six adults plus children and babes were found. The *Pant-y-saer hut group* (Iron Age) is $c.\ \frac{1}{2}$ mile to the east, at end of plateau. Protected by limestone cliffs and enclosure wall of limestone slabs.

Llanbedrgoch parish church. A pretty site on a hill; 15 and 17 c., violently restored. There are small slate 18 c. tablets in the floor, like pages from neat notebook. Reading desk made up of 15 c. bench-ends; one a mermaid with a comb and mirror.

The district was noted for its millstones.

Llanfairpwllgwyngyll (2) was extended to:

Llanfairpwllgwyngyllgogerychwyrndrobwllllandysiliogogogoch

by a publicity-minded tailor of that village in the last century. British Rail unimaginatively removed the world-famous name board when the station was abandoned recently. Picture post cards of it are still on sale.

[1] Since this was written, disaster has struck Britannia Bridge. In 1900 the two lines of tubes had been covered by a massive timber canopy (invisible from below) bearing a catwalk along its centre, as an aid to maintenance. It was roofed by pitch soaked canvas.

On 23rd May, 1970, two boys who were looking for bats on the bridge, ran off when they heard someone calling, dropping their lighted flare as they went. So began the fatal fire. An eye-witness of the inferno has described how, shortly after this, ". . . . not only smoke but also large orange flames could be seen issuing furiously forth from the tops of the tubes of the bridge. It was a beautiful clear evening with a strongish south-westerly wind blowing. As night fell the wind increased. The flames spread quite quickly to the first stone tower, but it was completely dark by the time they reached the central tower...". During the night there was seen "the terrifying sight of flames rising sometimes in a continuous mass, sometimes singly, at least as high as the tops of the towers. Between the bottom of the tubes and the water there was a continual display of 'golden rain'. Every now and then a loud crack would herald the dislodging of a section of the burning superstructure. This, perhaps six feet long, would then slowly somersault, brilliantly alight from end to end, into the water below, followed by smaller pieces. All the time there was the dull roar of the flames, and a faint smell of burning paint and hot metal . . . . The paint on the north side of the tubes had been burnt off in some places. Otherwise, except for the blacking of the tall tops of the towers, everything looked uncannily the same as before the fire. In fact, a close inspection revealed that each of the four central tubes had sagged no less than two and a half feet in the middle."

A steel arched structure is proposed for the new bridge: the quickest and cheapest method of dismantling the damaged tubes and spanning the gaps between the piers. An early Stephenson design for an arched structure was turned down since it would have obstructed navigation in the Straits; this was fortunate since aesthetically it was commonplace. The present grand piers with their strong Egyptian overtones had, of course, no place in Stephenson's arched design but they were ideally suited to support the great beams which his tubes essentially are. Although structurally unnecessarily high, they give visual weight and punctuate the spans in a way that is as satisfactory as it is unexpected. Light steel arches between the huge pylons are likely to make the stonework appear absurdly superfluous above track level. Egyptian architecture was essentially trabiated, arches being unknown along the banks of the Nile: it is feared that in this context they will look ridiculous spanning Menai. A road deck above the railway track is also contemplated.

The sign, and the lions guarding *Britannia Bridge*, were highlights of journeys on the Holyhead line.

This tremendous bridge (Robert Stephenson, 1845–50) is one of the great pioneering works of all time.[1] The rigorous conditions imposed by the Admiralty to safeguard shipping were similar to those for Telford's Menai Bridge. Britannia conveys confidence, resolution and a seemingly inevitable rightness of proportion exactly in tune with one's interpretation of the best of the Victorian age. But the Dee Bridge, for which Stephenson was also responsible to the same railway company, collapsed just when he was deciding how to span Menai. On top of the inevitable agony of mind Stephenson narrowly escaped being accused of manslaughter, and the disaster shattered the confidence of the Chester and Holyhead Railway Company. Then the only known methods of spanning were by arch or suspension. Stephenson, realising the principle of a rigid deck combined with suspension to be unsound, consulted experts. They gave diametrically opposite views. He decided against chains but kept his own counsel, allowing piers which could take suspension cables to go ahead while experiments were made.

The bridge as constructed (and as it now stands) consists of two rectangular boxes, side by side, each 1,511 ft. long. Their erection was a most hazardous affair witnessed by immense festive crowds. The longer spans were floated out on barges at exactly the right state of the tide, and gradually raised by hydraulic pumps.

The sides of the tubes are one plate thick, but the top and bottom are cellular and have to be painted inside every five years against corrosion. The painter lies on a special trolley, and propels himself along the 21 in. square by 1,511 ft. long iron tunnel: a more claustrophobic job would be hard to imagine. Francis Thompson, the architect to the railway company, was involved in the design of the masonry, but to what extent is obscure. The lions, reminiscent of Victorian politicians, are by John Thomas.

The best place for a close view of the bridge is from the Caernarvon shore (public path, west side). A fairly close view, unfortunately meshed by electric power lines, can be had from Llanfairpwll churchyard.

The *church*, rebuilt 1853, is not notable, but the obelisk at the top of the churchyard commemorates those who died in connection with the building of the bridge: eight men of injuries, the chief accountant of typhus fever in his twenty-seventh year, and one Emma Greaves who

Slate chimney-piece, Glyn, LLANFAIR-MATHAFARN-EITHAF

Britannia Bridge before the fire, LLANFAIRPWLL

died "at Britannia Bridge" in her fifth (how and why?).

The path below the churchyard leads to the seaweedy shore of the Straits, and a mid-19 c. monument to Nelson, appropriately a navigation mark, designed by Lord Clarence Paget, sailor-sculptor son of the 1st Marquess of Anglesey.

Right beside the bridge, Britannia Cottage, a charming white deep-eaved timber house of sensible classic design, is all that remains of the buildings erected for its construction.

The drystone wall (still standing to a height 8 ft. in places but only visible at low water) which runs from the small island immediately east of the bridge, for about 50 yards, parallel with the shore, is the remains of a fish-trap, one of the once thriving *Menai Fisheries*, probably dating from the 16 c. Remains of another trap (and sluice opening) also survive a few hundred yards further along towards Menai Bridge. This is an idyllic stretch of the Straits and is easily accessible by the footpath through the young plantation 50 yards west of the upper layby on A.5. On *Ynys Gorad Goch*, the island opposite, there is an ingenious system of weirs and traps and an old curing tower. Fish carried on the strong tides through the Straits swim into these enclosures and are stranded by the ebb. The traps can be seen through binoculars from the layby. The difference in the water level in and outside the trap, and the tide race, are tremendously dramatic. Wily herons perch along the top of its wall awaiting an easy meal.

The *Anglesey Column* is the chief landmark on the island. On top is One-Leg, the famous first Marquess, who lost the other while watching with Wellington the end of the battle of Waterloo, where he was second-in-command. "By God, Sir, I've lost my leg!" he exclaimed. The Duke, momentarily taking his telescope from his eye, is reported to have replied "By God, Sir, so you have!" and to have at once resumed his scrutiny of the retreating French. The column was designed by Thomas Harrison in 1816, and was not intended for a statue. It is by Matthew Noble and was erected in 1860. This tricky operation is described on the copper plate over the door at the top. (Mind your head.) The gallery gives tremendous views of Anglesey and Caernarvonshire, with Snowdonia as an ever-changing 18th-century-seeming backcloth, while immediately below your feet is a fascinating intricate plan view of tree-tops. A.5 lies like a ruler across the island, electricity grids spread east and west; the Straits flow like a great river with *Plas Newydd* (rebuilt by One-Leg's father) lying peacefully in a green clearing, just above the curving tideline which cuts the thickly-wooded banks with such satisfying precision.

Llanfair Gate is the best of the four surviving toll-gates on A.5: a small octagonal building of great charm; the deep eaves of the shallow pitched roof are echoed in the pretty verandah which surrounds the house. The toll board is still in position. This gate, with others on the Holyhead Road, were the last surviving in use in Great Britain (ceased 1 November 1895).

Llanfairpwll also has the distinction of having the first Women's Institute in the United Kingdom. It is nice to think that this most English-seeming institution began here in a Welsh village, having been introduced from Canada by a connection of the Anglesey family.

Plas Llanfair now houses the naval training establishment, *Indefatigable*.

Plas Newydd has a superb site; one of the best in Britain. Secluded yet open; set in civilised parkland against wild views of Snowdonia, with curlew whistling over the water just below. A new house was built here in the 15 c. on the site of the old one. The present house, 1800–1810, (open only on written application) results from the combined efforts of James Wyatt and Joseph Potter, who was Wyatt's assistant on Lichfield Cathedral at the time; he did the Gothic work.

It fuses a basic idea of classic order and symmetry with a romantic urge for the Picturesque, but was somewhat de-Gothicised in the 1930s: battlements and turrets lopped. It was then that a long, too-narrow dining-room was transformed by Rex Whistler's mural which gives the room an extraordinary illusion of depth. It has that remote clarity of something seen in a mirror, so that it is almost disconcerting to turn and see Snowdonia outside.

Below the house are two landing stages (*c.* 1800); the boats entered brick vaulted docks under Gothic arches. Store-rooms aired by open fires flanked the bigger one. The harbour and boathouse (now used by H.M.S. *Conway*) are late 19 c. The stables, uninhibited Gothic, are by James Wyatt. They, and the new buildings, are occupied by H.M.S. *Conway*, a cadet training school for the Merchant Navy; the splendid three-decker, alas wrecked, was moored in the Straits below.

Opposite the stables is the immense *Plas Newydd burial chamber*, with its capstone of over 11 by 9 ft.; there is a smaller ante-chamber adjoining it.

Bryn-yr-hen-bobl, another famous cromlech, lies about one mile west of the house. Still mostly covered by its earth mound; but the burial chamber itself is visible, and the remains of the forecourt to it.

Running out to the south (now covered) is a 330 ft.-long terrace, constructed in stone on a clay bed; perhaps a phallic symbol. The grave contained bones of at least thirty people, a baby, ox, sheep and pig, and shell and pottery fragments.

The home farm (1804) can be seen from the drive to the walled garden, which is now open as a garden centre. Attractive agricultural classic brick with no Gothic nonsense about the high barn doors.

On the road to *Llanedwen Church* (just inside the park wall above Moel-y-don) a gap has been left in the wall for viewing Snowdonia. It instantly evokes an old railway-carriage photograph: long shallow proportion and splendidly romantic scene. The church was rebuilt by H. Kennedy in 1856. Tall spire springs from the ground beside an aisleless nave; like a child's drawing, but a satisfactory composition. Inside unplastered and dark, but can be lit by 96 candles. Robust 15 and 17 c. carvings incorporated in reading-desk; particularly lively lion and griffin. Relics include dog tongs.

Llanfairynghornwy (2) is the windy parish in the north-west corner of Anglesey. It includes the *Skerries* whose light can be seen flashing two miles off Carmel Head. The first light shone in 1716. It was a coal fire in a conical grate, and a financial failure. But the dues levied on shipping increased steadily throughout the 18 c. From 1835 on, Trinity House made several offers for the light, which were declined. It was now the only surviving private lighthouse, its value increasing steadily with the importance of the port of Liverpool. Eventually, in 1841, the owners settled for £444,984 11s. 2d., the sum fixed by a special jury.

The parish church, much restored in Victorian times (particularly by Weightman and Hadley in 1847), has a 16 c. south chapel added to the early medieval building. Note the nicely worded memorial to Evan Thomas, "a most skilful Bone setter," who died in 1814.

Caerau, up its syecmore avenue, is a most attractive farmhouse; 17 and early 18 c. Plain exterior protects panelled rooms, with generous but simple built-in dressers, cupboards, etc. typical of the time.

Llanrhwydrys Church (322932) is close to the sea, but slightly sheltered by the rising headland. The farm track to this lonely little building crosses a causeway over a reedy marsh. The churchyard wall has a pretty arched gateway with a mounting block. Both it, and the little bell-cote, are brilliant with orange lichen. A very simple, light church. You enter under a gallery (beam dated 1776); pews are attractively placed to the south of the nave only.

85

The cruck which supports the chancel roof has been left free-standing in a very modern manner where the nave wall was demolished for a north chapel.

Cemlyn Bay (N.T.), with its shallow, almost land-locked lagoon and secretive, walled-in house (private) has a John Buchan-ish air. The garden wilderness is a refuge for all kinds of rare migrants on this bare coast, and the pool is renowned for wildfowl in the winter.

Llanfair-yn-neubwll (2) to the south of the Holyhead road, is largely submerged by Valley Airfield. Coastline: the great open sweep of Cymyran Bay, silver sand and thundering breakers; and the estuary-like waters leading up to Four Mile Bridge, brimming like a quiet river with gleaming wet mud or sand as the tide slips out (see Holy Island). The single-cell church, St Mary's, was restored by H. Kennedy, 1857; no frills, and brown with nice hessian matting on the floor and a 12 c. font with saltire pattern.

The R.A.F. has built vast housing estates in an R.A.F./New Town style. There is a car-park for plane watchers (at your own risk) to which many holiday-makers resort in non-seaside weather.

It was during contruction work on Valley Airfield in 1943 that the Llyn Cerrig Bach hoard was discovered. A mechanical scoop accidentally grabbed what has been presumed to be a hoard of votive offerings which had been thrown into a small lake: swords, scabbards, daggers, chariot-fittings and horse-trappings preserved in peat from the early Iron Age. No one knows what else may be buried.

Llanfechell (2) is a farming parish in the north, immortalised by that endearing 18 c. diarist, Mr Bulkeley, who lived at Brynddu. Early widowed he brought up his unsatisfactory children single-handed, only to be landed with a succession of grandchildren resulting from his daughter's yet more unsatisfactory marriage to a pirate. (See bibliography.)

The church is snug among houses in the middle of the village (so rare in Anglesey). It has a 16 c. tower, with a corbelled 18 c. stumpy apology for a spire. The rest medieval, restored 1846 and 1870 (Kennedy and O'Donoghue). Fragments of gold and buff 15 c. glass have been re-set in the transept windows.

Green marble (verd-antique) was quarried in this parish.

Llanffinan (see Penmynydd).

Llanfflewyn (2) (350891) (Llanbabo), a mile east of Llanrhyddlad. Remote church hidden from the road up half-mile track and sheltered by a rocky outcrop. Its eager bell (1642) still bids people to evensong. The roof fell in in 1932, and the R.C.A.M. Inventory coolly dismisses it as having no architectural features earlier than late 18 c. But there is an un-architectural timelessness about this church, perhaps deriving from its site and bell.

Llanfigael (2) (328828), three miles north-east of Valley, means the shepherd's parish. The small single-cell church was restored in the early 19 c. It looks unpromising, but has its 19 c. fittings undisturbed: box pews, bench pews (see St Mary's Tal-y-llyn), and standing space; oil lamps.

Plas Llanfigael, the sturdy Georgian-looking house next door, has shiny spun glass in its windows.

Llanfihangel Dinsylwy (see **Llani-estyn**).

Llanfihangel Esceifiog (6). An inland agricultural parish which straddles A.5 to the south of Llangefni, with no village of its name. The old parish church has been abandoned, and its tantalising ruins are impenetrably overgrown. The parish includes Gaerwen, and part of Malltraeth Marsh with its abandoned little coal-mine near Holland Arms, whose old brick chimney and deserted cottages emerge from a creamy sea of elder-flower and meadow-sweet.

Plas Berw, a remote and astonishing house recently restored with a grant from the Historic Buildings Council for Wales, so open on written application, is tucked under the steeply sloping bank at the edge of the marsh; hidden and secretive, with some lovely beeches beside the steep rocky drive. A 17 c. wing has been added to a 15 c. hall, on to which a three-storey tower (now ruined) had already been tacked. These two wings, with a high garden wall, form a forecourt against the bank.

Berea Congregational church with its caretaker's house (originally 1839) make a cheerful contrast: reassuringly straightforward, and of an open countenance.

Llanfihangel Tre'r-beirdd (2), inland to the north-east, includes part of *Mynydd Bodfan*, a diminutive mountain outcrop with little lakes. Particularly good when the heather is out, but inevitably discovered and very popular.

The church, nestling beneath electricity pylons, was largely rebuilt in 1888; but the plaster is uneven and washed light blue like a dairy, and enough monuments crowd the walls to allow a sense of continuity.

There is a big maen hir in the wall on the road to the south of the church.

Llangadwaladr (5), just south of Aberffraw, includes the lovely Cefni estuary and Malltraeth Sands where the tide runs out leaving sheets of shining sand drying pale in the sun with shallow pools between. The river mouth is guarded by *Twyn-y-parc;* a strategically sited Iron Age promontory fort, protected by a massive rampart on the landward side and by natural cliffs elsewhere. There is a sheltered creek below. Write to Bodorgan Estate Office for permission to see.

Bodorgan House (not open) by James Defferd, c. 1800, lies on the right bank of the river, well sheltered by woodland so untypical of Anglesey. Also on the Bodorgan estate, a little nearer the open sea, is all that remains of *Bodowen*, the 16 c. home of the Owen family (see chapel in church). Ruined walls of a courtyard, with arched gateways (17 c.) framing idyllic views of the estuary and distant mountains.

The left bank of the Cefni and the coast right round to Abermenai are a National Nature Reserve (see Newborough), to much of which access is restricted. *Malltraeth Sands* are alive with waders and wildfowl according to the season. A lot can be

Plas Newydd, LLANFAIRPWLL

seen from the public path on the Cob (see Trefdraeth) and the public path along the left bank of the estuary.

St Cadwaladr, himself a king, was the grandson of Cadfan ruler of Gwynedd who is described, in Latin, on the stone (*c.* 625) found in the churchyard and re-set in the church, as "the wisest and most illustrious of kings". The saint himself is portrayed with his royal sceptre and orb, below the Crucifixion in the fine 15 c. (re-set) east window. His crown also appears on the brass chandelier nearest the altar. The present nave probably represents the 12 c. church, but all is restored and the north chapel (Meyrick) completely rebuilt. Its Fuller Memorial (1858) should please Victorian gothicists. The south chapel (Owen) is 17 c. Gothic with a sturdy classical memorial (1660) to Colonel Hugh Owen of Bodowen. Llyn Coron (Bodorgan Lake) is an attractive stretch of water between the church and the Holyhead line.

Llangaffo (5). An agricultural parish on rising ground to the south of Malltraeth Marsh with fine open view. The church spire, rare in Anglesey, makes a good landmark across the marsh. The church was rebuilt by Weightman and Hadfield in 1847. A 15 c. doorway from the old church has been re-used as the churchyard entrance and a small iron gate, identical to those used by Telford for the footways on Menai Bridge, hung on it. The church has an attractive two-tier brass chandelier and a 12 c. font.

Llangefni (2) on the little river Cefni, once navigable, is almost in the middle of Anglesey, and is the county town. In the early 19 c. the Reverend Bingley described it as "a pretty little village", and shortly after this the Holyhead post road, which ran through Llangefni, was replaced by Telford's new highway a mile to the south. Llangefni looks its best in the bustle of market day (Wednesday and Thursday). The market centres on the "square" (not instantly recognisable as such) in the middle of the town: the main street sloping down to it from both east and west gives the town a focal point. The cattle market is a reminder that Llangefni is the centre of a very agricultural county. Post-war housing estates and small modern factories must have doubled its size in recent years. The enterprising Theatr Fach thrives in Pencraig.

The parish church (dedicated to St Cyngar) is withdrawn from the town among trees to the north. It was rebuilt in 1824 (an unfortunate 1898 chancel was added). It is attractively odd, and of unknown origin. The nave is ceiled by a shallow barrel vault, supported on arched beams decorated with open cusped work. There is a restrained gallery to the west, supported on tapering octagonal columns. The pews have recently been effectively scumbled in putty green. The tower is another given by that "most munificent friend of the Church, the late Lord Buckley".

Llangeinwen (5) is the parish at the southern end of the Straits, still sheltered woodland and river in feeling with views of Caernarvon less than a mile away across the water, Snowdonia behind, and the Lleyn running out to the west. Until the closing of the regular Foel Ferry near the Mermaid Inn, Caernarvon was the market town for this corner of the island; the place for shopping, piano lessons and city life. Now it is 17 miles away by too busy a road. The parish is separated from the great expanse of Newborough Warren (see Newborough) by Afon Braint, a secret-seeming stream which brings the tide up into the low meadows, and leaves wet mud for the heron's and dapper oyster-catchers.

The parish church of St Geinwen is basically the 12 c., restored in 1812. It is surprisingly light and spacious as you enter, because the eye is carried through the broad arch to the north chapel instead of focusing to the east up the narrow nave and chancel. The chapel and the endearingly humble pinnacled tower (despised by experts) were added in 1839. 9 and 11 c. carved grave slabs have been re-set in the tower buttresses (north). Font early 13 c. with attractive fleur-de-lys and palmette pattern. Nice early 19 c. brass chandeliers, and an 18 c. memorial to Margaret Williams ". . . whose remains are deposited beneath in hopes of resuming the same At the general Ressurrection with greater lustre".

Llanfair-y-cwmwd church is prettily sited up a shady lane with high stone hedges, a mile to the north-east.

Llangoed (3), the most easterly peninsula in Anglesey, at the entrance to the Menai Straits, thrusts out into the sea towards the Great Orme with Puffin Island at its tip.

Penmon Priory, with its sturdy church and handsome dovecot, is sheltered by the massive limestone headland. It lies at the mouth of the Straits; a haven of civilisation in a now remote, much-quarried land. In medieval times, easily accessible by sea.

The Priory was not given to the Augustines until 1414. It is believed to have been founded by Cynlas in the 6 c., who put it in charge of his brother Seiriol. The remains of an oval hut above the well beside the Priory could have been his cell. The well, under a little cliff, is an idyllic spot on a hot summer day; a clear rectangle of pure water over rounded pebbles in a tiny stone-benched cell.

The Priory was burnt by the Danes in the 12 c., and rebuilding following this period gives an immense sense of strength and shelter. The low tower has a pyramidal stone roof, which makes it seem hewn-out rather than put-on. Through the south doorway, under the dragon in its tympanum, you enter the Middle Ages; the nave is a dim, mysterious world, which glows secretly when the afternoon sun shines through the diminutive west window. It is then possible to see the bold Norman carvings on the tower arches. The south transept has simple round-headed arcading and a cross, *c.* 1000, has been re-erected here. The font is the base of a similar cross. The chance is an astonishing contrast to the nave; almost emaciated by comparison. It was originally added when Llewelyn the Great granted the monastery to the Prior of Priestholm (see Puffin Island), but has been thoroughly rebuilt by Weightman and Hadfield (see Llanfaes).

The great dovecote, *c.* 1600, has a corbelled bee-hive dome, crowned by an open lantern through which the pigeons flew. The massive circular pillar with corbelled steps carried a ladder which spanned the gap to the nests.

The *deer park* behind the Priory is enclosed by an immense limestone wall (18 c.); it stretches like a silver ribbon above the ripening barley. The much-weathered cross which juts out of this golden sea was set up around 1000; its principal scene is said to represent the Temptation of St Anthony.

The *quarries* by the Priory (Flagstaff and Park) were those used by Telford for the construction of the piers of the Menai Bridge (q.v.). Those on the head itself are now worked and supply stone for dock walls, which is taken away by barges which may be seen off-shore.

There is a tolled road to the Point, where the clanging bell of the unmanned light (NO PASSAGE LANDWARD) and the standard design of the coastguard cottages (1836) give an out-post-of-empire flavour.

Puffin Island (Priestholm or Ynys Seiriol) lies about half a mile off the point, and is only accessible by special arrangement. It was the site of an early Christian monastic settlement, and remains, probably from the 7 c. onwards, have been found. Now a ruined church with a 12 c. tower is said to survive. Puffin Island had a signal staff for the Liverpool telegraph; a lonely station. The cliffs have long been noted for sea-birds; a popular feature of the early steam-packet excursions from Liverpool was the spectacle resulting from discharge of a fowling-piece as the vessel passed the island.

West of the headland the north coast drops to a long low sweep of limestone cliffs, which climb again under the hill fort of Dinsylwy. There is a coastal path (accessible near Fedw fawr). Isolated ruined

The dovecote, Penmon Priory

quarry buildings lie by a tiny creek. North of the village and looking out over the sea is *Tros-y-marian* (not open); one of those remote late 17 to 18 c. Anglesey houses with big farm buildings and a dovecot, sheltered by outcropping rock and salt-bitten sycamore.

The upper part of *Llangoed village* has 19 c. cottages stepping neatly up the hill where the Calvinist Methodist chapel looks across to the Edwardian school. St Cawdraf's church has been harshly restored, but the black bricks round the windows give it an original consistency of character. Inside there is a lovely eight-branch candelabra with a dove and real candles; and a finely carved hexagonal pulpit, though much restored, 1662.

Castell Aberlleiniog (616793) is on the edge of thick woodland, ¾ mile from the coast. A forerunner to Beaumaris; a very steep motte thrown up by Hugh of Avranches, Earl of Chester *c.* 1090; it is still impressive despite nettles and undergrowth. His timber castle was replaced by a stone one in late medieval times. This, square on plan with corner turrets (one missing), survives. Rather like a toy. Garrisoned during the Civil War.

Llangristiolus (5). A central parish astride A.5 which includes a large slice of Malltraeth Marsh. The church, whose fine austere 16 c., east window looks to the main road, stands above the reclaimed land, aloof from the traffic that grinds up Telford's highway. But when you reach it, via a handsome iron field gate, it is timelessly agricultural and deep in cow-parsley. The approach is nicely enclosed by a caretaker's cottage (disused) and stable. The church, reconstructed in the 13 c., was restored by Kennedy in 1852. The chancel is wider than the nave, and separated from it by a generous arch which gives an unexpected sense of space. The east window, with its lilac and light blue glass, seems Gothic-revival from within, and with a mixed bag of other windows makes a surprisingly successful whole. The 12 c. font is particularly attractive, with vigorous interlaced patterns of rope and strapwork below an embryonic arcaded cornice.

There is a big lime kiln in the field on the opposite side of A.5; a grander version of the many which must have burnt lime on the island in the last century for both agriculture and building.

Henblas barn, a building of monumental proportions, can be seen shortly after passing the astonishingly un-Anglesey round Gothic lodge of Henblas on B.4422. It stands alone, open to the sky. The date, 1776, and a lion rampant decorate one of the segmental arches over the great doorways designed to take wagons high with hay or corn. These, and its narrow slit ventilation, give it massive simplicity and scale.

Llangwyfnan (see Aberffraw).

Llangwyllog (2) claims to be the centre of the island, and certainly feels like it. The church is reached by a farm track with grass down the middle, off the Llangefni–Llanerchymedd road. It lies in a hollow, beside a marsh through which a stream and the Amlwch railway wind their lonely way. 15 c. nave and chancel in one, with a separate room added to the west end in the 16 c. Restored in 1854 by D. Roberts of Beaumaris, who spared the 18 c. fittings. These include a combined pulpit and reading-desk, dated 1769, with a pew below and a box pew to the east. These are splendidly scumbled in black treacle on a golden syrup background. Other seating is late 18 c., and the communion rails are 1769. Good memorials flank the late

Inside the dovecote at Penmon Priory, LLANGOED

90

15 c. east window, and the round tubby font is 13 c., carved with a leaf pattern and cable moulding.

Llaniestyn Rural (3) is the small coastal parish to the west of the Penmon headland and Llangoed. The steep limestone cliffs contain old quarries. At 586825, the hill fort, *Dinsylwy* encloses about 17 acres of limestone plateau; a lawn tilted gently towards the sea. It is protected where natural defences are not enough by an 8 ft. thick wall, made up of limestone slabs on edge filled with rubble; now much overgrown. The main entrance is to he south. A lovely site with views of Red Wharf Bay below, miles of sand at low tide, and the great sweep of sea between Point Lynas and the Great Orme. 1–4 c. A.D.; possibly earlier. Roman coins and pottery found. To get in, find the stile near bend in road in south-west corner, sharp right along hedge to old quarry, path up from here. Otherwise impenetrable.

Sheltered snugly under the eastern shoulder of the fort is the church of *St Michael* (*Llanfihangel Dinsylwy*); small and grey, with orange lichen on the roof. Bracken pushes up between the great flat slabs in the graveyard, casting lovely shadows on the smooth purple slate. Early 15 c., restored 1855. The finely carved hexagonal oak pulpit is dated 1628.

A mile to the south, in open country is *Llaniestyn:* 14 c. church; humble, with an inviting open porch. Doorway 1510. Inside whitewashed and simple, with a whopping beam across the opening to the 15 c. south chapel. Here is the austere but lovely low relief of St Iestyn, carved on warm grey stone. The almost severe treatment of figure and the folds of his hermit's tunic are set off by the intricate pattern under the cusped arch. A brilliantly restrained use of surface pattern; 14 c. Perhaps by the sculptor who carved St Pabo? (see Llanbabo).

Llanrhyddlad (2) to the north-west has a rocky coastline with popular picnicking bays, Church Bay being specially well-known in this respect. The church above the bay, dedicated to St Rhyddlad, was rebuilt by Kennedy near the old site in 1858. Rather emaciated; spire like an oversharp pencil. A 9–10 c. cast bronze handbell, like a camel-bell, is kept in the church.

The Holyhead–Liverpool telegraph had a station one mile north-west of the village at Craig-y-gwynt, where the cottages and remains of a signal mast can be seen. An inscription set in the wall of the telegraph cottage reads: Cefn du Telegraph. Built in 1841 by the trustees of the Liverpool Docks.

◁ *far left* St Iestyn, LLANIESTYN church
◁ ▽ *opposite* Penmon Priory, LLANGOED, the cross and (*below*) the font

MENAI BRIDGE with the walls of a fishtrap in the foreground

This telegraph system, dating from one of 1810, was inaugurated to bring news of shipping to the Liverpool owners and merchants in the days of the tea and wheat races. On a trial run it was claimed that a signal was transmitted in one minute; five to six minutes was usual. The first station was on Holyhead Mountain; this was the second. Others included Mynydd Eilian, Puffin Island, the Great Orme and Hilbre Island (in the Dee estuary).

Llansadwrn (3). An agricultural parish west of Beaumaris. The church must once have enjoyed a fine mountain back-cloth, now obscured by immense corrugated asbestos farm shed. A stone, *c.* A.D. 520, to Saturnius and his saintly wife, found in the churchyard and now in the chancel, is claimed to be the oldest memorial stone in Wales. This now thoroughgoing Victorian church was restored five times during the 19 c.; the last being when the chancel was refitted and re-roofed, 1895, by Demaine and Brierley (York). Barrel vault in olive, gold and red. Nice memorials include one to John Williams, who died 1825, aged 88; he "blended the active discharge of every social duty with a liberality of sentiment, a piety and cheerfulness rarely united".

Hafotty (not open), a tantalising 14 c. house with a great hall flanked by solar and kitchen, slowly crumbles among hayfields (1968). It has absorbed several alterations, including a floor and immense 16 c. fireplace in the hall, but seems to be basically unimproved, unloved, and protected by thistles.

Llantrisant (2). The old parish church (349841) is now an unloved ruin (late 14 c. with 17 c. south chapel). As recently as 1946 it had one of the most attractive interiors on the island. Now it is open to the sky, its coved ceiling collapses, and its 19 c. box pews rot, but some good 17 c. wall memorials remain, including a charming marble cartouche with flowers and cherubs' heads to Hugh Williams, 1670. The churchyard may be impenetrable. Who knows what is buried under the brambles? This church may yet be saved.

Lechylched (2). A large parish astride A.5, with a mile of sandy coastline north of Rhosneigr (see Llanfaelog). No village of this name, but *Bryngwran* has grown along the main road.

Salem is a pleasant, plain chapel, 1824, 1839 and 1900, with raking floor and side pews slanted down to face the pulpit, but no gallery.

Llanbeulan Church (372755), reached by a grassy causeway across the fields, is now disused and very overgrown. 14 c. chancel and deep south chapel added to an earlier nave. Vigorously carved rectangular font, decorated with wheel cross and arcading; 12 c. Nice Creed and Commandment boards on west wall.

Llechcynfarwy (2), inland and agricultural, 6 m. north-west of Llangefni. The church (382811) itself is dullish but there is a smart skull-bedecked monument, 1631, in the south chapel; and a round 12 c. font decorated with saltires, rather weathered.

Menai Bridge (6), in the parish of Llandysilio, came into being after the construction of Telford's great suspension bridge, 1819–26. Schemes for a bridge had been mooted since 1785, but had foundered through local opposition and lack of money. Even the union of Ireland and England had little effect because of the war. The technical difficulties were indeed formidable. The great importance of coastal shipping caused the Admiralty to rule that there must be a minimum headway of 100 ft. for the whole length of the bridge, and that neither the piers nor the bridge's construction should cause any obstruction. From 1801 John Rennie produced four designs, all with cast-iron arches. Then the principles of suspension bridges in rope and timber were known, but no iron bridge of any size had been constructed. In 1810 Telford, who was working on the survey for the Holyhead Road, produced two designs, both for cast-iron arches. They were to be constructed on suspended shuttering to avoid interference with shipping, but the Admiralty was not satisfied. In 1814 he produced his fantastic design for the Runcorn Bridge, which was to be an iron suspension bridge spanning 1,000 ft. This came to nothing, but the Commissioners, having seen the scheme, approached Telford about the possibility of a suspension bridge over Menai. Discussions dragged on, the endless opposition continued, but fortunately "explanations satisfied the noble marquess". Others, however, "would listen to no compromise whatever".

Meanwhile Telford surveyed for good limestone for the suspension piers; this was found at Penmon (q.v.). Eventually the masonry was to go ahead before the method of spanning was settled. In 1817 two suspension bridges were constructed over the Tweed; one collapsed, but that using chains designed by one, Samuel Brown, had not. More experiments were made, with chains of long flat links and pins: the type eventually used on Menai. At last, in 1819, Parliament authorised the bridge. The links were forged in Shropshire, brought by the recent Shropshire Union Canal (see Chirk) to Chester, and shipped to Menai. Intensely thorough testing and counter-checking took place at all stages. Eventually, in April 1825, both suspension towers and chains were ready. The Admiralty authorised the closing of the Straits to shipping, and Telford waited at Bangor for the weather and the tide. April 26th dawned fine and still; high water was at 3.30 p.m. Menai was thronged with boat-loads of sightseers, and the shore-line thick with people. The first chain lay ready on a long raft moored to the Caernarvon shore. It was floated out on the tide in dead silence; and then, to the tune of a fife band, hoisted to the top of the Anglesey pier where Telford drove in the pin joining the links only 2 hours 20 minutes after the operation had begun. He raised his hat as a signal that it was home, and a mighty cheer resounded from shore to shore. The capstan crews were liberally refreshed by quarts of ale, and three of them celebrated by running across the 9 in. wide curving chain to the opposite side.

The bridge was open to traffic on a wild wet night the following January: 41 years after the first petition to Parliament, and six since it had actually begun.

Telford's troubles were not over. On 7th February the bridge was struck broadside by a tremendous gale. It moved so violently that the coachman refused to cross. "The bridge certainly laboured very hard," it was reported to Telford, "and the night being dark and the wind whistling thro' the railings and chains made it appear rather terrific". Twenty-four roadway bars and six suspension rods were broken. But it was so successfully strengthened that, despite the greatly increased loading of modern traffic, Telford's wrought-iron was only replaced by steel 1938–40 (Engineer: Alexander Gibb, a descendent of Telford's Engineer for Aberdeen Harbour).

The iron gates, typical of those designed for turnpikes on the Holyhead Road, are also most carefully detailed (see on Caernarvon shore).

St Tysilio's is the old parish church. Its secluded island site lies at the mouth of a small inlet, ¼ mile west of Telford's bridge, originally dammed for a tide mill which was working here anyway in the 16 c. The stretch between the island and the bridge seems to be Edwardian arcadia. You can walk from the Tea Gardens (off A.5) through coppery-barked Scots pine which frame postcard-worthy views, to the Belgian Promenade which runs along the edge of the water below the wooded bank. It was built by Belgian refugees in the 1914–18 war.

The church is reached by a causeway at the beginning of the Promenade. A very small 15 c. church, restored, single-cell, candle-lit. Inside there is a robustly lettered 17 c. grave slab to GRPHITH ROBYNS aged 2½, and another with 18 c. lettering appropriately more feminine, to a small girl also two. In a window facing down the Straits one of the leaded lights has been allowed to be larger than the rest, to give a period lilac-tinted view of Britannia Bridge (see Llanfairpwll). The graveyard is full of fine slate slabs. The rather upstage broken column is for John Hemingway, 1872, presumably of the firm who built that bridge.

Dinas Cadnant, a mile to the north, is accessible by footpath. A fine site on a 300 ft. hill with commanding views to the mainland. The huts and terraces are difficult to distinguish under bracken in summer. Pottery of A.D. 6 c. found.

Menai Bridge Town non-precious, Victorian and later, even has red brick. Shops, holidays, boats and pier. Steamer trips: Llandudno, Caernarvon, and Round-the-Island. *St Mary's* church: 1858, from designs by H. Kennedy, dark and carpeted. The Georgian Victoria Hotel is c. 1852 (W. Dew). The Tregfryn Gallery (Beaumaris end of town) shows contemporary paintings throughout the year. Menai Bridge fair was originally a pony fair; herds of wild ponies used to graze the dunes and commons of the island.

Newborough (5), in the south-west corner of Anglesey, includes the coastline from the mouth of the Cefni to the Straits. Tremendous low-tide beaches with the ever-changing Lleyn peninsula lying just across the water: sometimes so blue and close that you could touch each crack in the rock, often dimmed by rain or sea-mist, very occasionally transformed by snow. The scale of this stretch of coast is immense; distant figures walking over the wet sand are lilliputian. The Cefni salt-marsh (see Llangadwaladr), the coastline and the vast sandy peninsula are the *Newborough Warren-Ynys Llanddwyn National Nature Reserve* (Nature Conservancy), but the northern part, between the estuary and the present warren, has been transformed since 1947 by the planting of *Newborough Forest* (Forestry Commission): mostly Corsican pine for dune-fixing and sitka spruce in the wetter areas. They grow slowly in the sand, and tricks of scale can change a glimpse of Snowdonia into the Rockies or Alps; an illusion soon disturbed in a south-west wind by the booming surf. There are several public rights of way through the forest and the conservancy area and local N.C. maps should be consulted. Written permits necessary to wander elsewhere.

The great sweeps of Malltraeth and Llanddwyn Bays are separated by *Llanddwyn Island*, a low rocky (very ancient pre-Cambrian) peninsula accessible, except at the highest tides, from the Forestry Commission car-park in the south corner of the forest about a mile along the shore, or by the edge of the Cefni salt-marsh and another mile of beach. Sadly, the very possessive colony of terns which inhabited the island until the war has gone, and the Caernarvon pilot cottages have long ceased to shelter pilots. Oyster-catchers naturally claim its thrift-covered turf; but Arctic and common terns still fish off-shore, diving with supreme elegance and precision.

The rocky coast shelters lower land in the middle of the island where there are traces of old fields and the ruins of *St Dwynwen's church* (16 c. chancel). St Dwynwen is thought to have lived here in the 5 c. She seems to have been a kind of Aphrodite of the new religion: her great concern was for lovers, that they should not deceive each other. The island, and particularly her well, became a great place of pilgrimage: hence the size of the church. The plain Latin cross near the lighthouse commemorates the saint; and the Celtic cross, also modern, all those who died here.

The lighthouse, 1845, was built when the old landmark on the point to the south was found to be too low. The lifeboat station dated from 1840. The crew were summoned from Newborough by the cannon which still rusts on Gun Cliff near the pilot cottages; this was answered by another close to the village. The cottages are marvellously sited under sheltering outcrop, basking in the sun with one of the best views on earth. Their drab khaki rough-cast is transformed by the black margins round their windows and white-painted woodwork.

The land between the island and the village is now forest. Once, the three-mile walk through the great dunes (which can reach 60 ft.) seemed to be nothing but immense skies alive with sky-larks, rabbit-nibbled turf bright with heart's-ease, prickly marram grass, and sand in your sand-shoes. This enormous sandy warren, and the marram and rabbits it supported, had been vital to Newborough's economy since the borough was settled by Edward I with people displaced from Llanfaes at the building of Beaumaris, q.v. (The dunes had begun to encroach on these corn lands of the Princes of Gwynedd in the 14 c.; and Aber Menai, their landing place, had begun to silt up.) Until myxamatosis the Newborough people were still great rabbit-catchers and the marram grass industry can be remembered in the village. Ropes, mats and cordage were made. So important was the industry (and presumably the stability of the dunes) that the marram grass became protected during the reign of Queen Elizabeth.

Newborough has an independent feel about it. The village street frames splendid views of Snowdonia, meshed in telegraph wires and flanked by the grand Ebenezer Chapel and the cheerful-looking White Lion pub. The Pritchard Jones Institute (clock tower and half-timbered almshouses) was built by Pritchard Jones who made good in the clothing trade in London in the late 19 c. and did not forget his home village. A more socially than architecturally conscious benefactor.

St Peter's church on the road to Llanddwyn Bay stands on high land, with splendid views of both Caernarvonshire and the Bodorgan peninsula. Chancel and nave are probably early 14 c., extended around 1600 and much restored in the 1850s. The first impression of being in a long tunnel is not suprising since. nave and chancel walls run through, making a church over 90 ft. long and under 17 ft. wide. No aisles. Tunnel effect is greatly increased by the curved roof braces. Good 12 c. font in gritstone, with interlaced loop, knot and cross patterns. Interesting 14 c. carved grave slabs in the chancels.

Penmon (see Llangoed).

Penmynydd (3), between Llangefni and Llanfairpwll, inland and agricultural, claims fame as the home of the Tudors. Henry VII's great-grandfather lived at Plas Penmynddd, even if his grandfather Owen Tudor, who married Henry V's widow, was not brought up there, as tradition hopefully suggests. The present farmhouse (not open) dates from 1576, and has been altered and added to (17 and 19 c.). 16 c. Tudor arms and a saracen's head have been re-set above the north door.

In Penmynydd church there is a fine altar tomb (*c.* 1385) with Tudor arms to Gronw Fychan and his wife, believed to have come from Llanfaes at the Dissolution. The alabaster is translucent against the light in this rather dark church. The church is in a hollow among withered evergreens; 14 and early 15 c., restored 1848 and not enticing. The recently restored almshouses, 1620, are fulfilling their original function: a terrace of five by themselves in open country. The out-buildings opposite the front doors give a sense of enclosure, and seem vital to the success of the very lineal layout. Minute scale. Whitewashed walls with limestone dressings to the mullioned windows.

Llanffinan Church (495755), ¼ mile north of Plas Penmynydd is Romanesque revival, 1841, by John Welch. A nice change from pointed. An isolated site in a hollow down a farm road; hens clucking. The church is straightforward single cell with rather small windows. Victorian

NEWBOROUGH ▷
above Llanddwyn Bay
below Llanddwyn Island

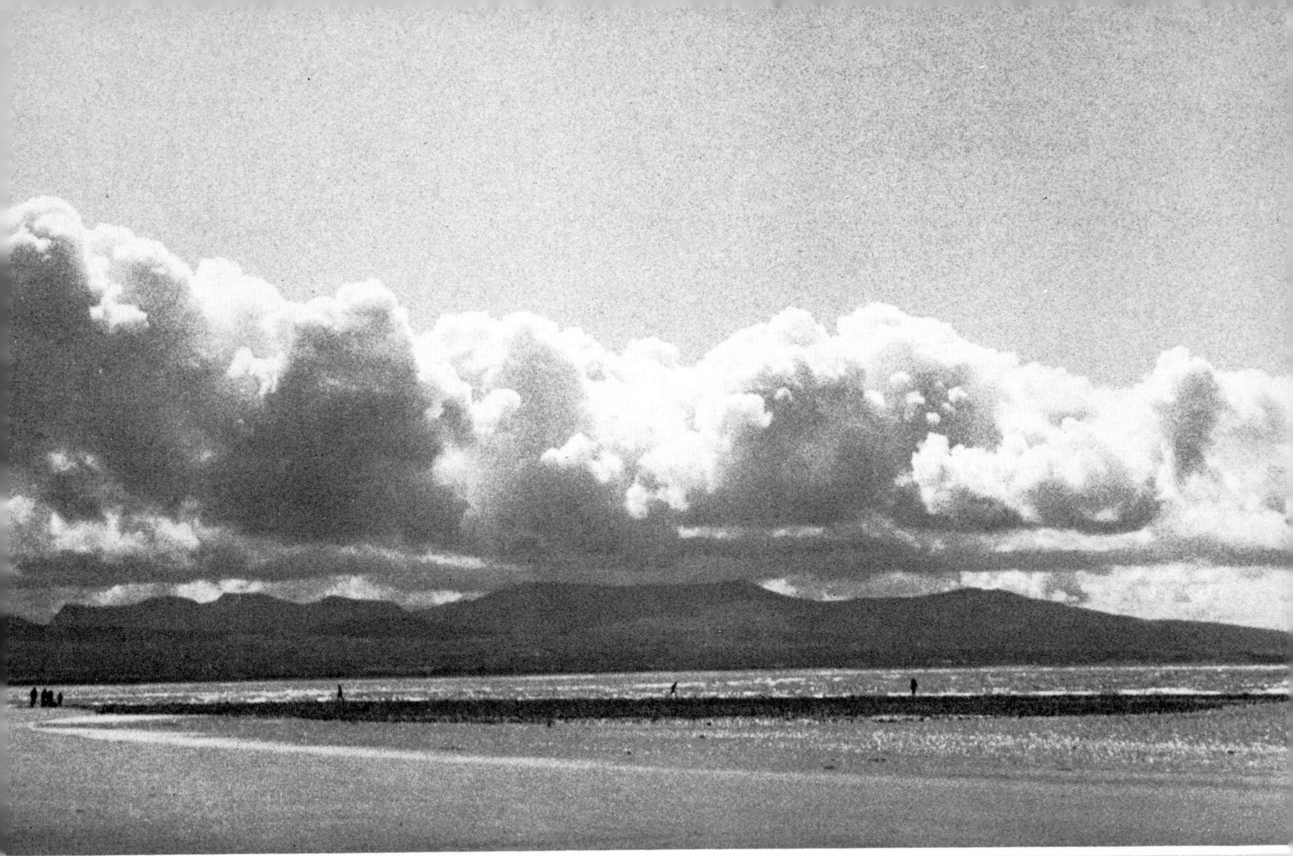

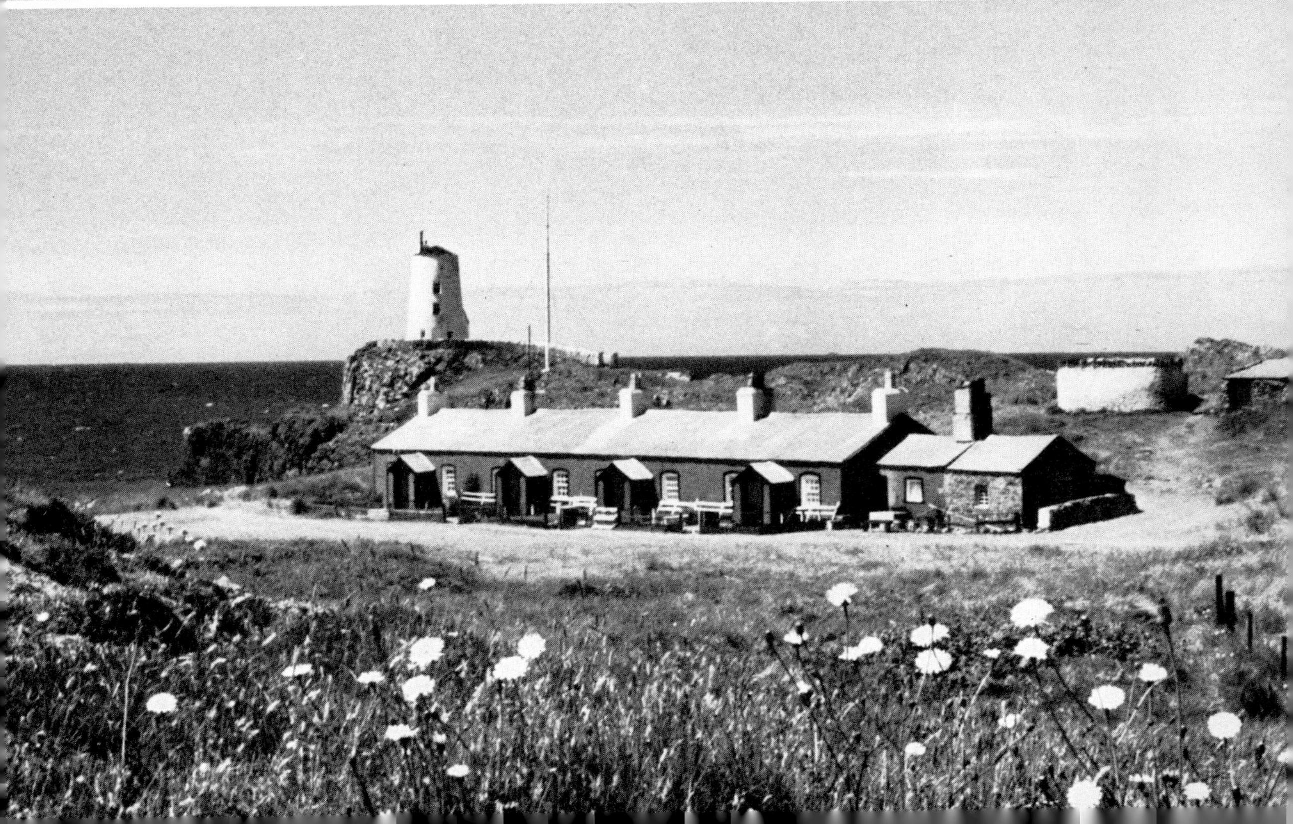

box pews and pulpit. A splendid 1705 memorial with coat of arms commemorates John Lloyd of Hirdefraig Esq., aged three. Brass chandelier and wall candle-holders, but main lighting by electricity and oil.

Penrhosllugwy (3) is a wooded and hummocky parish in the north-east, much enjoyed by caravanners. It includes the southern bank of lovely Traeth Dulas (see Llaneilian). The Mona marble (a fine building limestone quarried in the parish), was shipped from the creek at the head of the Traeth. The north part of Mynydd Bodfan (see Llanfihangel Tre'rbeirdd) is in this parish.

Din Llugwy (496862) is an astonishing Iron Age village, probably fortified in the 4 c. by an Anglesey chieftain. The path from the road leads across a field and then up through a small wood. Suddenly you are face to face with the enclosing wall: limestone facing slabs filled with rubble, 4–5 ft. thick; it is more clearly defined than many modern villages. There are remains of rectangular and two circular huts: some of the walls standing to 6 ft. The silver limestone has brown grasses and the fine blood-red stems of herb-robert springing from every crevice. The village is sheltered by trees, with a break towards the sea a mile away. It makes one want to settle.

Capel Llugwy, a sturdy roofless chapel probably dating from the 12 c. The walls, brownish-grey limestone with white and orange lichen, were rebuilt in the 14 c., and a south chapel added in the 16 c. A fine site, looking north over land falling to the sea.

The Llugwy burial chamber (501860), 3000–2500 B.C., is beside a road ½ mile south. A gigantic capstone, 18 by 15 by 3 ft. is supported on stumpy-seeming uprights, now partly buried. A tremendous monument, reduced to the ridiculous by public park-type railings; like a whale in a shrimping net.

The parish church of *St Michael* (481859) has a pleasant setting in sheltered fields: medieval, very much restored by Kennedy and Rogers, 1865, e.g. the roof timbers "remodelled and made ancient throughout". Simple mid-17 c. communion table. An inscribed stone, *c.* 550 A.D., has been set in the chancel.

The Morris Memorial (478873) is on rising ground a short stroll off A.5025 above the Pilot Boat Inn. A pretty view point. It commemorates the three 18 c. Morris brothers, who came from this farm. They were men of many parts, useful and scientific, and were patrons of literature and founders of the Cymmrodorion Society.

Lewis Morris published that excellent coastal survey, *Plans of Harbours, Bays and Roads in St George's and the Bristol Channels*, 1748.

Pentraeth (3) is shown on early 17 c. maps at the head of Traeth Coch (Red Wharf Bay), but it has long been about a mile inland. The woodland slopes above the bay to the east of the village rise to the 500 ft. contour; rare in Anglesey. The village is at a crossroads. The Panton Arms is pleasant, unassuming, black-and-white: the impressively dock-like building with rounded corners rising out of new housing was once a chapel. The church received a lot of attention in Victorian times; and again in a limed-oak, blue-carpet period.

Plas Gwyn (not open) is inappropriately named; an imposing redbrick, white-sash-windowed, Georgian house which seems to have escaped from Herefordshire. The sturdy stone barns of its home farm (true Anglesey) can be glimpsed on the way to the market garden.

Pentre Berw (6). A village on A.5 centred on the Holland Arms, with a ruined windmill and mine-workings. See Llanfihangel Esceifiog.

Rhodogeidio (2) has been partly flooded by the Alaw reservoir, and has two humble, unwanted churches.

St Ceidio's is very small but has a commanding site, the circular churchyard being well above the general ground level. It was rebuilt in 1845 with old materials by the Rector, Hugh Wynne Jones. Single cell with bell-cote. It has Victorian box pews and brass candle-holders.

The church of *St Mary* (398855) is the most remote in Anglesey. On an island whose sites tend to overwork adjectives like solitary, lonely or isolated, this is a serious claim. In farmland, about ½ mile from the reservoir; not even a path remains. Only likely to be known to curlews and fishermen. The bell, dated 1717, hangs from the little bell-cote, but the west gable end is falling out.

Rhoscolyn (1) has two sandy bays and a very attractive rocky coast south to the gut which separates Holy Island from the main island (see Llanfair-yn-neubwll). *St Gwenfaen* founded her church here in the 6 c. Her well (259754) is near the sea on the lonely headland west of the church (take the path past Plas). It has two pools; the first has a small paved cell or forecourt with slab benches across its corners. Very simple and unexpectedly orderly in this remote place. Fine cliff scenery north to Holyhead Mountain.

The church was rebuilt 1875–9; a 15 c. font survives. It is very uninviting architecturally, but some good late stained glass (presumably Morris and Co., and Kemp) commemorates some of the select late-Victorian families who discovered Rhoscolyn and saved it from development. The cromlech in the field above the bay was erected by one of these gentlemen. A thriving oyster fleet was then based here. The lifeboat station (1830–1929) had a long distinguished record.

Rhosneigr (see Llanfaelog).

Trearddur Bay (see Holy Island).

Trefdraeth (5) (the place on the sands) includes the south-west end of *Malltraeth Marsh*. The cob (embankment) across the estuary was eventually completed in 1818 after various attempts in the late 18 c. which foundered for lack of funds. The pool between the cob and A.4080 is alive with waders and wildfowl which can be seen from the public path on the cob and the main road. Indeed, in spring and early summer, redshank whizzing low across this road may scare the unaccustomed motorist. It is under the protection of the Nature Conservancy (see Newborough). Shipbuilding went on in a small way at *Malltraeth Yard*, the small village where the canalised Cefni escapes through sluice gates to the estuary. The village has well designed modern stone sewage-pumping stations. Unfortunately the bridge here had to be widened (1968), but Pont Marquis still has its single handsome round arch and the long, low viaduct of the Holyhead railway is grand in a quietly determined way. The marsh here has a fenny feeling, the river being cut off from the road by high banks. Now much of it is half-heartedly drained, with wet green fields bright brown with reeds, flecked with bog-cotton; ditches thick with meadow-sweet and patches of yellow flags.

St Beuno's church has a sheltered rural site on the higher land; silvery stone against dark trees. Probably 13 c., windows renewed 14 and 15 c.; all much restored 1846. Lovely fragments of glass, *c.* 1500, have been re-set in tiny south window by the altar.

Trefeilir (not open) is the attractive house seen among trees from B.4422. Mainly *c.* 1735.

Tregayan (2), north of Llangefni, is an attractive hamlet consisting of a farm, church and Plas Tregayan (not open). Sheep bleat. Simple single-cell church with bell-cote; nicely textured stone. The inside face of the south wall is battered, giving a dynamic cross-section to the 17 c. square-headed windows. Small east window, 14 c., with tracery similar to those at Llanbabo, Rhodogeidio and Llandrygarn. The Gothic revival arcaded panelling which screens the vestry came from Llangefni.

It has been recorded that in 1581 a man died in Tregayan aged 105. About 300 of his descendents attended his funeral. He married three times, and had two concubines. His eldest son was 84, and the youngest $2\frac{1}{2}$. He was "of middle Stature, of good Complexion, never troubled with Cholick Gout or Stone, seldom sick, of moderate Diet, liv'd by Tillage, exercised himself much in Fishing and Fowling and had his Senses perfect to the Last".

Trewalchmai (see Gwalchmai).

Valley (2). A recent village on A.5 at the crossing to Holy Island. Toll-house survives. See also Llanfair-yn-neubwll.

The home of the Tudors: Plas PENMYNYDD

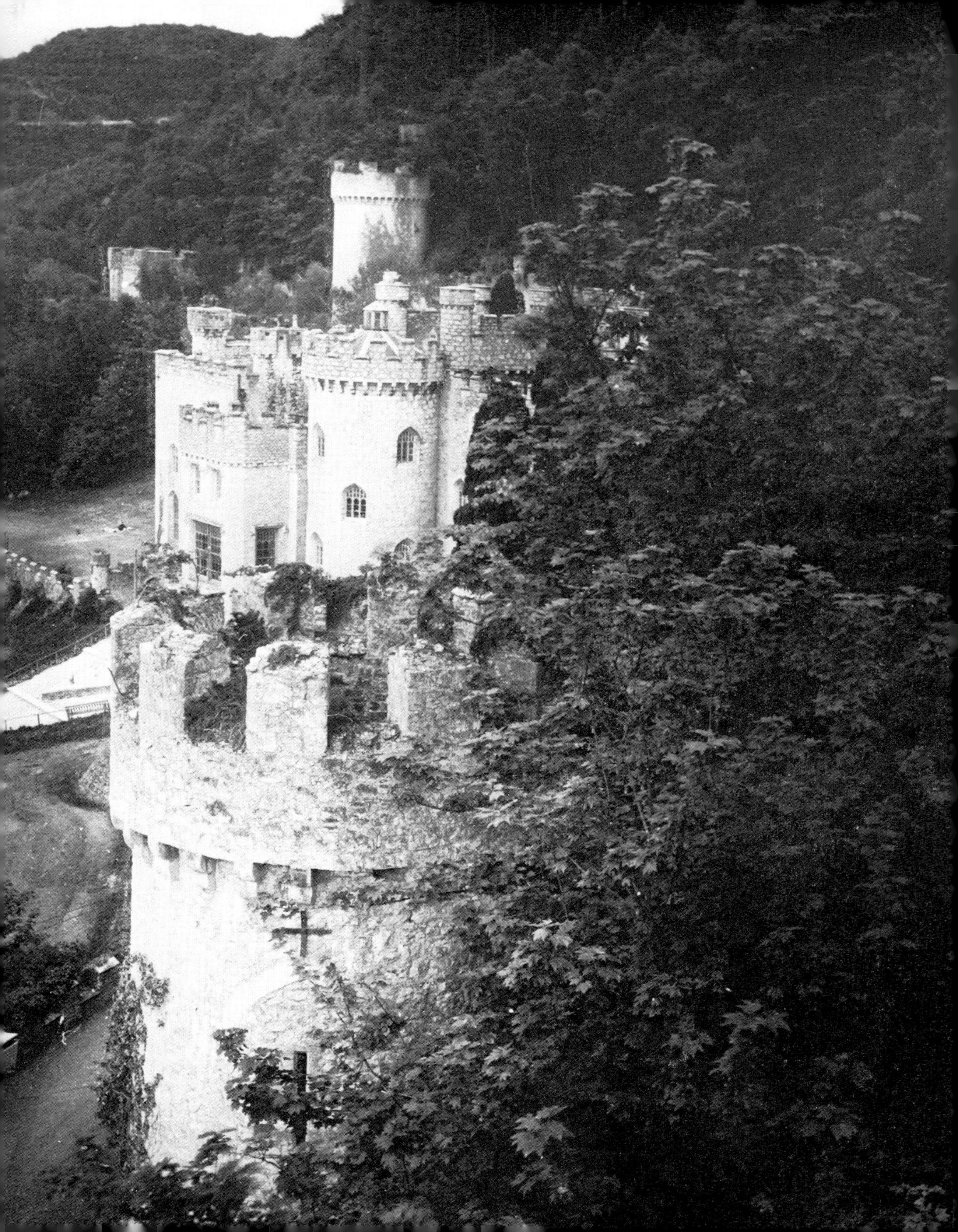

Denbighshire: Gazetteer

The number after each entry refers to the square on the map following page 144 *where the place is situated.*

Abergele (12). A market town now swamped in seaside subtopia, with a fine beach at Pensarn. The restored parish church, large for Denbighshire, is basically 16 c., but without much architectural character. The vestry contains some 16 c. glass, but the 19 c. glass is poor. The tower was heightened in 1879. The churchyard contains two mass graves, one the result of the wreck of an emigrant ship in 1848, the other of a train smash in 1868.

Abergele's only picturesque feature, but a remarkable one, is *Gwrych Castle*, a piece of pure romantic scenery: its castellated walls and eighteen turrets strung along the wooded hillside above the coastal plain have a silvery unreality. Designed by C. A. Busby in 1814 Gothic for L. B. Hesketh, it is now on popular display.

Three miles east is *Kinmel Park*, the grandest country house in the county. The estate was bought in the early 19 c. by Edward Hughes, who made a fortune out of a copper mine under Parys Mountain in Anglesey and became Lord Dinorben. The pink brick mansion, seen through handsome wrought-iron gates in the manner of Tijou, is the third on the site, but closely follows the earlier plan by Samuel Wyatt. It was designed in 1870 by W. E. Nesfield, the younger partner of Norman Shaw, in a gay and graceful style reminiscent of F. Mansart's Chateau of Balleroy. (But note the un-French off-centre chimney.) The richly-carved gate-lodge and the farm at Plas Kinmel are by the same architect. At right-angles to the entrance front, the splendid Vanburgh-like stable block was built in 1855 by William Burn. The house is now a school and is not open to the public: the interior is in any case of less interest.

The old estate village of *St George*, with another lodge probably by Samuel Wyatt, has in the churchyard the early Victorian Gothic mausoleum of Lady Dinorben, and there is an Iron Age fort on the crest above.

Lodge at Kinmel Park, ABERGELE

Bersham (23), near Wrexham, is strongly industrial with unexpected patches of agriculture. To the west lie the wonderful empty spaces of Esclusham mountain. Some of the

◁ Gwrych Castle, ABERGELE

finest wrought-iron gates in Britain were made at the Croes Foel Smithy by the three Davies brothers (e.g. the Golden Gates at Eaton Hall; and, see Chirk Castle, Leeswood Hall and Wrexham church). Robert Davies (1675–1748) is believed to have been a pupil of Tijou (who made the Hampton Court gates). A plaque on the wall of Croes Foel farm (Bersham turning off A.483), near the gate of the smithy, explains that it was demolished for road improvements in 1967.

With the arrival of the Wilkinson family in the mid-18 c., Bersham grew in importance for a very different type of iron production: smelting and casting. The juxtaposition of coal, iron and water-power made it an ideal site for their great iron works (no remains).

St Mary's, the parish church (1873), is by John Gibson who did the famous marble church at Bodelwyddan (q.v.). Bersham is quite different with its square campanile and apsidal east end: a version of continental romanesque. It stands opposite the site of the nicely named Plas Power.

Betwys-yn-Rhos (12). Modern accretions spoil this popular excursion from the coastal resorts. St Michael's church (J. Welch, 1838) has an eccentric double bell-turret and a charming interior with bright early Victorian glass. The pretty house, Ffarm, perhaps by the same architect, is now a hotel. Further west, in a broad park studded with oaks, is the late Georgian *Coed Coch*, renowned for the world-famous stud of Welsh mountain ponies of that name, started here in 1923 by Miss Broderick and her head groom Mr John Jones: perhaps the most attractive of all British ponies, particularly here in their home setting.

Bodnant (11). One of the three or four great romantic gardens of Britain, wholly created in the last 100 years. It was begun by Henry Pochin in the late 1870s as a Victorian arboretum and shrub garden. The central terraces were inserted by his grandson, the second Lord Aberconway, in the classical manner of Lutyens and Jekyll; they were cleverly placed off the axis of what was by then thought to be an ugly house, and so as not to disturb the ancient beeches and Mr Pochin's maturing cedars. In the same Edwardian period the Dell was planted up with the famous rhododendrons (including Chinese and Himalayan species), azaleas and magnolias. Lord Aberconway gave the garden to the National Trust in 1949. and it has since been further improved under the supervision of his son; it now extends over 70 acres, and on a May day, when it is at its most spectacular, all of it should be visited. Note particularly the astonishing Laburnum Arch, the lily pool, where a thousand flowers have been counted in midsummer, the Canal Terrace, with the 1730 Pin Mill brought from Gloucestershire in 1938 at one end and the Italianate yew theatre at the other, and the marvellously romantic Dell of the little river Hiraethlyn; the flour mill at the foot was built in 1837. The head gardener is Mr Charles Puddle, who succeeded his father in 1947.

BETWS-YN-RHOS

BODNANT ▷

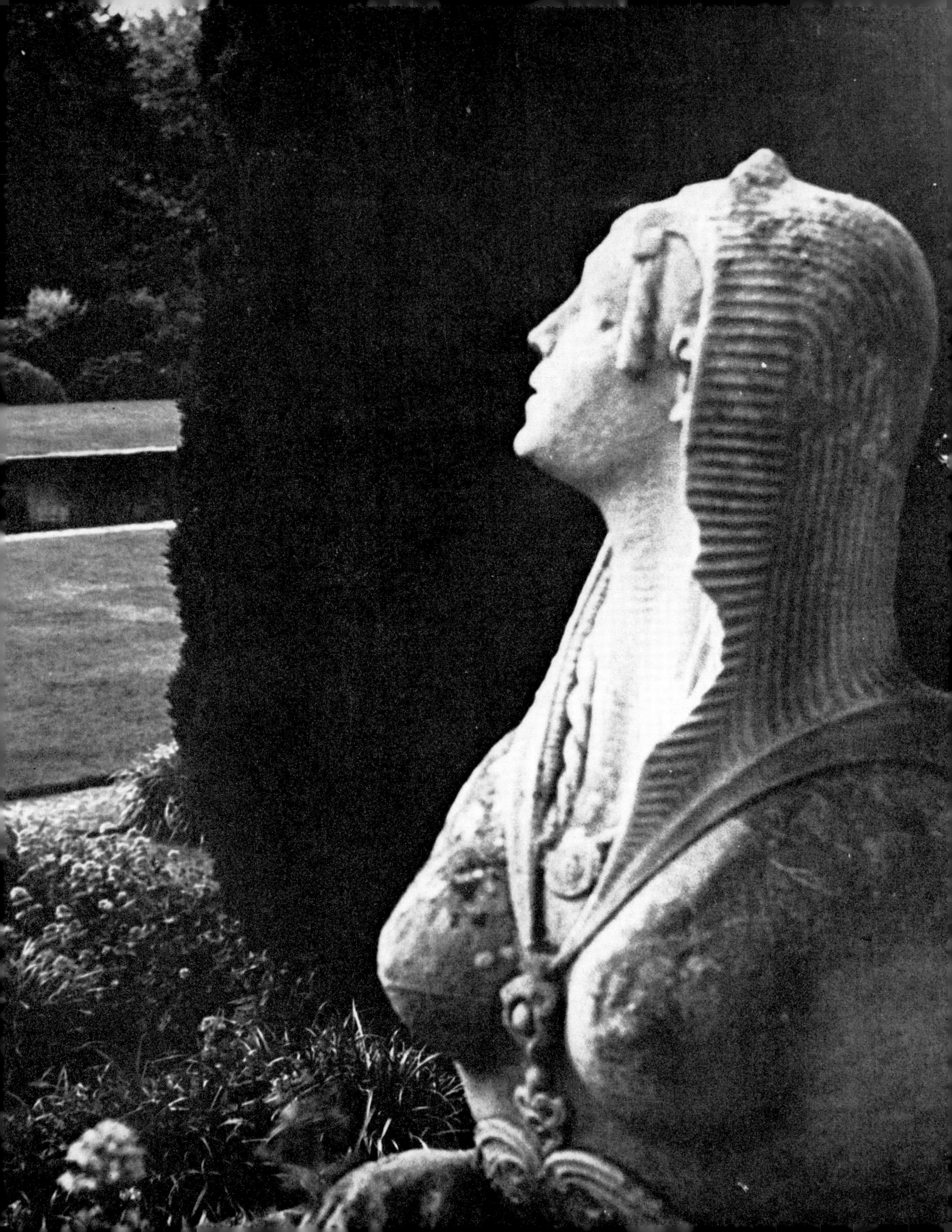

Bryneglwys (22). The round walled churchyard with its lo*w* grey church and black yews stands finely on its green knoll above the A.5104. In the Victorianised interior, behind thick wooded piers, is the chapel of the Yale family, from which the founder of the University was descended.

Capel Garmon (14). A mile south of the village, behind the farm Tyn-y-coed, is the "cromlech", a Bronze Age (*c*. 1800 B.C.) burial chamber in the form of a figure 8 which retains one of its immense roof-slabs. Magnificent views towards Snowdonia, particularly from the lay-by at 827575.

Cefn Mawr (23). Cefn's pink roofs and chemical works look down over the lower end of the Vale of Llangollen. Here the pastoral scene changes abruptly to industry. Telford's marvellous iron aqueduct, *Pont Cysyllte* (1794–1805), aloof and separate, strides across the valley, 127 ft. above the Dee. It is not to be missed. Contemporaries aptly named it "the stream in the sky". The 1,000 ft. long aqueduct, with a towpath cantilevered over it, consists of massive embankments at each end with nineteen airy arches in cast iron between. The daring use of this material caused the committee many doubts which delayed the work, but by 1797 Telford was able to write that the aqueduct was "already reckoned one of the wonders of Wales" and that his resident engineer "now thinks nothing of having three Carriages at his Door at a time". The ironmaster, Hazeldine, opened a foundry on the site of the present chemical works when the ironwork contract was awarded to his firm in 1802. Remains of a boat-building dock can be seen on the north side where the canal basin has taken on a new life with pleasure craft. The primary purpose of the aqueduct was to carry the Shropshire Union Canal across the Dee. The Llangollen Canal which joins it here, was primarily a feeder for the English system.

The great stone viaduct (1848) which carries the railway across the mouth of the Vale is less dramatic but splendidly telling in landscape terms. Engineer: Henry Robertson.

Pont Cysyllte, CEFN MAWR ▷

Burial chamber, CAPEL GARMON

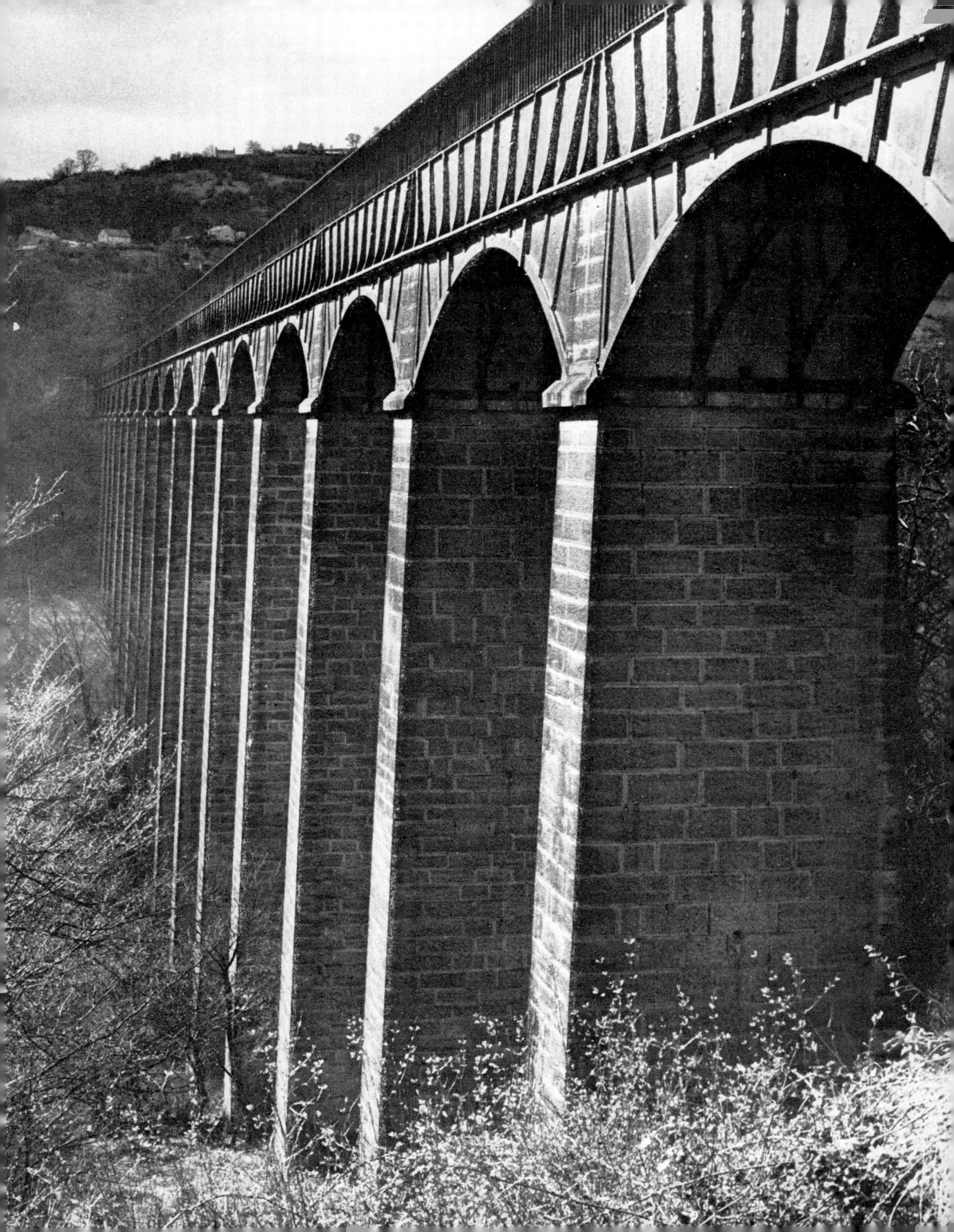

Cefn Meiriadog (12). Arcadian country in the crook of the Elwy. High on the ridge, a tiny, beautifully placed church of 1864 by Benjamin Ferrey has vast views over the Vale of Clwyd. It was wholly built of stone quarried on the spot. Good glass by Lavers and Barraud in the charming apsidal chancel. In the limestone gorge is a ruined Well Chapel (Ffynnon Fair) and caves which contained both palaeolithic and neolithic remains.

Cerrigydrudion (15). "The Stones of the Daring Ones." A bleak place now, with the widened A.5 roaring past it and many garages, etc. The clock on the bell-turret of the much-altered parish church is an attractive memorial of the '39–45 War.

Chirk (26). Here, where A.5 enters Wales and crosses the Ceiriog by Telford's handsome but small span, single-arched stone bridge, there are fine views of his aqueduct and the railway viaduct above it. A pub sign says "the last in England" and you climb the hill into the very English-seeming village of Chirk, with its pollarded chestnuts, brick and stone houses and some quietly Gothicised cottages; it then spreads north up the main road less attractively.

The site of the original motte which guarded this important crossing of the Ceiriog, and thus the way into Wales, lies behind the red brick Georgian house by the church which is built in its bailey. The church is double-aisled with a west tower: a 12 c. building to which the north aisle and tower were added in the 15 c. and the whole brought up to date. The Myddelton family of Chirk Castle are well commemorated, particularly by an early 18 c. monument in the south aisle (by Robert Wynne of Ruthin). Parts of the village school by A. W. Pugin (1844) survive; and the parish hall, a nice Jacobean building, 1902–4, is by Grayson and Ould (Liverpool). The war memorial is by Eric Gill.

To the west of the village a footpath drops down through woodland to *Chirk Aqueduct* (Thomas Telford, 1796–1801) and the *railway viaduct* (1848) which cross the valley side by side. This is a tremendously exciting five-minute walk. First you see the bright ribbon of the aqueduct shining through the trees. As you get nearer it appears to be a canal at ground level with the railway just above. Only on reaching the grassy towpath is one really aware that the Ceiriog is rushing 70 ft. below. The canal opens into a boat pool and then disappears into a tunnel immediately to the north, ¼ mile long, and on to Pont Cysyllte three miles further up. Chirk aqueduct consists of ten stone arches, each of 40 ft. span. The bottom of the channel is formed of iron plates bolted together. This was an entirely new departure from Brindley's method of using puddled clay to form the channel. Part of Telford's brief for this branch of the Shropshire Union Canal was to reduce locks to a minimum; hence a route favouring aqueducts.

Chirk Castle (open) is approached by a very fine pair of wrought-iron gates and screen made by Robert and John Davies of Bersham 1719–21. It is a border castle of Edward I's reign, completed 1310 but domesticated at various periods since. It stands in fine parkland cut by Offa's Dyke on the edge of romantic hilly country and has all that a castle of this sort should: grand, grey walls, entrance to courtyard under portcullis; dungeons. Also a suite of 18 c. rooms by Joseph Turner of Chester, and 19 c. Gothic work (in the private part of the house) by Thomas Harrison and by A. W. Pugin. There are also formal gardens with clipped yew.

The Ceiriog joins the Dee in the eastern corner of the parish: wooded river banks and undulating farmland with sudden glimpses of mines.

Clocaenog (22). The village gives its name to one of the earliest and largest of North Welsh forests, intersected by enticing minor roads. Large areas are now mature and give a wholly welcome new character to the bleak moorlands north of the A.5. At 065552 a conspicuous monument records that

"As a memorial of his having completed the large range of mountain plantations which in part skirt the base of this hill, William, second Lord Bagot, erected this pile of stones in the year 1830."

The village church has a simple 15 c. rood-screen and a fine big east window of 1538 with fragments of old glass.

Clwydian Range (19 and 22). A long wall of hills which shelters the Vale of Clwyd from the north-east. The Flintshire/Denbighshire county boundary runs along much of the ridge, swerving off it in a seemingly arbitrary fashion at various points. The splendid profile of these hills, specially when seen across the wet sands of the Dee estuary at ebb tide from the Wirral peninsula, beckon the suburb-bound to a promised land. They are crowned by *Moel Fammau*, justly "Mother of Mountains," although only 1,820 ft. The distinctive squarish top is the vast but collapsed Jubilee Tower, erected in 1810 to commemorate George III's fifty-year reign, designed by Thomas Harrison: a two-tiered obelisk standing on a battered base, of Egyptian inclination; it was not blown down until 1862 (a policeman on the walls of Denbigh Castle happened to witness this local catastrophe and noted "the strong breeze" blowing at the time). But on 25th October, 1810, "the sun shone upon the undertaking . . ." and a great procession on horseback, "accompanied by a constellation of beautiful Welsh ladies", made its way to the summit (already thickly peopled) where "the Military then fired several rounds and a *feu de ioie*; and the musick breathed forth our national pathetic air of *God save the King*, with a most enchanting effect". Dinners were eaten in all the local towns and the evening spent "with the utmost hilarity and loyalty".

The ridge is cut by public roads at several points which lead to lovely hill walks but few are on truly public footpaths; some of the heather covered hills are grouse moors. The best known way up the mountain is via Bwlch Pen Barras (where the 1810 procession formed up). From here a clear stony track leads to the

▷ Viaduct, aqueduct
and tunnel, CHIRK

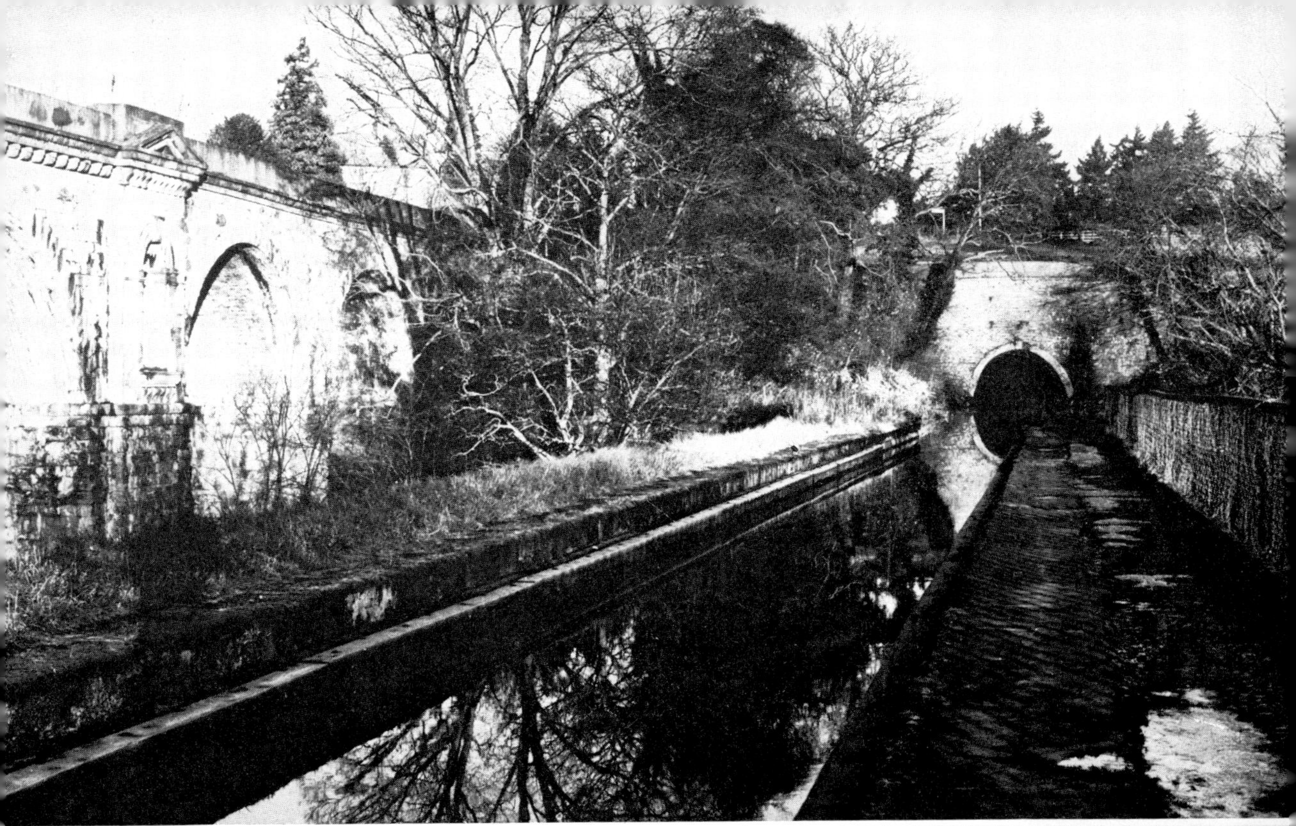

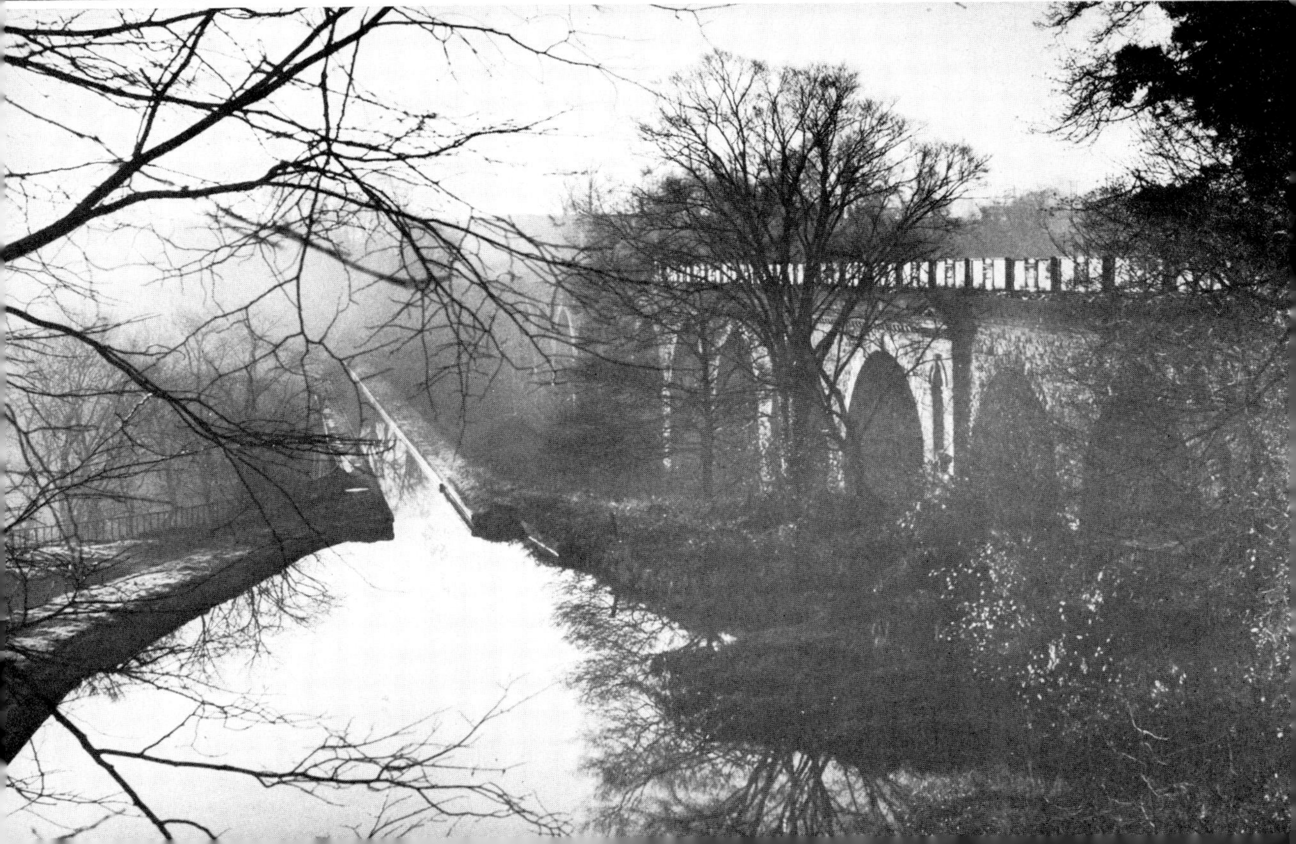

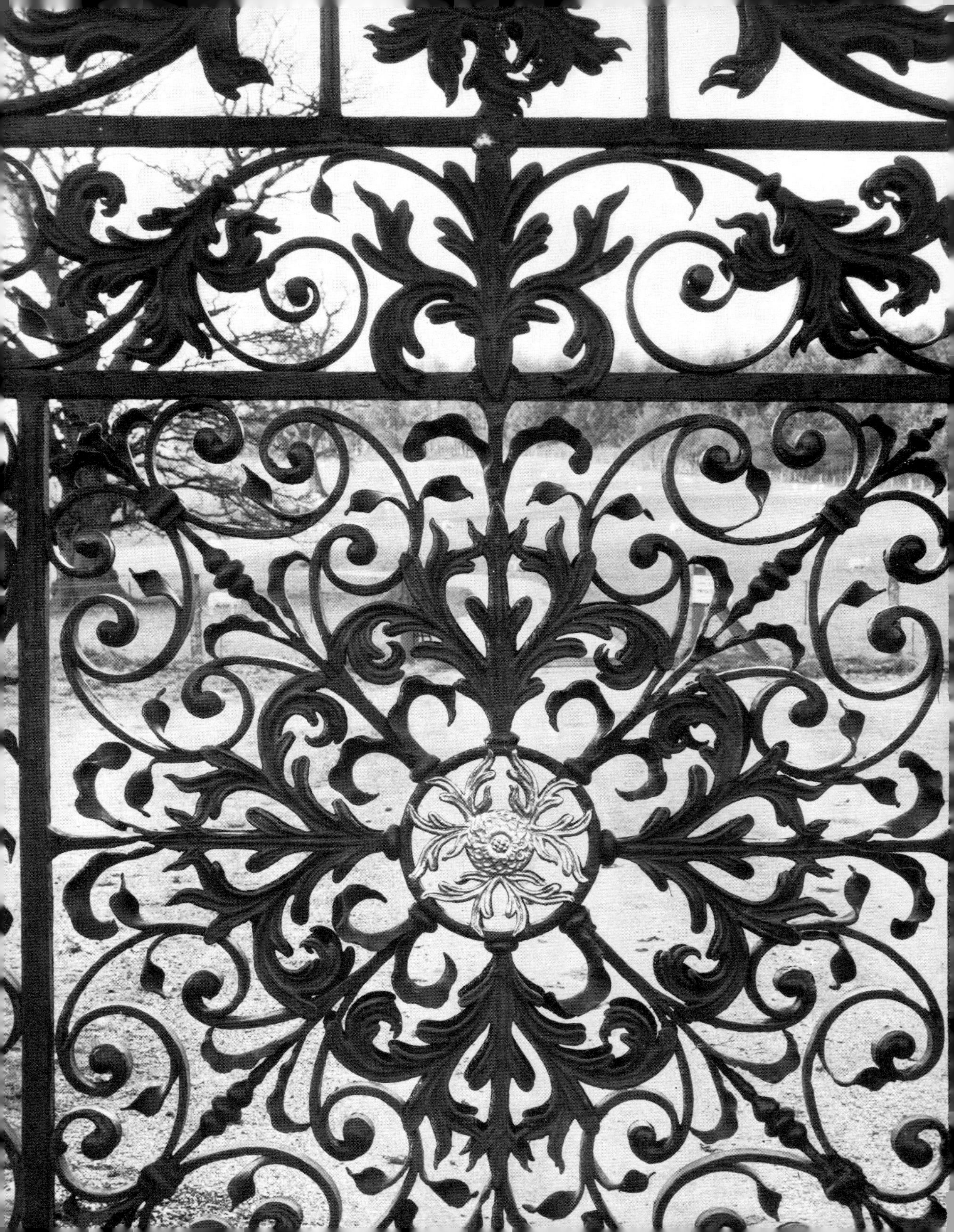

summit. The views, particularly those further into Wales towards Snowdonia, are magnificent.

The Forestry Commission has planted *Clwyd Forest* on the east slopes of the mountain. *Moel Fenlli*, one of the Iron Age chain of hill forts built along the range, c. 350 B.C.–A.D. 400, is on the opposite side of the cwm, crowning the hill above the Forestry Commission car park. Chief defences are on the north and east; banks 25 ft. above the exterior ditch. In 1816, after a heather fire, 1,500 Roman bronze coins were found on the inner rampart.

Other forts (all marked on the 1 in. O.S. maps) are: *Moel Hiraddug* (064783), the most northerly, above Diserth: now being excavated before being quarried out of existence. *Moel-y-Gaer* (095708) above Bodfari, and, also in Flintshire, *Pen y Cloddiau* (130675), not excavated and one of the largest in North Wales. And *Moel Arthur* (145660), where coarse Roman pottery and a hoard of Early Bronze axes have been found.

Colwyn Bay (12). The cheerful red-roofed conurbation is strung out for five miles along the A.55. Entirely un-Welsh in character, it has the look of a little Reading by the side of a brown sea. Its best features are its many neat and verdant suburban streets and its backcloth of hanging woods. Every building is post-1865, the date when old Lady Erskine, née Jane Silence Williams, finally decided to sell her estate of Pwllycrochan. By then the railway had already been there for 17 years and the influx of prosperous Lancashire folk was rapid. There was an energetic bout of sandstone church building for the large retired population, and the preferred architect was Mr Douglas of Chester (the architect of the Colwyn Bay Hotel) whose parish church of St Paul (1888) has a conspicuous, powerfully-buttressed square tower, added in 1910. St John's (1899) in Old Colwyn, also his, has a more interesting interior. For charm, some will prefer the naïve St Catherine's of 1838, with an east window by Clutterbuck. On the steep hills behind the town, both conspicuously sited, are the old parish church of *Llanelian*, an elementary 16 c. double-aisled structure, and the square-towered *Bryn y-maen* (1897), again by Douglas: church and vicarage were built by a devout servant girl who married the local squire. *Rhos-on-Sea*, now a breezy suburb of Colwyn with the advantage of isolation from main road and railway, has on its own hilltop the basically mid-Gothic parish church of *Llandrillo*, with a square battlemented tower used as a sea beacon, and a later (16 c.) south aisle.

Denbigh (19). Edward I's plan for pacifying Wales at the end of the war in 1282 was to build royal castles commanding the estuaries, with walled towns attached to them and organised as English boroughs, and to control the border by appointing Lords of the Marches, who were to build and garrison their own castles. In the Vale of Clwyd two such border barons were appointed, Henry de Lacy, Earl of Lincoln, for the lower Vale, and Reginald de Grey for the upper. For de Lacy the choice of the limestone bluff of Denbigh was inevitable, and he placed his castle on its highest point, with the walled town sloping away to the north.

Today it is a huddled, lively market town of considerable character, best entered across the Clwyd from the east whence the silhouette of the ruined castle stands up well on its wooded bluff. The first feature of arrival from this direction, and still on the fringe of the town at 072663, is the parish church of St Marcella, known as *Whitchurch* or Eglwys Wen, a well-restored 15 c. two-aisled structure with a plain, earlier tower. The interior has hammer-beam roofs, slightly mutilated, and a fine series of primitive corbels, now crudely painted. It also contains the naïve but impressive monument of Sir John Salusbury of Lleweni and his wife (1578). On the walls are a number of 18–19 c.

◁ ▽ CHIRK Castle; the wrought-iron gates, 1719–21, by Robert and John Davies

DENBIGH

monuments, many hatchments and the 16 c. brass of the Myddelton family (9 sons, 7 daughters). The simple pulpit is 18 c.

Continuing through suburbia, stop just short of the railway to note the ruined 13 c. church of the White Friars, absurdly concealed behind a Shell filling station in a private garden. Then climb Vale Street, which contains a number of good mid-18 c. houses (esp. the police station and solicitors' offices opposite). The High Street, really a market place, has been notably improved by a Civic Trust face-lift, and contains a delectable selection of country-style buildings of all periods, many of them arcaded (No. 26 the best of the 16 c., No. 2 of the 18 c., No. 32 of the 19 c.). Note also the two Lion pubs in Back Row.

The Castle is best approached on foot via Broomhill Lane (east side of High Street), and the impressive Burgesses' Gate, the main entry into the fortified town. Beyond, one passes the aqueduct-like ruin of "*Leicester's Church*" (a failed project of Queen Elizabeth's Robert Dudley) and a tower which is all that remains of St Hilary's. On the steeply sloping greensward hereabouts stood the little medieval town. Crowning it is the fine abstract shape of the Castle Gate, almost church-like with its powerful receding Gothic arches. Nothing much else survives but a rough circle of lumpish ruins. *The Castle*, held for the King by Salusbury in 1645 until it was starved out by General Mytton, was effectively ruined by Charles II. It is now a marvellous viewpoint for the Vale of Clwyd, aptly described by Dr Johnson as "embellished with woods and diversified with inequalities".

North-west of the Castle at the far end of High Street is *St Mary's* gloomy church of 1874, with a good modern window in the north aisle. *St David's* (1840, rebuilt 1894) has a Burne-Jones.

Half a mile north on the A.525 is Plas Clough, a stuccoed manor house with stepped gables, built for Sir Richard Clough in 1595. Half a mile south, at Pont Ystrad, is the abrupt grassy mount (Llys Gwenllian) thought to have been the original fort of Dinbych.

"Dr Johnson's Cottage" on the Ystrad is a spot he liked when he spent three weeks with Mrs Thrale's relations at Lleweni in 1774. It has some verses of his over the door, and nearby a classical urn (to his dismay) commemorates the visit.

More remote is Lleweni, where little remains of what was one of the biggest houses in North Wales except some immense columns in the kitchen of the farmhouse of that name. The large, red brick building nearby may have been quarters for workers at the Bleach Works (now demolished) by Thomas Sandby, or stables for the house. Now mournful and uncherished.

Derwen (22). The plain and powerfully modelled church, bleakly situated, is spick-and-span black-and-white inside, with a delicate 16 c. rood-screen. In the churchyard is a fine late 15 c. cross, now so worn that the moment of restoration or write-off cannot be long delayed.

Efenechtyd (22). A modest hamlet among water-meadows just south of Ruthin. The simple and charmingly situated little church has an oak porch and the only wooden font in Wales, a good rough bit of carving.

Eglwysbach (11). A village of terraced houses in a beautifully wooded valley, whose main street leads straight to the 1782 Gothick church, with square stone nave columns.

Erbistock (23) lies in a loop of the Dee just before it flows under Overton Bridge. By now it is a swift and level, broad determined river, brown after rain, flowing between steep wooded banks. Arcadian in character but mostly private property. The pretty stretch by Erbistock church and the Boat Inn (now fashionable) is accessible.

St Hilary's, 1860), pink sandstone, small and without memorable features except a good brass chandelier, has a marvellous leafy site by the water.

Erbistock Mill and its weir can be seen from the very pleasant road leading to Overton Bridge.

Gresford (23), whose colliery suffered one of the worst mining disasters of the century has much 19 and 20 c. housing development and in the nucleus of the old village, one of the best parish churches in Wales. It was built by Lady Margaret Beaufort. Perpendicular, pinnacled and buttressed, its tower whose peal is one of the Wonders of Wales, looms above 18 c. yews. Inside it is glassy, light and high; chiefly second half of 15 c., well restored by G. E. Street, 1867–8. Excellent glass 1498–1510, restored by Clayton and Bell 1868 and 1870: the east window in the north aisle (Llay chapel) dates from 1498. The choir screen and oak stalls are contemporary with the church. There are lovely brass chandeliers and interesting monuments: 17 c. alabaster in the Trefor chapel; a bust of W. Egerton by Chantrey (1827) and a monument by R. Westmacott Jr. 1797. A church not to be missed.

Gwytherin (15). Unspoilt village in the remote sheep country of the upper Elwy, the site of St Winifred's nunnery, until in the reign of Stephen her body was stolen by the English and removed to Shrewsbury. The 1867 church is of little interest.

Gyffylliog (22). Snugly and charmingly situated near the head of the Clywedog valley 4 miles west of Ruthin, the hamlet has nothing of architectural interest.

Henllan (12). Picturesquely situated in the hills west of Denbigh, the church on its warm slope has a detached castellated bell-tower, the four angle buttresses of which face precisely N.S.E. and W. The wide rubble-walled interior contains some rich Victorian glass. Just outside the village and visible from the Denbigh road, the house Garn has a good red brick 1739 façade by Robert West.

Holt (24) was a medieval borough built round its castle at the end of the 13 c. at the next crossing of the Dee above Chester. The present eight-arched sandstone bridge (from early 15 c.) links it to Farndon (Cheshire) which, with its Georgian houses, seems grand and West End compared with humble, bricky Holt.

The castle built by John de Warren, Earl of Surrey, is on a small boss of rock by the riverside too low for safety, adjoining red sandstone cliffs which have been quarried away to isolate it: a pentagon with corner towers, now much ruined and overgrown.

The church is most satisfyingly straightforward and symmetrical, reminiscent of a sampler. Two yew trees frame the west tower from the gate and a path, flanked by a plain brick wall, leads straight to the west door under the tower. Perpendicular, but dating from the 13 c., refashioned

Whitchurch, DENBIGH; Sir John Salusbury and his wife, 1578

in the 15 c. (including new aisles) and sympathetically restored by John Douglas and Ewan Christian (who did the chancel). There are steps down from the west door into the nave and this approach, from a higher level, reinforces its satisfactory symmetry. The octagonal font is elaborately carved with arms of successive lords of Holt Castle. 17 c. memorial tablets include a brass to Thomas Crue (died 1666) of Wrexham (see Gwydir chapel, Llanrwst). The verse is an acrostic on the name.

The site of a very large Roman tile and pottery factory lies northwest of the village.

Is-y-coed (24). A surprising hamlet which seems to be in the depths of English buttercup meadows less than a mile from the vast industrial estates to the east of Wrexham. Flat country: big skies over Welsh and Cheshire hills.

The 18 c. church (opposite the Plough Inn) is a plain, unassuming, brown brick building; cheerful in aspect with a low square tower with octagonal upper storey topped by a cupola and weather vane (dated 1742). Unfortunately it has been refitted inside but a wheel chandelier (now with mock candles) remains.

Llanarmon Dyffryn Ceiriog (25). Excellent and secluded walking and pony-trekking centre in the upper Ceiriog valley, deep in the foothills of the Berwyns. The steepled 1846 church (T. Jones of Chester) is approached between yews of immense antiquity. 600 ft. above the village is Llanarmon "Camp", possibly a prehistoric cattle enclosure, with wide moorland views.

Llanarmon-yn-Iâl (22) is a pleasantly austere stone village in impressive outcropping limestone country below the Clwydian range on its Wrexham side. The River Alyn runs through it.

The double-aisled church was rebuilt in 1736 but restored in 1870 and since. The arcades are supported by octagonal timber columns with Ionic capitals. There is a fine early-16 c. three-tier brass chandelier with a figure of the Virgin. Mid-14 and curious 17 c. tombs. Opposite the cheerful whitewashed Raven Inn.

The word "Iâl" in Welsh means a cultivated region. This word was adopted by a local family as a surname, one of whom was Elihu Yale, the founder of Yale University.

Llanbedr Dyffryn Clwyd (22) lies on the Ruthin-Mold road where it enters the Vale. It has a pleasant stone toll house with romantic iron windows and the Griffin Inn (early 19 c. charm with latticed casements). The amazing high-Victorian church, Decorated, and cheerful with a striped slate roof and striped stone walls, a very crotcheted spire and apsidal east end, is by Poundley and Walker, 1863. It contains a monument by John Gibson.

The by-road to Bwlch Pen Barras below Moel Fammau winds along the wooded hillside from the village: holiday bungalows are hidden in the trees.

The hill fort of *Moel Fenlli* (see Clwydian Range) is the parish.

Llanddulas (12). Roadside village in a cwm running into the sea. High above are G. E. Street's dour little church of *Llysfaen* (1868), with huge sea views and the vast Iron Age fortress of *Pen y Corddyn*, embracing 37 acres of the limestone hilltop.

Llandegla (22) is a small stone village on the edge of the Llandegla moors (grouse). The 1866 church is surprisingly dull: Goodhart-Rendell says it is probably by John Gibson (see Bodelwyddan). The fine brass chandelier is traditionally from Valle Crucis over the mountain. There is a weird east window from St Asaph Cathedral by Francis Eginton, 1800. Subject matter repellant; technique of painting skilful.

Llanddoget (14). Perched on the escarpment above Llanrwst with great views across the Conway, the church was rebuilt in 1838 with square wooden columns (regrettably encased in plywood) and pointed plaster arches separating the two aisles. Box pews. Behind the two-decker pulpit are two naïve early Victorian paintings. 60 yards to the north the Saint's well, Ffynnon Ddoged, still flows copiously.

Llandyrnog (19). The ugly church has an Art-and-Crafts porch of the nineties and a beautiful late 15 c. "Seven Sacraments" window with a crucifixion in the wholly Victorianised interior.

Capel y Dyffryn, 1836, was the first Presbyterian Methodist church in the Vale. Before, the congregation met in a field near the Sanatorium. This plain Georgian building makes an attractive group with its house and Sunday school. Its founder lived at Plas Ashpool, the rather Dutch-looking brick house on the Bodfari road, nicely framed by its outbuildings, which include a barn on crucks. At *Waen Bodfari* the Calvinistic Presbyterian chapel, 1822-62, painted in putty grey with white and crimson, looks cherished and trim.

The "Georgian" Baptist church on the corner below Llandyrnog, with windows uninhibitedly out of line, was the gift of John Madocks, 1836, of Glan y wern, the big house of the parish which he had remodelled some years earlier.

Llanelidan (22). Three buildings in a peaceful pastoral valley of the upper Clwyd. The church has a sprucely restored interior with a primitive 16 c. pulpit and fragments of late 15 c. glass; alongside, a good 17 c.–19 c. group, all with white diamond panes —now an inn.

One mile north and visible from the A.494 is *Nantclwyd Hall*, a basically late 17 c. house with 1857 additions, altered and embellished by Clough Williams-Ellis. It lies in a prosperous pastoral parkscape of great beauty.

Llanfair Dyffryn Clwyd (22). Roadside hamlet with some early 19 c. almshouses, a good Vestry House of 1831 and a large Perp. church, thoroughly restored by Sedding in 1872, with plain square tower. There is a patchwork window of old glass dated 1500 and an attractive 1890 window in the south aisle. The 17 c. font was removed to *Jesus Chapel*, a mile south up the main road, when the church was restored. The chapel is a 17 c. design rebuilt with its original door and windows in 1787.

GRESFORD ▷

110

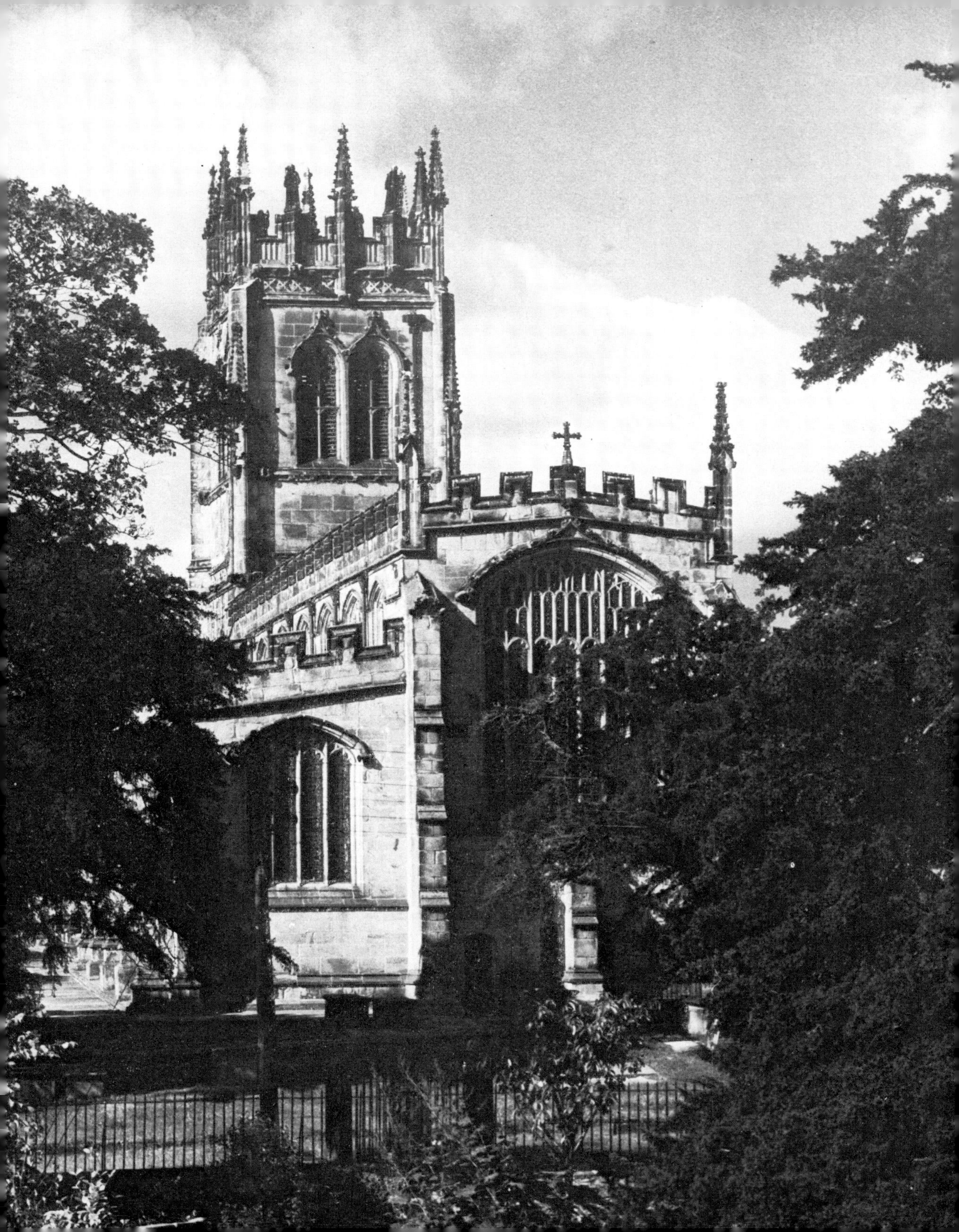

Llanfair Talhaiarn (12). Presumed home of the bard Talhaiarn, who is buried in the churchyard. Now an unspoilt fishing village, with streets that climb steeply from the Elwy bridge, and a weather-fish on the belfry of its otherwise unremarkable church. The best centre for exploring the Elwy valley.

Llanferres (22) is on the Flintshire side of the Clwydian Range and includes the famous *Loggerheads Inn* and the Crosville Motor Company's Tea Gardens: a survival of Edwardian arcadia within bus and bicycling distance of Liverpool, beside the little River Alyn, here a mere stream, which glides through wooded glades under the sheer and splendid limestone crags to disappear dramatically in dry weather into swallow holes. After leaving the slot machines in the tea gardens (in 1968 it was still possible to test strength, skill, weight or fortune at 1d. per time) the path idles along the stream where wagtails flash, sulphur yellow. It leads through to Cilcain with branches up to Moel Fammau.

Richard Wilson, who spent his last days at Colomendy Hall (his brother was agent to the estate) is reputed to have painted the inn sign (now elsewhere). The house is a school and has several simple modern buildings by Colwyn Foulkes and Partners.

Llanferres church and the Druid Inn are attractively sited farther up the Ruthin road. Retirement dream bungalows of the '30s are perched here and there above the road with gentle hilly views, pastoral and Welsh. The church was largely rebuilt in the 18 c. but has since been put into thorough order by the late Victorians.

Llanfihangel Glyn Myfyr (15). A hamlet on the B5105 from Ruthin. The tall arch of Thomas Penson's bridge over the Alwen and the 18 c. Crown Inn group well together.

Llangedwyn (25). The manor house, basically Elizabethan, but much altered and stuccoed, with Georgian windows and sundial, is seen at the end of a tall lime avenue off the main road through the impeccable Tanat valley. The church opposite, wholly rebuilt in 1869, contains (on the right of the altar) a 14 c. recumbent figure, and the churchyard contains a memorial to a man who died in 1734 at the age of 110. There is a handsome early 19 c. bridge over the Tanat, with niched abutments.

Llangernyw (12). Compact main-road village in the Elwy valley. The restored 16 c. church has attractive barn-like transepts and a rich red 1830 window by Clutterbuck. It retains its original quatrefoiled font. A mile up the hill to the east is Sir Gilbert Scott's *Hafodunos*, one of his most important country houses, in his St Pancras manner of the 1860s.

Llangollen (23). *The Vale of Llangollen* is as romantic as its name is evocative: the picturesque dream in unawful mood. The Dee flows swiftly through green meadows walled by magnificent limestone cliffs (notably the Trefor and Eglwyseg Rocks), so vertical and architectural in form as to seem man-made. The woodland makes one long for the first October frosts, but the Vale is good at any season and sets off its medieval ruins and industrial monuments to perfection (e.g. Pont Cysyllte, which spans it to the east and Valle Crucis Abbey ½ mile to the north. The small town centres on the Trefor Bridge, which probably dates from Elizabethan times but has been widened several times. Bishop Trefor (1300–57) built the first bridge here. There are remains of old mills by the river, but the International Eisteddfod (held in a field upstream) and the tourists, now provide Llangollen's *raison d'être* and, judging by its buildings, have done so increasingly since early in the last century when it was a popular posting station on the Holyhead Road.

St Collen's is a typical double-aisled church to which a third (now the south) was added in 1863; its square tower is mid-18 c. It has an open roof with angels on the hammer-beams; the central aisle is particularly finely carved. The spacing of the trusses does not match those of the arcading, so it was presumably taken from another church (Valle Crucis?).

The famous Ladies of Llangollen and their maid have an imposing tomb in the churchyard. Lady Eleanor Butler (". . . Aunt to the late and to the Present Marquess of Ormonde") had arrived with Sarah Ponsonby and their maid, Mary Caryll, in 1780 from Kilkenny, where the prospect of country life and suitable but uncongenial marriages bored them. They set up house at *Plas Newydd* (open), which is still a place of great curiosity and considerable charm. From a gazebo in the garden they spied the coaches on the road below. Anyone who was anybody visited them but was not invited to stay. (Scott, Wordsworth, Shelley . . . and the Duke of Wellington himself, who got them a pension from the Privy Purse.) It became customary for guests to bring wood carving as a present so the black and white house is decorated, rather like a sampler, with carvings from all over Europe.

Plas Newydd also commands a suitably romantic view of *Castell Dinas Bran* perched high on its isolated outcrop in the Vale below, eyrie of the beautiful Myfanwy Fechan. Short, sharp climb and lovely views. The present castle has an 18 c. feel about its ruins but the romance can be dulled by an all-pervading smell of chemicals from the factory at Cefn. It is thought to have been built on an Iron or Late Bronze Age site by Gruffyd ap Madoc (d. 1270) whose father founded Valle Crucis. Up on the springy turf of the bailey one is almost level with the fascinating limestone terraces and quarries of Trefor and Eglwyseg and the remains of the dramatic inclines constructed to lower the stone to the valley. The grass on the terraces is like a mown lawn, level and idyllic.

The Llangollen Canal, designed by Telford as a navigable feeder to the Ellesmere Canal (part of the Shropshire Union) can be explored on foot along its towpath or by boat. The stretch leading up towards Horseshoe Falls has rock cuttings of miniature grandeur; unaware birds creep among the young larch and a sturdy road bridge and railway viaduct cut through each other's masonry arches. It is all very unexpected and separate in the fashion of canals. Most unexpected of all are the *Horseshoe Falls*: not the tearing cataract one might expect of picturesque Wales but a beautiful, curved weir, with a fall of about 18 in., designed to bring the waters of the Dee into the canal. Downstream from Llangollen the canal winds its pastoral way above the Dee to Pont Cysyllte. It runs below *Trevor Hall* (now crumbling). The simple 1717 chapel in the grounds has been disappointingly restored at various times but still has its 19 c. box pews, and a good chandelier among tasteless electric fittings. *Plas-yn-y-peutre* (1634) with black and white first floor makes a nice group between the Dee and the canal with its mill (disused; 30 ft. wheel survives), round house and dovecot. Treasure from Valle Crucis is said to have been hidden here after the dissolution.

Llangwm (15). A parish of wide sheep-walks straddling the A.5 west of Corwen. The shrunken village is crossed by a stream handsomely bridged. Alongside the decent 18 c. church (dull interior) is a fine white-washed farmstead grouped round the monumental bole of a long-dead sycamore.

Llangwyfan (19). Persevere past the hospital to the little stucco church perched above the Vale of Clwyd, with the village stocks beside the churchyard gate. The delightful 18 c. interior has box pews and a gay east window by Gibbs, dated 1853.

Llangynhafel (22). A hamlet at the foot of Moel Fammau. Up a lane to the east is the attractive church, with a round and monumental bell-turret. It is the usual double-aisled Denbigh type, newly stuccoed without and smoothly plastered within. The central Perp. arcade is more graceful than most and the hammer-beam roof retains several of its carved angels. There is a primitive 17 c. pulpit, a group of early 19 c. monuments and a pelican over the altar. Behind the church is a romantically composed half-timbered house.

Llannefydd (12). In the rolling country between Elwy and Aled valleys, this

Hafodunos, LLANGERNYW, ▷
by Sir Gilbert Scott

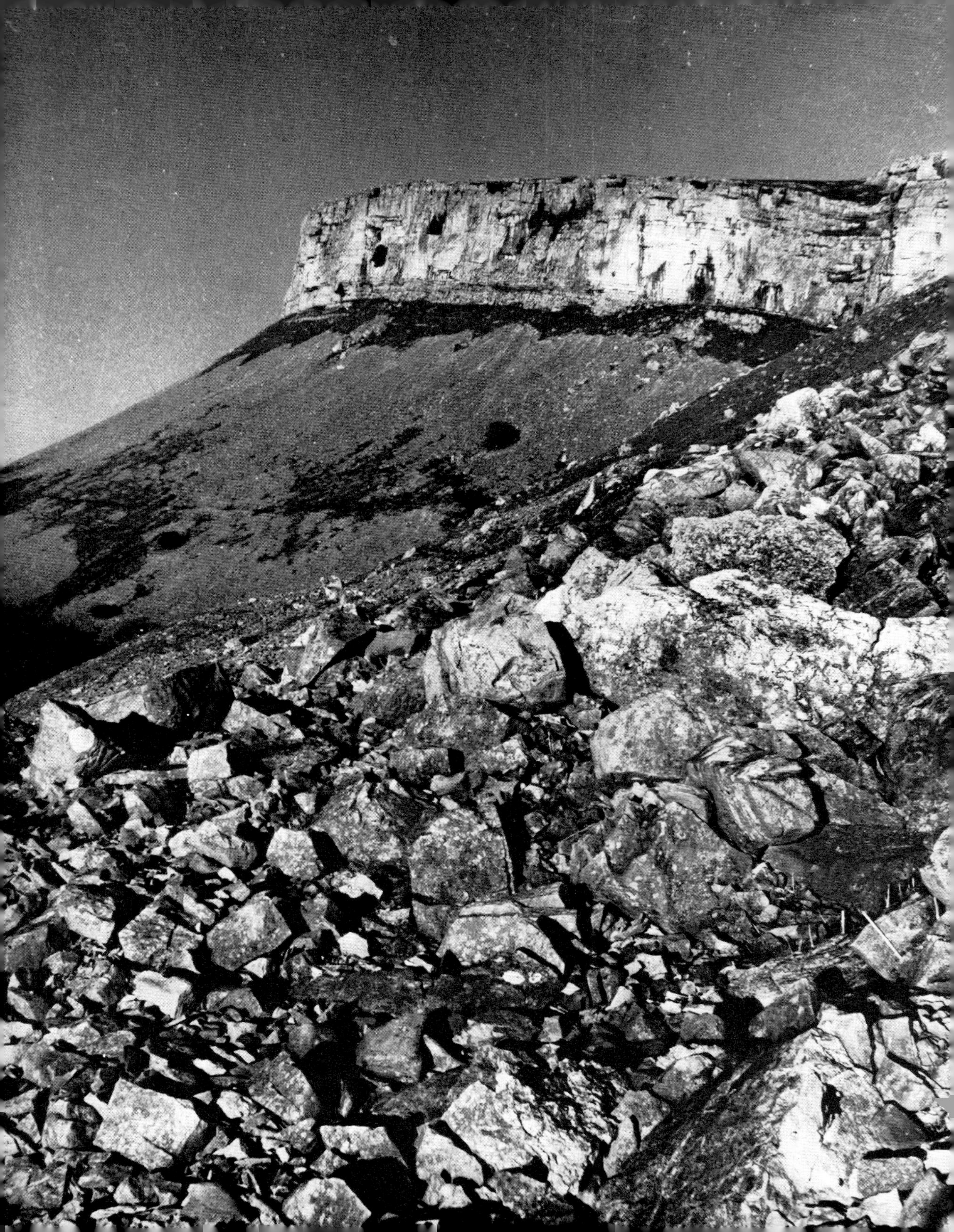

LLANTYSILIO-LLANGOLLEN
◁ Craig Arthur
△ Eglwyseg Rocks
Derelict quarry building; Trefor ▷ Rocks

wholly 'Chapel' community has a late 15 c. church of some size, now closed because its congregation was reduced to two (key at Henllan vicarage). The spacious interior is well-lit by plain-glazed Perp. windows with some fragments of original glass.

Llanrhaiadr-yn-Cinmerch (22). The white-washed 17 c. almshouses, smithy and inn on the main Denbigh–Ruthin road, embosomed in trees, are grouped round a typical 15 c. double-aisled church which should on no account be missed. It is entered by a finely-carved 15 c. oak porch, unusual in Wales. The rather dark interior has over the chancel a 15 c. panelled barrel roof of exceptional elegance, with carved angel corbels, a west window containing a patchwork of glass of the year 1508, and the great Jesse window of 1533, unquestionably the finest in the county and a good deal more sophisticated than the work of the York school of the same period. Below it is the chest hollowed out of a single oak in which the glass is said to have been buried during the Civil War. In the south-east corner

LLANRWST

is the cheerful 1705 monument to Maurice Jones, recording his "fine parts both of body and mind and diverting conversation".

Llanrhaiadr Hall (not open), seen from the road at the end of an avenue, is a dignified Victorian mock-up of an Elizabethan E-plan manor house. It was built by T. Penson of Chester in 1841.

Llanrhaiadr-yn-Mochnant (25). This large market village, snugly situated in the foothills north of the Tanat, has been much changed for the worse by 20 c. extensions. From the tiny market place, largely late-Victorian, one sees the basically 17 c. Wynnstay Arms, with carved bargeboards, and the square keep-like tower of the parish church, whose narrow nave is now a useless appendage to the original three-aisled structure, added to it in the 15 c. and restored in the 19 c. The interior's only attraction to the traveller is a 10 c. sepulchral slab incised with a movingly primitive Celtic cross.

Three miles up the romantically wooded valley of the Rhaiadr, is *Pistyll Rhaiadr*, to our eyes the most

LLANGWYFAN

beautiful and spectacular waterfall in Wales—amply described by George Borrow, who had it to himself without car park or litter. From the rustic temple portico at its foot, now in a precarious condition, the cataract seems to fall out of the sky into a richly wooded chasm, then tumbles through a natural (rebuilt) rock arch into lower pools and falls. The scene, minus our 20 c. corruptions, is all that Richard Wilson or Rex Whistler could have desired.

Llanrwst (14). Memorable because of the fine church–bridge–river relationship, rather than for any special personality in the town itself. The graceful bridge of 1663, attributed without evidence to Inigo Jones, with an attractive 17 c. cottage at its far end, is the most elegant in North Wales before the Second Iron Age. The much-restored church is approached between two sets of almshouses, 17 c. on the right, 19 c. on the left. The only important internal feature in its main body is the black, intricately carved 15 c. rood-loft and screen, comparable with the Conway one and probably built by the same craftsmen. The Gwydir Chapel, recently restored with the aid of the Pilgrim Trust, is an elegant and harmonious late Gothic structure, added to the church by Sir Richard Wynn of Gwydir in 1633–4. It has an elaborate flat oak ceiling and stalls with surprisingly naïve carved female heads, contrasting with the sophisticated Lely-like brass to Dame Sarah Wynn of 1671 (see Holt). In the centre of the chapel is a 14 c. stone sarcophagus of great size, probably brought from Maenan Abbey, with boldly carved quatrefoils on its sides. Other monuments are more fun but less fine.

The town contains a National Westminster Bank in a Frenchified Edwardian manner (cp. the equally outlandish Llandudno branch) and a prize-winning housing scheme of the 1950s by Colwyn Foulkes, reached via Llanddoget Road.

Llansannan (12). The only sizable community in the Aled valley, which is of extreme and unspoilt charm both

Pistyll Rhaiadr, ▷
Llanrhaiadr-yn-Mochnant

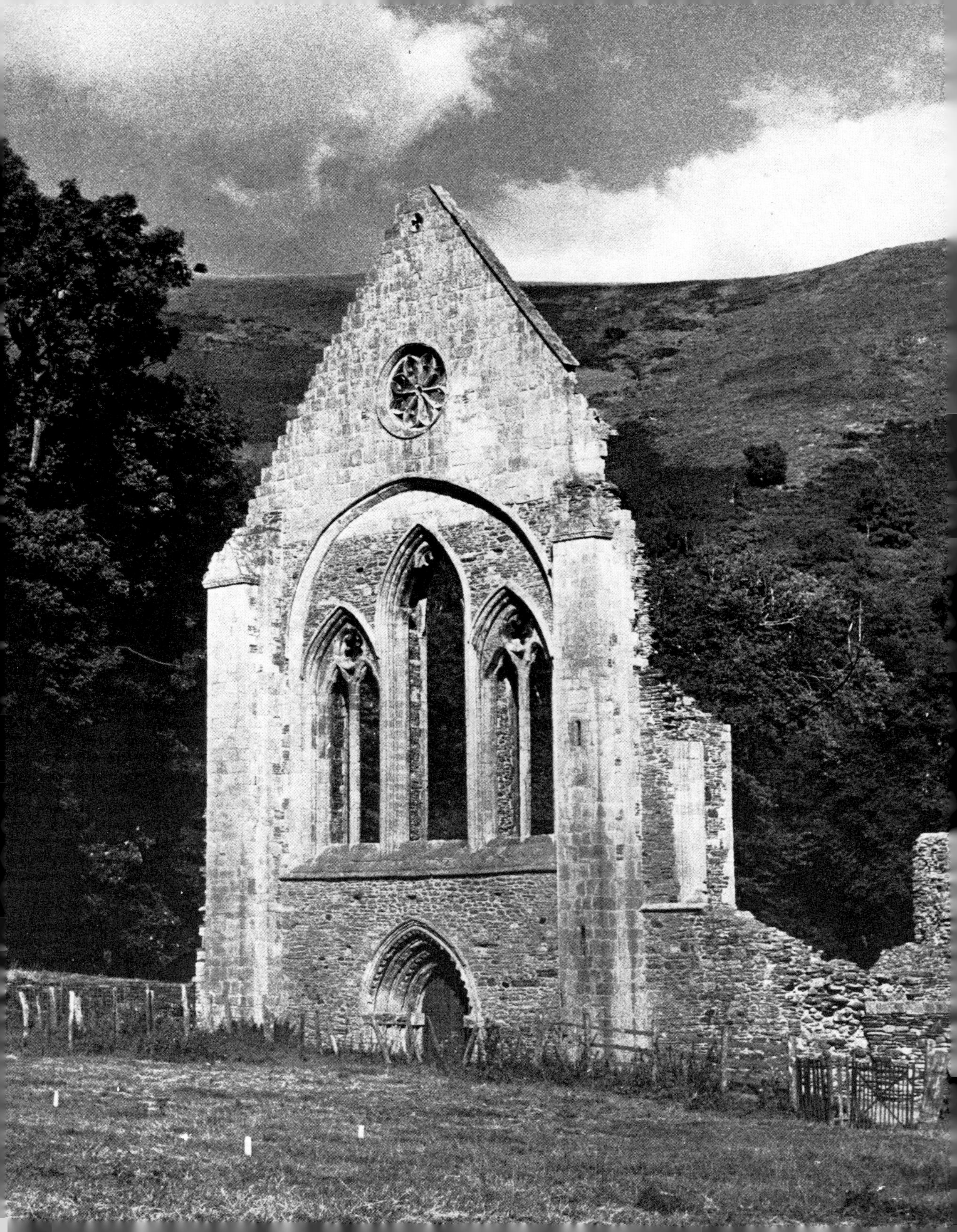

◁ Valle Crucis Abbey, LLANTYSILIO

above and below the village, though more accessible below. The church, wholly rebuilt in pitch pine on its old foundations by Sir Stephen Glynne in 1869, contains a late 17 c. carved pulpit brought from Liverpool, and a number of Yorke family monuments.

Llansantffraid (11) (Glan Conway). The naive church, rebuilt 1839, has two fine windows of about 1500 representing St John Baptist and St Catherine, preserved from its predecessor. It has some even finer 19 c. glass, including an exceptionally beautiful east window of 1839, probably by Clutterbuck.

Llansantffraid Glynceiriog (26). A straggling townlet with ugly modern accretions housing workers in the Ceiriog quarries. The older part climbs steeply (1 in 4) to the largely 1839 church, with a gloomy interior of some character virtually untouched since the 19 c. There is some pleasant early Victorian armorial glass by David Evans. Church Hill climbs even more steeply on to the watershed of the Vale of Llangollen, into which it descends spectacularly, through impeccable landscape; a drive not to be missed, and to be treated with respect.

Upstream of the town the valley narrows into a prettily wooded glen, where the hamlet of *Pandy* is a good base for riders and walkers.

Llansilin (26). Chief village in the remote and beautiful pastoral valley of the Cynlleth, a tributary of the Tanat, among rounded grassy hills just inside the English border. It has some good houses in its compact centre and a mainly 14 c. well-restored double-aisled church with 1830 tower standing prominently in a large churchyard with many ancient yews. A monument commemorates seven children of one family who died of diphtheria within three weeks in 1892. The interior is fully described in an excellent parish history displayed on large panels in the porch. The chancel has a fine barrel-shaped panelled roof (14 c., restored) and the altar-table and rough timber gallery are 17 c. There are a few good monuments, including an unusual panel studded with brasses commemorating some 17 c. churchwardens. The handsome brass candelabra was donated in 1824 by a local man who made good in Birmingham.

A mile to the south is "*Owen Glendower's Castle*", a conspicuous green mound on which there is evidence that his timber house originally stood. Here in 1858 George Borrow sat down and recited a long ode by the bard Iolo Goch, a contemporary of Glendower's.

"And when I had finished repeating these lines I said, 'How much more happy innocent and holy I was in the days of my boyhood, when I translated Iolo's ode, than I am at the present time.' Then covering my face with my hands, I wept like a child."

The site is symbolically dominated by the much higher ground along which runs the English border.

▽ Corn mill on the Alyn, ROSSET

119

Llantysilio (22) is the hilly parish just north of Llangollen (q.v.) and includes much that might logically be included in the Vale, the lovely valley of Eglwyseg being a northerly branch of it. This cuts the high empty tops of Llantysilio Mountain from Eglwyseg and Ruabon Mountains. The narrow wooded valley winds up under the limestone cliffs past the appropriately named World's End and Plas Eglwyseg, originally an Elizabethan house, to the remote plateau of Esclusham Mountain so surprisingly close to industrial Wrexham.

Valle Crucis lies just above the junction of the Dee and the Eglwyseg, its site sheltered and secluded in the great tradition of the Cistercians, and now also enjoyed by caravanners. The abbey was founded here in 1201 in the heart of the kingdom of Powis; its choir is said to have rivalled Salisbury. It is now a ruin, with hills framed in its empty windows. The west end was repaired by Sir Gilbert Scott. The pilaster buttressing dividing the windows of the east end is most unusual. An 18 c. cottage looks over this and the formal fish-pond to the north.

The *Pillar of Eliseg* stands on a tumulus about ¼ mile up the valley close to the road. Its inscription is of scholarly rather than visual interest and was copied in 1696. It recorded the ancient glories of the house of Powis and was erected in honour of King Eliseg.

The *parish church* has an attractive site above the Horseshoe Falls but is very much restored. A tiny single-light window on the north side has 1460 York type glass.

There is also a very attractive narrow road above the wooded north bank of the Dee which runs close to the river in places.

Llanynys (22). In the heart of the Vale, next to Ruthin, its meadows watered by the Clwedog as well as the Clwyd, whence its name (ynys = island). The church and its yew trees are attractively grouped with the Cerrigllwdian Arms and the vicarage. On the oak door the oldest carved initials are dated 1598. The central arcade was replaced in 1770 by a tall closely-spaced row of square fluted oak columns, and the Gothick windows are also probably of that date. On the north wall, above the sadly mutilated effigy of an ecclesiastic, is a remarkable 15 c. mural painting of St Christopher, recently uncovered; it has a striking stance and scale. The church also possesses an unusual hexagonal headstone of the 14 c. with a crucifixion on one side and a bishop on the other.

Maenan. See Caernarvonshire.

Marchwiel (23) is a small village which has miraculously avoided being smothered by Wrexham. The church was entirely rebuilt in 1778, the tower being reported to be "upon a plan of Mr James Wyatt's"; a transept was added in 1829. Outside it is plain, pleasant and classic; inside, dull, having been refurbished in the 19 c. There is an armorial window of the Yorke family by Francis Eginton made in 1788, and a very nicely worded monument to Simon Yorke of Erthig Esqr., 1767: "A pious temperate sensible country Gentleman, / of a very mild, just and benevolent Character, / as the concern for his Death did best testify; / An Advantage which amiable Men have over great Ones." His late 17 c. house, Erddig (not open), is precariously undermined by recent coal mining.

Nantglyn (15). Remote white-washed place near the head of the Ystrad valley. The modest 18/19 c. church is partly slate-hung, and in its yew-shaded churchyard are buried several 19 c. Welsh scholars.

Pentrefoelas (15). Neat 19 c. roadside hamlet on the A.5 with a Georgian

Congregational chapel, RUTHIN, 1820

△ Ruthin and the Clwydians (*see also* The Clwydian Range, p. 104)

▽ St Peter's Square, Ruthin

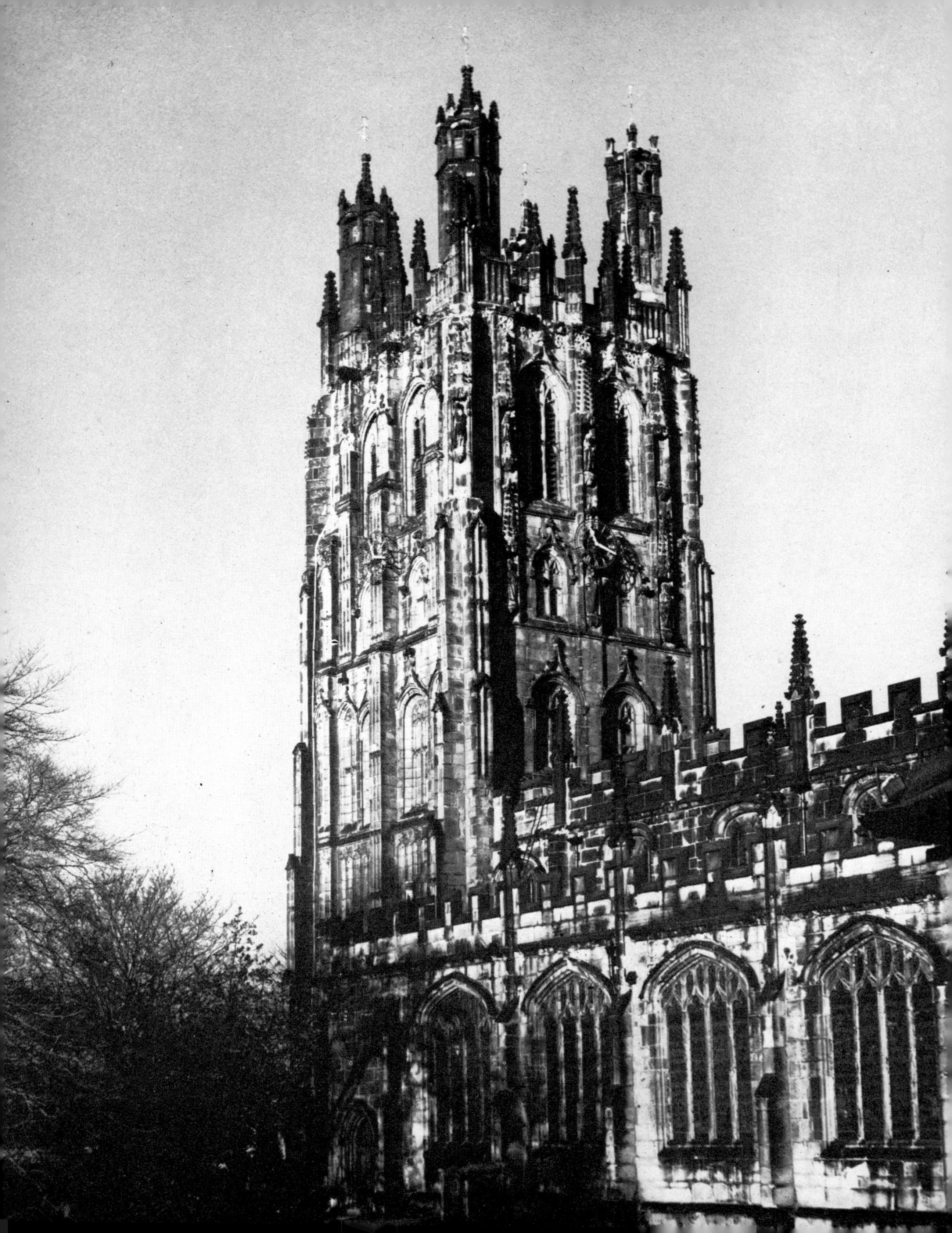

coaching inn and a glum stuccoed church by Sir Gilbert Scott.

Rhosllanerchrugog (23) is proudly Welsh, partly perhaps because of its position straddling Offa's Dyke. To the west it is wedged against the wide tops of Ruabon Mountain (heather and grouse). A nineteenth century town brilliant with orange/red Ruabon brick and purple slate shining after rain. The variety of terracotta mouldings to be seen might provide fodder for a thesis writer. It has, like other towns and industrial villages around Wrexham, a generous share of chapels and it is a great place for choirs. The rather withdrawn stone church (Thomas Penson, 1853) has unexpectedly open views from the graveyard.

Rossett (23), only a mile from the border, feels like a Cheshire village. There are two corn mills, until recently driven by the River Alyn; the weir is beside the Hope road. The black-and-white mill dates from the 14 c.; extended in 1661. Much of the black is painted on for decoration in the local tradition. Its great wheel and machinery survive; last worked in 1961. On the opposite side of the road the big brick mill is from 1791, now worked by electricity. The church, 1875, is by John Douglas; rather dull.

Trevalyn (open on written application), 1576, was built by John Trevor, who has a curious monument in Gresford church (q.v.). Basically an Elizabethan house with classic details as befitted the *avant-garde* of the day: note the porter's lodge (now moved from its original position). Brick (now rendered) with stone quoins and a comfortable human scale. Unexpected views both of Beeston Castle and the Welsh hills.

Ruabon (23) is justly famous for most diverse reasons; for Wynnstay, for generations seat of the Williams Wynn family, landowners of such extent as to be known as the kings of Wales; for Ruabon brick, whose fierce red has adorned buildings far beyond the Principality. Collieries and chemical works are close by, giving a sharp mixture of industry and agricultural border country.

Approaching from the south with the railway viaduct, 1848, striding across the east end of the Vale of Llangollen, the park wall of *Wynnstay* is soon visible on the right. The park was laid out by Capability Brown. James Wyatt's great column, topped by a copper vase, which commemorates the Sir Watkin who died in 1789, is one of the few survivals of his work at Wynnstay. A small bath-house may also be Wyatt's. His house was burnt. The present house and chapel (occupied by Lindisfarne College) are by Benjamin Ferrey, who had the good fortune to travel in the same railway compartment as Sir Watkin Williams Wynn shortly after the fire. Result: a François I château of the 1860s. The handsome stable block (now a school dining hall, open during the school holidays on written application, but best seen from outside) survived the fire.

The Waterloo Tower, visible from Pont Cysyllte, is by Wyattville; an inhabited folly, good as a landmark but coarse on closer inspection. He is said to have designed lodges at Wynnstay; so is Benjamin Gummow (who worked at Eaton Hall, near Chester). The only one of note is at Newbridge (where A.483 crosses the Dee) and it is indeed remarkable. A small pavilion on a boldly arched plinth (which contains the gatekeeper's living rooms), its forecourt marked by big stone piers, balancing those of the gate. Architect: C. R. Cockerell.

The main entrance to Wynnstay from the village is dull but the broad street, which turns off the main road at the Wynnstay Arms, hospitable-looking brick Georgian, is flanked by pleasant stone cottages.

St Mary's church, opposite, is an 1877 restoration, dark and not very attractive, but containing much of interest. The pretty marble bowl, used as a font, is by Robert Adam (1772) who was working on the Wynn town house at that time. Wynn memorials include work by Rhysbrack and Nollekens. The splendid 16 c. tomb in the north chapel commemorates John Eyton and his wife. He fought at Bosworth and was rewarded with Ruabon estates which eventually became the Wynnstay property. The robustly restored wall-painting was discovered in 1870.

The *round house* by the main road below the church was used as a lock-up for prisoners being taken from Chester to Shrewsbury gaol.

The plain stone building with a hipped roof (seen when travelling south), dramatically wedged between the curve of the road and the great railway viaduct, is a *nonconformist chapel*, 1826.

Ruthin (22). De Grey's 13 c. castle is now the sort of ruin the Romantics built as a garden ornament, and is appropriately the basis of a mature Victorian garden crowned by a rust-red Gothic pile. To explore it you must buy a meal or a drink at the hotel.

The little town climbs steeply up both sides of its sandstone ridge, with the market place (St Peter's Square) perched on the saddle between the castle and church. It is a delightful small space, dominated by the mid-18 c. Castle Hotel with its multi-dormered annexe (said to have been built by Sir Richard Clough) and a group of determinedly Tudorbethan banks (Barclays, in fact, a restoration of the early 16 c. Exmewe Hall). At the far end, through modern wrought-iron gates, rises the 1859 broach spire of *St Peter's church*, originally that of a small priest's college. Red sandstone dressings give it a Victorian air, though its core is 14 c. The interior has some character, with a richly-panelled 16 c. oak roof over the north aisle and a number of interesting monuments, including the self-made memorial carved in bog-oak and mutton-bone of a castle porter who died in 1874. The old cloisters contain two roundels of Flemish glass of about 1500.

The best secular buildings outside the Square are in Castle Street (Nantclwyd House) and Well Street (Plas Coch) at the foot and above it the Wynnstay Arms, where Borrow's guide first tasted duck. The bow-fronted 1820 Congregational chapel, also in Well Street, has character. A feature of old Ruthin houses is their timber pillared porches, some supporting oversailing upper floors. Most are 17 c. Of several 19 c.

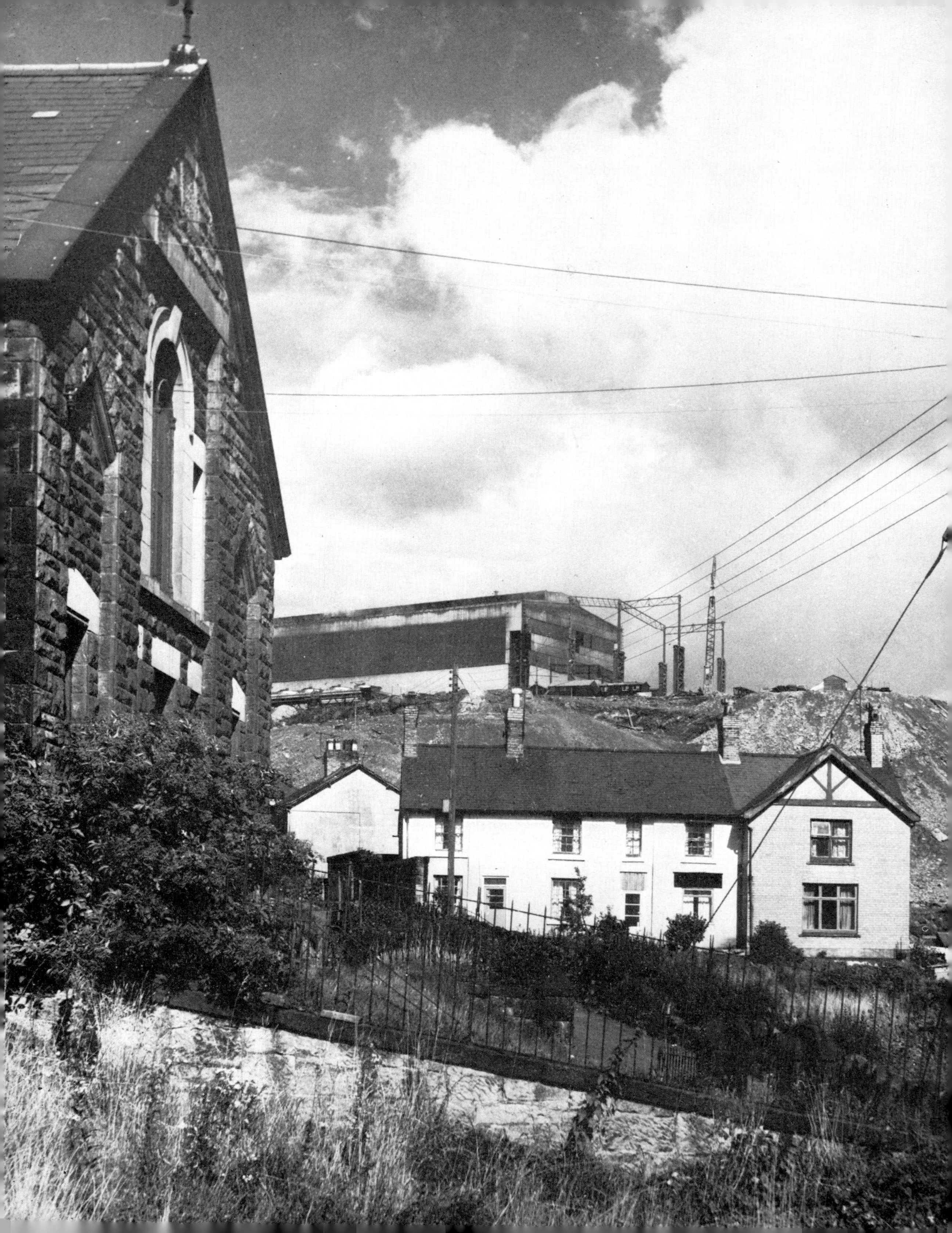

Towyn church and school by G. E. Street 1873

buildings of considerable personality occupied by the County or District Councils, the great mill on the Clwyd and the ferocious Richardsonian Fire Station (1863) in Market Street are the most striking.

On the western fringe at 113578 is *Llanfwrog* church with a strong square tower, and on the eastern fringe at 140578 is *Llanrhudd* church (mother church of Ruthin), with a 1586 monument with the Thelwalls' 14 children kneeling below them.

Towyn (12), on the flat coastlands between Rhyl and Abergele, has a remarkable group of buildings by G. E. Street, church, vicarage and school, which give a feeling of permanence in this caravan and bungalow land. The church, 1873, perhaps more admirable than lovable, is nicely linked to the vicarage by its vestry. It was built for Robert Bamford-Hesketh of Gwrych.

Trefnant (19). A Victorian village at the crossing of main roads with a richly detailed and finely maintained church of 1855 by Gilbert Scott: grey Anglesey marble columns and font. "For the capitals" (wrote the

◁ Brymbo Steel Works near Wrexham

Builder) "every group of leaves was carved by Mr Blinstone of Chester from natural specimens gathered from the woods and hedges around." Opulent late Victorian windows.

Wrexham (23), bustling with shops, shoppers and long-established market, seems Victorian/Edwardian. This is hardly surprising since the 19 c. saw the transformation of the agricultural setting of this most important market town to a land of coal and iron. Wrexham had long been the clearing house for Welsh and English goods. Its *parish church*, a 1480s rebuilding, suggests this early prosperity. It is nicely sited, just off the High Street, protected by handsome gates by Robert Davies of Bersham (q.v.). The splendid tower was copied for the chapel of Yale University. The memorial to the much-travelled Elihu Yale, one of Yale's founders, is in the churchyard beside it. The church has a strong Perpendicular character (the chancel arch shows remains of tracery of an earlier window). Restored 1867. Interesting memorials within.

Wrexham's back lanes are worth exploring for the earlier character of the town. The brick Wynnstay Arms suggests its 18 c. character.

There are several Victorian churches. *Our Lady of Dolours* (Roman Catholic) in Regent Street is by E. W. Pugin, 1857.

Commercial buildings by architects noted in North Wales for their churches include a very sober National Westminster Bank by John Gibson, Gothic shops in white brick by H. Kennedy, 1875, and several buildings by Thomas Penson including the Jacobean market hall, 1848. There is a surprising glass and slate roof over another part of the market.

Except to the east where an industrial estate interrupts the pastoral scene, Wrexham is set in a network of extraordinarily individual villages and townships which have grown up with the iron and coal industry since around 1800. Each has its stamp and character to the insider but they are visually confusing to the stranger: chapel, terrace, mine, co-op, bosky wood, iron works, farmland, miners' well-fare, terrace, chapel, more tips, more open country, detached bungalows. . . . He may have the luck to stumble on the classical remains of some great house like Brymbo Hall, stranded in industry, but sight-seeing in these parts is exploration best pursued without a guide.

125

Flintshire: Gazetteer

The number after each entry refers to the square on the map following page **144** *where the place is situated.*

Bagillt (20), an industrial village on the Dee estuary, is compressed between the marshes and steeply-rising limestone upland. This instantly remote country is riddled with lead workings and was once alive with small mining settlements (e.g. Gadlys). White-washed farms and cottages hide away up sheer brambly lanes a few hundred yards above the relentless traffic of the coast road which has by-passed what must once have been a pleasantly plain brick and stone village too late.

Bagillt was the heart of the lead ore smelting industry, not only of Flintshire but for imports from South Wales and Ireland. A quarter of the output of the United Kingdom was smelted here and there were also extensive collieries. Hey-day 18 and 19 c. *Parry's Railway Guide* (1848) describes reverently how "the dark columns of smoke, rising high to the heavens and then spreading its sable cloud through a vast expanse, indicate the large trade transacted here". The grandiose church (John Lloyd, 1839), built immediately above the village, reflects this period of prosperity.

Bodelwyddan (12), famed for its gleaming Marble Church, is on A.55 on the edge of the flat water-meadows of the Clwyd estuary; fenny country where whitebeam and poplar shine white against great grey skies.

The church, 1856–60, is by John Gibson, who for nine years had been Barry's only pupil working on the Houses of Parliament. He chiefly designed banks, including the National Westminster in Wrexham. His few churches include Bersham. Bodelwyddan's magnesium limestone spire glints in the sun, a silver pointer for miles around, 202 ft. high. It was erected by Margaret Lady Willoughby de Broke in memory of her husband in "the best period of the Decorated" and no cost spared. Marbles, including red Belgian, and alabaster, give a hard polished interior, high and rich. Caen stone "artistically wrought and choicely carved" was also imported. The soldiers' graves, tidily to the east of the bowling-green-like lawn on which the church sits, commemorate men camped locally in the First World War who unhappily died of 'flu or, some say, in a riot. The village and school are the same date as the church.

Bodelwyddan Castle, now Lowther College, lies behind the great park wall. For permission to see, write to the Bursar. Its nucleus is said to be Elizabethan. Several rebuildings include a thorough early 19 c. reconstruction. The remarkable Gothic work is all said to date from J. A. Hansom's transformation (c. 1830–42), although some parts are finer than others. It was at this period that the house was castellated and the great park wall with its huge rustic capping stones erected.

Bodfari (19) lies just above the Vale of Clwyd (q.v.) where the Mold–Denbigh road cuts through the Moel Fammau range. *Moel-y-Gaer* an Iron-Age hill fort, commands the pass. The church, largely rebuilt by T. H. Wyatt in 1865, is attractively grouped on the steeply sloping hillside with the Dinorben Arms and a white stuccoed house. A black-and-white lych-gate (rather riverside in feeling) leads by a flight of steps up to the sturdy 13 c. tower on its boldly battered base. *Bach-y-graig*. Nothing, except parts of the grand stable now incorporated in the pleasant farmhouse of that name, remains of the astonishing 16 c. "Flemish chateau" built by Sir Thomas Gresham, agent to Sir Richard Clough: a six-storey pyramid if you include three floors in the roof space. But old prints and the many-dormered Clough town house (see Ruthin) give an idea of what it was like. Sir Richard Clough was the second of Katherine of Berain's four husbands. It was said that he had proposed to her on the way to her first husband's funeral. This was as well since on the return journey she received another proposal; fortunately this suitor agreed to wait his turn and become her third. It was later the home of Gabriele Piozzi, who demolished it to build Brynbella.

Buckley (23), three miles east of Mold, sprawls haphazardly among vast clay pits now used chiefly for the brickworks. Buckley potteries, mostly producing a coarse ware, were locally famous in the 18 c. when a system of tramways took materials for export down to the newly-canalised Dee.

The parish church, St Matthew's is very cheerful indeed; almost hilarious. It is a rebuilding, 1874–1904, by John Douglas of an 1821 church by John Oates. Even the half-timbered clerestory of this pink sandstone building does not give sufficient warning of the lack of inhibition within. Light and open: the thin steel pillars, cased in oak, supporting brightly painted panels below the clerestory windows; rosettes and angels and the Beatitudes. The clock is by Lord Grimthorpe, who designed Big Ben, and the porch was built with the proceeds of the sale for publication of Ruskin's letters to the vicar's wife.

Beside the Mold road, near the U.D.C. sign, a huge hen, in ivy topiary, covers the whole wall of a cottage. It has a beady white eye and is the creation of an eminent rat-catcher.

Caerwys (19); a rectilinearly planned stone village with some plain cottages and a 19 c. feel, but dating, as a town, from 1290. It is famed for having been the seat of the Eisteddfod, instituted by royal sanction of Queen Elizabeth I in 1568 to test the claims of vagrants and others calling themselves bards and harpists, some with little justification.

The church, on the edge of the village has a sturdy tower; top added

1769. Double-aisled. Glass in window on south side of chancel includes York-type figures, *c.* 1460; Tree of Jesse fragments *c.* 1400.

The *Piccadilly Inn* was built (or enlarged) as a result of a successful bet placed on a horse named Piccadilly at the Holywell Races.

Cilcain (19). An attractive stone and whitewash village on the north slope of Moel Fammau near the limit of cultivation. Nutty lanes contour the mountain and tracks lead up to the open moor and on to the summit.

The double-aisled church with a square tower stands in its oval churchyard sheltered by sycamores at the top of the village. The north aisle, rebuilt 1746, is now screened off and used for a Sunday school. The south (restored by Ambrose Poynter in 1845) has tremendous angels on its hammerbeams (perhaps from Basingwerk Abbey). Perpendicular east window has 16 c. figures re-set in clear glass; the Virgin, SS John and Peter and, surprisingly, St George. The plain stone schoolhouse opposite the church is dated 1799.

The wooded valley of the Alyn, below Cilcain, has been suburbanised by a sewage works, very municipal in white concrete and viridian green chain-link fencing. The stream here at times runs dry, having disappeared mysteriously into a swallet near the Loggerheads. A mile to the south of the village, near the head of a remote valley running up towards Moel Fammau, is *Brithdir Mawr*, a small hall house, thought until recently, when a medieval central hearth was discovered, to be late 16 c.; altered and a floor put in 1638–42. It has timber mullioned windows of the pre-glass type.

Penbedw stone circle: remains of a stone circle, probably *c.* 2,500, now in an oak copse, can be seen from the lay-by on A.541, in Penbedw Park. It was not mentioned by writers before the 18 c.

Clwydian Range, the (see under Denbighshire).

BODELWYDDAN ▷

Looking towards Snowdon from the Vale of Clwyd near CWM

Cwm (19) is appropriately sited in a little cwm at the north end of the Clwydian Range immediately below Moel Hiraddug.

The church is wedged into the side of the wooded hill, buttressed by its sturdy west wall, crowned by a double bell-cote; single cell, stepping up with the contours. The deep porch has generous benches. The Perpendicular east window has fragments *c.* 1500.

There are several good springs in the parish; Ffynnon Asa produces four to five million gallons a day.

Diserth (19). The good springs and the falls, in the miniature limestone gorge in the middle of the village, which feed the stream which runs through it, are as attractive to tourists seeking relative quiet during a seaside holiday at nearby Rhyl or Prestatyn as they were to those who made use of this abundant waterpower for Diserth's numerous mills (all now gone).

The church is below the falls; G. G. Scott restored it in 1875. The Perpendicular east window is very golden and has many early fragments: upper part *c.* 1498; lower (a Jesse), early 16 c.

Diserth Castle's military life was short-lived: built 1241 and destroyed by Henry III, 1263. Little remains. The town was established in 1248.

Bodrhyddan Hall, ½ mile west (open to the public), consists of W. E. Nesfield's confident red brick additions (1872–3) to a brown brick rebuilding of 1696, to which a new dining-room had been added in the late 18 c. Attractively cheerful, and lots to look at.

Ffynnongroyw (19) on the coast road has a late and astonishingly dull-looking church by G. E. Street, 1883; evidently an off-day. Only historians and addicts will risk their lives among the traffic which grinds through this unfortunate industrial village to park and find the key. It is not easy on this stretch of the estuary to imagine Mary calling the cattle home across the sands of Dee.

Flint (20). "It is scarcely worth the traveller's while to visit the poor town of Flint . . ." wrote the usually enthusiastic Henry Wyndham (1781). He might not change his mind today, although Flint's new housing may be cheering the inhabitants. This is the more disappointing since Flint sounds so promising; created a chartered borough and built to a rectilinear plan by Edward I who began his castle here on the banks of the Dee, in summer 1277.

The castle was built on a rocky platform, "the Flint", which jutted into the channel: now green salt marshes have taken over. In spite of being cheek by jowl with enormous industry and spreading housing, the castle gives a powerful sense of remoteness, looking out over the river with three empty miles between it and the Wirral peninsula. It is square on plan with corner turrets: one a detached donjon originally connected by a drawbridge. It was at Flint that Richard II was taken after his capture by Bolingbroke and where even his greyhound deserted him (Froissart).

The gaol (in 1968 the local Territorial H.Q.), hard by the castle and

Landscape near DYSERTH ▷

128

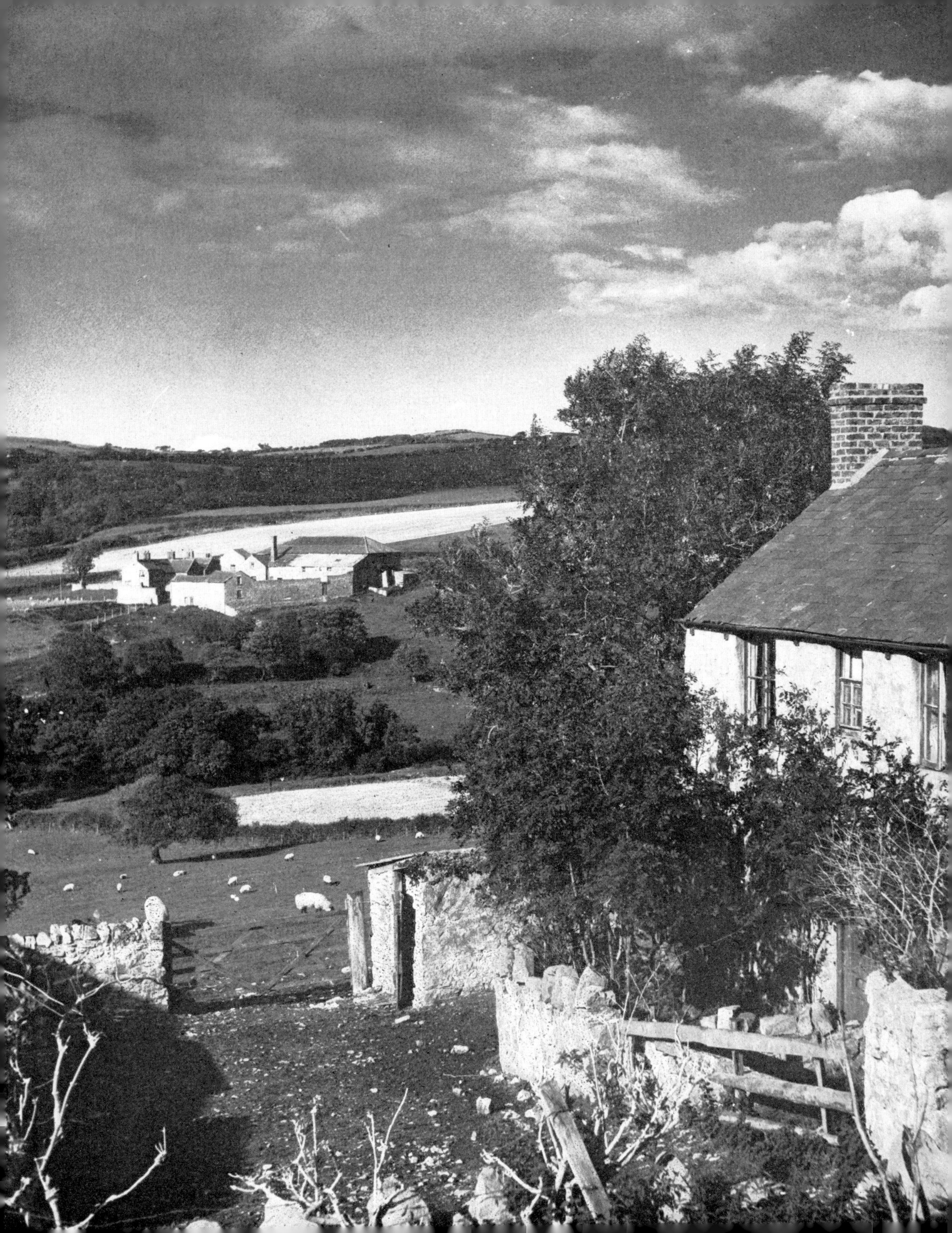

FLINT Castle

partly masking its entrance, is by Joseph Turner of Chester, 1785.

The attractive ex-town hall, Gothic revival freely interpreted, is by John Welch (1840).

Flint was a port for Chester as recently as 1876, if not later. Vessels discharged into lighters here.

Gwaenysgor (19). This remote-seeming hamlet is only one mile from Prestatyn (q.v.) as the herring-gull flies, but 600 ft. above it. High thorn hedges and narrow lanes blocked by cows coming home for milking, above; bungalow avenues below.

The parish church is small and unexpected; single cell with unusually deep south porch. There is a curious timber arch or frame in the doorway: massive oak boldly carved with a childish but attractive incised pattern of flowers, crosses and other decoration. Inside, carved stone coffin-lids. A walled, four-acre Neolithic village was found on the summit of Bryn Llwyn just north of the village.

Halkyn (20). *Halkyn Mountain* is sparse limestone country spattered with cottages (built for quarrymen and lead miners), sheep and gorse and riddled with old shafts and rights of way; distant and separate, rising above the 900 ft. contour.

Moel-y-Gaer, an Iron Age fort, 600 ft. diameter and nearly circular, is only a five-minute stroll from Rhosesmor on B.5123, but it feels like the roof of the world. Patrol the earthworks for enormous views. Flintshire seems remarkably wooded and agricultural; laid-out country sheltered from the south-west by the long Clwydian Range which blocks the way to the rest of Wales and bounded on the north-east by the broad Dee estuary with the Wirral, the Mersey and Liverpool beyond. The heavy industry of the coastal strip clings to the river bank: a pink ribbon of tiled roofs with dramatic cooling towers and high chimneys standing out of the haze.

Halkyn, below the mountain, is an attractive estate village. Plain stone houses often with hooded lintels, the Britannia Inn, and a large yellow stone parish church by J. Douglas, rather harsh-textured but handsome. The castellated lodges belong to *Halkyn Castle* (not open), which is by J. C. Buckler (watercolour painter), 1824, extended by Douglas. It was built by the Grosvenors, when once they were refused admittance at a local inn where they normally stayed for the Holywell Races.

Hawarden (20) is only six miles west of Chester and is a fairly compact, stone and brick English type of village at the gates of the castle. For centuries Hawarden controlled the route into North Wales (Chester–Conway): the road then ran immediately east of the *Old Castle*, which was originally a Norman structure destroyed and rebuilt in the 13 c., eventually to be made untenable by Cromwell and into a satisfactorily romantic ruin (stone faced brickwork where necessary) in the early 19 c. Now it is sympathetically overgrown with ivy and bracken, and not overtrim.

Hawarden Castle (not open) lies a few hundred yards below the Old Castle so can easily be seen from it. It is the result of the Gothicising of Broadlane Hall, the 18 c. house of the antiquarian, Sir Stephen Glynne. Nash put forward a scheme in 1807 but it was actually done by Thomas Cundy, 1809–10. The castle's claim to fame is probably more historical than architectural because, through marriage into the Glynne family, it became the home of Mr Gladstone, the Prime Minister. The Gladstones are commemorated in the *parish church* in no half-hearted manner, and this building contains much for the 19 c. enthusiast. It had been restored by James Harrison, 1855–6, only to catch fire the following year. It was then rebuilt by Sir Gilbert Scott: sandstone Perpendicular with a low tower at the crossing which also had a spire and pinnacles. The Gladstone memorial, by Sir William Richmond, depicts Mr and Mrs Gladstone in a marble ship ploughing their way through the sea of life. The east and west windows are by Burne-Jones (the west said to be his last). Reredos by Scott. Rood by Giles G. Scott, who also designed the candlesticks in the memorial chapel. Other windows by Frampton and Richmond and Wailes.

St Deiniol's Library, close to the church, was designed by John Douglas of Chester, 1899–1906, to house Gladstone's books which had long overflowed from the Temple of Peace, his study at Hawarden Castle.

Hawarden civil airport (Chester) is a mile east of the village.

Ewloe Castle is a romantic ruin built by the Welsh Princes; a D-shaped tower supposedly dates from the time of Llewelyn the Great and the remainder was probably built by Llewelyn ap Gruffydd in 1257. The Ministry has sensitively rescued it from an unintelligible bramble-choked thicket. It lies across fields, off A.55, three miles west of Hawarden. A sudden surprise: open oakwood with mossy lawns and, below among the trees, a steep moat and the curtain wall and towers built above the junction of the two streams which can be heard rushing through the woods far below. It was in this dingle that the Welsh had defeated Henry II's troops many years before.

Holywell (19) was long famed both for its holy well and for the industry which harnessed this abundant source of water. It was also a coaching station on the North Wales road. The busy high street, cheerfully plastered and painted, is at the top of the town. Religion and industry are sited by the springs and water courses which fed the grand series of factory pools below, dropping down to the Dee at Greenfield. One source of this tremendous quantity of pure water is said to be the River Alyn (see Cilcain).

Panton Place, 1816, brick and architectural (just off the High Street) is fortunately now being restored for Old People's Homes.

Bank Place is among the last surviving terraces of pre-brick workers' housing; humble and vernacular.

The Roman Catholic church (between High Street and parish church)

HALKYN

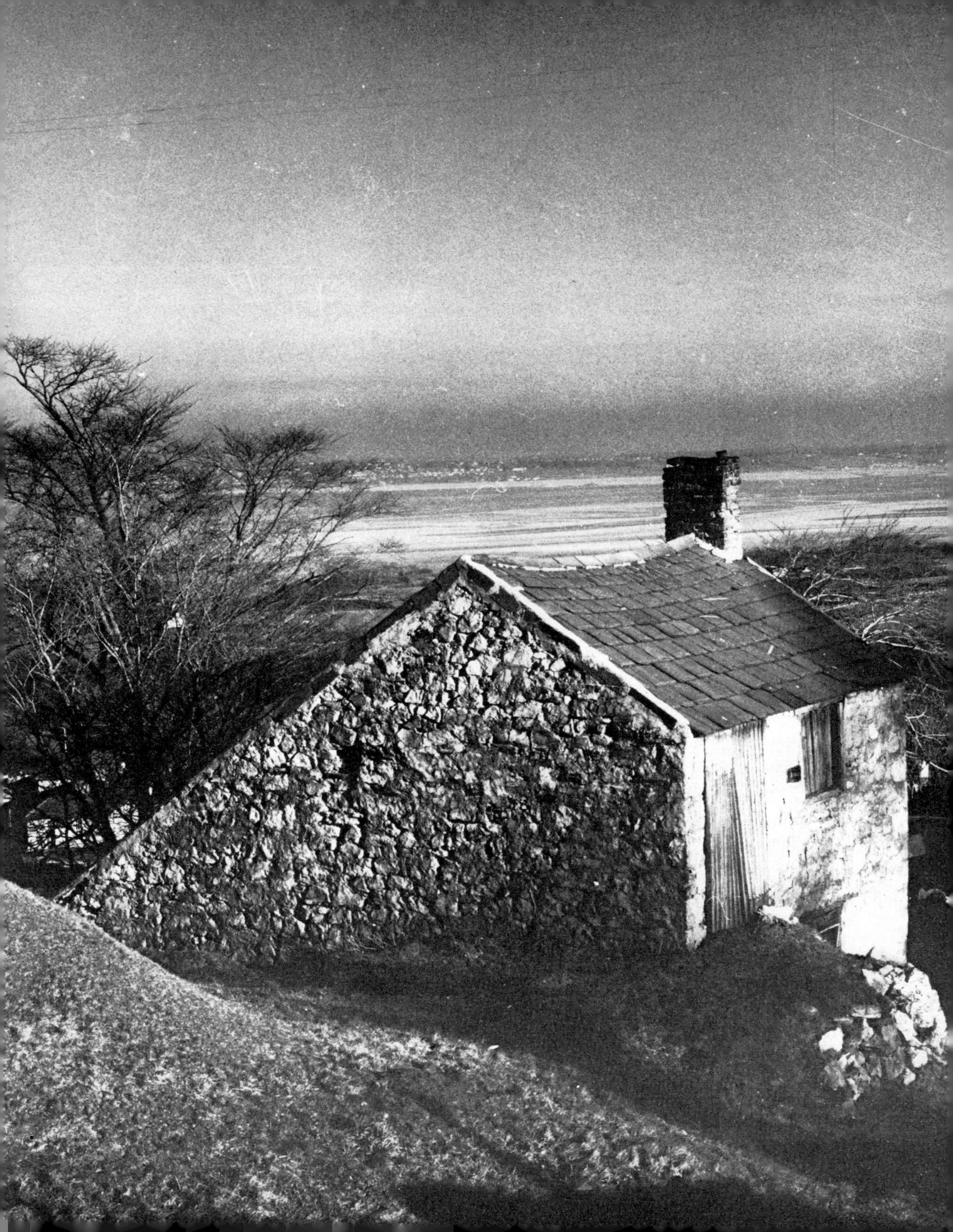

is by Joseph Scoles, 1833, but in his classic manner. Much altered 1895 by the parish priest (Beauclerk).

St Beuno's, the parish church, 1770, but founded by the saint, is close to St Winifred's Well; this plain 18 c. building makes a nice contrast to the glassy late medieval chapel. It is reached by a steep path and is so tucked under the hill that a peal from its tower could not be heard in the town; instead a bell (still kept in the church) was rung round the streets to call people to services. Inside the church is disappointingly dingy and the galleries swoop down oppressively. Restored and modernised by Matthew Wyatt of London, 1884–5, after which "It was difficult, even for regular members of the congregation... to conceive that the old building with its box-pews, in which they had worshipped, was capable of being so thoroughly transformed."

St Winifred's Chapel stands over the well on the sloping hillside. It was rebuilt in 1490–1500 by Lady Margaret Beaufort, Countess of Derby, who also built several churches in the district (Mold, Hope, and Gresford). As might be expected from such a patroness, the chapel is elegant and sophisticated but has been under repair for so long that no one, when asked, seemed to remember what it is like inside. But its undercroft—the shrine of the well—which is at ground level when approached from below, is very fine. Fan vaulting shelters the star-shaped pool; the boss over the centre is richly carved with details of the surprising life of St Winifred. At the base of the star there is a small rectangular pool with steps down into it for those who come to be healed. This they have done for centuries; indeed it is the only shrine in Britain to have an unbroken record of pilgrimage. Until recently a heap of abandoned crutches lay by the pool. The moss and candles give a sense of continuity. The water is cloudy from the limestone through which it flows, but tastes good.

Below the shrine is the great succession of factory pools which

◁ The Dee Estuary from Brynford Hall above HOLYWELL

provided power for the copper sheet-rolling (see Parys Mountain in Anglesey), wool and other mills. What was until recently an industrial archaeologist's dream site now provides little of interest. These pools drop down past the ruins of *Basingwerk Abbey*, chiefly 13 c., which was founded here 1132. Little of the church survives but the monastic buildings give an idea of its importance. Now an oasis among gasometers and factory sheds.

Holy Trinity, *Greenfield* (an industrial village at the junction with the coast road) is by Ewan Christian (1870).

Holywell Junction is bold brick with plaster decoration, a once-grand though small station by Francis Thompson for the Chester–Holyhead Railway. The engine shed is attractively plain with blank arcading.

Pantasaph, a mile to the west of Holywell, is a Franciscan Friary founded in 1858. Architecturally North Oxford. *St David's Church*, (1849–52), beside the Friary, was designed by T. H. Wyatt for Viscount Feilding, then a Protestant (who had inherited Downing). He was converted to the Roman Catholic faith and wished the building to be so too. A lawsuit followed which he won. He then employed A. W. Pugin to give a Catholic finish to Wyatt's design (Brynford and Gorsedd were built for the Anglicans to replace Pantasaph). Pugin designed various statues and other fittings (exhibited in the Great Exhibition) for Pantasaph: some have disappeared, as has his pulpit. Those of the Virgin Mary, St David and St Asaph survive. There are two recent glowing windows by Harry Clarke, Dublin. The poets Francis Thompson, Coventry Patmore and Alice Meynell all stayed at Pantasaph.

(The site of Holywell Racecourse, now abandoned, is to the south of the monastery).

Hope (23), on the river Alyn, is only five miles north of industrial Wrexham and is linked to it by strange country: industrial, mining, housing and pockets of agriculture. The parish had an early colliery and mixes industry with mountain and farmland. Best appreciated from *Caergwrle Castle*, a short steep walk above Caergwrle village. It was constructed in the late 13 c. to command the pass; now unkempt. Caergwrle boasted a spa around 1890; its life was brief.

The parish church is in Hope: its square stone tower stands high above the village street of red and grey houses. A Stanley church, that is, built by Lady Margaret Beaufort; it has an excellent brief guide. Double-aiseld and Perpendicular with a fine but incomplete east window in the south aisle (now incorporating the Te Deum from the north aisle), 1498–1500. Early 17 c. pulpit and 17 c. effigy of Sir John Trevor and his wife who built the great house of *Plas Teg*.

Bryn Yorkin is the attractive 17 c. stone farmhouse with interesting outbuildings (barns on crucks and 1796 corn kiln) on a little limestone plateau near the top of Hope Mountain. Not open but seen from farm road.

There is a weir and derelict mill at *Bridge End* on the Alyn where the new bridge was constructed in 1838.

Llanasa (19) is a snug stone village in a small valley on the limestone plateau. Only two miles from the coast but, like Gwaenysgor (q.v.) in another world.

The double-aisled church with its very flat arched arcade is 16 c., restored 1739 and again in 1877 by G. E. Street. The Perpendicular east windows have early 16 c. glass which traditionally came from Basingwerk Abbey. Good octagonal font, probably of same date. The furnishings also include a fine twelve-branched chandelier (the inscription, "This candelstick was erected solely by the industry of Edw. Foulkes 1758", suggests possible lack of harmony in the parish at that period); and two small but attractive polished brass memorial plates, 1830 and 1836, in the west end.

Unfortunately the village school has recently been closed, taking life out of the heart of the village, but a racy red lion decorates the pub.

The parish has two attractive early 17 c. stone houses (with 19 c. additions) on prominent sites. They are not open and are considerably altered or modernised within. Hen-

133

blas (1645) is in the village, and Golden Grove (*c*. 1600) basks in the view from the Gop Hill. It was built by Edward Morgan a Flintshire gentleman who had interest in "cole workes" in Bagillt.

Maelor, the (Flintshire Detatched) (24, 27) (see page 141).

Marford (24), even more curious than the Maelor, since Marford and Hoseley form another much smaller enclave of Flintshire, this time entirely surrounded by Denbighshire, accounted for by an ancient boundary dispute.

Marford is an all-out Gothic hamlet astride the Chester–Wrexham main road. Built 1805 by George Boscawen whose wife had inherited her share of the Trevor estate (see Trevalyn, Rossett) in 1795. He is said to have known Horace Walpole. The gingerbread cottages with their iron lattice windows, eyes and cross decoration, were originally thatched. The Trevor Arms, an exceptionally attractive inn, has ogee arches over the iron windows and coach-house door.

Moel Fammau (22) (see Denbighshire, page 104).

Mold (23), the small county town, is a no-nonsense place whose authenticity is somehow underlined by the fact that it featured in that fantastic Intelligence enterprise of World War II, retold in the story *The Man who Never Was*.

The town is set in wooded farmland on the little River Alyn which once turned its important cotton mills. The main street is a down-to-earth mixture of brick, stone, plaster and mock half-timbering. The market held in it, is equally diverse in its offerings: spools of yarn, plastic lace, dahlias and cabbages.

The *parish church* stands proudly at the top of the street; recent civic "improvements" have made its slightly withdrawn setting rather open and obvious. A fine town church built by Lady Margaret Beaufort; yellow-grey sandstone; big windowed; Perpendicular; finely carved and battlemented; beasts natural and imaginary run round the string courses. The tower, rebuilt in convincing 1773 Gothic, is said to be by Joseph Turner, who seems to have been sacked from Chirk Castle that year. Inside it is broad, spacious and civic and again thoroughly Perpendicular, except for Sir Gilbert Scott's 1856 shallow pentagonal east end. Restored by John Douglas of Chester 1878 and later. Resurrection window by Burne Jones. Richard Wilson, the painter, is buried in the churchyard.

Just above the church, facing down the street, is the very attractive *Wesleyan church* (1828) with a paper-like façade of yellow-grey sandstone, beautifully grained; pinnacled with angle buttresses; very restrained and rather Soanesque.

Bailey Hill, which dominates the town, is the site of the *c*. 1100 motte and bailey castle which was Mold's *raison d'être*. It constantly changed hands in border warfare. Now a public park crowned by a beech-ringed clump. Below there is a 20 c. stone circle, an Eisteddfod Gorsedd, beside which the U.D.C. has erected a sign: THROWING OF STONES IS PROHIBITED.

The Welsh Presbyterian Church on the Ruthin road with a big Corinthian portico is by W. W. Gwyther of London, 1863, who also built the Free Church (Gothic) on the way in from Chester.

The vast new *County Offices*, 1967, designed by the County Architect, are outside the town to the east. It is a puzzling reflection on 20 c. computerisation and the streamlining of office techniques that so much floor space should be required to administer Flintshire. At its best where the design is straightforward: sympathetically sited in wooded parkland. Had the offices been built in Mold they would certainly have overpowered their county town.

The Allelujah Monument is about one mile west of Mold in a field by the Cilcain road. An obelisk, erected by Nehemiah Griffith, Esq., in 1736 near his seat Rhual, to mark the spot where, early in the 5 c., the Britons, under St Garmon defeated the combined armies of the Saxons and the Picts. Warner describes how the Britons, "repeating the word Allelujah as they rushed upon the foe, with a full persuasion of its powerful efficacy, so terrified the Pagan host, that they fled at the third repetition of it, and were pursued by the conquering Britons with terrible slaughter". The double echo, peculiar to this site, may also have added to their terror.

Several good houses (open on written application only) were built near Mold in the 16 and early 17 c.: peaceful times following the Tudor accession. Plas Teg, Nerquis Hall, Fferm and *Rhual*. This attractive three-gabled house, 1634, which can be seen across the road from the obelisk, is brick which was rendered in the early 19 c. A charming walled formal garden survives in front of the house, with wrought-iron tulip decoration surmounting its corner summer-houses.

Pentrehobyn Hall (not open), the stone 16–17 c. house seen from the Pontblyddyn road, has long been famed for its llettyau; eight small cells, each 7 by 5 ft., with low entrance and brick vaulted roofs. They are believed to have been for poor travellers, but it seems more likely that they were storage rooms. There is a guardian's (? steward's) room up a flight of steps at the end.

Tower (may be open on written application), to the south of the town, 1380 with later additions and enthusiastic Victorian embellishment, was a small fortified border house. The Mayor of Chester was hanged from the barrel vaulted roof of the hall in 1450, having been captured in Mold Market. Much altered inside.

Mostyn (19) is on the Dee estuary near its mouth. The Mostyn family has been part of the history of Flintshire since medieval times. *Mostyn Dock*, now modernised, still plies a busy trade, although the entrance is a very narrow gutter at low water. Mostly imports of pulp and exports of scrap. It was originally a colliery port trading with Ireland, but the Dee channel shifted in the 18 c. and with it much shipping. There was also passenger trade; the Liverpool ferry ran until the 1890s. Mostyn was important for copper smelting, cockles, shrimps and flatfish, and its coal mine. The coal here is very near the surface. Indeed, within recent memory a miner appeared through the scullery floor in one of the cottages near the river; the mangle disappeared into the hole. The mines are now closed but sinister air shafts, flooded by the tide, can be seen near the dock. Mostyn Park is riddled with mine workings where surface coal has been dug for centuries.

Mostyn Hall (not open) has been described by generations of Tourist Guides, including of course, Pennant. The present 17 c. hall (considerably enlarged in the 1840s by Ambrose Poynter who did the church) is an extension of an earlier house, itself very close to another, Porth Mawr. The whole makes a very attractive group.

Tradition has it that the Earl of Richmond (soon to be Henry VII) narrowly missed capture at Mostyn Hall. His pursuers found his place laid for dinner but were told it was a custom of the house always to set an extra place for unexpected visitors. They were then themselves delayed by the practice of this hospitality while he made his escape from the port below.

Dry Bridge Lodge at Rhual Mostyn is a hilarious (inhabited) 19 c. folly, easily seen since it tops a tunnel on the Mostyn–Whitford road. A ride through the park, crossing the road at right-angles, tunnels through the lodge. This ride runs from Mostyn Hall to Whitford near the church. (*Mostyn Railway Station*, disappearing, was by Francis Thompson.)

Nannerch (19). A pleasant small off-the-mainroad village. Stone houses and trees. The church is by T. H. Wyatt, 1852, and is very period. It also has a Grinling Gibbons monument, 1693, a cherub weeping for a member of the Mostyn family, and a lovely brass chandelier with a dove bequeathed 1826. The glass of the small Royal arms in the north aisle is *c.* 1500.

Nerquis (23), two miles south of Mold. A hamlet consisting of church, farm, cottages and pub.

St Mary's, very restored and enlarged in the 19 c. and since, has a neat domesticated broached shingled spire; a good brass chandelier; well-lettered panels, giving list of benefactors, under the tower; and a sedilla made out of old rood screen material, known as the Cadnair Fair, the Virgin Mary's Seat.

Nerquis Hall 1638–40 (open on written application) is an upstanding 17 c. house to which battlemented wings and stable were added in 1797. The folly (a small castle) and orangery, with cast-iron Gothic tracery (Benjamin Gummow), are *c.* 1815. The 19 c. porch has been rescued by Clough Williams-Ellis and is now at Portmerion.

Leeswood Hall (not open) has two remarkably fine iron gates by the Davies brothers of Bersham (q.v.) known as the Black Gates and the White Gates, which separate the park from the public road.

Newmarket (see Trelawnyd).

Northop (20). A small village busy road junction has a big Perpendicular church with an impressive five-stage tower, pinnacled and battlemented. Much restored 1839 and later by John Douglas, 1877, who

Drybridge Lodge, MOSTYN

135

designed all the pews and woodwork. Dark inside, because of rubble walls and much Victorian glass. In the corner of the graveyard is a simple stone building with three-light mullioned windows and the roof giving in. This was the old Free School, founded in 1606.

Offa's Dyke (19, 23, 26) was constructed during the reign of Offa, King of Mercia (757–96). It follows the fringe of hill country from *Prestatyn*, where it met the sea in the north, to the Bristol Channel, and defined the westerly limit of English settlement. It thus divided the coastal strip of Flintshire, along the Dee estuary, from the main part of the county. This great earthwork can be picked out on the 1 in. O.S. map. E.g. in the parishes of Trelawnyd, Whitford and Treuddyn (Flintshire); and Llanfynydd, Coedpoeth, Rhosllanerchrugog (here it is only ¾ mile from Wat's Dyke) and Chirk in Denbighshire.

Overton (24) (see the Maelor).

Penley (27) (see the Maelor).

Penymynydd (23). *St John's* church is at the cross-roads two miles south of Hawarden. It is a spiky 19 c. building 1843, designed by J. C. Buckler. The rector, the Rev. John Ellis Troughton entirely decorated it (from designs by Pullan), without detriment to his parochial duties. He evidently enjoyed himself enormously. His chancel screen, arcaded gallery, murals, painted ceiling and glass have all been restored with loving care and are in sparkling condition.

Pontblyddyn (23), four miles southeast of Mold, has its name spelt out in a hedge in the village which is on the River Alyn. The land above rises towards Hope Mountain: wooded valleys and fields interspersed with old industry. Pleasant plain stone cottages result from local quarrying. The parish church, 1836, is by John Lloyd. Two houses which may be open on written application are:

Fferm (visible behind its orchard from the road) is a very attractive 16 c. passage house with its original screen and a slightly later porch. It became a farm house in the 1790s. The scale of its fireplaces is huge in its pleasantly modest rooms.

Plas Teg is a *tour de force*, particularly if seen on a late summer evening when the sun lights its four corner turrets. At other times its

Plas Teg, PONTBLYDDYN ▷

sunless site gives it a grim aspect, which may be why no one has ever lived there for long. This handsome Jacobean house was built by Sir John Trevor (a son of Trevalyn) *c*. 1610. A square plan with a great hall down the centre, now divided. Not of interest inside.

Prestatyn (19) is seaprated from the sea and its caravan and holiday camps by the Holyhead Railway. Anyone doubting that trees will survive on this coastal plain might spare a glance for the beeches to the east of the town. Prestatyn is for retirement to one's dream bungalow and holidays. It also has an Edwardian feel. Offa's Dyke (q.v.) joined the sea near here.

Christchurch and the vicarage, 1863, are by T. H. Wyatt. Viewed from the railway footbridge the old retort house of the gasworks looks as if it could have provided inspiration for the 1960s' avant garde.

Talacre Abbey, 1824–7, high above Point of Air, is a Benedictine nunnery (the church is open). The house was designed by Thomas Jones of Chester for Sir Pyers Mostyn; it

Fferm, near PONTBLYDDYN

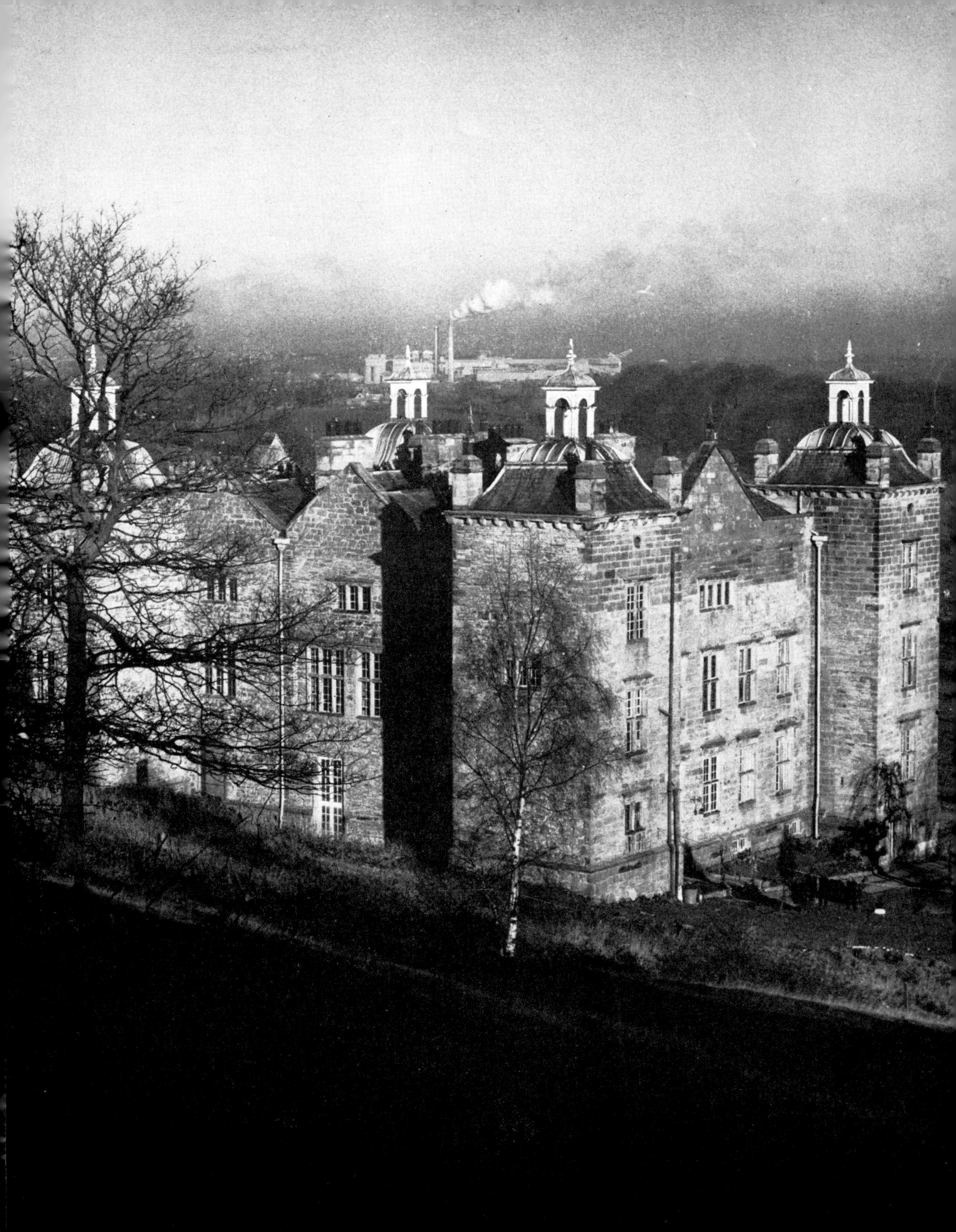

was immediately burnt down and rebuilt. Parry says it is "after a design of the late Thomas Harrison". Pleasant stables.

Point of Air, once so well named when nothing but miles of dunes, is now bungalowed and caravanned. It was a station on the Liverpool–Holyhead telegraph system. The lighthouse is disused but the coalmine operates. The huge expanse of the Dee estuary is famous for waders and wildfowl, particularly during passage and in winter.

Rhuddlan (12), at the lowest crossing of the Clwyd, and just on the Welsh side of Offa's Dyke, was a key point in English–Welsh wars until 1300. Only a mile from Rhyl, but in a different world. The English won the Battle of Rhuddlan in 796 and intermittently held sway over parts of Flintshire, but probably not much beyond the Dyke. Rhuddlan was the royal seat of Gruffydd ap Llewelyn in 1063 when it was sacked by Harold. The Normans constructed a motte and bailey castle: a town with church and mint was centred on the castle. After two more centuries of skirmish and warfare Llewelyn surrendered to Edward I here in 1277 and in 1278 his Master of Works, James of St George, began new castles at Rhuddlan and Flint (q.v.). In August that year 1,800 ditchers were employed in canalising the Clwyd so that the castle could be supplied from the sea (the river then ran close under its walls). It is concentrically planned: square inner ward with great round towers and gatehouses at the corners, making it look diamond-shaped on plan; protected by a curtain wall and wet and dry moats. 17 c. demolition following the Civil War has left parts of the masonry in a grotto-like state which must have delighted the 18 c. tourists. Originally the walls were plastered and painted white. Edward I established a chartered borough. The present streets to the north and north-west of the castle are roughly on a line of those of 1278.

Rhuddlan Bridge was remodelled in 1595 and since. The 14 c. stone bridge had already replaced an earlier timber one. The town quay, just below, was used until the railway took its business.

St Mary's Church lies downstream of the bridge; double-aisled, large and much restored. There are pale murals of illuminated manuscripts on the aisle walls.

A *Dominican friary* stood on the site of the farm, Plas Newydd. Edward I wanted to build a cathedral in Rhuddlan to replace St Asaph as head of the see. Unfortunately this came to nothing.

Rhyl (12). A Victorian resort at the mouth of the Clwyd; bright and breezy, but without the architectural stamp of Llandudno (q.v.). The sense of horizontal sprawl is perhaps inevitable in flat country with almost no high buildings. Bay windows abound in Rhyl; a surprising number, restrained "Georgian" in character, survive above much-modernised shop fronts. Acres more, out-and-out Victorian, in yellow and pink brick terraces, advertise holiday flatlets with television. Beyond are miles of holiday camp and bungalow development.

Rhyl's churches reflect her prosperity:

Holy Trinity, 1835–37, by Thomas Jones of Chester; humble, with cast-iron Perpendicular tracery in the windows; transepts enlarged to its present cruciform plan 1851–2. In 1861, Sir Gilbert Scott built *St Thomas's* on the next-door plot, its immense and rather extraordinary spire (203 ft.) completely dwarfing the earlier church. Rather grand inside. As the town spread west *St John's*, 1885–6, was built by David Walker of Liverpool. Dullish outside, but its octagonal nave makes an interesting space within.

St Asaph (19), on the Clwyd, 2½ miles upstream from Rhuddlan, should be a quiet little town now that it is by-passed, and its pleasant sloping High Street be restored to equanamity.

The small *Cathedral*, cruciform with a low tower from 1385 at the crossing, sits on a tidy lawn which borders the High street (NO SMOKING in the precincts.) It has had an exceedingly chequered history. 1869–75, Sir Gilbert Scott thoroughly restored the cathedral; the exterior was recased and the stone choir screen removed, as were the nave and aisle ceilings which Lewis Wyatt had stuccoed in 1822. In 1809, a "Mr Turner" (see Chirk and Mold) had restored the choir screen. Presumbaly the cathedral suffered 18 c. neglect. It was burnt by the Roundheads and also by Owen Glendower (roofless for most of the 15 c.), having been rebuilt after burning by Edward I's men. After all this it is churlish not to love the restored building rather more. The nave gives a great sense of width, but the total effect seems to lack climax. In the south transept there is good heraldic glass by Francis Eginton of Birmingham, formerly in the east window.

The *parish church*, lower down the High street, is double-aisled of Perpendicular character with some good 17 and 18 c. memorial tablets.

The *Ebenezer Chapel*, 1845, is a good brown brick building in the Gamig (turning by the Red Lion).

Sealand (20) is on the right bank of the Dee, really in the Wirral peninsula. As the name indicates it is flat reclaimed land. The Dee itself was canalised in the 18 c. The Dee bore, a straight wave coming up with the tide is well worth seeing. Roads are ruled lines. There is a garden city and a pre-war airfield with 1930-ish R.A.F. buildings. Driving down the main road from Liverpool to the Queensferry Bridge there are most heartening views of the Welsh hills.

St Bartholemew's Church, isolated near a windy road-junction, is by John Douglas, 1867.

Shotton is a sea of industry (notably Summers' immense steelworks), Edwardian industrial housing in Ruabon brick, and later development. The saltings and pools in the steelworks are renowned for migrant and river birds. 25,000 swallows roost in the reed-beds in August. Queensferry Bridge is a bottle-neck for traffic coming into Wales. There are good views of the old bridge from the new; like a giant's Meccano construction with seemingly over-heavy sections.

St Ethelwold's, 1898–1902, is a very good John Douglas church, ("Douglas early-pointed"). Likeable, simple and open in form and thoroughly well thought out in detail.

Trelawnyd (Newmarket) (19) is in the

high limestone country, steep valleys and stone walls.

St Michael and All Angels restored in 1724 was very thoroughly gone over by John Douglas in 1895. Result gloomy and overdone. There is a medieval stone cross in the churchyard.

The *Gop Cairn* is an enormous cairn crowning the Gop Hill, turf-covered and hollowed out. A place for a summer's day. Vast views. Never properly excavated; no finds, but thought to be Bronze Age.

The *Gop Bone Cave*, nearby, was explored 1886 and 1908. It was used in the 4th and 3rd millennia B.C. Bones found included those of woolly rhino and hyena. There was also a chamber of regularly coursed limestone packed with human bones.

Tremeirchion (19) looks down on the Vale of Clwyd from the east. The church is attractively sited in the village. Single cell, once divided by a rood screen, with a musicians' gallery at the west end. North transepts added 1864. Interesting tombs and glass. See 15 c. St Anne in curtained-off vestry; and 1625 portrait on south of nave. Mr Piozzi, whose memorial is in the church, was Mrs Thrale's (Dr Johnson's friend) Italian music master whom she married after Mr Thrale's decease. They demolished the stables of Bach-y-graig (see Bodfari) to build Brynbella (not open), hence its attractive Welsh–Italian name. Drawings for this house, perhaps the most civilised in the Vale, were exhibited by J. C. Meade in the Royal Academy, 1794.

St Beuno's Well is beside the cottage (once an inn) with the glass name plate. Water gushes through a gargoyle. This spring probably gave the site importance from time before memory. Behind, in the Paleolithic caves many animal remains including a mammoth tooth and a rhino jaw, and a flint knife were found (say 25,000 B.C.). In Ffynnon Beuno, the lower cave, stratification may have been confused by flooding, but Man was definitely in Cae Gwyn cave before the final advance of the ice.

St Beuno's College is a Jesuit foundation where Gerard Manley

RHUDDLAN castle

Brynbella, near TREMEIRCHION

Hopkins lived for a time. Joseph Hansom and Son made considerable additions, 1873–4. A spiky chapel crowns the nearby hill: Our Lady of Sorrows.

Treuddyn (23), 1873, must be one of T. H. Wyatt's most uninviting churches, but it is worth penetrating for the very good early glass which has been set in the side windows of the apsidal east end. The strong glowing colours in the left lower north panel are said to be the earliest glass in North Wales (very early 14 c.). The tracery light of this window and the heraldic glass of the south window are c. 1330. Finely drawn Virgin in south window, late 14 c.

Wat's Dyke (23), an intermittent earthwork, was constructed before Offa's Dyke (q.v.) as an earlier conception of the Mercian Frontier, constructed after Mercia broke through to the sea at Chester. It met the Dee estuary at Holywell and ran south and east. It can be picked out on a 1 in. Ordnance Survey map in the Flintshire parishes of Buckley and Hope. In Denbighshire: Llay and Ruabon.

Whitewell (24) (see Iscoyd, the Maelor).

Whitford (19) was the parish of the intrepid 18 c. traveller and antiquarian, Mr Thomas Pennant. Downing, his house, has gone, but his memorial graces the parish church, a disconsolate muse kneeling below (Westmacott jr., c. 1798). The church is in an attractive hamlet of solid stone houses standing above a road junction. The steps up to it lead under a lych-gate with a room built over it. The church was rebuilt, 1843–6, by Ambrose Poynter, embodying much of the old. Spacious; four-centred arches separate nave and aisles. Much of antiquarian interest, as might be expected in Pennant's church, including inscribed stones, 6–10 c. Also fine brass chandelier, 18 c. Memorials include that of Pennant's "friend and servant", Louis Gold, and one Caroline Griffith who died at Downing "at an awfully sudden hour but in holy peace".

Maen Achwyfan (128788) stands at a junction of early tracks; it may be simply St Cwyfan's stone; others claim it to be a stone of lamentation, a station on the Holywell pilgrimage. It stands near the road 1½ miles east of the village. It was erected c. 1000: a wheel cross about 11 ft. high covered with Celtic patterns (also, it is said, the figure of a man treading on a serpent; this is very difficult to see, partly on account of the unsympathetic spiky municipal fencing which surrounds the monument).

Garreg, a hill (809 ft.), ¾ mile west of Whitford, is topped by a ruined tower of gleaming white rubble: fine view-point (13 counties are said to be visible) and landmark, fast disappearing in forestry. Pennant thought it was a pharos; others, 16 or 17 c. A plaque states that it was restored in 1897 "in commemoration of the 60th year of the Glorious Reign of VICTORIA Queen and Empress". In 18 c. prints it is shown with four stages and regular rectangular openings. (Approached by several public paths.)

Garreg Uchaf is a very attractive, unspoilt limewashed stone smallholding with an astonishing sense of remoteness. Once typical, now rare.

Gelli Fawr (128781), a small stone house beside the road below, was a 16 c. grange to Basingwerk Abbey (open on written application).

Worthenbury (24) (see the Maelor).

Ysgeifiog (19) is a silvery grey village on a breezy hill, bare and open above wooded valleys, ½ mile north of the Mold–Denbigh road. The church, 1837, by John Welch, has a most promising exterior. Its west end looks squarely down a walled village road; grey, vertical and symmetrical, a pinnacled and battlemented tower with lancet windows, like a child's drawing and very inviting. Dismally disappointing within. In the vestry a drawing shows a treble-aisled church with a square tower; 1792.

The big lake below the village is a fish hatchery.

The English Maelor or Flintshire Detached

This is that surprising part of Flintshire on the English side of the Dee, separated from the rest of the county by ten miles of Denbighshire. It is real farming country where cows graze in deep summer meadows. Sir Watkin Williams-Wynn's hounds hunt over its winter landscape: thorn fences, and big coverts cherished by landowners who live there; not hilly but far from flat. The buildings are brick, stone, or black and white: Cheshire (of which it was part at the time of Domesday) and Shropshire flow into the Maelor with no visible distinction, but there are always glimpses of the Welsh hills.

Its name perhaps derives from Mael+lawr, the territory that belonged to the Mael or prince, but this is no help in explaining its existence which, as an administrative entity, seems to spring from confusion. However, most people ask for an explanation. When Edward I created his Welsh counties he turned the land of the princes into shires but could not take that of the marcher lords who had supported him. Much of the border country therefore remained as independent lordships but, in 1283, the English Maelor was restored to the Crown and became part of Flintshire. Then, when Henry VIII finally suppressed the lordships marcher and divided their land between the Welsh counties, he surprisingly gave the Welsh Maelor (i.e. great lordship of Bromfield and Yale) to Denbighshire, thus dividing Flintshire from the English Maelor which was already part of it.

The Maelor is less than 4 miles from Wynnstay round which a most spirited and enjoyable social life orbited in the 18 and early 19 c. Several houses had their private theatres and at Wynnstay Garrick and the Sheridans were among the guests. Emral, Bryn-y-pys, Pickhill and other houses of the Anglo-Welsh gentry have gone and estates are broken up, but the life is both recorded and epitomised by Nimrod (C. J. Apperley) who never went on a fox-hunting tour without a copy of a Latin poet in his pocket. The country still has the feel of well-farmed, well-managed land belonging to big estates.

Bangor Is-coed (Bangor-on-Dee) (24), a pleasant brick and stone village, stands at an important crossing of the Dee where it is spanned by a fine 5-arched sandstone bridge dating from *c.* 1500. The bridge is very narrow so its parapets are constructed of thin single stone slabs to avoid stealing space from the roadway.

The church stands on the river bank close to the bridge. The pink sandstone tower, adorned with honey-coloured stone, is by Richard Trubshaw, 1723. He was a Staffordshire quarry-owner and master-builder who became very interested in architecture, and a champion wrestler; he also built Worthenbury church (q.v.) in the Maelor. The church has been thoroughly restored and partly rebuilt by John Douglas: broad nave and aisles, rather dark; attractive Decorated east window, but with unattractive glass by Gibbs (1868).

The site of the great Celtic monastery of Bangor Is-coed, is uncertain but it is thought to have been between here and Overton. It is reputed to have been one of the earliest in Britain and in the 6 c. to have housed 2,400 monks. Contemporary propaganda has it that these were mostly slain by Aethelfrith, King of Northumbria, in 615 at the battle of Chester, but the remnant went to found the monastery on Bardsey Island.

The pleasant racecourse lies in a loop of the river to the south of the village.

Bettisfield (27) is the southern tip of the Maelor between Whitchurch and Ellesmere, cut by the Shropshire Union Canal (neat bridge) and bounded by Fenn's Moss to the east. The khaki-coloured church, by G. E. Street, 1874, has a big roof, and a spire: important in this flat country. Inside: spacious with a broad nave and no aisles. All very well thought out and detailed. Oil lamps survive in the choir.

Bettisfield Hall, now a farm, is the early 17 c. house opposite the church: good red-brown brick and vast mullioned windows. Not open.

The Primitive Methodist Ebenezer church, 1879, is endearingly unassuming but rich in colour. Red brick with blue and white headers and a purple slate roof. Iron windows.

Bronington (27) is a brick village whose parish church is detached from it in trees across a field (the War Memorial marks the turning off the main road). Goodhart-

141

BETTISFIELD (G. E. Street, 1874)

Rendel says it was made by a William Smith in 1836 "by adding transepts to a barn", to which a chancel and tower were added in 1864. Restored by F. Shayler in 1901. The result of this activity is brick building with generous Tudor arched iron windows (not so Gothic as those in the vicarage next door). The 19 c. box pews have survived in the transepts but sadly not in the nave. The clock had stopped at five to four and there is a forgotten far-awayness about the place which suggests thinly cut bread and butter and China tea, although the church itself is more muffins and Indian.

Halghton (24), in the middle of the Maelor, is a farming parish with neither village nor church. Halghton Hall (now a farm-house, open on written application) is handsome brown brick of the mid-17 c.; it does not seem to have been finished. It has a flamboyant doorway and voluted window decoration. It stands on an older moated site.

Halghton forge, the attractive group by the main road, was worked by the same family for 200 years until 1965 when Mr Suckley died.

Hanmer (27) is a compact village above Hanmer Mere, an attractive stretch of water about ½ mile long, which makes an unusual prospect from the church porch. New old people's bungalows have been sited by the mere and it is a popular place for motorists to stop. The church was burnt out in 1889 and rebuilt in 19 c. Perpendicular by G. F. Bodely and Thomas Garner, except, it seems, for the 1720 chancel; this was rebuilt in 1936 and feels quite separate from the church. There are interesting sepia pre-fire photographs in the porch and some nice brass wall memorials in the church. The churchyard gates are said to have been the chancel gates within the church, by Robert Davies, 1721. Village houses make a plain but attractive setting to the east end of the church.

Iscoyd (24). The parish church, 1829, by John Butler, is on the site of the half-timbered chapel of Whitewell (there is a spring of limey water below the church), a chapel of ease to Malpas, Cheshire; hence its remoteness. An interesting sketch of this building survives in the vestry; unusually domesticated with flights of outside steps leading up to the galleries. The 19 c. stables and cottage and the unusual thatched 17 c. carriage shelter (this for the parson's conveyance) are grouped like a Victorian water-colour with the church which looks surprisingly Swiss: whitewashed brick with a west tower with a pointed roof. It has a cruciform plan with deep galleries.

Overton (24) is a big, attractive village whose main street has all types of architecture, but the general impression is of Georgian brickwork; this includes terraced cottages with Gothic iron windows and a good deal else which is not 18 c. New speculative housing has been carefully integrated in the middle of the village behind a traditional garden wall and a line of chestnut trees in front of the church. Pensioners' flats and bungalows are also knit in at the north end.

St Mary's church, surrounded by its famous yews, is sandstone Perpendicular with a late Decorated tower all much restored/rebuilt in the 19 c. (north aisle 1819, south aisle 1885; restored W. M. Teulon 1870).

Overton Bridge, across the Dee, has one splendid stone arch. In 1810 a design by Thomas Penson (senior) was adopted, the idea of an iron bridge put forward by Mr Hazeldine being rejected. The bridge collapsed during its construction and Thomas Penson (junior) contracted to finish it. Here the Dee is big and deep with wooded banks (see Erbistock).

Worthenbury (24) is a compact village of red-brown brick with an 18 c. church, red brick with stone quoins and architraves, an apsidal east end and a square tower at the west, by Richard Trubshaw (see Bangor Is-coed), 1736–9. Inside, the 18 c. fittings are astonishingly intact except the altar. Pulpit, reading desk, west gallery, brass chandeliers. Box pews become grander as they work east; two have fireplaces ("All that" said the farmer's wife, with some asperity, who directed us to it "to worship a God who came on earth a carpenter"). Unfortunately the east window is very dark (Betton and Evans, probably 1823).

Anglesey farm

Bibliography

Beavan-Evans, E.: *The Farmhouses and Cottages of Flintshire; The Industrial Archaeology of Flintshire.*
Black's: *Picturesque Guide to North Wales, 1876.*
Borrow, George: *Wild Wales,* Dent. 1953.
Bowen, E. G.: *Settlements of the Celtic Saints in Wales,* University of Wales Press., 1964.
Carr and Lister (ed.): *The Mountains of Snowdonia, 1925.*
Clarke, M. L.: *Anglesey Churches in the Nineteenth Century,* Anglesey Antiquarian Society 1961; *Church Building and Church Restoration in Caernarvonshire During the Nineteenth Century.* Caernarvonshire Historical Society, 1961.
Colvin, H. M. (ed.): *The History of the King's Works,* Chapter VI: The King's Works in Wales, 1277–1330. H.M.S.O.
Condry, W.: *The Snowdonia National Park.* Fontana, 1968.
Dodd, A. H.: *The Industrial Revolution in North Wales.* University of Wales Press, 1951.
Evans, G. Nesta: *Social Life in Mid 18th Century Anglesey.* University of Wales Press, 1936.
Glazebrook, F. F.: *Anglesey and North Wales Coast.* Bookland & Co. Ltd. 1964.
Goodhart Rendel, H. S.: *Card Index of 19th Century Churches,* R.I.B.A.
Grose, Francis: *Antiquities of England and Wales* (Vol. 7), 1786.
Hughes and North: *The Old Churches of Snowdonia, 1924.*
Hughes, D. L. and Williams, D. M.: *Holyhead, The Story of a Port,* 1967.
Jackson, Thomas: *A Visitors' Handbook to Holyhead.* Smith & Sons, 1873.
Lewis, M.: *Topographical Dictionary of Wales,* 1833.
Llwyd, Angharad: *A History of the Island of Mona,* Ruthin, 1833.
Murray's Guide to North Wales, 1885.
Pennant, Thomas: *A Tour in Wales,* 1778.
Ramsay, A. C.: *Old Glaciers of Switzerland and North Wales,* 1860.
Roberts, Dew.: *Mr. Bulkeley and the Pirate,* Oxford University Press, 1936.
Rolt, L. T. C.: *George and Robert Stephenson,* Longmans 1960. *Thomas Telford,* Longmans 1958.
Roscoe, Thomas.: *Wanderings in North Wales,* 1836.
Rowlands, Henry.: *Mona Antiqua Restaurata,* Dublin, 1723.
Rowlands, John.: *Copper Mountain,* Anglesey Antiquarian Society, 1966.
Royal Commission Reports on the Historic Monuments of *Anglesey, Caernarvonshire, Denbighshire, Flintshire.*
Senogle, D.: *Ynys Gorad Goch and the Menai Fisheries,* 1968.
Thomas, the Rev. D. R.: *A History of the Diocese of St. Asaph,* 1874.
Ward, F.: *The Lakes of Wales,* 1931.
Watson, Katherine.: *North Wales* (Regional Archaeology series), Corie, Adams, McKay, 1965.

1
The Skerries
Carmel Hd
Cemaes B.
Porth Wen B.
Bull Bay
Bull B.
Amlwch
Point Lynas
Llaneilian
Cemaes Bay
Burwen
Tre-gele
Llanfechell
Bodewryd
Pensarn
Nebo
Ynys Dulas
Llanwenllwyfo
Dulas B.
Llanfair-ynghornwy
Parys Mountain
Llanrhyddlad
Rhyd-wen
Church B.
Rhos-y-bol
Lligwy Bay
Moelfre
Llanfaethlu
Alaw Resr.
Llanbabo
Penrhos Lligwy
Llandyfrydog
Llanallgo
Llanddeusant
Llanerchymedd
Llanfihangel Tre'r Beirdd
Benllech
Brynteg
Llanfwrog
HOLYHEAD
HOLYHEAD BAY
N. Stack
Holyhead Mount
S. Stack
Llaingoch
Llanfugail
Llyn Llywenan
Coedana
Capel Coch
Red Wharf Bay
Llanfachraeth
ANGLESEY
Llanbedr-goch
Penmon Priory
Llangoed
Kingsland
Llanynghenedl
Bodedern
Trefor
Llangwyllog
Tregaian
Pentraeth
Llanddona
Llanfaes
Valley
Caer-geiliog
Tyn-lon
Rhos-meirch
Talwrn
Baron Hill
Tre-Arddur Bay
Four Mile Br.
Bryngwran
Llanfaes
Bod-ffordd
Llyn Frogwy
Llangefni
Llansadwrn
Bryn-minceg
Beaumaris
HOLY ISLAND
Rhoscolyn
Gwalchmai
Heneglwys
Penmynydd
Lavan Sands
Tywyn Trewan
Cymmeran Bay
Llanfaelog
Rhosneigr
Tycroes Sta.
Llangwyfan
Groeslon
Cerrigceinwen
Llangristiolus
Pentre-berw
Llanfair-pwllgwyngyll
Menai Br.
Garth
Port Penrhyn
BANGOR
Penrhyn Cas.
Aberffraw
Llyn Coron
Bodorgan
Llangadwaladr
R. Cefni
Malltraeth Marsh
Gaerwen
Llanddaniel Fab
Plas Newydd
Glan Adda
Waen Wen
Glasynfryn
Tal-y-bont
Llanllechid
Hermon
Malltraeth Yard
Llangaffo
Bryn-Siencyn
Port Dinorwic
Pentir
Rhiwlas
Bethesda
Aberffraw Bay
Malltraeth Sands
Newborough Woods
Newborough Warren
Llangeinwen
Saron
Bethel
Llanddeiniolen
Deiniolen
Penrhyn Slate Quarries
CAERNARVON BAY
Malltraeth B.
Llanddwyn Is.
Llanddwyn Bay
CAERNARVON
Abermenai
Llanbeblig
Cae-athraw
Llanrug
Cwm-y-glo
Llyn Padarn
Llanberis
Dinorwic Quarries
Elidyr Fawr
Llyn Peris
Y Garn
Nant Peris
Llanfaglan
Foryd B.
Dinas
Llanwnda
Bont-newydd
Waunfawr
Rhostryfan
Moel Eilio
Snowdon Mt. Rly.
Betws Garmon
Llyn Cwellyn
Glaslyn
Snowdon
Rhyd-ddu
Llandwrog
Groeslon
Glynllifon Park
Carmel
Mynydd Mawr
Pen-y-groes
Nantlle
Llyn Nantlle-uchaf
Y-Garn
Tal-y-sarn
Llanllyfni
Yr Aran
Caen-y-morfa
Capel Uchaf
Clynnog-fawr
Carnedd goch
GWYNEDD
Beddgelert
Pant-glas
Moel Hebog
Pass of Aber Glaslyn
Pont Aber Glaslyn
Nantmor
Bwlch Mawr
Y Gyrn-ddu
Mynydd Cenin
Brynkir
Garn Dolbenmaen
Dolbenmaen
Moel Ddu
Afon Glaslyn
Trefor
Yr Eifl (The Rivals)
Llanaelhaiarn
Llithfaen
Llyn Glasfryn
Cefn-caer-Ferch
Penmorfa
Pentre-felin
Tremadoc
Portmadoc
Morfa Nefyn
Nefyn
Garn Boduan
Llangybi
Llanarmon
Afon Dwyfawr
Rhoslan
Criccieth
Moel-y-Gest
Borth-y-gest
Edern
Greestfordd
Ceidio
Four Crosses
Chwilog
Llanystumdwy
Rhos-y-llan
Tudweiliog
Bodfuan
Llannor
Efail-newydd
Abererch
Holiday Camp
Traeth Bach
Harlech Pt.
Llanfihangel-y-traethau
Ynys
Madryn Cas.
Rhyd-y-clafdy
Pwllheli
South Beach
Morfa Harlech
Penllech
Carn Fadryn
Llaniestyn
Penrhos
TREMADOC BAY
Porth Golmon
Llangwnnadl
Meyllteyrn
Sarn
Pig Street
Llanbedrog
Llanbedrog Pt.
Harlech
Bryncroes
Rhos-hirwaun
Tyddyn
Methlem
Llandegwning
Mynydd Rhiw
Mynytho
Llangian
Llanfair
Llandanwg
Llidiardau
Abersoch
St. Tudwal's Bay
Mynydd Anelog
Bwlch-y-Rhiw
Rhydolion
Llanfaelrhys
Llanengan
Aberdaron
Porth Neigwl or Hell's Mouth
Sarn bach
East St. Tudwal's Is.
West
St. Mary's Ch.
Aberdaron B.
Porth Caered
Pen-y-cil
Pencilan Hd.
Bardsey Sd.
St. Mary's Abbey
Bardsey

2
Benllech
Red Wharf Bay
Red Wharf
Puffin I. or Priests Holm
Penmon Priory
Llangoed
Llanddona
Llanfaes
Baron Hill
Beaumaris
CONWY BAY
Lavan Sands
Llansadwrn
Bryn-minceg
Llandegfan
Port Penrhyn
Penrhyn Cas.
BANGOR
Llanfair-Pwllgwyngyll
Menai Br.
Llandegai
Glan Adda
Glasynfryn
Port Dinorwic
Saron
Pentir
Rhiwlas
Llanddeiniolen
Deiniolen
Bethel
Llanrug
Cwm-y-glo
Llyn Padarn
Llanberis
Waun-fawr
Rhostryfan
Moel Eilio
Betws Garmon
Snowdon
Rhyd-ddu
Llyn Cwellyn
Y-Garn
Llyn Nantlle-uchaf
Carnedd goch
Moel Hebog
Moel Ddu
Garn Dolbenmaen
Dolbenmaen
Penmorfa
Tremadoc
Portmadoc
Pentre-felin
Criccieth
Moel-y-Gest
Borth-y-gest
Portmeirion
Minffordd
Penrhyndeudraeth
Maentwrog
Traeth Bach
Talsarnau
Llanfihangel-y-traethau
Eisingrug
Morfa Harlech
Harlech
TREMADOC BAY
Harlech Pt
Llanfair
Llandanwg
Llanbedr
Morfa Dyffryn
Llanenddwyn
Dyffryn
Llanddwywe
Tal-y-bont
Afon Ysgethin
Llawr Llech
Diphwys
Y Garn
Llyn Bodlyn
Moelfre
Y Llethr
Rhinog Fach
Rhinog Fawr
Llyn Cwm Bychan
Afon Artro
Y Graig-ddrwg
Afon Crawcwellt
Crawcwellt
Trawsfynydd
Trawsfynydd Lake
Tomen-y-mur
Afon Eden
Afon Gamlan
Tyn-y-groes Inn
Ganllwyd
Llanelltyd
Moel Offrwm
Llyn Cynwch
Llanfachreth
Rhobell Fawr
Dduallt
Moel Hafod Owen
Moel Cors-y-garnedd
Afon Mawddach
Moel-y-Fiedlog
Nant Gwnol
Mynydd Bryn-llech
Ffridd Trawscoed
Afon Lliw
Llanuwchllyn
Pant Gwyn
Aran Benllyn
Aran Mawddwy
Foel Ddu
Wnion Valley
Moel Llyfnant
Arenig Fawr
Llyn Arenig Fawr
Arenig Fach
Migneint
Llyn Celyn
Afon Tryweryn
Fron-goch
Bala
Llanycil
Afon Lliw
Llyn Tegid or Bala Lake
Llangower
Gwastadros
Llanfor
Llandderfel
Rhos-y-gwaliau
Rhiwaedog-is-afon
Pont Cwm-bychan
Cwm Hirnant
Moel-y-Geifr
Bwlch Rhiw Hirnant
Tynant
Rhiwargor
Eunant
Hirddu Fawr
Lake Vyrnwy
Moel Rhudd
Bwlch y Groes
Craiglyn Dyfi
Dyrysgol
Cyrniau Nod
Cefn-ddwysarn
Moel Emoel
Llyn Gaer Euni
Foel Goch
Llangwm
Cader Benllyn
Carnedd y-Filiast
Garn Prys
Glasfryn
Cerrigydrudion
Mwdwl Eithen
Llanfihangel Glyn Myfyr
Pont Alwen
Cefn-brith
Alwen Reservoir
Mynydd Hiraethog
Llyn Alwen
Llyn Aled
Sportsmens Arms Inn
Llyn Bran
Nantglyn
Bylchau
Moel Seisiog
Gwytherin
Pandy Tudur
Llangernyw
Llansannan
Deunant
Wenlli
Pentre-Tafarn-y-fedw
Llanddoget
Llanrwst
Trefriw
Llyn Geirionydd
Llyn Crafnant
Llyn Cowlyd
Swallow Falls
Betws-y-Coed
Capel Garmon
Pentrefoelas
Foel Cas
Ysbytty-Ifan
Penmachno
Llyn Conwy
Blaenau Ffestiniog
Ffestiniog
Bethania
Tanygrisiau
Moelwyn
Moelwyn Bach
Tan-lan
Rhyd
Vale of Ffestiniog
Cynfal
Graig Wen
Dolwyddelan
Roman Br. Sta.
Ro-wen
Moel Siabod
Pont-y-pant
Capel Curig
Mymbyr
Llyn Ogwen
Glyder Fach
Glyder Fawr
Y Garn
Llyn Peris
Nant Peris
Pass of Llanberis
Dinorwic Quarries
Elidyr Fawr
Carnedd Dafydd
Carnedd Llewelyn
Foel Grach
Foel Fras
Drum
Llanbedr-y-Cennin
Dolgarrog
Pont Dolgarrog
Tal-y-Bont
Caerhun
Tyn-y-groes
Ro-Wen
Tal-y-fan
Carreg Fawr
Aber
Aber Falls
Moel Wnion
Llanllechid
Bethesda
Gerlan
Braich-melyn
Penrhyn Slate Quarries
Nant Ffrancon
Tal-y-bont
Crymlyn
Llanfairfechan
Moelfre
Llangelynin Ch.
Penmaen-mawr
Capelulo
Moel-Llys
Gyffin
Conwy
Deganwy
Conwy Sands
Gogarth
Gt. Ormes Hd.
Llandudno
Lit. Ormes Hd.
Penrhyn Bay
Rhos-on-Sea
Llandudno Junc.
Llansantffraid Glan Conwy
Pentre-felin
Tal-y-cafn
Graig
Eglwys-bach
Moel Gyffylog
Mynydd Llanelian
Mwdwl Eithin
Colwyn Bay
Old Colwyn
Llysfaen
Llanelian-yn-Rhos
Dolwen
R. Dulas
Rhyd-y-foel
Llanddulas
Betws-yn-Rhos
Wern-fach
Mynydd Bryn
Moelfre-uchaf
Llanfair Talhaiarn
Pentre
Tre-pys-llygod
Pen-y-mwdwl
Abergele
Pen-sarn
Towyn
Kinmel Bay
Rhyl
Morfa Rhuddlan
Bodelwyddan
St George
Kinmel
Moelfre-isaf
Llannefydd
Cefn Meiriadog
Bryn Rhyd-yr-arian
Vale of Conwy
GWYNEDD
Nant Gwynant
Llyn Gwynant
Llyn Dinas
Beddgelert
Pass of Aber Glaslyn
Pont Aber Glaslyn
Nantmor
10
11
12
13
14
15
16
17
18
A 5
A 55
A 470
A 487
A 496
A 494
A 4212
A 4085
A 4086
A 498
A 497
A 543
A 544
A 547
A 548
A 546
B 4391
B 4401
B 4402
B 4403
B 4406
B 4407
B 4410
B 4418
B 4366
B 4547
B 4573
B 4501
B 5106
B 5113
B 5381
B 5382
B 5383
B 5384
B 5427
B 5109
B 5108
B 4393

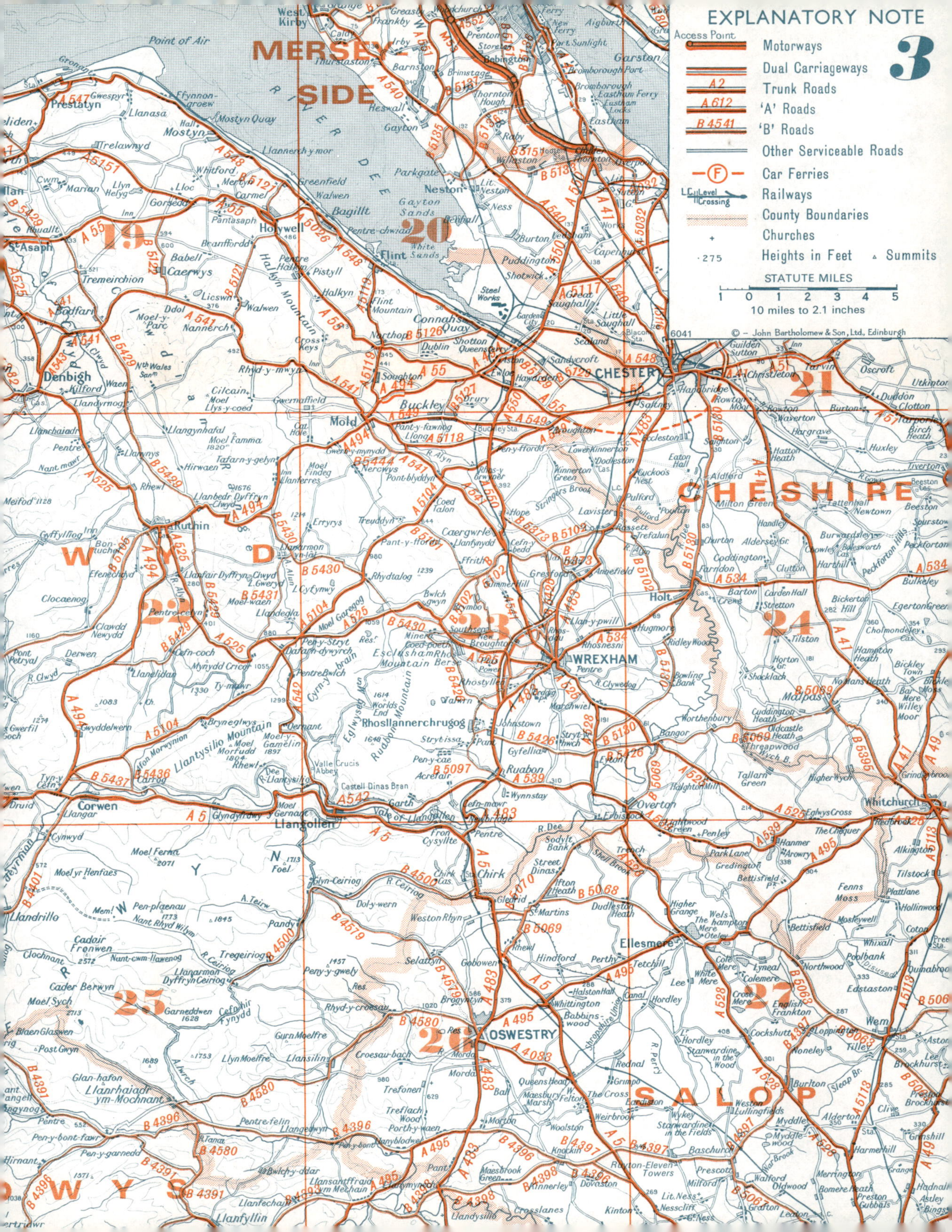
EXPLANATORY NOTE
3
Access Point
Motorways
Dual Carriageways
A 2 Trunk Roads
A 612 'A' Roads
B 4541 'B' Roads
Other Serviceable Roads
F Car Ferries
L.C. Level Crossing
Railways
County Boundaries
Churches
·275 Heights in Feet
▲ Summits
STATUTE MILES
1 0 1 2 3 4 5
10 miles to 2.1 inches
6041
© – John Bartholomew & Son, Ltd., Edinburgh
MERSEY-SIDE
RIVER DEE
CHESHIRE
SALOP
POWYS
19
20
21
22
23
24
25
26
27
CHESTER
WREXHAM
OSWESTRY
Llangollen
Corwen
Ruthin
Denbigh
Mold
Flint
Holywell
Prestatyn
St. Asaph
Buckley
Ellesmere
Whitchurch
Malpas
Chirk
Ruabon
Overton
Holt
Bangor
Llanfyllin
Point of Air
West Kirby
Heswall
Neston
Connah's Quay
Queensferry
Hawarden
Saltney
Rhosllannerchrugog
Llanrhaiadr ym-Mochnant
Ruabon Mountain
Halkyn Mountain
Mostyn
Llandrillo
Gresford
Tattenhall
Tarporley

Index

(C) *indicates Caernarvonshire section,* (A) *Anglesey,* (D) *Denbighshire,* (F) *Flintshire, and* (FD) *Flintshire Detached. Lakes are shown by prefix Llyn.*

Abbeys, *see* Monasteries
Aber Menai, *see* Newborough (A)
Aberconway family, *see* Maenan (C) and Bodnant (D)
Aberglaslyn, *see* Beddgelert (C)
Adam, Robert, *see* Ruabon (D)
Admiralty, The, *see* Menai Bridge (A)
Aethelfrith, King, *see* Bangor Is-coed (FD)
Afon Llugwy, *see* p. 51
Alaw reservoir, *see* Carreglefn (A), Llanbabo (A) and Rhodogeidio (A)
Aled valley, *see* Llansannan (D)
Alexander, Daniel, *see* Holy Island (A)
Alexander, George, *see* p. 15, Betws Garmon (C) and Llanwnda (C)
Allelujah Monument, *see* Mold (F)
Alyn, river, *see* Rossett (D), Llanarmon-yn-Ial (D), Llanferres (D), Cilcain (F), Holywell (F), Hope (F), Marford (F) and Pontblyddyn (F)
Ambrosius, *see* Beddgelert (C)
Ancaster, Lord, *see* p. 60
Anglesey Column, *see* Llanfairpwllgwyngyll (A)
Anglesey Hunt, *see* Beaumaris (A) and Cerrigceinwen (A)
Anglesey, Lord, *see* Caernarvon (C) and Llanfairpwllgwyngyll (A)
Antemorius, *see* Llanfaglan (C)
Apperley, C. J., *see* p. 141
Arthur, King, *see* p. 63
Assheton-Smith family, *see* p. 15 and Deiniolen (C)
Augustinians, *see* Beddgelert (C), Brynsiencyn (A) and Llangoed (A)

Bach-y-graig, *see* Bodfari (F)
Bagot, Lord William, *see* Chirk (D)
Bailey Hill, *see* Mold (F)
Baker, C. L., *see* Holyhead (A)
Bamford-Hesketh, Robert, *see* Towyn (D)
Bangor, Bishop of, *see* Tremadoc (C)
Bank Place, *see* Holywell (F)
Barcloddiad-y-gawres, *see* p. 10 and Aberffraw (A)
Bardsey, *see* Aberdaron (C) and Clynnog Fawr (C)
Baron Hill, *see* Beaumaris (A)
Basingwerk Abbey, *see* Holywell (F), Llanasa (F) and Whitford (F)
Beauclerk, *see* Holywell (F)
Beaufort, Lady Margaret, *see* p. 13, Gresford (D), Holywell (F), Hope (F) and Mold (F)
Beaumaris, *see also* Newborough (A)
Beddgelert, *see also* p. 58
Belan Fort, *see* Glynllifon (C)
Benedictines, *see* Prestatyn (F)

Benllech, *see* Llanfair-Mathafarn-Eithaf (A)
Berea Church, *see* Llanfihangel Esceifiog (A)
Berwyn Moors, *see* p. 9
Betton and Evans, *see* Worthenbury (FD)
Bingley, the Rev., *see* Holyhead (A) and Llangefni (A)
Black Ladders, *see* p. 51
Black Prince, *see* Pwllheli (C)
Blinstone, Mr., *see* Trefnant (D)
Blomfield, Sir Arthur, *see* Bangor (C)
Bodegroes, *see* Llannor (C)
Bodeley, G. F., *see* Beaumaris (A) and Hanmer (FD)
Bodelwyddan, *see* p. 14
Bodewryd Church, *see* Carreglefn (A)
Bodorgan House, *see* Llangadwaladr (A)
Bodowen, *see* Llangadwaladr (A)
Bodrhyddan Hall, *see* Diserth (F)
Bodvean, *see* Bodfuan (C)
Bodvel, *see* Llannor (C)
Bodwrdda, *see* Aberdaron (C)
Bodysgallen, *see* Llandudno (C)
Bolinbroke, *see* Flint (F)
Borrow, George, *see* Llanfair-Mathafarn-Eithaf (A), Llanrhaiadr-yn-Mochnant (D), Llansilin (D)
Borth-y-Gest, *see* Portmadoc (C)
Boscawen, George, *see* Marford (F)
Braich-y-Pwll, *see* Aberdaron (C)
Braint, Afon, *see* Llangeinwen (A)
Bridge End, *see* Hope (F)
Bristly Ridge, *see* p. 55
Britannia Bridge, *see* p. 14, Llanfairpwllgwyngyll (A) and Menai Bridge (A)
Brithdir Mawr, *see* Cilcain (F)
Broadlane Hall, *see* Hawarden (F)
Broderick, Miss, *see* Betwys-yn-Rhos (D)
Bronwen, Princess, *see* Llanbabo (A)
Broom Hall, *see* Pwllheli (C)
Brown, Capability, *see* Ruabon (D)
Brown, Samuel, *see* Menai Bridge (A)
Brymbo Hall, *see* Wrexham (D)
Bryn Bras Castle, *see* p. 14 and Llanrug (C)
Bryn Celli Ddu, *see* p. 10 and Llanddaniel Fab (A)
Bryn Llwyn, *see* Gwaenysgor (F)
Bryn Yorkin, *see* Hope (F)
Brynbella, *see* Bodfari (F) and Trelawnyd (F)
Brynddu, *see* Llanfechell (A)
Bryngwran, *see* Lechylched (A)
Brynkir, *see* Pennant, Cwm (C)
Brynteg, *see* Llanfair-Mathafarn-Eithaf (A)

Bryntwrog, *see* Bodwrog (A)
Bryn-y-maen, *see* Colwyn Bay (D)
Bryn-yr-hen-bobl, *see* Llanfairpwllgwyngyll (A)
Buckler, J. C., *see* Halkyn (F) and Penymynydd (F)
Buckley, Lord, *see* Llangefni (A)
Bulkeley family, *see* Beaumaris (A), Llandegfan (A) and Llanfechell (A)
Burn, William, *see* Abergele (D)
Burne-Jones, E., *see* Holyhead (A), Denbigh (D), Hawarden (F) and Mold (F)
Busby, C. A., *see* Abergele (D)
Butler, John, *see* Iscoyd (FD)
Butler, Lady Eleanor, *see* Langollen (D)
Butlin Holiday Camp, *see* Pwllheli (C)
Bwlch Main, *see* p. 58
Bwlch Cwm Llan, *see* p. 58
Bwlch Pen Barras, *see* Clwydian Range (D) and Llanbedr Dyffryn Clwyd (D)
Bwlch Tryfan, *see* p. 55
Bwlch y Saethau, *see* p. 58

Cader Idris, *see* Abersoch (C) and Rhiw (C)
Cadfan, *see* Llangadwaladr (A)
Cadnair Fair, *see* Nerquis (F)
Caerau, *see* Llanfairynghornwy (A)
Caergwrle Castle, *see* Hope (F)
Caerhun, *see* p. 11
Caernarvon Castle, *see also* p. 51
Caer-y-twr, *see* Holy Island (A)
Caer Gybi, *see* Holyhead (A)
Caer Leb, *see* Brynsiencyn (A)
Caesarea, *see* Pen-y-Groes (C)
canals, *see* p. 14; *see also* Ellesmere Canal, Llangollen Canal and Shropshire Union Canal
Canovium, *see* Caerhun (C)
Capel Curig, *see* p. 51
Capel y Dyffryn, *see* Llandyrnog (D)
Capel Llugwy, *see* Penrhosllugwy (A)
Capel Newydd, *see* Llandegwning (C)
Careglwyd, *see* Llanfaethu (A)
Carmel, *see* Pen-y-Groes (C)
Carmel Head, *see* Llanfairynghornwy (A)
Carn Fadron, *see* Llaniestyn (C)
Carnedd Dafydd, *see* p. 51
Carnedd Llewelyn, *see* p. 51
Carnedds, the, *see* pp. 9, 51, Bangor (C), Penmaenmawr (C) and Penrhyn Castle (C)
Caryll, Mary, *see* Llangollen (D)
Castell Aberlleiniog, *see* Llangoed (A)
Castell Bryn-gwyn, *see* Brynsiencyn (A)
Castell Dinas Bran, *see* Llangollen (D)
Castellmarch, *see* Abersoch (C)

145

Castle of the Winds, see p. 55
castles, see pp. 13, 14, Caernarvon (C), Conway (C), Criccieth (C), Dolbadern (C), Dolwyddelan (C), Llanberis (C), Llanrug (C), Beaumaris (A), Llangoed (A), Abergele (D), Chirk (D), Denbigh (D), Holt (D), Llangollen (D), Ruthin (D), Bodelwyddan (F), Diserth (F), Flint (F), Halkyn (F), Hawarden (F), Hope (F), Mold (F), and Rhuddlan (F)
Cefnamlwch, see Tudweiliog (C)
Cefni, river, see Llangadwaladr (A), Llangefni (A), Newborough (A) and Trefdraeth (A)
Ceiriog, quarries, see Llansantffraid Glynceiriog (D)
Ceiriog, River, see Chirk (D) and Llanarmon Dyffryn Ceiriog (D)
Cellar Mill, see Llanddeusant (A)
Celts, see p. 11
Cemaes Bay, see Llanbadrig (A)
Cemlyn Bay, see Llanfairynghornwy (A)
Cistercians, see Conway (C) and Llantysilio (D)
Chantrey, see Gresford (D)
Chester and Holyhead Railway, see Llanfairpwllgwyngyll (A) and Holywell (F)
Chirk Castle, see p. 14 and Chirk (D)
Christian, Ewan, see Holt (D) and Holywell (F)
Clarke, Harry, see Holywell (F)
Clayton and Bell, see Bangor (C) and Gresford (D)
Clough, Sir Richard, see Denbigh (D), Ruthin (D) and Bodfari (F)
Clutterbuck, see Llanllechid (C), Colwyn Bay (D), Llangernyw (D) and Llansantffraid
Clwyd Forest, see Clwydian Range (D)
Clwydian Range, see also Cwm (F)
Clwyd, Vale of, see p. 9, Clwydian Range (D), Denbigh (D), Llanelidan (D), Llangwyfan (D), Llanynys (D), Bodelwyddan (F), Bodfari (F), Rhuddlan (F), Rhyl (F), St. Asaph (F) and Tremeirchion (F)
Clywedog, river, see Gyffylliog (D) and Llanynys (D)
Cnicht, see Beddgelert (C) and p. 51
coal, see pp. 9, 14, Wrexham (D), Mostyn (F) and Prestatyn (F)
Cob, the, see Portmadoc (C)
Cochwillan, see Llanllechid (C)
Coed Coch, see Betws-yn-Rhos (D)
Colomendy Hall, see Llanferres (D)
Colwyn Bay, see Llandudno (C)
Colwyn Foulkes & Partners, see Llanferres (D) and Llanrwst (D)
Conway Falls, see Betws-y-Coed (C)
Conway, H.M.S., see Llanfairpwllgwyngyll (A)
Conway, river, see p. 9, Caerhun (C), p. 58 and Llanddoget (D)
copper, see Amlwch (A)
Crafnant valley, see Trefriw (C)
Craigybera, see p. 51
Craig-y-gwynt, see Llanrhyddlad (A)

Craig-yr-Ysfa, see p. 51
Creigiau Gleision, see p. 51
Crib Goch, see pp. 48 and 58
Croes Foel farm and smithy, see Bersham (D)
Croesor, see p. 51
Cromwell, see Hawarden (F)
Crosville Motor Co., see Llanferres (D)
Crowe, Sylvia, see Llanbadrig (A)
Crue, Thomas, see Holt (D)
Cruickshank, see Cerrigceinwen (A)
Cundy, Thomas, see Hawarden (F)
Cwm Cloch, see p. 51
Cwm Pennant, see p. 51 and Dolbenmaen (C)
Cwm y Llan, see p. 58 and Beddgelert (C)
Cwm Ystradllyn, see Pennant, Cwm (C)
Cymmrodorion Soc., see Penrhosllugwy (A)
Cynlas, see Llangoed (A)
Cynlleth, river, see Llansilin (D)

Davies bros., see p. 14, Bersham (D) and Nerquis (F)
Davies, John, see Llansadwrn (A)
Davies, Robert, see Hanmer (FD)
Davies, Robert & John, see Chirk (D)
Davies, Thomas, see Llandegfan (A)
de Broke, Lady Willoughby, see Bodelwyddan (F)
de Grey family, see Denbigh (D) and Ruthin (D)
de Lacy, Henry, Earl of Lincoln, see Denbigh (D)
de Warren, John, see Holt (D)
Dee Bridge, see Llanfairpwllgwyngyll (A)
Dee, river, see Cefn Mawr (D), Chirk (D), Clwydian Range (D), Erbistock (D), Holt (D), Llangollen (D), Llantysilio (D), Bagillt (F), Flint (F), Mostyn (F), Offa's Dyke (F), Prestatyn (F), Sealand (F) and Wat's Dyke (F)
Defence, Ministry of, see Aberffraw (A)
Defferd, James, see Holy Island (A)
Demaine and Brierley, see Llansadwrn (A)
Dew, W., see Menai Bridge (A)
Dickens, Charles, see Llanallgo (A)
Din Dryfol, see Aberffraw (A)
Din Llugwy, see Penrhosllugwy (A)
Dinas Cadnant, see Menai Bridge (A)
Dinas Cwnfor, see Llanbadrig (A)
Dinas Emrys, see Beddgelert (C)
Dinas Promontory Fort, see Holy Island (A)
Dinbych, see Denbigh (D)
Dinorben, Lord, see Abergele (D)
Dinorwic quarries, see p. 14 and Llanberis (C)
Dinsylwy, see Llangoed (A) and Llaniestyn Rural (A)
Dodd, Professor, see p. 14
Domesday, see p. 141
Dolbadarn Castle, see Llanberis (C)
Dominicans, see Rhuddlan (F)
Dorothea pit, see Nantlle (C)
Douglas, John, see p. 15, Criccieth (C),

Deganwy (C), Colwyn Bay (D), Holt (D), Rossett (D), Buckley (F), Halkyn (F), Hawarden (F), Mold (F), Northop (F), Sealand (F), Trelawnyd (F), Bangor Is-coed (FD)
Douglas-Pennant family, see p. 14
Doyle, J. F., see Llandudno (C)
Druids, the, see p. 11 and Brynsiencyn (A)
Druid's Circle, see Llanfairfechan (C) and Penmaenmawr (C)
Drws-y-Coed, see p. 51
Dry Bridge Lodge, see Mostyn (F)
Dudley, Robert, see Denbigh (D)
Dwyfor, river, see Pennant, Cwm (C)
Dwygyfylchi, see Penmaenmawr (C)

Eaton Hall, see p. 14 and Holyhead (A)
Ebenezer Chapel, see Abererch (C)
Ecclesiologist, The, see Sarn-Mellteyrn (C)
Edward I, see p. 11, Caernarvon (C), Conway (C), Maenan (C), Beaumaris (A), Newborough (A), Colwyn Bay (D), Flint (F), Rhuddlan (F) and p. 141
Edwards family, see Aberdaron (C)
Egerton, W., see Gresford (D)
Eginton, Francis, see Llandegla (D), Marchwiel (D) and St. Asaph (F)
Eglwys Wen, see Denbigh (D)
Eglwyseg, river, see Llantysilio (D)
Eglwyseg rocks, see Llangollen (D)
Eisteddfod, see Llangollen (D) and Caerwys (F)
Eisteddfod Gorsedd, see Mold (F)
Eliseg, King, and Pillar of, see Llantysilio (A)
Elizabeth I, see Caerwys (F)
Ellesmere Canal, see Llangollen (D)
Elwyn valley, see Llanfair Talhaiarn (D) and Llangernyw (D)
Erch, river, see Abererch (C)
Erddig, see Marchwiel (D)
Erskine, Lady, see Colwyn Bay (D)
Eryri, see pp. 48-58
Esclusham, see Bersham (D)
Evans, David, see Bangor (C) and Llansantffraid Glynceiriog (D)
Evans, Margaret, see Llanberis (C)
Everest expeditions, see Capel Curig (C)
Ewloe Castle, see Hawarden (F)
Excalibur, see p. 63
Eyton family, see Ruabon (D)

Fairy Glen ravine, see Betws-y-Coed (C)
Farmer and Dark, architects, see Llanbadrig (A)
Feilding, Viscount, see Holywell (F)
Ferrey, Benjamin, see Cefn Meiriadog (D) and Ruabon (D)
Ffarm, see Betws-yn-Rhos (D)
Fferm, see Pontblyddyn (F)
Ffestiniog quarries, see Portmadoc (C)
Ffraw, river, see Aberffraw (A)
Ffynnon Asa, see Cwm (F)
Ffynnon Ddoged, see Llanddoget (D)
Ffynnon Llugwy, see p. 51

Flagstaff and Park, *see* Llangoed (A)
Foel Fawr, *see* Llanbedrog (C)
Foel Ferry, *see* Llangeinwen (A)
Forestry Commission, *see* Gwydir Castle (C), p. 51, p. 60, Newborough (A) and Clwydian Range (D)
Fort Williamsburg, *see* Glynllifon (C)
Foulkes, Edward, *see* Llanasa (F)
Four Mile Bridge, *see* Holy Island (A) and Llanfair-yn-neubwell (A)
Franciscans, *see* Llanfaes (A) and Holywell (F)
Fuller Memorial, *see* Llangadwaladr (A)
Fychan, Gronw, *see* Penmynydd (A)

Gaerwen, *see* Llanfihangel Esceifiog (A)
Gallt-y-Wenallt, *see* p. 58
Garn, *see* Henllan (D)
Garndolbenmaen, *see* Dolbenmaen (C)
Garneddwen Farm, *see* Llangelynin (C)
Garner, Thomas, *see* Hanmer (FD)
Garreg, *see* Whitford (F)
Garreg Uchaf, *see* Whitford (F)
Garrick, David, *see* p. 141
Gelli Fawr, *see* Whitford (F)
George III, *see* Clwydian Range (D)
George IV, *see* Holyhead (A)
Gibb, Alexander, *see* Menai Bridge (A)
Gibbons, Grinling, *see* Nannerch (F)
Gibbs, *see* Llangwyfan (D) and Bangor Is-coed (FD)
Gibson, John, *see* Conway (C), Bersham (D), Llanbedr Dyffryn Clwyd (D), Llandegla (D), Wrexham (D) and Bodelwyddan (F)
Gill, Eric, *see* Chirk (D)
Gimblet Rock, *see* Pwllheli (C)
Giraldus Cambriensis, *see* pp. 60 and 63
Gladstone family, *see* Penmaenmawr (C), p. 58 and Hawarden (F)
Glan Conway, *see* Llansantffraid (D)
Glanogwen, *see* Bethesda (C)
Glanywern, *see* Llandyrnog (D)
Glaslyn, *see* p. 58
Glaslyn estuary, *see* Portmadoc (C)
Glaslyn, Llyn, *see* pp. 60, 62
Glendower, Owen, *see* Owen Glendower
Gloddaeth, *see* Llandudno (C)
Glyder Fach, *see* p. 55
Glyder Fawr, *see* p. 55
Glyders, the, *see* pp. 51–55
Glyn, *see* Llanfair-Mathafarn-Eithaf (A)
Glynllifon, *see* p. 14
Glynne family, *see* Llansannan (D) and Hawarden (F)
Goch, Iolo, *see* Llansilin (D)
Gogarth Bay, *see* Holy Island (C)
Golden Gates, *see* p. 14
Golden Groove, *see* Llanasa (F)
Goodhart-Rendel, *see* Llandegla (D) and Bronington (FD)
Gop Bone Cave, *see* Trelawnyd (F)
Gop Cairn, *see* Trelawnyd (F)
Gordon, Alex & Partners, *see* Aberffraw (A)
Gorphwysfa, *see* Capel Curig (C)

Gorseddau quarries, *see* Pennant, Cwm (C)
Grayson & Ould, *see* Chirk (D)
Grefor, Bishop, *see* Llangollen (D)
Gregory, P. S., *see* Gaerwen (A)
Gresham, Sir Thomas, *see* Bodfari (F)
Griffith family, *see* Tudweiliog (C)
Griffith, Caroline, *see* Whitford (F)
Griffith, Nehemiah, *see* Mold (F)
Griffith's Crossing, *see* Brynsiencyn (A)
Gribin ridge, *see* p. 55
Grimthorpe, Lord, *see* Buckley (F)
Grosvenor family, *see* Halkyn (F)
Gummow, Benjamin, *see* Ruabon (D) and Nerquis (F)
Gun Cliff, *see* Newborough (A)
Gwrych Castle, *see* p. 14, Abergele (D) and Towyn (D)
Gwydir Chapel, *see* Llanrwst (D)
Gwynedd, *see* p. 11
Gwynedd, Princes of, *see* Newborough (A)
Gwyther, W. W., *see* Mold (F)
Gyffin, *see* Conway (C)

Hafod Dwryd, *see* Penmachno (C)
Hafod Llwyfog, *see* Beddgelert (C)
Hafodunos, *see* p. 14 and Llangernyw (D)
Hafotty, *see* Llansadwrn (A)
Hall, John, *see* Beaumaris (A)
Hansom, Joseph A., *see* Bodelwyddan (F) and Tremeirchion (F)
Hansom and Welch, *see* Beaumaris (A)
Harbour Act, *see* Amlwch (A)
Hare, Henry T., *see* Bangor (C)
Harold, King, *see* Rhuddlan (F)
Harrison, James, *see* Hawarden (F)
Harrison, Thomas, *see* Holyhead (A), Llanfairpwllgwyngyll (A) and Clwydian Range (D)
Hazeldine, Mr., *see* Cefn Mawr (D) and Overton (FD)
Hebog group, *see* p. 51
Hen Weliau, *see* Caernarvon (C)
Henblas, *see* Llanasa (F)
Henblas barn, *see* Llangristiolus (A)
Henllan vicarage, *see* Llanefydd (D)
Henry II, *see* Hawarden (F)
Henry III, *see* Diserth (F)
Henry VII, *see* p. 11, Penmynydd (A) and Mostyn (F)
Henry VIII, *see* p. 141
Hesketh, L. B., *see* Abergele (D)
Hill Walking in Snowdonia, *see* p. 48
Historic Buildings Council for Wales, *see* Llanfihangel Esceifiog (A)
Holy Island, *see* Rhoscolyn (A)
Holyhead Mountain, *see* Aberffraw (A), Holyhead (A), Holy Island (A), Llanrhyddlad (A) and Rhoscolyn(A)
Holyhead–Liverpool telegraph, *see* Llanrhyddlad (A) and Prestatyn (F)
Holywell Races, *see* Caerwys (F) and Halkyn (F)
Hope Mountain, *see* Pontblyddyn (F)
Hopkins, Gerard Manley, *see* Trelawnyd (F)
Hopper, *see* Penrhyn Castle (C)
Horner of Liverpool, *see* Bangor (C)

Horseshoe, the, *see* p. 58
Horseshoe Falls, *see* Llangollen (D)
Hugh of Avranches, *see* Langoed (A)
Hughes, Edward, *see* Abergele (D)
Hughes, H., *see* Aberffraw (A)

Ibbetson, *see* Amlwch (A)
Idwal outlet, *see* p. 55
Idwal Slabs, *see* p. 55
Indefatigable, *see* Llanfairpwllgwyngyll (A)
iron, *see* p. 14 and Wrexham (D)
Iron Age remains, *see* pp. 11, 12–13, Beddgelert (C), Llaniestyn (C), Penmaenmawr (C), Pen-y-Groes (C), Llanbadrig (A), Llanfair-Mathafarn-Eithaf (A), Llangadwaladr (A), Penrhosllugwy (A), Abergele (D), Clwydian Range (D), Llanddulas (D), Bodfari (F), and Halkyn (F)

Jesus College, Oxford, *see* Llaniestyn (C)
Joan, Princess, *see* Beaumaris (A)
Johnson, Dr., *see* Llannor (C), Denbigh (D) and Trelawnyd (D)
Jones, Inigo, *see* Llanrwst (D)
Jones, John, *see* Betws-yn-Rhos (D)
Jones, J. Wynne, *see* Gwalchmai (A) and Heneglwys (A)
Jones, Maurice, *see* Llanrhaiadr-yn-Cinmerch (D)
Jones, Rev. Peter, *see* Llanddona (A)
Jones, Thomas, *see* Aberffraw (A), Llanarmon Dyffryn Ceiriog (D), Rhyl (F) and Prestatyn (F)

Katherine of Berain, *see* Bodfari (F)
Keating, Misses, *see* Llanbedrog (C) and Rhiw (C)
Kemp, *see* Beaumaris (A) and Rhoscolyn (A)
Kennedy, Henry, *see* p. 15, Bangor (C), Bodfuan (C), Llanbedr-y-Cennin (C), Llandwrog (C), Llanllechid (C), Llanystumdwy (C), Sarn-Mellteyrn (C), Gaerwen (A), Llanerchymedd (A), Llanfaelog (A), Llanfaes (A), Llanfairpwllgwyngyll (A), Llanfair-yn-Neubwll (A), Llangristiolus (A), Llanrhyddlad (A), Menai Bridge (A) and Wrexham (D)
Kennedy & O'Donoghue, *see* Aberffraw (A), Amlwch (A), Bodedern (A) and Llanfechell (A)
Kennedy & Rogers, *see* Llandyfrydog (A) and Penrhosllugwy (A)
Kinmel Park, *see* p. 14 and Abergele (D)
Kyffin, Maurice, *see* Maenan (C)

Lavers & Barrand, *see* Cefn Meiriadog (D)
lead, *see* p. 9, Bagillt (F) and Halkyn (F)
Leeswood Hall, *see* p. 14 and Nerquis (F)
Lindisfarne College, *see* Ruabon (D)
Lingwy burial chamber, *see* Penrhosllugwy (A)

147

Liverpool Docks, *see* Llanrhyddlad (A)
Llanbedrgoch, *see* Llanfair-Mathafarn-Eithaf (A)
Llanberis Pass, *see* Capel Curig (C) and p. 55
Llanberis track, *see* p. 58
Llanbeulan Church, *see* Lechylched (A)
Llanddwyn Bay and Island, *see* Newborough (A)
Llandrillo, *see* Colwyn Bay (D)
Llandudwen, *see* Tudweiliog (C)
Llanedwen Church, *see* Llanfairpwllgwyngyll (A)
Llanelian, *see* Colwyn Bay (D)
Llanfaes, *see* Beaumaris (A) and Newborough (A)
Llanfair Gate, *see* Llanfairpwllgwyngyll (A)
Llanfair-y-Cwmwd, *see* Llangeinwen (A)
Llanfihangel Dinsylwy, *see* Llaniestyn Rural (A)
Llanfwrog Church, *see* Llanfaethu (A) and Ruthin (D)
Llangollen Canal, *see* p. 14 and Cefn Mawr (D)
Llangwyfan, *see* Aberffraw (A)
Llanidan, *see* Brynsiencyn (A) and Llanddaniel Fab (A)
Llaniestyn Church, *see* Llanddona (A)
Llanrhaiadr Hall, *see* Llanrhaiadr-yn-Cinmerch (D)
Llanrhos Church, *see* Llandudno (C)
Llanrhudd Church, *see* Ruthin (D)
Llanrhwydrys Church, *see* Llanfairynghornwy (A)
Llanrhychwyn, *see* Trefriw (C)
Llanwenllwyfo, *see* Llaneilian (A)
Llay Chapel, *see* Gresford (D)
Llechog, *see* p. 58
Lledr, river, *see* Dolwyddelan (C)
Llewelyn the Great, *see* Deganwy (C), Dolwyddelan (C), Beaumaris (A), Llanfaes (A), Llangoed (A) and Hawarden (F)
Llewelyn ap Gruffydd, *see* p. 11, Hawarden (F)
Llewelyn, Gruffydd ap, *see* Rhuddlan (F)
"Llewelyn's old church", *see* Trefriw (C)
Llewenni, *see* Denbigh (D)
Lleyn peninsula, *see* p. 10, Bardsey Island (C), Llanaelhaearn (C), Llanengan (C), Llaniestyn (C), Pistyll (C), Pwllheli (C), Sarn-Mellteyrn (C), Tudweiliog (C), p. 51, Aberffraw (A), and Newborough (A)
Lliwedd, *see* p. 58
Lloyd, John, *see* Caernarvon (C), Bagillt (F) and Pontblyddyn (F)
Lloyd of Hirdefraig, John, *see* Penmynydd (A)
Lloyd George, *see* Caernarvon (C), Llanystumdwy (C) and Pwllheli (C)
Llugwy Valley, *see* Betws-y-coed (C)
Llwyd, *see* Llanbadrig (A)
Llyn Bach, *see* p. 62
   Bochlwyd, *see* p. 58
   Cerrig Bach hoard, *see* Llanfair-yn-neubwll (A)
   Conwy, *see* p. 58
   Coron, *see* Llangadwaladr (A)
   Cowlyd, *see* pp. 51 and 58
   Crafnant, *see* pp. 51 and 58
   Cwellyn, *see* pp. 51 and 58
   Cwm Dulyn, *see* p. 58
   Cwm Silin, *see* p. 58
   Cwm y Stradllyn, *see* p. 58
   Dinas, *see* Beddgelert (C) and p. 58
   Diwaunedd, *see* p. 58
   Dulyn, *see* p. 60
   dur Arddu, *see* p. 60
   Dywarchen, *see* p. 60
   Edno, *see* pp. 60 and 62
   Elsi, *see* p. 60
   Ffynnon Lloer, *see* p. 60
   Ffynnon Llugwy, *see* p. 60
   Geirionydd, *see* p. 60
   Glas, *see* pp. 51 and 60
   Gwynant, *see* Beddgelert (C) and p. 62
   Idwal, *see* pp. 55 and 62
   Llagi, *see* p. 62
   Llydaw, *see* pp. 58 and 62
   Llywenan, *see* Bodedern (A)
   Maelog, *see* Llanfaelog (A)
   Marchlyn Mawr, *see* p. 62
   Mymbyr, *see* p. 62
   Nantlle Uchaf, *see* p. 63
   Ogwen, *see* pp. 51 and 63
   Padarn, *see* Deiniolen (C) and p. 63
   Padrig, *see* Aberffraw (A)
   Peris, *see* Llanberis (C) and p. 63
   y Cwn, *see* pp. 55 and 63
   y Dywarchen, *see* p. 51
   y Foel, *see* p. 63
   y Gadair, *see* p. 63
   y Parc, *see* p. 63
Llynon Mill, *see* Llanddeusant (A)
Llysdulas House, *see* Llaneilian (A)
Llysfaen, *see* Llanddulas (D)
Loggerheads Inn, *see* Llanferres (D)
Lords Marcher, the, *see* p. 13
Lowther Castle, *see* Bodelwyddan (F)

Machno, river, *see* Betws-y-coed (C)
Madocks family, *see* p. 14, Nefyn (C), Portmadoc (C), Tremadoc (C) and Llandyrnog (D)
Mael, *see* p. 141
Maen Achwyfan, *see* Whitford (F)
Maenan Abbey, *see* Conway (C), Gwydir Castle (C) and Llanrwst (D)
Malltraeth Marsh, *see* Llanfihangel Esceifiog (A), Llangaffo (A), Llangristiolus (A) and Trefdraeth (A)
Malltraeth Sands, *see* Llangadwaladr (A)
Man Who Never Was, The, *see* Marford (F)
Mansart, F., *see* Abergele (D)
Marble Church, *see* Bodelwyddan (F)
Meade, J. C., *see* Trelawnyd (F)
Melius Medicus, *see* Llangian (C)
Menai Bridge, *see also* p. 14, Bangor (C), Llangaffo (A) and Llangoed (A)
Menai Fisheries, *see* Llanfairpwllgyll (A)
Menai Straits, *see* p. 10, Bangor (C) Conway (C), Port Dinorwic (C) Beaumaris (A), Llanddaniel Fab (A) and Menai Bridge (A)
Mercians, *see* Offa's Dyke (F) and Wat's Dyke (F)
Middle Ages, *see* p. 13, Caernarvon (C), Conway (C), Aberffraw (A), Beaumaris (A), Llangoed (A) and Cilcain (F)
Millionaire's Mile, *see* Llandegfan (A)
Moel Arthur, *see* Clwydian Range (D)
Moel Fammau, *see* Clwydian Range (D), Llangynhafel (D) and Cilcain (F)
   Fenlli, *see* Clwydian Range (D)
   Hebog, *see* Pennant, Cwm (C) and p. 51
   Hiraddug, *see* Clwydian Range (D) and Cwm (A)
   Meirch, *see* p. 60
   Siabod, *see* p. 51
Moelfre, *see* Llanallgo (A)
Moel-y-don ferry, *see* Llanddaniel Fab (A)
Moel-y-Gaer, *see* Clwydian Range (D), Bodfari (F) and Halkyn (F)
Mona, *see* Cerrigceinwen (A)
Mona Antiqua Restaurata, *see* Brynsiencyn (A)
Mona marble, *see* Penrhos Llugwy (A)
Mona, the Mother of Wales, *see* p. 10
monasteries, *see* Beddgelert (C), Conway (C), Llanfaes (A), Llangoed (A), Llangollen (D), Holywell (F), Bangor Is-coed (FD)
Moore, David, *see* Beaumaris (A)
Morfa Bychan, *see* Borth-y-gest (C)
Morfa Nefyn, *see* Nefyn (C)
Morgan, Bishop, *see* Dolwyddelan (C)
Morgan, Edward, *see* Llanasa (F)
Morris Memorial, *see* Penrhosllugwy (A)
Morris, William, *see* Holyhead (A) and Rhoscolyn (A)
"Mostyn Christ", *see* Bangor (C)
Mostyn family, *see* Llandudno (C), Nannerch (F) and Prestatyn (F)
Murray's Guide, *see* Conway (C), Llandudno (C), and Penrhyn Castle (C)
Myddelton family, *see* Chirk (D) and Denbigh (D)
Myfanwy Fechan, *see* Llangollen (D)
Mynydd Bodfan, *see* Llanfihangel Tre'r-beirdd (A) and Penrhosllugwy (A)
Mynydd Drws-y-Coed, *see* p 51
Mynydd Eilian, *see* Llaneilian (A)
Mynydd Mawr, *see* Betws Garmon (C) and p. 51
Mynydd Rhiw, *see* Rhiw (C)
Mytton, General, *see* Denbigh (D)

Nanhoron, *see* Llandegwning (C)
Nant Ffrancon, *see* p. 15, Bethesda (C) and Capel Curig (C)
Nant Peris, *see* Llanberis (C)
Nantclwyd Hall, *see* Llanelidan (D) and p. 14

Nantgwynant, *see* Capel Curig (C) and p. 58
Napoleon, *see* Glynllifon (C)
National Museum, *see* Llanddaniel Fab (A)
National Trust, *see* Aberdaron (C), Beddgelert, Conway (C), Dolwyddelan (C), Llanbedrog (C), Penrhyn Castle (C), Rhiw (C), Ysbyty Ifan (C), Llanbadrig (A), Llanfairynghornwy (A) and Bodnant (D)
Nature Conservancy, *see* Newborough (A) and Trefdraeth (A)
Nature Reserve, National, *see* Llangadwaladr (A); *see also* Newborough
Nazareth, *see* Pen-y-Groes (C)
Nebo, *see* Pen-y-Groes (C)
Nelson, Lord, *see* Llanfairpwllgwyngyll (A)
Nelson, John, *see* Bardsey Island (C)
Nerquis Hall, *see* p. 13
Nesfield, W. E., *see* Llandudno (C), Abergele (D) and Diserth (F)
Newborough, Lord, *see* Bardsey Island (C), Glynllifon (C) and Llandwrog (C)
Newborough Nature Reserve and Forest, *see* Newborough (A)
Newborough Warren, *see* Llangeinwen (A)
Nimrod, *see* p. 141
Noble, Matthew, *see* Llanfairpwllgwyngyll (A)
Nollekens, *see* Ruabon (D)
Nonconformists, the, *see* p. 12

Oates, John, *see* Buckley (F)
Offa's Dyke, *see* also Chirk (D), Rhosllanerchrugog (D), Prestatyn (F), Rhuddlan (F) and Wat's Dyke (F)
Ogwen Cottage, *see* Capel Curig (C)
Orme, Great and Little, *see* Llandudno (C)
Overton Bridge, *see* Erbistock (D)
Owen family, *see* Llangadwaladr (A)
Owen Glendower, *see* p. 11 and St. Asaph (F)
Owen Glendower's castle, *see* Llansilin (D)
Owen, Goronwy, *see* Bethesda (C), Capel Curig (C), Llanfair-Mathafarn-Eithaf (A)
Owen, Col. John, *see* Tremadoc (C

Paget, Lord Clarence, *see* Llanfairpwllgwyngyll (A)
Paley & Austin, *see* Betws-y-coed (C)
Pandy, *see* Betws-y-coed (C) and Llansantffraid Glynceiriog (D)
Pantasaph, *see* Holywell (F)
Panton Place, *see* Holywell (F)
Pant-y-Saer burial chamber and hut group, *see* Llanfair-Mathafarn-Eithaf (A)
Parciau, *see* Llaneugrad (A)
Parry, Harry, *see* Llanrug (C)

Parry's Railway Guide, *see* Holyhead (A) and Bagillt (F)
Parys Mine Co., *see* Amlwch (A)
Parys mountain, *see* Amlwch (A), Abergele (D)
Parson's Nose, *see* p. 58
Pen Llithrig, *see* pp. 51 and 58
Penbedw Park stone circle, *see* Cilcain (F)
Pencraig, *see* Llangefni (A)
Penllech, *see* Tudweiliog (C)
Penmon Priory, *see* Llangoed (A)
Penmorfa, *see* Tremadoc (C)
Pennant, Thomas, *see* pp. 11, 12, Aberdaron (C), Caernarvon (C), Conway (C), Dolwyddelan (C), Llanberis (C), Tremadoc (C), Ysbyty Ifan (C), pp. 51, 63, Brynsiencyn (A), Holy Island (A), Mostyn (F) and Whitford (F)
Pennant, Richard, *see* Bethesda (C)
Penrhos House, *see* Holy Island (A)
Penrhyn Castle,*see* p. 14 and Bangor (C)
Penrhyn, Lord, *see* Bethesda (C), Capel Curig (C), Llandegai (C) and Penrhyn Castle (C)
Penrhyn Old Hall, *see* Llandudno (C)
Penrhyn quarry, *see* p. 14 and Bethesda (C)
Pensarn, *see* Abergele (D)
Penson, Thomas, *see* Llanfihangel Glyn Myfyr (D), Llanrhaiadr-yn-Cinmerch (D), Rhosllanerchrugog (D), Wrexham (D) and Overton (FD)
Pentrehobyn Hall, *see* Mold (F)
Pen-y-Bryn, *see* Aber (C)
Pen-y-Cloddiau, *see* Clwydian Range (D)
Pen-y-Corddyn, *see* Llanddulas (D)
Pen-y-Gwryd, *see* p. 12 and Capel Curig (C)
Pen-y-Pass, *see* Capel Curig (C) and p. 58
Pen-yr-helgi-du, *see* p. 51
Pen-yr-oleu-wen, *see* p. 51
Pilgrim Trust, *see* Llanrwst (D)
Piozzi, Gabriele, *see* Bodfari (F) and Trelawnyd (F)
Pistyll Rhaiadr, *see* Llanrhaiadr-yn-Mochnant (D)
Plans of Harbours, Bays and Roads etc., *see* Penrhosllugwy (A)
Plantagenets, *see* p. 11
Plas Berw, *see* Llanfihangel Esceifiog (A)
Clough, *see* Denbigh (D)
Coch, *see* Llanddaniel Fab (A)
Eglwyseg, *see* Llantysilio (D)
Gwyn, *see* Bangor (C) and Pentraeth (A)
Kinmel, *see* Abergele (D)
Llanddyfnan, *see* Llanddyfnan (A)
Mawr, *see* p. 13, Conway (C) and Maenan (C)
Newydd, *see* p. 14, Llanfairpwllgwyngyll (A) and Llangollen (D)
Penmynydd, *see* Penmynydd (A)
Power, *see* Bersham (D)
Teg, *see* p. 13, Hope (F) and Pontblyddyn (F)

Tregayan, *see* Tregayan (A)
-yn-Rhiw, *see* Rhiw (C)
-yn-y-pentre, *see* Llangollen (D)
Pochin, Henry, *see* Bodnant (D)
Point Lynas, *see* Llaneilian (A)
Ponsonby, Sarah, *see* Llangollen (D)
Pont Cyfyng, *see* p. 51
Cysyllte, *see* p. 14, Cefn Mawr (D) Llangollen (D)
Marquis, *see* Trefdraeth (A)
-y-Pair, *see* Betws-y-coed (C)
Port Penrhyn, *see* Penrhyn Castle (C)
Porth Colmon, *see* Llangwnnadl (C)
Dafarch, *see* Holy Island (A)
Dinllaen, *see* Nefyn (C)
Llanlleiana, *see* Llanbadrig (A)
Mawr, *see* Mostyn (F)
Trecastell, *see* Aberffraw (A)
Trefadog, *see* Llanfaethu (A)
Wen, *see* Llanbadrig (A)
Porthamel Hall, *see* Brynsiencyn (A)
Portmerion, *see* Nerquis (F)
Potter, Joseph, *see* p. 14 and Llanfairpwllgwyngyll (A)
potteries, *see* Buckley (F)
Poundley & Walker, *see* Llanbedr Dyffryn Clwyd (D)
Powis, *see* Llantysilio (D)
Poynter, Ambrose, *see* Cilcain (F), Mostyn (F) and Whitford (F)
Prehistoric remains, *see* pp. 10, 12–13, Clynnog Fawr (C), Dinas Dinlle (C), Llanaelhaearn (C), Aberffraw (A), Brynsiencyn (A), Holy Island (A), Llanddaniel Fab (A), Llandegfan (A), Llanfaelog (A), Llanfair-Mathafarn-Eithaf (A), Llanfairpwllgwyngyll (A), Llangoed (A), Llaniestyn Rural (A), Menai Bridge (A), Penrhosllugwy (A), Capel Garmon (D), Cefn Meiriadog (D), Clwydian Range (D), Llanarmon Dyffryn Ceiriog (D), Llangollen (D), Cilcain (F), Gwaenysgor (F) and Trelawnyd (F); *see also* Iron Age
Presaddfed burial chamber, *see* Bodedern (A)
Priestholm, *see* Llangoed (A)
Prince of Wales' quarry, *see* Pennant, Cwm (C)
Pritchard Jones Institute, *see* Newborough (A)
Publicius, *see* Caernarvon (C)
Puddle, Charles, *see* Bodnant (D)
Puffin Island, *see* Llangoed (A)
Pugin, A. W., *see* Chirk (D), Wrexham (D) and Holywell (F)
Pwllheli, *see also* p. 15
Pwll-y-crochan, *see* Colwyn Bay (D)

Queen Mab, *see* Tremadoc (C)
Queensferry Bridge, *see* Sealand (F)

railways, *see* pp. 12, 13; *see also* Chester & Holyhead Railway Co. and Snowdon Railway
Ramsay, A. C., *see* Llanberis (C)
Red Wharf Bay Sailing Club, *see* Llaneugrad (A)

149

Rennie, John, *see* Holyhead (A) and Menai Bridge (A)
Rhaiadr river, *see* Llanrhaiadr-yn-Mochant (D)
Rhianva, *see* p. 14
Rhosbeiro church, *see* Carreglefyn (A)
Rhosneigr, *see* Llanfaelog (A)
Rhos-on-Sea, *see* Colwyn Bay (D)
Rhual, *see* Mold (F)
Rhyd-Dhu, *see* p. 51
Rhysbrack, *see* Ruabon (D)
Rhythallt, *see* Llanrug (C)
Richard II, *see* Flint (F)
Richard III, *see* Betws-y-coed (C)
Richmond, Sir William, *see* Hawarden (F)
Rio Tinto, *see* Holyhead (A)
Rivers, *see* Alyn, Cefni, Ceiriog, Clywedog, Conway, Cynlleth, Dee, Eglwyseg, Erch, Ffraw, Rhaiadr, Tanat and Ystrad
Roberts, D., *see* Llangwyllog (A)
Roberts, David, *see* Bangor (C)
Roberts, Rev. R. D., *see* Clynnog Fawr (C)
Robyns, Grphith, *see* Menai Bridge (A)
Roman remains, *see* pp. 9, 11, 13, Beddgelert (C), Caerhun (C), Caernarvon (C), Amlwch (A), Brynsiencyn (A), Holyhead (A), Llaniestyn Rural (A), Clwydian Range (D) and Holt (D)
Roose, Jonathan, *see* Amlwch (A)
Rowland, *see* p. 48
Rowland's almshouses, Bishop, *see* Bangor (C)
Rowlands, Henry, *see* Brynsiencyn (A)
Royal Charter, *see* Llanallgo (A)
Ruabon mountain, *see* Rhosllanerchrugog (D)
Runcorn Bridge, *see* Menai Bridge (A)
Ruskin, *see* Buckley (F)
Russell, Bertrand, *see* Llanbadrig (A)

St. Asaph, *see also* Rhuddlan (F)
St. Beuno, *see* Clynnog Fawr (C), Trefdraeth (A) and Holywell (F)
St. Beuno's Wall, *see* Trelawnyd (F)
St. Cadwaladr, *see* Llangadwaladr (A)
St. Ceidio, *see* Rhodogeidio (A)
St. Cwyfan, *see* Whitford (F)
St. Cybi, *see* Langybi (C)
St. Cyngar, *see* Llangefni (A)
St. Deiniol's library, *see* Hawarden (F)
St. Dwynwen, *see* Newborough (A)
St. Garmon, *see* Mold (F)
St. Geinwen, *see* Llangeinwen (A)
St. Gwenfaen, *see* Rhoscolyn (A)
St. Maethlu, *see* Llanfaethu (A)
St. Pabo, *see* Llanbabo (A)
St. Peblig, *see* Caernarvon (C)
St. Rhyddlad, *see* Llanrhyddlad (A)
St. Tudno, *see* Llandudno (C)
St. Tudwal's Islands, *see* Abersoch (C)
St. Tysilio, *see* Menai Bridge (A)
St. Winifred's Chapel and Well, *see* Holywell (F)
"Saints' Road", *see* Llanaelhaearn (C)
Salt Island, *see* Holyhead (A)
Salusbury family, *see* Denbigh (D)

Salvin, Anthony, *see* Caernarvon (C)
Sandby, Thomas, *see* Amlwch (A) and Denbigh (D)
Saturnius, *see* Llansadwrn (A)
Scoles, Joseph, *see* Holywell (F)
Scott, G. C., *see* Diserth (F) and Hawarden (F)
Scott, J. O., *see* Llandudno (C)
Scott, Sir Gilbert, *see* p. 15, Bangor (C), Tudweiliog (C), Holyhead (A), Llangernyw (D), Llantysilio (D), Pentrefoelas (D), Trefnant (D), Hawarden (F), Llanasa (F), Mold (F), Rhyl (F), St. Asaph (F)
Sedding, *see* Llanfair Dyffryn Clwyd (D)
Segontium, *see* pp. 11, 13 and Caernarvon (C)
Seiont, river, *see* Caernarvon (C)
Seiriol, *see* Llangoed (A)
Shayler, F., *see* Bronington (FD)
Shelley, P. B., *see* Tremadoc (C)
Sheridans, the, *see* p. 141
Shotton, *see* Sealand (F)
Shropshire Union Canal, *see* Menai Bridge (A), Cefn Mawr (D), Chirk (D) and Bettisfield (FD)
Siabod, *see* Dolwyddelan (C) and p. 51
Skerries, the, *see* Llanfairynghornwy (A)
Skevington, Bishop, *see* Bangor (C)
Skinner's Memorial, *see* Holyhead (A)
slate, *see* pp. 14–15, Bethesda (C), Nantlle (C), Pennant, Cwm (C), Port Madoc (C), and Llanddaniel Fab (A)
Smith, William, *see* Bronington (FD)
Snowdon, *see also* pp. 9–10, Aberdaron (C), Abersoch (C), Capel Curig (C), Deiniolen (C), Dolwyddelan (C), Llanberis (C), Nantlle (C), Pen-y-groes (C), Portmadoc (C), pp. 51, 55–58
Snowdon Railway, *see* Llanberis (C)
South Penrallt, *see* Caernarvon (C)
Stanley Embankment, *see* Holy Island (A)
Stanley family, *see* Holyhead (A)
Stanley of Alderley, Lord, *see* Bodedern (A), Holy Island (A) and Llanbadrig (A)
Stephen, King, *see* Gwytherin (D)
Stephenson, George, *see* Conway (C) and Holy Island (A)
Stephenson, Robert, *see* p. 14 and Llanfairpwllgwyngyll (A)
Street, G. E., *see* p. 15, Gresford (D), Llanddulas (D), Towyn (D), Ffynnongroyw (F) and Bettisfield (FD)
Suckley family, *see* Halghton (FD)
Suetonius, *see* Brynsiencyn (A)
Swallow Falls, *see* Betws-y-coed (C)
Swift, Jonathan, *see* Holyhead (A)
Sychnant Pass, *see* Penmaenmawr (C)

Tacitus, *see* p. 11 and Brynsiencyn (A)
Talacre Abbey, *see* Prestatyn (F)
Talhaiarn, *see* Llanfair Talhaiarn (D)
Talysarn, *see* Nantlle (C)
Tanat, river, *see* Llangedwyn (D)

Tan-yr-allt, *see* Tremadoc (C)
Telford, Thomas, *see* pp. 10, 14, Bethesda (C), Betws-y-Coed (C), Conway (C), Bodedern (A), Cerrigceinwen (A), Holy Island (A), Llanfairpwllgwyngyll (A), Llangaffo (A), Llangefni (A), Llangoed (A), Llangristiolus (A), Menai Bridge (A), Cefn Mawr (D), Chirk (D) and Llangollen (D)
Temple of Peace, *see* Hawarden (F)
Teulon, W. M., *see* Overton (FD)
Theatr Fach, *see* Llangefni (A)
Thelwall family, *see* Ruthin (D)
Thetis, H.M.S., *see* Llaneugrad (A)
Thomas, John, *see* Llanfairpwllgwyngyll (A)
Thomas, Percy & Sons, *see* Bangor (C) and Llandegfan (A)
Thomas, R. G., *see* Beaumaris (A) and Llanfaes (A)
Thompson, Francis, *see* Conway (C), Holywell (F) and Mostyn (F)
Thorneycroft, Hamo, *see* Holyhead (A)
Thrale family, *see* Llannor (C) and Trelawnyd (F)
Tijou, *see* Bersham (D)
Tour in Wales (Pennant), *see* p. 11; *see also* Pennant, Thomas
Traeth Bychan, *see* Llaneugrad (A)
Traeth Coch, *see* Pentraeth (A)
Traeth Dulas, *see* Llaneilian (A) and Penrhoslugwy (A)
Traeth Mawr, *see* Portmadoc (C)
Trearddur Bay, *see* Holy Island (A)
Trefeilier, *see* Trefdraeth (A)
Trefignath burial chambers, *see* Holy Island (A)
Trefor Bridge, *see* Llangollen (D)
Trefor Chapel, *see* Gresford (D)
Trefor rocks, *see* Llangollen (D)
Tregfryn Gallery, *see* Menai Bridge (A)
Trer Ceiri, *see* Llanaelhaearn (C)
Trevalyn, *see* Rossett (D)
Trevor estate, *see* Marford (F)
Trevor Hall, *see* Llangollen (D)
Trevor, Sir John, *see* Hope (F) and Pontblyddyn (F)
Trinity House, *see* Holyhead (A) and Llanfairynghornwy (A)
Tros-y-marian, *see* Llangoed (A)
Troughton, Rev. John Ellis, *see* Penymynydd (F)
Trubshaw, Richard, *see* Bangor Is-coed (FD) and Worthenbury (FD)
Trum-y-Ddysgl, *see* p. 48
Tryfan, *see* Capel Curig (C) and p. 51
Tudor, Owen, *see* Penmynydd (A)
Turner, Joseph, *see* Chirk (D), Flint (F) and Mold (F)
Twt Hill, *see* Caernarvon (C)
Twyn-y-parc, *see* Llangadwaladr (A)
Ty Mawr, *see* Dolwyddelan (C) and Holy Island (A)
Ty Newydd burial chamber, *see* Llanfaelog (A)
Tyn-y-coed, *see* Capel Garmon (D)
Tyn-y-Maes, *see* Bethesda (C)

University College, *see* Bangor (C)

Valle Crucis, *see* Llantysilio (D) and Llangollen (D)
Valley Airfield, *see* Llanfair-yn-neubwll (A)
Vaynol Chapel, *see* Caernarvon (C)
Verelst, Charles, *see* Holyhead (A) and Llandegfan (A)
Verney family, *see* Llanddona (A)
Victoria, Queen, *see* Holyhead (A)
Visitor's Handbook for Holyhead, *see* Holy Island (A)
Vortigern, *see* Beddgelert (C) and Llithfaen (C)

Waen Bodfari, *see* Llandyrnog (D)
Walker Art Gallery, *see* p. 63
Walker, David, *see* Rhyl (F)
Walpole, Horace, *see* Marford (F)
Ward, Frank, *see* p. 58
Warner, *see* Mold (F)
Waterhouse, A., *see* Penmaenmawr (C) and Holyhead (A)
Waterloo Tower, *see* Ruabon (D)
Watkin path, *see* p. 58
Weightman & Hadfield, *see* Llanfaes (A), Llangaffo (A), Llangoed (A) and Llanfairynghornwy (A)
Welch, Edmund, *see* Beaumaris (A)
Welch, John, *see* p. 15, Llandudno (C), Penmynydd (A), Brynsiencyn (A), Betwys-yn-Rhos (D), Flint (F) and Ysgeifiog (F)
Well Chapel, *see* Cefn Meiriadog (D)
Wellington, *see* Llanfairpwllgwyngyll (A)
Wern, *see* Llanddona (A)

West, Robert, *see* Henllan (D)
Westmacott, *see* Llandegai (C)
Westmacott jr., *see* Gresford (D) and Whitford (F)
Wheeler, Mortimer, *see* Caernarvon (C)
Whistler, Rex, *see* Llanfairpwllgwyngyll (A)
Whitchurch, *see* Denbigh (D)
Whitewell, *see* Iscoyd (FD)
Wilkinson family, *see* Bersham (D)
Williams, Archbishop, *see* Conway (C) and Llandegai (C)
Williams, Hugh, *see* Llantrisant (A)
Williams, Jane Silence, *see* Colwyn Bay (D)
Williams, Margaret, *see* Llangeinwen (A)
Williams-Ellis, Clough, *see* Aberdaron (C), Llanystumdwy (C), Pentrefelin (C), Llanelidan (D) and Nerquis (F)
Williams-Wynn family, *see* Ruabon (D) and p. 141
Wilson, Richard, *see* Llanferres (D) and Mold (F)
Women's Institute, *see* Llanfairpwllgwyngyll (A)
Woodward, B., *see* Llaneilian (A)
Wyatt, Benjamin, *see* Bethesda (C), Caernarvon (C) and Penrhyn Castle (C)
Wyatt, James, *see* p. 14, Llanfairpwllgwyngyll (A), Marchwiel (D) and Ruabon (D)
Wyatt, Lewis, *see* St. Asaph (F)
Wyatt, Matthew, *see* Holywell (F)
Wyatt, Samuel, *see* Penrhyn Castle (C), Beaumaris (A) and Abergele (D)

Wyatt, T. H., *see* Bodfari (F), Holywell (F), Nannerch (F), Prestatyn (F) and Treuddyn (F)
Wyattville, *see* Ruabon (D)
Wylfa Atomic Power Station, *see* Llanbadrig (A)
Wyn, Eifion, *see* Pennant, Cwm (C)
Wyndham, Henry, *see* Flint (F)
Wynn family memorials, *see* Bodfuan (C)
Wynne family, *see* Dolwyddelan (C), Gwydir Castle (C) and Llanrwst (D)
Wynne family memorials, *see* Llandudno (C) and Llandwrog (C)
Wynne, Robert, *see* Chirk (D)
Wynne Jones, Hugh, *see* Rhodogeidio (A)
Wynnstay, *see* Ruabon (D)

Yale, Elihu, *see* Llanarmon-yn-Ial (D) and Wrexham (D)
Yale family, *see* Bryneglwys (D)
Yale University, *see* Llanarmon-yn-Ial (D) and Wrexham (D)
Y Garn, *see* pp. 51 and 55
Ynys Dulas, *see* Llaneilian (A)
Ynys Gorad Goch, *see* Llanfairpwllgwyngyll (A)
Ynyspandy, *see* Pennant, Cwm (C)
Yr Eifl, *see* Llithfaen (C)
Yr Eifl, *see* Llanaelhaearn (C)
Yorke family, *see* Marchwiel (D)
Yorke monuments, *see* Llansannan (D)
Ystrad, River, *see* Denbigh (D) and Nantglyn (D)